THE
AWAKENED

SARA ELIZABETH SANTANA

To Robby, Jessica, Dink, Joey and Stevey:
I would fight a million Awakened for you guys.
Love you!

THE

AWAKENED

PROLOGUE

I'M PRESSED AGAINST THE COLD tile of the floor, and I can't breathe. I can't remember how long I've been here. Has it been hours? Days? Weeks? Time is lost, and all I can feel are the shivers going through me.

I'm hungry. They brought me food earlier, and the smell wafted over me. It's been so long since I've had real food, and I want nothing more than to eat it, to fill myself up, scrape the plate with my fingers. Screw utensils. Utensils are for a civilized world. That doesn't exist anymore.

I can't eat their food. *I can't.* I don't know what's in it. But I'm hungry. I'm so hungry, I can barely stand it; I can barely think, and the smell is overwhelming, and I feel like I'm going to throw up but there's nothing there. I can't throw up. But I can't eat it. I don't know what they've put in it, and I'm tired of the darkness. I'm scared of sleeping when I'm not tired, and I'm scared of what is going on outside the door that I can't get out of.

I think of Dad. Mom. Bandit. Madison.

I miss Ash.

I'm so cold.

There's a click, and I spring up. The door begins to creak open, but I'm too exhausted and too hungry to do anything about it.

They've finally come for me.

PART 1

CHAPTER
ONE

MY AIM WAS GETTING BETTER.

And okay, sure, I hadn't hit the actual head on the target in at least a few rounds, but who was counting? I definitely wasn't.

Zoey, you need to lift your arm just a little bit. I'm glad you can shoot the target now, but let's try actually hitting what we aim for.

I sighed, trying to ignore my dad's voice in my head. It was because of him that I was even learning how to shoot a gun. I've lived my entire life in Manhattan in the great state of New York, and yeah, sometimes things aren't all sunshine and rainbows here, but it wasn't exactly the worst place to live either. But my dad is a police chief, and he tends to be a little overprotective sometimes.

"You're thinking of your dad right now, aren't you?" my

best friend Madison called over the partition that separated us. As soon as my dad signed me up for gun lessons, Madison's dad had jumped on board. We both thought it was incredibly stupid, until Madison started to do infinitely better than me. Madison was good at a lot of things, and she loved being good at things. Success was her biggest talent, not that I had noticed or anything. But at least we were together. Anything was manageable as long as I was with Madison.

I raised my gun. My eyes were intent on the target a few yards in front of me. I was determined to actually hit the target that I was aiming for this time. I breathed in and out and then fired. The bullet hit the paper right in the square of the chest.

"Nice," Madison complimented right before firing her own gun.

"Except that I was aiming for the head," I grumbled. "You know, if I ever need to actually *use* a gun, I'm going to be absolutely useless."

About fifteen minutes later, we were walking outside, heading toward the subway. Madison was gushing about the praise she had received from our instructor today. I was massaging my arm and feeling sorry for myself. My dad is on the New York police force, so he's amazing with a gun, yet I couldn't fire one to save my life, which I think was kind of the point.

"You're going to get better at this," Madison insisted, breaking into my thoughts.

"I would love if I didn't have to do it at all," I answered, sliding my Metro card through the slot and stepping through. We jogged a bit to make the train that had just pulled in and made our way through the car, looking for some empty seats. We found some near the back and collapsed in them.

Madison shrugged, pulling out her phone and typing a quick text message to her boyfriend Brody. I was surprised it had taken her this long to have the phone in her hand. The only times the two of them were NOT texting each other were when we were in school, at gun practice and while sleeping. "In a few months, we're going to be in college! COLLEGE, Zoey! Your dad just wants you to be protected."

"Yeah, except for the fact that I can't exactly keep a gun in my dorm room, Maddie. And we applied to Colombia and NYU. We could live at home if we wanted to."

"We are not living at home! Dorms! Roomies! We've been talking about this for years," she said, fiercely. I raised my eyebrow at her, and she smiled. "And as for using a gun, how 'bout this?" She placed the phone in her lap, and used her hands to talk. "What if someone on campus attacked you, and they had a gun, and somehow you got the gun? You should be able to use the actual gun."

"I'm surrounded by paranoid people. It's bad enough that I have gun lessons, self-defense, kickboxing and mixed martial arts classes. Not to mention school, homework and cheer practice. Please do not encourage my dad to add more to my plate," I said, rolling my eyes. "Come on; let's go."

We got off the subway and started making the short walk home in silence. Madison typed furiously on her phone, and

I watched a couple kids playing soccer in the street.

As we walked up to our houses, standing next to each other, I got a strange feeling like someone was walking right behind me. I turned around quickly, and seeing no one there, I frowned. I turned back around and ran right into someone and shrieked.

"Hello, Z," Ash Matthews said grinning.

"It's Zoey, Ash. Zoey, not Z. My name does contain more than one letter. And stop doing that," I said, stepping around him.

"Aw, come on, Z. I know you're happy to see me," Ash said, falling into step with us. From the corner of my eye, I saw Madison's lips quivering with a barely concealed smile.

"Actually, Ash, not everyone is always happy to see you," I replied.

"Not true," Madison whispered under her breath. I shot a glare in her direction but didn't say anything.

"Are you ladies going to the dance on Friday night?" he asked.

"As head of the dance committee, I'm obviously going to be there," Madison said, finally looking up from her phone at the same time I said, "No."

Ash stopped, sticking his arm out to stop me, his hand curved around my hip. I flinched at the contact between us and raised my head to look at those big gorgeous blue eyes. "Now, why wouldn't my girl be going to the dance on Friday?"

"Let go of me," I said, trying to wriggle from his grasp. "And I'm not your girl."

Ash laughed as he let me go. I grabbed Madison's hand and started dragging her away. "See you at school tomorrow, Z."

"You are SO in love with him," Madison laughed as I yanked her down the street.

I growled in response. She laughed again before turning to climb the steps of her own brownstone apartment. I stuck my tongue out at her and walked past the three apartments that separated my house from the one Madison's family shared with a couple other families. I kept my head down as I passed Ash's house, hoping that he had already made his way inside. I didn't care what Madison said; I was definitely not in love with him. The guy drove me crazy.

Ash and I had lived next door to each other for as long as I could remember, even before my parents divorced and my mom went back to her hometown in Nebraska where she had grown up. He has always been the bane of my existence. When we were nine, he made me eat a mud pie. When we were eleven, he used to snap the straps of my bra, because I was the only girl that young who needed to actually wear one. And now that we're eighteen, he continues to drive me absolutely insane.

But the guy was ridiculously good looking. He was the tallest guy at my high school, no question, with dark brown hair and these stupid big blue eyes that caused most girls at the school (and some teachers) to swoon. He was also the captain of the football AND the baseball teams, which gave him a body that even I couldn't help but admire.

I slipped my key into the lock of my own brownstone

and felt it click. Some people in my neighborhood had really great jobs, ones where they could afford to live in a brownstone by themselves. But most brownstones were split into apartments amongst at least two families. We had our own brownstone, left behind to my dad when my granddad died. It was garishly big for the two of us, but it was home.

It was empty at the moment though, but that was to be expected. As a police chief in New York, my dad tended to not be home very often.

I called for Bandit, my dog. He's a purebred German shepherd who, despite being a few years old, acted like an overgrown pup. He came bounding down the stairs. I fitted a leash on him and took him for a quick walk around the block, making sure that he did his business. I got Bandit from my mom for my 12th birthday; she had tried to use Bandit as a tool of persuasion during my parents' divorce. Unfortunately for her, the plan backfired since I chose to remain in New York with my dad.

When I got back, I dumped the leash in the entryway closet and kicked off my shoes. One flew across the open hallway. I shrugged, not wanting to chase after it. Bandit showed signs of wanting to go after it but instead trotted away toward the basement. I made my way into the kitchen and opened the refrigerator to see what I could scrounge up for dinner.

About twenty minutes later, I was plopping down on the couch in front of the television, ready to watch some trashy TV until the Mets game came on. I lifted the burger I'd fixed to my mouth just as my phone lit up beside me, blasting out the theme song from *Battlestar Galatica.*

"Hey, Dad," I said, cradling the phone between my ear and shoulder, eager to dive into my hamburger.

"Hey, champ," came the booming answer, "how did lessons go tonight?"

"Great!" I forced cheerfulness in my voice.

"Oh yeah?"

"Yeah, definitely! I'm definitely improving!" I assured him.

"You are such a liar," he laughed.

I laughed. "I know. I swear, though, I think I *am* getting better."

"Yeah, we'll see about that," he answered. "Have you eaten?"

I looked down at my hamburger, which was getting colder each second that I was on the phone with him. "No, but I…"

"Awesome. Craig gave me tickets to the Mets game tonight. You wanna go?"

I sat up. "Yeah, definitely."

"All right, give me time to get home and we'll head over there, okay?"

"Perfect!" I sprang up off the couch and flew into the kitchen, where I wrapped up the burger and stuffed it into the fridge. I went upstairs, put my Mets jersey on, threw my messy brown hair into a ponytail, slipped my worn out Chucks on, and then went downstairs to wait for my dad on the front porch.

"Zoey-bell!"

I groaned, putting my head in my hands and wondering,

not for the first time, how I got myself into situations with Ash Matthews. I wish he would just move away so I didn't have to see him. Every. Single. Day. "Go away, Ash."

"You going to the game tonight, Z?" Ash said, ignoring me and coming to sit next to me on the stoop.

"No, I just like wearing my jersey randomly while waiting on my front stoop," I said, sarcastically.

"You're so mean! Why you always gotta be such a heartbreaker with me?" he said, leaning back on his palms. I glanced over, catching a glimpse of his toned abs between his shirt and jeans.

I blushed and turned away. "If you leave me alone, Ash, I promise I'll be nicer to you."

"Come on, we've been next door neighbors for, like, our whole lives. Aren't we friends?"

I burst out laughing at that one. "Do you call shooting spit balls at me during fourth period 'being friends'?" I asked.

"All fun and games, Z, all fun and games," Ash said dismissing it with a wave. "Don't you remember that boys are mean to the girls they like because they're too awkward to actually do anything about it?"

I shook my head, looking back at him and getting sucked into those stupid, stupid, *stupid* blue eyes. "You don't like me, Ash Matthews."

He sat up and leaned toward me. He was only a few inches away from me, and his breath smelled perfect, like spearmint Listerine mouthwash. I sucked in a breath, ignoring how hard my heart was pounding in my chest.

"Now, wouldn't you like to know?"

I rolled my eyes, trying to diffuse the tension between us. I could feel the warmth coming from him, and his blue eyes were fixated on me. "You have a girlfriend, Ash. Heather Carr, remember?"

"Heather doesn't hold a candle to you, baby," he said in a low voice. He came closer, even closer, and my body began to betray me. I leaned toward him and closed my eyes.

Suddenly, my face was wet. I opened my eyes in shock only to see Ash pointing a small squirt gun at my face. He was laughing hard.

I wiped my hand across my face. "I hate you so much, Ash."

"Lies, all lies," he said, still laughing. "One day, you'll admit how much you love me and then maybe you'll get that kiss that you seem to want so much."

I stood up, folding my arms across my chest. "Ugh. You wish."

He placed a hand on his chest, looking forlorn. "Oh, but I do wish, Zoey Valentine."

I shrieked in frustration, bounding down the stairs, ready to walk all the way to Citi Field if it got me away from him. I ran right into someone with so much force that I bounced back and almost lost my balance. A hand reached out and grabbed me before I reached my imminent doom on the sidewalk.

"Heya, champ."

"Sorry, Dad," I said, still fuming.

"Hey, Mr. Valentine!"

I groaned again. "Hey, Ash, how's it going? Season is going pretty well, isn't it?" Dad asked, eagerly. My dad *loved* Ash and spent way too much time talking to him about football and baseball. Ash wasn't just the captain of the football team, he was the quarterback. He wasn't just the captain of the baseball team, but the star pitcher. He was everything my dad would have wanted for me, if I didn't have, you know, boobs and stuff.

"Dad, can we go?" I hissed at him under my breath.

My dad looked down at me with a familiar look on his face. He thought I was being "dramatic." My mom had given my dad a lecture when I turned thirteen. She told him all about the "terrors of raising a teenage girl." Since then, he seemed to take that to heart and every reaction I had to anything was "overdramatic" and "irrational." "I'm talking to Ash, Z."

My mouth dropped open, and I turned to Ash who was trying and failing not to laugh. "God, not you too. My name is Zoey. Z-O-E-Y! Not Z. You can call me champ, if you'd like. But not Z. I am more than one letter." I glared at Ash. "Will you just stop?"

Ash shoved his hands in the pockets of his jeans and started walking backward toward his own house. "One day, Mr. Valentine, your daughter is going to figure it out, and it's going to be all good from there," he called before disappearing into his apartment. Sometimes I felt really bad for his neighbors in the brownstone. It was bad enough living next door to him.

I turned my glare on my dad, who was chuckling. "Why

do you have to encourage him?"

He had already changed into a comfortable outfit, which I was grateful for. I checked his jeans, noticing the bulge of the gun and tried hard not to sigh. My dad brought his gun everywhere with him, and I should have learned not to be so surprised at this point. "That guy is crazy about you, Zoey. I don't know why you hate him so much."

I grabbed his arm and started pulling him in the direction of the subway. "Seriously? No...just, no. He's awful. Do you know that he told Ol' Barb the lunch lady that he was pining for her, and she gave him extra pie? I mean, it's disgusting." I made a face. "And he just tried to trick me into kissing him and squirted water in my face. Like I wanted to kiss *him*."

"Denial ain't just a river in Egypt," he said, as we descended the steps.

"Shut up, Dad," I said, but only half-heartedly. "Let's just go enjoy the game, okay?"

Later that night, while on the subway home after a crushing defeat at the hands of the Yankees and my dad I were arguing different points of the game, I realized how lucky I was. I had a great dad, a great place to live, a great best friend, and I was a senior in high school, with an impressive grade point average which guaranteed me admission into a decent college. Life was good, and the future was looking bright.

It was the right moment for the shit to hit the fan.

CHAPTER
TWO

MOST TEENAGE GIRLS DIDN'T HAVE the sort of schedule that I did. I was in honor society, always making sure that I had the best grades. I helped Madison with whatever cause she was currently on, whether it was decorating for the latest dance or collecting food for the local food banks.

But most of my time was spent in classes. My dad is extremely protective of me. This wasn't a bad thing of course, but it had led to me being way more equipped to protect myself than was actually necessary.

Mondays were karate, Tuesdays were kickboxing, and so on. I was proficient in so many forms of self-defense and fighting that it was almost embarrassing.

It was Thursday and as soon as I was done with cheer practice and homework, I packed up my bag, and hopped on the subway to that day's class: mixed martial arts. MMA was just the newest of my dad's obsessions. I had been taking it for a couple months now and was getting fairly good at it.

I spent most of my time there with the punching bag, practicing my kicks, punches and blocks. I had slipped on my ear buds, turning up the volume of my iPod so that the music was the only thing that I heard. Even though I constantly gave my dad a hard time for making me take these lessons, I kind of liked it. I had muscles in places I didn't know could become muscle and I knew that I could take care of myself, if anyone came my way. Sure I had absolutely no social life outside of these various martial arts studios but who needed a social life?

Lost in my music and the satisfying smack of my skin against the rough fabric of the punching bag, I didn't notice when the room had gone silent and the practice fights had begun. Someone went careening into me, causing me to wrap my arms tightly around the bag to keep from falling over. I turned around and noticed the fight. I smiled sheepishly and took a seat on the floor by the mirrors, using a towel to wipe the sweat from my brow.

Two girls were already in a practice fight, and I watched them carefully, mentally correcting a step or a punch when it went the wrong way. It had always come as a surprise to me that despite never having the desire to learn to be a fighter, I was kind of a natural. I wasn't really good at anything. I liked to read, but past second grade, they didn't exactly hand out awards for being able to read. I wasn't social and intelligent like Madison, and I definitely wasn't able to try out for basketball or swimming or anything. I reluctantly cheered for the football and basketball teams because Madison was head cheer captain, and she always managed to convince me, year after year, that it was a good way for us to spend time together.

And to find cute boys to date. That part was true at least.

I wasn't musical, and I couldn't sing. I could recite entire scenes from *The Lord of the Rings* series from memory, and I knew the current batting average for every player on the Mets. I was fashionable enough to know how to dress myself well, with the odd shape that I was. But I wasn't talented, not until I started taking defense lessons.

So, yeah, I wasn't always fond of the next form of fighting my dad had found for me, but secretly, I was a little excited every time. It was a challenge. I liked challenges, and each form of fighting was met as a challenge I wanted to defeat.

I had spaced out a bit, my eyes glazing over as I watched the fight in front of me, which meant I had missed seeing my dad enter the studio. The room erupted into fierce whispers, and I felt my face flush.

Dad was something of a celebrity, in the only way that a police chief could actually be a celebrity. He had worked his way up the ranks fairly quickly and was a really young police chief. New York City was an impossible place sometimes as a cop: people died every day, there was crime everywhere, and you couldn't solve every crime. But that didn't stop my dad from trying, and it didn't stop him from making a small dent in that crime rate. He was also known for not always following the rules, which got him into trouble but the city saw him as a hero. They loved hearing that he had beaten a serial rapist in the face until he bled.

"Valentine, you're up," my instructor shouted at me and I resisted the urge to roll my eyes. I didn't fight most classes because I usually ended up winning, and the other girls didn't learn anything from receiving a beating. I was only being thrown into a fight because my dad was here to watch.

He stood against the wall, his arms folded tight across his chest. He was in civilian clothes, but he was never truly a civilian, and you could see the outlines of his guns beneath the fabric of his jeans. Dad was in his late thirties, young to have an eighteen-year-old daughter. He and my mom had married young, after finding out they were expecting me. A lot of girls at school were always finding ways to come to my house and I suppose it was because he was good looking or something. He was my dad, though, and that was something I avoided thinking about it.

Right now, for instance, I could see more than a few of the girls stealing glances his way. He had his "serious cop" face on that made him look intimidating and a bit mysterious as well, as if there was a wall that couldn't be broken down, a wall that any woman would just be dying to break down.

To me, he was just my dad. He was the guy who helped me pick out my prom dress, took me to baseball games, and challenged me to eat an entire medium size Hawaiian pie all by myself, which I accomplished thank you very much. He was the guy who sat on the couch drinking a beer, watched crappy action movies and had a weird addiction to professional wrestling.

I pushed myself off the ground, making sure the tape around my hands was still tight and ready. I jumped around loosening myself up a bit. My opponent was a girl named Stacy, who was good but doubted her own abilities. She could pack a punch, no problem, but she didn't want to and that was her weakness. I felt bad every time I stepped up to fight her.

Her arms were up in a block, and I paced in a circle, my arms up and ready. I threw a punch, and she dodged it. Her leg came up in a kick, and I grabbed it, twisting it so she fell to the ground. She scrambled backward, trying to gain the momentum to stand back up, but I was quick, and I had her pinned down to the ground.

"Good work, Zoey," my instructor said, sounding anxious, tossing a glance at my father.

"Thanks," I said, standing up and offering a hand and an apologetic smile to Stacy. She smiled back, taking my hand, and I hoisted her up.

"You weren't evenly matched," Dad said, his deep voice carrying across the room. Everyone turned to look at him, and then back at me. "You win because you're fighting those who aren't matched to you or, frankly, just don't want to fight." He offered Stacy a smile and she smiled shyly in return. "You should be in a boy's class. They would at least offer you a challenge."

I felt a wave of irritation roll through me. He was the reason I was even in these classes and when I was good, I still wasn't good enough. "Well," I said, sarcasm seeping into my voice, "you could always arrange that, couldn't you? I think my Wednesdays might be free."

I was being sassy and pushing buttons, and I knew it. My dad had a small smirk at the corner of his mouth. I heard a girl sigh behind me, and I resisted the urge to roll my eyes.

"Well, I don't know that I have to go that far," he said, uncrossing his arms, and coming toward the mats. He rolled up his sleeves, and I heard a few laughs behind me. I was totally in trouble now. "Why not try fighting someone who is a challenge?"

I felt a wave of doubt wash through me. The last person that I wanted to fight was my dad, a guy who took down drug dealers on a daily basis. I sighed like I was bored. "I don't want to hurt you, old man."

His smirk grew a bit more, and I nearly stopped. I nearly backed down and admitted that there was no way I could actually try and take down my dad. My pride always got the better of me though. I was the star of this class, and there was no way I was admitting defeat. "Defense position," he ordered, nodding at me.

I rolled my eyes, but raised my arms, fists clenched. He was standing there, not even in position. I knew I had to act quickly, catch him off guard before he could take me down in one swipe. I stepped closer. He studied me, his eyes intent on mine. I threw a left punch, and he dodged it effortlessly. My right hook was coming up not even a split second later, aimed for his throat. He reached almost lazily for my fist and twisted my arm around. His hand grabbed my leg, and

I flipped, landing with a hard "oomph" on my back, seeing stars.

"YOU KNOW, YOU DIDN'T HAVE to flip me," I said.

Dad laughed, his hands shoved deep in his pockets. He stopped in front of a street vendor, handing over a wrinkly five-dollar bill. "Want one?" he said, pointing to the admittedly tempting hot dogs spinning in the case. I shook my head. "Someone had to teach you a lesson in humility."

"I have plenty of humility," I grumbled, shifting the strap of my bag so it fit more comfortably on my shoulder.

"No, you really don't," he said, taking an enthusiastic bite out of the hot dog that was just handed to him. "Your real weakness is your pride. You're good, so you think nobody can beat you."

"Well, I'm obviously wrong about that," I said, wincing at my sore back.

He laughed again. "I wasn't kidding when I said I would put you in a men's class. Maybe going up against those who are much stronger than you would make you better and less cocky and flashy."

I scowled. He was mostly right about that. "I *am* good."

"Yeah. Yeah, you are," he said, looking down at me appraisingly. He wrapped his arm tightly around my neck. "Come on, let's go get pizza." He finished the last couple bites of his hot dog. "I'm starving."

"IT'S SUPPOSED TO BE DRAPING! How do you even consider that draping? They're vines. It's supposed to look effortless!" Madison stomped her foot down, her small face red with exhaustion and frustration. I knew a meltdown was probably coming soon.

Brody, high atop a ladder, paused for a moment in the middle of his work and looked at Madison. "Babe, this is not effortless."

"Well, it should be," she said, not meeting his eyes but consulting her clipboard instead. "Zoey, have we heard from the DJ?"

"Hmm?" I said, vaguely. I was sitting on one of the black iron benches that lined the open courtyard in the middle of the square buildings that were St. Joseph's Prep. A book was open in my lap, *American Gods* by Neil Gaiman, one of my absolute favorites.

"Get your head out of the book for like an hour, can you, please?" Madison begged. She had pulled her slick black hair in a perfect bun, and had no less than three or four pens stuck in the bun. She was still wearing her workout clothes from cheer practice. "The DJ, Zoey, the DJ?"

"Last I heard, he'd be here at 6 p.m., to be ready in time for doors opening at 7 p.m.," I said. "Everything is going to be fine."

"Yeah, right," she said. "Does anyone have a pen?" My eyebrow rose in response, and she immediately reached for her bun. She smiled sheepishly, and then her eyes went wide. "Ash, no, seriously? What are you doing?"

I turned and glanced over my shoulder. Ash had been put in charge of draping the Christmas lights that Madison had purchased, a task that I had thought was way too optimistic for him. True to form, none of the lights were put up, and instead were wrapped around his body, lighting him up like a Christmas tree. I rolled my eyes and turned back to my book.

"Please, will you go help him?" Madison said, her hands over her eyes. "I can't handle this. I'm a wreck."

"Maddie, it's going to be great, just like every single dance turns out great," I said, irritated at being interrupted again. I was only present at the setup for the dance under duress. Madison had signed me up herself, of course. She did that for most of her committees.

She turned her evil eye on me for a moment. "This is a pivotal dance, Zoey. The fall dance sets the tone for the entire school year. It shows everyone here at school whether I am capable of planning Homecoming or Winter Formal or prom. This is the beginning and end of our entire year as seniors."

I held my hands up in surrender, biting back the laugh that was threatening to burst out. "All right, all right," I said, looking at all the action around us. Brody was on the ladder, draping the vines, and it looked just fine to me. Everything else was coming together very nicely. "I'll go help Ash."

I placed a bobby pin on the page I was reading and set the book aside. I hopped up off the bench and walked over to Ash, who was laughing at his own obviously hilarious situation. Not saying a word, I just started unwrapping the lights from his body.

"What are you doing?" Ash said, watching as I moved around him, removing the lights as best I could without getting them tangled up. If they got tangled, it would be a disaster almost instantly, and I'd be stuck on the bench untangling the stupid mess until the doors opened in a few hours.

"We have to decorate the courtyard, Ash, not ourselves," I said, as my hands brushed along his hipbones. I blushed and avoided eye contact.

"Nah, you just wanted an excuse to touch me," he laughed. "That's exactly why I did it, you know. I knew Madison would send you over here to untangle me, and I couldn't get past that thought."

"You're revolting," I answered indifferently. I didn't have a lot of effort to spare on Ash today, not when a classic Madison Wu breakdown was imminent. "Just help me with these, okay?"

"Yeah, sure, Z, whatever you say," he said, stepping out of the last bits of lights that were wrapped around his legs. How did he even manage to do this to himself?

"Zoey?"

I turned around and saw my ex-boyfriend, Joel, standing behind me, a stack of tablecloths in his arms. "Oh, hey, what's up?"

"When you get a chance, can you help me with this?" he asked, motioning over where the food and beverage tables were set up under a breezeway.

"Yeah, definitely. Just let me help Ash finish these lights

first, okay?" He nodded, smiling, and walked away.

"So what's up with you and Joel over there?" Ash asked, helping me to set up a ladder. As I climbed up, I felt a blush cross my cheeks. I was wearing the clothes I wore to cheer practice and the shorts left very little to the imagination. Ash would be one to take advantage of this situation.

I glanced at Joel, talking casually with Jaida, the junior dance committee rep. We had dated for a little over a year and had parted without any drama, the easiest breakup in the history of all breakups. We'd had a few hot and heavy months, but our friendship was stronger than our chemistry, and we decided to remain friends. "We're friends," I said, reaching for the lights and the staple gun.

"That's not the way I see it, Zo-Zo," Ash said, grinning at me, his arms gripping the ladder tightly. "The way I see, Joelskies over there is still pining for you."

I stapled a section of lights to the breezeway and glanced back over at Joel, who was laughing at something Jaida said. Ash and I were not even a blip on their radar. "If you say so." I felt myself slip a little on the ladder as it shook slightly, and Ash's hand came up to steady me, just under the hem of my shorts. A tingle spread through my legs down to my toes, and I glared down at him. He smiled lazily back up at me.

"I know jealousy when I see it," Ash assured me. "He's heartbroken that you've left him in the dust, leaving him to run to underclassmen like Jaida."

"Last I had heard," I said, putting my body weight forward and stapling another section, "Joel was dating Kat

Mitchell." Ash's hand was still on my leg, and it was incredibly distracting.

"Kat," he scoffed. "She's missing something. Or maybe has an extra couple somethings. She's not quite as good as my girl Z."

"Zoey," I said, automatically, as the ladder shook again. I descended quickly and shoved the staple gun back into his hands. "And I think you're perfectly capable of finishing this."

He took the staple gun, surprised, watching as I walked away, the slick bottoms of my beat up converses slipping on the smooth cement of the courtyard. "I hope you save me a dance tonight, Z!"

"DO YOU THINK EVERYTHING LOOKS okay?" Madison asked me, wringing her hands together and glancing around the room.

"It looks beautiful," I assured her. "So do you by the way." After we had spent a good couple of hours setting up for the dance, we'd finally descended upon the girls' locker room. Using it as a makeshift beauty room, we changed from our practice clothes to the dresses we'd bought a couple weeks ago.

She beamed, but I could still see the anxiety building in her eyes. Her hair was still pulled back in a bun, but she'd added glitter to her sleek black strands, and it caught in the twinkling lights stretched across the courtyard. Her pink flowing dress hit right above her knee and made her look like a tiny ballerina. "Thanks. You do too. Scandalous. I hope Headmistress Dweller doesn't see you."

I rolled my eyes and looked down at my dress. It was red, which was already an alarming thing that might cause our old fashioned and conservative headmistress to lose her cool. It was a halter and accentuated the fact that I had large boobs, but in a good way, of course. I had started getting boobs when I was nine years old and had taken to wearing baggy shirts and jackets to cover them up. Now that I was older and enjoyed dressing up, especially when Madison and I went dancing, I dressed for my body type. No use in letting them hide when they were so nearly impossible to do so anyway. The dress hit at least a hands width above my knee but it wasn't *that* short.

Plus, I had left my long hair down for once, in messy waves so my shoulders were even covered. "What's wrong with it?"

"It's like a shirt, Zoey," Madison said, smirking a little.

"It's a dress," I protested. "But I will take your compliment and forget your doubt in my dress. This cost a good chunk of my monthly allowance."

"Also known as the mom guilt money," Madison finished. "You think it looks good, really? The dance, I mean."

"It does," I said, firmly. "You worked really hard on it. I still don't really get the apples hanging from vines when apples grow on trees but it looks good."

She threw me a glare. "It's fall. The apples add a fall ambience."

"Okay," I agreed. "Fall ambience, sure."

Madison looked like she wanted to say more but was momentarily distracted as her boyfriend Brody approached us. She lit up, and I shook my head again at the endearing yet vomit-inducing love they shared.

Sometimes, Madison treated dating like another thing to tackle on her never-ending to-do list. I remember the first day of freshman year, sitting on the steps that led up to St. Joseph's and planning which boys would be the best to date—and would help her lift her social strata. This was basically part of her plan for world domination. She had the grades, the fashion sense, the family pedigree, and the determination and ambition. She needed a boy to fit into that.

But Brody snuck up on her. He was nondescript, according to the list she had made of attributes necessary for a perfect boyfriend. There was no denying that he was good-looking with his shaggy blond hair and green eyes. But he was from Brooklyn and a scholarship student, and my dear social-climbing friend just couldn't handle that sort of reputation for her future boyfriend.

He was always there though: volunteering to help her campaign for class president, helping her bake cupcakes for the Honor Society bake sales, and helping her to study math, her hardest subject. It wasn't long before she dropped the cold method of finding someone suitable to her list and fell madly in love with Brody Levitt. That was three years ago, and she has never lost that dreamy look on her face when he came near her.

"Dance with me?" he asked, holding his hand out to

her.

She grinned, taking his hand. She looked at me. "You okay over here?"

I nodded. "Go."

"Have fun, wallflower," she called behind her as Brody led her to the dance floor.

"Hey, that's a good book," I retorted, but she was too far away and the music was too loud for her to hear. I stood around for a moment, watching my classmates dancing on the dance floor before deciding to walk over to the dessert table and grab a cupcake. Madison had managed to get the cupcakes donated by Crumbs, and I had been dying to try one all night.

I was peeling the wrapper off a dark chocolate cupcake when Ash came up to me. "And here I thought you weren't coming to the dance."

I shrugged, trying to ignore how good he looked. None of the guys at St. Joseph's looked particularly good in the uniforms, but once they were out of them, it was a completely different story. "I helped put the decorations up, might as well see my hard work in action."

He laughed, reaching for a cupcake himself. "Don't lie. You may act all cool and aloof, but I know that you love to dance."

"And how do you know that?" I asked, swiping a glob of cream cheese frosting off the top of the cupcake and stuck it in my mouth. I nearly moaned; this was delicious.

"I pay attention, Z," he said, biting into his own cupcake. Unlike me, he didn't hold back and a moan escaped his lips. "Jesus, these are amazing."

"What do you want, Ash?" I asked, shaking my hair out of my face.

"Come dance with me."

I burst out laughing. "Yeah, I don't think so."

"I know you love to dance, Z, and I know you're dying to right now," he said, wagging his eyebrows up and down suggestively. "So come dance with me."

I shook my head, a grin still on my face. "No, Ash, I'm smart enough to know that accepting a dance with you is a bad idea. I've seen *Carrie*. I've seen *Never Been Kissed*. It never works out well for the geeky girl when the popular boy asks her to dance."

"You don't look very geeky in that dress," Ash said, looking me up and down, his eyes lingering over my breasts, hips and legs. I felt a blush creep up on my cheeks, and I knew my face probably matched my dress perfectly.

"Zoey, do you want to dance?"

I turned and saw Eddie Ward standing there. He had been considered as a perfect match for Madison when she was obsessed with that sort of thing, until he had announced that he was gay, to the disappointment of Madison and pretty much every eligible bachelorette in New York City. Eventually he became incredibly close friends with Madison and, in turn, with me as well. He often went out to the clubs with us, dragging his boyfriend Trent along with us. He was a fantastic dancer.

I grinned and put the cupcake back on the table, away from the clean, untouched ones. "I would love to." I took his outstretched hand and let him lead me down to the dance floor. I tossed a victory smile over my shoulder at Ash. The DJ picked a faster paced song, and I felt the music pouring through my body.

"Was Ash bothering you?" Eddie shouted in my ear, his hands on my hips.

I rolled my eyes. "He's always bothering me. It's fine."

We stayed on the dance floor for a few songs before Trent came up to us. He looked awful. His face was incredibly pale, and sweat dripped through his hair and was running down his cheeks.

"Oh my god, Trent. Are you okay?" I shouted. I grabbed his arm, and Eddie and I guided him through the crowd to a seat on the outside.

He immediately collapsed on a bench, his head in his hands. He groaned loudly. "I feel awful."

"Please don't throw up on the shoes," I begged, and Eddie laughed. "Seriously, I worked hard for these. And Madison will kill you because she picked them out."

Eddie threw me an amused but exasperated look and turned to his boyfriend. "What did you have to eat?"

"Pancakes at the diner. And I had about three of those cupcakes," Trent said, looking like he was going to blow chunks at any moment.

Eddie laughed a little at that. "I told you that pancakes for dinner was a bad idea," he scolded him. He hooked his arm through Trent's and hauled him to his feet. "Sounds like a trip to the little boy's room is in order." He smiled apologetically at me, and I smiled back, watching them walk away.

"What's wrong with Trent?" Madison said, coming up from behind me and looking worried.

"He's sick. He's probably throwing up right now," I explained. Madison looked panicked for a moment. "He had pancakes before the dance apparently and three of the cupcakes, so it's really not a surprise."

"Oh god, the cupcakes," Madison moaned, looking around. "There are a couple girls in the bathroom throwing up too."

"Yeah, that's probably not the cupcakes," I said drily. Brody laughed, and I grinned widely.

"Zoey Elizabeth Valentine, be seriously!" Madison shrieked. "This is a disaster."

"It's not a disaster," I said, breezily. "A couple people are sick. It's not a big deal, and it's most likely not the cupcakes. Did you have a cupcake?"

"Yes," she answered, slowly and uncertainly.

"And are you sick?" I said, just as slowly.

"Well, no, but…"

"It's not the cupcakes," I said firmly.

"There's been some guys throwing up too," Brody piped up.

"You're not helping, Brody," I laughed. "We're trying to *avoid* a meltdown." Brody laughed again, and even Madison showed a small smile.

At that moment, a few freshmen girls came bursting out of the dance crowd. Two girls had a third supported between them. She had a distinct green tinge to her face, and I had a bad feeling immediately. She stopped her friends, her hands clutching her stomach tightly. I winced as she pitched forward and threw up all over the concrete floor.

Madison ran forward and grabbed the arm of one of the friends. "Did she have a cupcake?"

The girl looked from Madison to me, looking shocked, but nodded. Madison threw me a triumphant look, and I resisted the urge to throw my shoe at her. We jumped back a moment later as she joined her friend in vomiting.

"This is a disaster," Madison said again, her voice full of anger and disappointment.

I looked at Brody and saw that he was giving up as well. "Yeah, I think it's time to cut the party." I sighed and headed over to the DJ, taking the reins away from my disappointed friend.

CHAPTER

THREE

Five Weeks Later

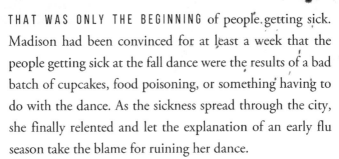

THAT WAS ONLY THE BEGINNING of people getting sick. Madison had been convinced for at least a week that the people getting sick at the fall dance were the results of a bad batch of cupcakes, food poisoning, or something having to do with the dance. As the sickness spread through the city, she finally relented and let the explanation of an early flu season take the blame for ruining her dance.

No one thought anything of it. It was October in New York. People get the flu; they take medicine, and they get over it. It was not a big deal. It was not rocket science: in a city of millions, germs spread easily and so did the flu season.

I guess it was hard to pinpoint the moment that the virus hit us, because we were so unaware of it. It started out just like your normal flu: fever, chills, vomiting. When it lasted more than a couple of days, people started going to doctors.

That's when it got worse. That's when we knew it was different.

It started affecting more people. Everyone went nuts, trying to get their hands on a flu vaccine, but they were running out, and it was becoming clear that it wasn't just the flu. The flu didn't turn your skin so pale that it was nearly blue or cause bright red sores that bled incessantly when they burst. The flu didn't kill people, not like this, not this quickly.

Two kids died at St. Joseph's within a few weeks of the virus, including one of the sick girls from the dance. Trent followed a week later. This was only the beginning.

"Zoey, I've been thinking…"

I paused in the middle of pouring milk into my cereal bowl. "Well, I don't like the sound of that."

"Just hear me out," my dad said, laying down his newspaper. I avoided looking at the headlines; they were just too depressing to look at. After seeing Trent's obituary in the paper, it held no appeal to me. "People are getting sick all over the place, champ, and no one has really figured out what it is."

"Dad…" I had a feeling I knew where this conversation was heading and I was also sure that I didn't like its direction.

"And it's not just New York anymore. There are cases of the virus all over the place: Los Angeles, Chicago, Philadelphia, Denver, Seattle, everywhere."

I sat at the table, taking a bite of my cereal. "Dad, we've discussed this. I'm not dropping out of school. I'm not sitting at home, by myself, all the time."

"It would just be a break," he insisted. His hazel eyes met my own very different deep brown eyes. "I just want to make sure you're safe."

"I'm already getting gun lessons," I grumbled. "I've already learned every type of self-defense there is." He gave me a look, one that clearly said I was acting like a brat. "I *am* safe. It's not like it's the black plague, Dad. People aren't walking down the street with a wheelbarrow and piling bodies into it. We don't have ring around the rosie or anything. I'm fine."

He sighed, exasperated, and I knew that I was pushing my luck. He was genuinely worried about me and if the virus didn't get under control soon, I'd be spending my days on the couch watching early afternoon talk shows. "Zoey Elizabeth, one of your friends has already died. I'm just trying to protect you."

"You're always trying to protect me. Hence the gun lessons," I pointed out, thinking about the pamphlet about some boot camp he had slipped under my door a few weeks ago. It seemed to be the only class on this island that I hadn't taken.

"Well, it's my job."

I gave him an ill-amused look and a small smile appeared on his lips. "It's your job to protect everyone, Dad."

"You're the most important, champ," he answered, then taking a sip of his coffee. He folded the newspaper back into place, with perfect creases, the way he always did before leaving for work.

"I'm not going to get sick," I said, firmly.

He stood up and grabbed his coat off the back of his chair. "If it gets worse, you're staying home." He came over and kissed the top of my head. "I'll see you after work."

I waited until I heard him pull away before getting up. I washed my dishes, leaving them in the drying rack, and grabbed my coat from the front closet. I made sure the dog door was open and gave Bandit a kiss on the head before leaving.

Madison was waiting on the front stoop for me when I opened the front door. She was talking to Ash, using her hands to animate the story. I sighed, turning to lock the front door before turning back to them. "Madison!"

She looked up, a big smile on her small face. Everything about her was small. I wasn't exactly tall at 5'4", but I towered over her. "Hey, Zoey. You ready?"

I nodded, shifting my backpack so it lay comfortably between my shoulder blades. I walked down the steps, avoiding any eye contact with Ash. He had booby trapped my locker with glitter two days earlier, and I had walked around in my St. Joseph's uniform the rest of the day looking like a fabulous Catholic school girl out of some weird anime movie. To say I was still a bit angry would have been a vast understatement.

We made it a few blocks in silence before Madison finally spoke. "Did you hear about Xavier Campos? He went to the hospital last night. He was already covered in sores, but I guess his mom didn't want to take him. His dad snuck him out in the middle of the night."

"Oh god," I said, feeling sick. Xavier sat behind me in Algebra II, and I had known him since kindergarten. "How on earth did you find this out?"

"Victoria," Madison said, referring to Xavier's girlfriend. "She texted him this morning and his brother told her. He's sick as well, but not as bad."

"Oh god," I repeated. "No one tell my dad. He really wants me to stay home."

"I don't know, Zoey," Madison said, looking worried as we slushed through the gray puddles along the sidewalk. It was already turning into a gloomy winter. "Maybe it's not such a bad idea. People are getting sick everywhere."

"Not you too," I groaned, stopping for a moment to pull up one of my knee socks. "We aren't getting sick. There's no need for everyone to get so panicky."

"If you get sick, Z, I could take care of you."

I jumped, looking over my shoulder at Ash. "Geez. You're still here?"

"We do attend the same school," he pointed out, a big grin on his face. His hair was windswept, and his cheeks had turned red from the cold, making his blue eyes stand out even more. "And take the same subway."

"Go away, Ash," I said, giving him a withering look before turning back around.

As usual, he ignored me. He fell into step next to me, forcing Madison to walk in front of us. She tossed an amused look over her shoulder but kept walking. Ash was Brody's best friend, and Madison had been convinced for months, years even, that Ash and I would work out and the

41

four of us would live happily ever after. Not likely. Not in this world.

"I would take care of you if you were sick. I'd fluff your pillows and tuck you in and make you chicken soup and read you a bedtime story." He grabbed my hand held it to his chest. I tried very hard to ignore the hard muscles I could feel even through his coat. "Maybe, if you're lucky, I'll even give you a sponge bath."

"You're disgusting," I answered, trying to pull my hand back. He held fast, grinning at me.

"Ash!"

The two of us turned and saw Heather Carr, Ash's girlfriend, standing over at the entrance to the subway, their usual meeting spot. She had her arms folded tight across her chest, looking angry. Ash dropped my hand like it was on fire and strode over to her, where she immediately started speaking heatedly to him.

Madison came back to stand next to me, looking at the couple arguing. Heather looked angry, her posture tense, while Ash had his hands shoved in his pockets, unconcerned and bored. "Can you please just make out with him already? The tension is too much for even me to handle."

"Really, Madison? I'm not putting my mouth anywhere near his. Especially since it's been on *hers*," I said, nodding my head in Heather's direction.

"Just think, Zoey," she said, as we snuck past them and down the stairs. "If you dated Ash, you could totally be prom queen."

"I thought you wanted to be prom queen," I said,

raising my eyebrow at her.

She thought about it for a moment, her nose wrinkled in concentration. "Okay, maybe just the prom court then." I laughed, and she smiled mischievously at me.

I COULDN'T SLEEP.

It was hot in my room, stifling. I tossed and turned for hours before finally pushing the covers aside and walking across my room to my window. I pushed it open, letting the air fill my room. Bandit looked up from his corner of the room with one sleepy eye open. Once he had determined that I was okay and safe, he closed his eye again, and his soft dog snores filled the room.

I took a deep breath and sat on my window seat for a moment, enjoying the breeze on my sweat covered body. I realized how dry my throat was, and I made my way downstairs to get something to drink.

I had barely opened a bottle of water when I heard a crash upstairs. I shrieked, and water went everywhere, including down my shirt. I waited, and heard more movement upstairs. The clock on the oven read 2:52, and I furrowed my brow, confused. What on earth was my dad doing up at this time?

I waited for a few moments at the bottom of the stairs before calling out, "Dad?"

He came rushing down the stairs, his shirt on inside out. He looked frazzled and stressed out; he hadn't even bothered to comb his hair. "Zoey? Why aren't you in bed?"

"I couldn't sleep," I said. "What's going on? Why aren't *you* in bed?"

"There's been a homicide down at the morgue," he said, rushing past me to grab his coat and scarf from the closet.

"At the morgue?" I asked, confused. "But isn't everyone there already…" I didn't finish the thought.

"Dead? Mostly. They brought in a bunch of doctors from the CDC to examine the bodies of those dying from the virus. They're dying too fast to be tested while alive."

"Okay…" I said, unsure of why he was telling me this or how this could possibly be important.

He looked at me. "The three doctors at the morgue are dead."

"Oh my god," I said, horrified. "Why? Why would that even happen? Aren't they there to fix the problem?"

He sighed. "Well, we're going to try and find out." He opened the front door, but paused before leaving. "Don't wait up for me. And Zoey? Stay home from school today, okay?"

"Dad," I started to protest.

He had a pained expression on his face. "Please, for me."

I swallowed hard, and nodded. "Okay."

"See if you can convince Madison to stay home as well. I'll be home later." Then he was gone.

I cleaned up the water in the kitchen before heading back upstairs. I typed out a quick message to Madison, urging her to stay home from school at the request of my dad. I hesitated for a moment, before sending another to Ash. I tossed my phone to the side before I could regret my momentary lapse of judgment and crawled back into bed, no longer feeling warm.

I woke later, feeling even more exhausted than I had felt earlier. I yawned widely and reached for the remote sitting on top of a crumbled bag of Doritos on my nightstand. Hoping to see something about the murders at the morgue, I flipped on the TV and found a channel showing the local news.

Instead I found what seemed to be the beginning of a press conference. The headline at the bottom of the screen read "Head of CDC to Address Concerns about Virus," and an empty podium, presumably waiting for the head of the CDC, was the focus of attention. I turned up the volume, eager to find out more about the virus that was sweeping through our country like a tornado.

The woman representing the CDC came on the screen and immediately there was a hushed tone, as she approached the podium. She shuffled a few papers and smiled at the crowd of reporters in front of her. Her name flashed quickly across the bottom of the screen: Razi Cylon.

"Good morning everyone," she began, her clipped British accent obvious right off the bat. There was also a little something else there, perhaps Indian. "My name is Razi Cylon and I'm a representative of the CDC. I have been very close to the work and study that we have been doing on this virus. As of right now, we know very little. The symptoms seem to be similar of what we know of the routine stomach flu: fever, chills, vomiting. However, the symptoms, as we have found out, tend to worsen and lead to the loss of blood, through vomiting or urination and the red sores that break out across the body. We are working hard to determine how the virus is transmitted. It is becoming more likely, as days pass, that it is not airborne. However, only with more time and more study will we begin to understand the nature of this.

We are working diligently to learn more about the virus in order to figure out a method of fighting it off or even curing it. We urge everyone to go about your normal business but with caution. Remember to wash your hands constantly. Do not share drinks. Keep yourself as healthy and active as possible. Go to the doctor or your local hospital the minute you start feeling the symptoms and together, we can progress forward toward a solution."

She smiled at the cameras again, but the smile not quite reaching her eyes. She didn't look much like a doctor, someone capable of spending days responsible for the Center of Disease Control. She was dressed impeccably in a smart business suit, and looked more like a lawyer than a doctor. I briefly remembered when my mother took me to Europe after my eighth grade graduation, and I sprained my ankle. The doctor in Leeds was dressed similarly, less like the normal picture I had for a doctor. There was something very poised and calculated about this woman though, and I was drawn to her eyes, that just didn't match the tone of her voice or the smile on her full lips.

The reporters immediately launched into a flurry of questions, talking over one another. I had had enough and switched off the TV. No sooner had my room fallen into silence again when there was a loud pounding on the door.

I jumped, startled, and then laughed at myself. This virus was making me paranoid and easily spooked.

I climbed out of bed and went bounding down the stairs. I stood on tiptoe to see through the peephole and sighed when my line of sight was just underneath. I opened the door and immediately saw Madison and Ash standing on my doorstep.

"Hi, Madison," I said, flashing an impatient look at Ash.

"I come bearing snacks and Buffy," Madison said, holding up a full grocery bag. She jerked her head toward Ash. "He invited himself." She gave me a knowing look as she came in.

"Nice bed head, Z." My hand went immediately to my hair. I hadn't even thought to run a brush through it. "I invited Brody, too," Ash said cheerfully, coming in as well, uninvited. "Where's Bandit?

At the sound of his name, Bandit came bounding down the stairs, skidding across the wood floor and crashing into Ash's legs. Ash bent over, and scratched him behind the ear. Bandit's tongue fell out, his foot stomping in happiness. I sighed.

"You weren't invited, Ash," I said, "Which means you can't just invite others."

Ash looked over at Madison, his eyebrow raised. She smiled sheepishly and didn't protest.

"I hate you both," I said, rolling my eyes and shutting the door. I was already beginning to shiver. It was freezing out there. "And besides, is it okay to invite Brody over? I thought his mother was sick. We don't know how the virus is spread."

"Brody's mom is sick," Ash admitted, wandering over to the couch and plopping down on it.

"Yes, she is," Madison said, glaring at Ash. "But his mom lives in Queens. He hasn't even seen her since she got sick."

I opened my mouth and then closed it, finding nothing to say.

"I think we won," Madison smirked, taking up residence on my dad's favorite armchair, a bag of Cheetos on her lap.

I grabbed the bag that Madison brought and dug through the contents, looking for the package of gummy worms that were absolutely necessary for my part in a *Buffy the Vampire Slayer* marathon. "I don't think this is what my dad had in mind when he said to stay home from school." I sighed. "But it *is* Buffy. I'm going upstairs to change."

"I think I'd rather you stay in those pajamas, Z," Ash called from the couch. "Much easier to take off."

I blushed furiously and turned away, stomping up the stairs. Ash was so infuriating! I thought about his comment and his hands sliding up to remove my flannel pajama bottoms, and I felt my blush deepen. Ash had a way of getting under my skin, and I hated it. I yanked on a pair of jeans and a soft gray sweater. I brushed my brown hair, which was sticking up in places. It was so long that it tended to do wild things when left to fend for itself.

By the time I got back downstairs, Brody had arrived and was canoodling on the armchair with Madison and nearly half of the first episode had passed.

"Come sit with me, my beautiful Manhattan babe," Ash said, patting the space on the couch next to him.

I rolled my eyes. "Budge over, buddy," I said, sitting on the couch. I pulled up my legs, folding them, and grabbed a blanket, draping it over my legs.

Bandit came trotting into the room, settling on the ground right in front of me. I ran a hand over his head, immediately feeling comforted. Bandit was one of my best friends. Before Madison, I kept to my books, and sometimes after a particularly bad day (like Ash dumping pudding on my jeans during PE so it looked like I had pooped my pants for the rest of the day), I would come home and immediately go to my bed. Bandit would jump on the bed with me and put his head on my lap, and I would tell him about the awful day I had.

Pathetic, I know. But he was the best dog, such a loyal dog. He couldn't sit or stay or roll over to safe his life but he was loyal as hell and incredibly protective.

A pillow fell in my lap, followed by a head of perfectly styled brown hair.

"You're comfy," Ash sighed.

"Seriously?" I hissed at him, aware of how close he was to me.

"Shh," Madison said, glaring at me. "Number one rule of a Buffy marathon is that one does not speak during said marathon."

"Yes, ma'am," Ash said, saluting her as best as he could from my lap. He fell into silence and I reluctantly let him stay.

CHAPTER

FOUR

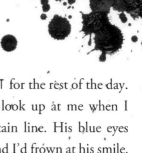

WE STAYED VIRTUALLY LIKE THAT for the rest of the day. Every once in a while Ash would look up at me when I laughed at a joke or quoted a certain line. His blue eyes would meet my dark brown ones, and I'd frown at his smile. I tried to ignore him, lying in my lap like he didn't find new ways to drive me insane every single day of my existence.

We all jumped when the front door swung open bringing in a gust of cold air and then slammed shut. I pushed Ash off my lap and ran to meet Dad in the foyer. He looked exhausted as he hung up his coat in the closet.

"Are you okay?" I asked, concerned. "Do you need anything?"

"A coffee would be nice," he said nodding. "Yeah, it was just a long day. I'm tired." We moved into the kitchen, and I started pulling the coffee canister out of the cupboard.

"What happened?"

Dad and I looked up and saw Madison, Brody and Ash framed in the stairway that led down to the basement floor, where we had been all day. My dad raised an eyebrow at me and I merely raised mine in response.

I turned to them. "Homicide. At the morgue."

"Zoey," Dad said resigned, collapsing in a chair and propping his feet on the table. I paused for a moment, wondering if I should reprimand him yet again but decided against it.

"Dad, we're adults. You can't keep hiding things from us," I said, firmly. I emptied the coffee grounds from the day before (he could never remember to do this) and put in a new filter.

He sighed. We all exchanged looks, wondering if he was going to say anything more. "This doesn't leave this room. A statement will be released but it won't be the whole truth." He looked at us each in turn, as we nodded in agreement. Madison and I both looked incredibly solemn while the boys had a certain gleam in their eyes. I rolled my eyes and turned back to my dad.

He took a deep breath and let it out slowly. "It was brutal. The doctors that were there to study the bodies? Well, they were torn to pieces. This wasn't a simple shooting or stabbing. This took time." He ran a hand through his thinning hair. "The coroner said the wounds looked like they were inflicted by teeth."

"Um, excuse me?" I asked, baffled, at the same time Brody and Ash said, "Awesome!"

I pushed Ash away from me and turned back to Dad. "I'm confused. What do you mean? Like an animal?"

He gave a sort of half-nod, half-shrug movement. "That's exactly what it looks like, but it just can't be. How would an animal capable of attacking and killing four grown adults get into a morgue in the middle of Manhattan? And you know, there were absolutely no signs of a break in."

"That's incredibly bizarre," Madison said, her pert little noise wrinkled in disgust.

"That's just the tip of the iceberg," Dad said, picking up the salt and peppershakers on the table and holding them in his hands. I knew my dad; he wasn't an idle person and his hands always had to be doing something.

"What else?" I was almost too scared to ask. What more could possibly be wrong with this crime? Vampires? Werewolves? A mad supervillain?

"The bodies are missing."

We were all quiet for a minute as we took in what my dad had said.

It was Madison who broke the silence. "What do you mean, 'the bodies are missing?' What bodies?"

"The bodies of the virus victims. There were at least twenty and they're gone. Disappeared, without a trace." I noticed a touch of unease in my father's voice and I felt my stomach drop. My dad dealt with crime every day, crime all over the city. There were some things he just got used to. To see him uneasy was a rarity. "We're getting word that this is happening all over the place too. Los Angeles. Phoenix. Denver. Chicago. It's been a nightmare."

I felt sick to my stomach. The death count of the virus had been climbing steadily over the past few weeks, and to think of all those bodies gone missing...I shuddered at the thought. "Are people stealing the bodies?"

Dad shrugged. "I don't know. Why would they? And it's not like they could get up and walk out on their own."

Ash's eyes went wide. "That would be pretty cool though. Animated corpses."

I looked over at my dad, pleading him to see the ignoramus that I was forced to deal with every single day. He smiled slightly, a corner of his mouth turned upward in amusement. I turned back to Ash, "Do you every take anything seriously?"

"I take you seriously, baby," he said, with a wink, and I threw my hands up in exasperation.

"Zoey?"

We all turned to Dad. "You're not going to school anymore. I'm sorry. It's just not safe." I nodded, swallowing hard. He looked over at the other three teenagers. "I'm not your parent, but I think it would be wise if you stayed home too."

All three of them nodded, suddenly solemn.

My dad suddenly stood up, walking over to dump the untouched coffee in the sink. "Zoey, I was also thinking that maybe you should go stay with your mom for awhile."

Madison suddenly looked alert. She knew what the three letter word "mom" would do to me. "Okay, that's my clue to leave." She grabbed Brody's shirt collar and started to tug him away." Let's go."

"No!" I burst out. "No, come on, Dad! I don't want to

live with Mom!"

"Told you," Madison said, tugging harder on Brody. "Let's go."

"I just think," he said, calmly, "it would be safer for you to be with your mother."

"Wait," Ash said, still standing there even though Madison and Brody had made their escape. "Why would Z go live with her mom?"

I ignored him. "Mom hates me."

"She doesn't hate you," Dad said, rolling her eyes. "She's hurt that you'd rather live here in New York with me, but she doesn't hate you."

"I can't live with her. I can't," I said, firmly. "My home is Manhattan."

"Why does Zoey have to move in with her mom?" Ash repeated.

"You have a home with your mom as well," Dad said gently.

"I don't want to," I said again.

"What is going on?" Ash said, looking back and forth between us.

Dad took pity on him, taking his eyes away from me. "Zoey's mother lives in a small town, Constance, in Nebraska. No one is sick there. It's safe." He directed the last line toward me pointedly.

I felt like I was losing. "No, Dad, really. I'll do anything. I'll drop out of school, I'll stay inside all day, and I'll stop breathing. Just please don't send me to Mom's. I want to stay here with you."

It was the truth, but I knew the words would have the desired effect. I was pulling the guilt card, the affection card. His resolve was beginning to crack. "I don't know, Zoey…"

"Dad, I'll stay inside all day. I'll be safe," I promised.

"I'm worried about you being alone with me gone all the time." He sounded uncertain, his shoulders sagging. I was getting closer and closer to a victory.

"It's never been an issue before," I pointed out.

"Yes, but people weren't getting sick from a mysterious virus, and bodies weren't disappearing," he pointed out. Okay, maybe I wasn't as close to a victory as I thought.

"I'll stay with her," Ash offered, sounding serious. "My parents have been pushing for me to stay home too. We can hang out together, keep each other company."

"Um, no," I said, automatically. "That's a terrible idea."

Dad sat up looking interested. "I like this idea."

"Dad!" I protested. Ash's face lit up with triumph, and I had to resist the huge urge to stick my tongue out at him.

"Zoey," he interrupted. "I would just feel safer about the both of you, if you were together."

"Yeah, Z, I can protect you," Ash said, sliding his arm around my waist. I pulled away from him, opening my mouth to protest again.

"It's either this or I'm shipping you off to Constance," my dad offered up.

I shut my mouth and glared at both of them. "You both suck," I said frustrated, turning on my heel to stomp upstairs.

"I THINK THAT WATCHING BUFFY is a better idea," Ash insisted.

"After the news, Ash, we can watch it after the news. I just want to watch the news," I said, through clenched teeth.

"Why would you want that?" he grumbled, smashing his face into a couch pillow. "It's so depressing."

"Five people from our school alone died in the last week! And we don't exactly go to a large school, Ash," I said, indignant. "It's kind of chaotic right now."

Ash sighed, exaggerated and loud, and I resisted the urge to throw the pillow at him.

It had been like this every day for about two weeks now. Ash came over in the morning and stayed until my dad came home, no matter how late it was. I tried staying away from him as much as possible, angry that I was hiding from him in my own house. At lunch, we came together and usually ordered in. I would take my food to the basement to watch the afternoon news. Ash usually followed and complained.

The death toll was mounting higher and higher, and the bodies kept disappearing. It was frightening. Panic was beginning to increase daily. People were choosing to die in their homes, afraid of their bodies being snatched. That only seemed to help the disease spread further. Most people had stopped going to work and school but there was still a great amount that carried on, like nothing was happening and everything was normal.

No one knew how the disease was spreading. Doctors were either sick themselves or too scared of the body snatchers. They were too scared to study the bodies long enough to figure out what was wrong.

People were dying, and I was scared.

Ash wasn't, not yet anyway. Instead, he was intent on driving me absolutely insane.

"What do you want for dinner, Z? I'm thinking Chinese."

"Yeah, whatever, fine," I said, vaguely. I felt my phone vibrate in my pocket and I yanked it out. It was Madison, and I immediately answered. "What's up?"

"What are you doing right now?" came the immediate response.

I looked over at Ash, bent over a takeout menu from Water Street Wok. "Contemplating the many ways to murder a high school quarterback."

"Don't murder Ash Matthews," Madison said, sighing. "There are only so many perfect specimens in the world, and it would be a shame to lose one of them."

I rolled my eyes but didn't respond.

"Seriously, Zoey, can you just admit that Ash is incredibly hot and that you're madly in love with him?"

I looked back over at Ash, noticing not for the first time how incredible he looked. You didn't live next door to that for nearly ten years without noticing. There was a reason he was one of the most popular guys at St. Joseph's and dating Heather Carr, one of the most popular girls. The deep, dark brown hair falling into impossibly pale blue eyes, broad shoulders, flat chest and stomach, slim hips and yes, the impressive backside in well-worn jeans, all added up to make Ash Matthews.

"I've never denied that Ash is hot," I said, dropping my

voice. "But I'm not in love with him."

"I heard that," Ash called. "And you not being in love with me is a debatable subject. I have many methods to convince you it's true."

Madison laughed, having heard him through the speaker.

"Thanks, Maddie. Now, was there a reason you called me? Besides to talk about Ash."

"Duh, we have tickets to see Strictly Take-Out tonight!"

I paused. A few months ago, Madison and I had bought tickets to see our favorite indie band Strictly Take-Out at a local club. We tried to see them every time they came to Brooklyn or Manhattan, sometimes even Jersey. It always involved a pull and tug with my dad, getting permission to spend my money on tickets, saving up for the tickets, and then getting permission to go to the show with Madison, without my father tagging along. I had been counting down the days until I'd simply just forgotten about it. "Yeah, Maddie, I don't think that it's such a good idea."

"Oh, come on, Zoey, why not?" she whined. "We've been waiting for this show for months, and remember the ordeal that we had to go through? We'll go, see the band and come straight home. We won't get sick."

"I'm not taking chances. People are dying and disappearing. Your boyfriend's mom just died." I grabbed the remote from the table and started flipping through the channels.

Madison was quiet for a moment. "I'm just so bored. I know that's wrong because of Brody's mom," she said, quietly. "But I'm cooped up inside all day with my sisters and I'm going insane. I can't just sit inside and wait for something to happen."

"I know," I said, "trust me. I know." I could hear Ash in the stairwell, ordering the Chinese food for us. I smiled slightly when I heard him order my favorite. "Come over. Ash just ordered Chinese; we'll watch movies." I laughed. "I really do need someone to keep me from killing Ash."

"The thing is," Madison said slowly, "I'm kind of already here."

"Madison!" I yelled abruptly. "What is wrong with you? It's not safe!"

"I'm sorry! I just had to get out. I had to keep living. I haven't had a real coffee in weeks, and all I eat is take-out and I'm tired of watching TV and movies. I had to get out." There were some muffled noises in the background. "I have to go."

"Madison? Maddie!" I held the phone out. Call ended. I shrieked in frustration and flew off the couch and up the stairs, bumping into Ash on the way up.

"Z, what are you doing?"

"Stupid Madison. Ugh," I said, slamming into my room. "She went out and now I have to go out and get her." I started pulling clothes out of my closet.

"Wait," Ash said, grabbing my arm to stop me midstride. He whipped me around to face him. "You can't go out there. Your dad wants you home; it's not safe."

"It's not safe for Maddie either." I tried pulling my arm away from his grip but he had a tight hold. "Let go of me."

"Z, you could get sick!" He looked uncharacteristically serious.

"I'm going, Ash, and I'm bringing my idiotic best friend home." I yanked my arm harder but it still didn't budge. I was strong but my strength relied mostly on my legs. His fingers flexed, gripping his arm tighter. His hands were so large that his thumb and fingers met together around my bicep. "Let. Go."

He released me from his grip but didn't leave. "Well, you know I'm going with you, right?"

I started shaking my head repeatedly. "No. No way."

Ash grinned. He grabbed one of the dresses I had tossed on the bed and shoved it into my arms, his fingertips lingering on my skin. "I'm your protector, remember? Now get dressed. We gotta go save Maddie." He winked and walked out of the room.

Moments later, I came down the stairs dressed in the little black lace dress Ash had pushed it in my arms. He had the uncanny ability to choose the shortest dress in my closet, of course. I had let my hair free of its usual ponytail, and I'd slipped on little boots.

Ash was at the front door, waiting for me. His face lit up. "Well, don't you look absolutely delicious? I picked a good one, didn't I?"

"Just stop it, okay?" I said, tired of his antics, tired of his teasing. I called for Bandit and put him in the basement, locking the door behind him. He whimpered slightly. I shook my head.

"Z," he said while helping me slip my coat on, his fingers light on my hips. "You do. You look gorgeous."

"Shut up," I said softly, avoiding his eyes. "Let's go. "

CHAPTER

FIVE

WE MADE IT DOWN TO the venue in no time at all. Ash paid the cover charge and I handed over my ticket. I passed my coat over to the guy just inside the doors and hoped I'd get it back at the end of the night.

Strictly Take-Out was already playing when we walked in, and I forgot my purpose for a moment. I had been waiting for this show for months, and now that I was here, all I wanted to do was listen to music and dance. They were my favorite band, and every time I saw them live, they seemed better and better. Plus, over the years, Madison and I had become friends with them. I looked forward to hanging out with them after the show.

"This is your favorite song, isn't it?" Ash shouted at me.

I turned to him, surprised. "How did you know?"

"I pay attention, Z." He shrugged. "Let's dance."

I hesitated. "We came here for Madison."

"Come on, it's one song," he said, walking backward toward the crowd dancing in front of the stage. "Besides, Madison is probably in there somewhere, so dancing would only be helpful to our cause."

I felt myself beginning to give in, and Ash seized his chance, taking my hand and dragging me into the crowd. I let myself be pulled in, feeling the beat of my favorite song flow through me. I wanted to dance. I wanted to dance so badly even if it had to be with him.

He stopped when we'd made our way to the stage. He took my shaking arms and wrapped them around his neck. His hands came to rest on my waist and he pulled me closer, right up against him, every part of us touching.

"We're too close," I shouted, swallowing hard.

Ash leaned down, the cocky grin in place. "Don't be nervous, Zoey," he whispered in my ear, causing me to shiver a little. He started off slow, his hips moving against mine, picking up speed to match the song. He was an amazing dancer and my hands were too tight around his neck. Overwhelming warmth was spreading through my body. My hands loosened and traveled down his shoulders to his arms. I knew I'd come here for a reason, but I couldn't remember what it was. I couldn't think of anything except the feel of his body against mine and the pulse of the music.

"What would your girlfriend think of you dancing with me?" I said, breathless, when the song ended.

He hadn't let me go. His arm was wrapped tightly around my waist, and his other hand was on my thigh right below the hemline of my dress, pushing it upwards. "I don't have a girlfriend." I gave him an exasperated look, trying to ignore the fact that my hands were still gripping his arms tightly.

"I don't," he repeated, "not anymore."

I suddenly felt uneasy about the serious expression on his face. Ash almost never looked like this, and it only made him look that much better. I started to pull away.

Ash's hand shot up, and his fingers wrapped around the back of my neck, holding me in place. "Now, where do you think you're going, Zoey?" he said, a small smile on his face.

He was leaning down to me, and all I could think was that he was going to kiss me and that I wanted him to. I didn't care that he was Ash Matthews or that I hated him or that he made my life miserable. He was inches away from me and incredibly sexy. He was an incredible dancer, and it had been a long time since a boy had kissed me. My heart was beating wildly in my chest, matching the beat of the song, and he was only a whisper away.

Then a scream rang out above the music.

And I knew exactly who it belonged to.

Madison.

I pulled away from Ash, my eyes wide. "Madison."

The band had stopped playing, and everyone was looking around in confusion. I started to push my way through, shoving people, Ash at my heels.

I found Madison by the entrance of the restrooms. She was sobbing, her hand pressed against her mouth, lipstick smeared across her lips and mascara running down her round cheeks. She was wearing a white lace dress, and she almost seemed to glow in the darkness of the club, surrounded by so many people dressed in black. A dark substance was spread across the front of her dress and I realized quickly that it was blood. She looked like an angel, a beautiful tiny avenging angel. I reached out to her at the same moment that she vomited blood all over the floor.

Ash yanked me back as blood splattered all over the floor. People behind us were starting to move quickly toward the door. I reached out for Madison, yanking her to her feet, careful not to touch any of the blood.

"Z, I don't think…" Ash said.

I glared at him. "It's Maddie, Ash." Her skin was burning hot to the touch, and I spotted a few sores on the back of her neck. "Mad, how long have you been sick? Maddie?"

She whimpered, bloody fingers pressed to her stomach, leaving red fingerprints on the white fabric. "Zoey, I don't feel good…"

"All right, honey, let's go home," I said, soothingly, trying to keep my panic under control. Madison was really sick, and I wasn't sure if it was too late to do anything about it. It was probably too late. But I couldn't think of that right now. "Ash, help me."

Ash came immediately to Madison's other side and hoisted her up. We made our way out and into the cold air. It blasted me, sending shivers up my body. My coat was still inside, but I didn't care. It was chaos outside. People were frantically hailing cabs or heading to the subway. A few people were on the phone, and several panicked voices filled the air.

"We have to get her out of here," I said, looking around.

"We should take her to the hospital," Ash insisted.

"No!" I said sharply. "We'll take her home."

"Zoey…"

"She's fine," I said, trying to keep the hysteria out of my voice. Someone shoved me from behind. He turned, his eyes widening when he saw Madison. He backed up quickly.

"Get her out of here. She's going to die," he said, his voice shaking. "I don't want to die too."

"Hey, back off," Ash said, stepping toward the guy, his fists clenched.

"Ash, please. Let's go," I begged. He looked at me and nodded. The two of us grabbed Madison again and started pushing our way through the crowd. Blood was dribbling out of her mouth and down her chin. I picked up my pace.

We hadn't made it more than a few blocks when a black van came screeching up next to us, bouncing up onto the sidewalk. Ash and I froze in shock.

Three men jumped out of the van. They were wearing all black, and their faces were covered in surgical masks. They walked straight to us, determined, reaching for Madison.

"Zoey…" Madison said uncertainly. Her voice was low and weak, and her eyes went wide at the men coming toward her.

"What are you doing?" I demanded. "Who are you?"

"Don't worry, dear," one of them soothed. His voice was too sweet, and his tone didn't reach his eyes. "We just want to help her." He pried my hands off Madison and, in one swift movement, swung her into his arms.

"No! She's fine!" I shouted. "We're just going to take her home. Please."

Another man stepped forward, a syringe in his hand, the needle looking sharp and bright in the faded light of the street lamps.

"No!" I shrieked. "Stop!" I stepped forward, but Ash took hold of my arm and pulled me back.

The needle pierced Madison's neck as her eyes met mine. They stared at me, blinking a few times until they closed completely. Her head lolled to the side, her lips parted.

"What did you do?" I trembled. "Is she…" I couldn't bring myself to finish the sentence. She looked tiny in the man's arms, like a doll. Her skin was so pale, it was nearly blue. How long had she been like this? When was the last time I had seen her?

"She's fine. She's sick," the man said again. "We're taking her to the hospital."

Fear washed through me. "No, please don't take her. Leave her. Leave her with me."

The third man, who had been standing off to the side, came over to me and grabbed my arm. He held me in place as they took Madison and loaded her into the van.

I strained against him. "No! Madison! Please! Please don't take her!"

The man shoved me, causing me to trip backward into Ash. Ash's eyes flashed, and he reached forward to peel the man's fingers off of my arm.

"Don't touch her, "Ash growled in a low voice. He pulled me away, his arm wrapped around my waist.

The man's eyes narrowed, and he looked for a minute like he really wanted to hit Ash. Instead, he turned on his heel and got back in the van. Before I could react, the van pulled away from the curb and sped down the street.

"No!" I screamed, straining against Ash's hold. "Maddie!"

"Zoey, let's go," he said, glancing around. "It's going to be okay, but we have to go home."

"It's not going to be okay." I ripped myself away from him and fumbled for my phone, tucked in my bra. My bloody fingers slipped on the screen as I dialed for my dad.

"Zoey!" Dad's voice was frantic and worried. "Zoey, where are you?"

"Dad!" I answered, choking back a sob. "Dad, we went to go get Madison, and she was sick. I wanted to bring her home, but these people came in a black van and gave her some kind of shot, and they took her! Daddy; they took her!"

There was a long pause. "Zoey, come home. Now."

"Daddy…"

"Is Ash with you?"

I nodded, and then remembered he couldn't see me. I was shivering in the late night. It smelled like rain and I had left my coat at the venue. "Yes."

"Tell Ash to bring you home right now." Ash nodded, having heard, and started pulling me toward the nearest subway station.

"But…Maddie. Dad, they took her!" I cried.

His voice softened. "I know, champ. Come home. We'll figure it out."

"Okay," I whispered and hung up.

The subway ride back was silent, the two of us having nothing to say. A few people gave us looks, but this was New York, and my frazzled hair, bloody hands and tear stained cheeks were nothing special. I couldn't stop shivering, the dead look in Maddie's eyes as they took her away playing over and over in my mind. Ash pressed his side against mine, allowing a little warmth to seep through me.

We said nothing as we walked through our neighborhood on the way home. Ash walked me to the front door. He faced me, and when our eyes met, I felt the tears sting my eyes.

"Hey, hey, hey," he said, softly, stepping closer to pull me against his chest. As if they had a mind of their own, my arms slid up and around him, my hands pressed flat against his back. "It's going to be okay."

"I'm scared," I whispered.

"You don't have to be," he said, firmly.

I felt a buzzing near my hip and pulled back slightly.

"Sorry, that's me." He pulled his phone out of his pocket and answered. "Hey, babe."

It took a moment for the words to seep through my panic, and my dramatics. But when it did, it hit me like a speeding train. I stepped back horrified, feeling a flush spread across my chest. Ash's eyes met mine, and I felt anger fill me up, making me shake even harder than before. I could feel the bile rise up in my throat.

"I know, I'm sorry," he was saying. "I promise I'll see you tomorrow. I know. I've been really busy…no, it's nothing important. I gotta go. Yeah, I'll see you tomorrow. I promise, baby." He hung up and slid the phone back into his pocket.

"You're an asshole," I spat out, backing up farther away from him.

"Zoey, come on," he started to say, following me.

"Get away from me." I placed my palms against his chest and pushed.

He stumbled, a bewildered, hurt look on his face, but he caught himself, and the look quickly disappeared. The arrogant smile was back. "I hope you weren't too encouraged back there at the club, Z," he said smoothly. "You're not exactly my type." He laughed.

I felt the words like a punch to the gut. "I hate you," I whispered humiliated. I danced with him. I let him touch me, and I had almost kissed him. I yanked my gaze away from his and turned, running into the house straight into the arms of my dad.

CHAPTER
SIX

FIRST THING IN THE MORNING, my dad rushed off to work, promising to find out as much as he could about Madison. Her parents had been calling us all night, in between calling hospitals and the police. No one knew where she was.

Like clockwork, Ash showed up at my door less than an hour after my dad had left. He had been given a key (thanks, Dad, for making it possible for Ash to walk in on me naked), but I'd already thought about that and had secured the chain lock. As soon as Ash unlocked the door, it merely swung open a couple inches. I sat on the bottom step of the stairs and wrapped my arms tightly around my knees, my head resting against the banister.

Bandit went to the door, his tail wagging. He looked behind him, right at me as if wondering why I wasn't opening the door.

73

"Zoey?" Ash sounded confused. "Let me in."

I squeezed my eyes shut. "Go away, Ash."

There was a long pause. "Come on, let me in, Z."

"No."

Ash laughed, his voice echoing through the small crack. "You're being ridiculous."

I felt the anger flare up in me, but I ignored it and took a deep breath to steady myself. "I said, go away," I repeated.

Bandit barked softly, looking between the wood of the door and me, a confused look on his face.

"See, Bandit wants me to come in."

I didn't answer. That didn't even deserve an answer.

"I told your dad I'd take care of you."

"Shut up, Ash." I gripped the bannister tightly in my hand. "I can take care of myself. Go take care of Heather."

Ash laughed again. "God, I knew you were jealous. Last night was all fun and games, Z. There's no need to get attached."

I sprung up onto my feet and went stalking toward the door, my heart pounding loudly in my head. "Last night was not fun and games. My best friend is sick and was taken away, you asshole." I slammed the door shut. "And I'm not jealous!"

I waited a moment for a response that didn't come. I raced to the front window just in time to see Ash walk up on his own front steps. I collapsed on the window seat and sighed, my head in my hands.

I stayed in the house for days, going through each as if on autopilot. I was unable to do more than eat, sleep and watch a lot of TV. I couldn't move, or function. We'd finally received some word of Madison but the barest of words. She was in the hospital, she was sick. No one, not even her family, was allowed to see her.

Ash came to my door three days in a row, knocking on the chain secured door. Each day, I sat on the stairs, waiting until he would eventually give up and go back home. On the fourth day, he stopped showing up. On the fourth day, everything changed.

On the fourth day, Madison died.

"You're lying."

My dad ran a hand over his face, looking tired. He had aged so much in the last few weeks; his skin was paler and looser, his dark hair filled with streaks of gray. "I wish I was, champ. But I'm not. We got the word today, myself and Mr. and Mrs. Wu. Madison passed last night."

I swallowed hard, everything turning red in front of my eyes. "No. Dad, she's not dead. She cannot be dead."

"I'm so sorry, champ."

"No!" I screamed, picking up my cup and throwing it against the wall. It hit the wall with a loud crash, scattering into a million pieces, across the counters, sliding on the floor, wedging underneath the fridge. I slid out of my chair, sinking to the ground.

He came down on his knees and pulled me into his arms. "You need to go, Zoey. I'm going to get you a car. You're going to drive to Nebraska."

I wiped the tears from my cheeks with shaky fingers. "No. Not without you."

Dad hesitated, and I saw a brief spasm of pain flash across his face, the way it usually did with my mother. "I don't know if that's a good idea. Your mother and I…"

"I know what she did," I said, viciously. "But I'm going without you. No way. I can't go there. I can't be around her without you." I felt the hysteria bubbling in my stomach.

"Okay," he agreed, quickly. "Okay. We'll go Friday." Three days away. "We need to get some things together, but we'll go. Together."

I hiccupped. "Thank you." A fresh wave of tears threatened to spill over. "I just can't…I can't. Madison…"

He pulled me closer and rocked me back and forth. "It's going to be okay, champ. We're going to be okay."

I didn't know if we were going to be okay. I didn't even know what that word meant anymore. Not when everyone was saying it over and over again. It was losing its meaning. Nothing was okay. Nothing could be okay again.

"Z!"

I froze in place on the couch, where I'd been watching a movie. I hadn't heard from Ash in days. And now, I could've sworn I heard his voice. My heart was pounding in my chest. I'd been alone for a couple days and every noise, every tiny sound was amplified in the empty house.

"Z! Please!"

His voiced sounded pleading. I stood up and tiptoed to the door. I cursed the fact that the peephole was over my head. I placed my palms against the cool wood of the front door, waiting to hear more. I jumped when a loud pounding sounded through the empty entryway.

"Let me in. Please. I'm begging."

I hesitated. He sounded different, almost as if he had finished crying or was about to. I had never heard that tone of voice from Ash in my life. "Are you sick? I can't let you in if you're sick."

"I'm not, Zoey. I'm not."

It was that, being called Zoey instead of Z, that changed my mind. I unlocked the front door and let him in. He pushed past me and went straight to the staircase and sunk onto the bottom step, his head cradled in his hands.

I looked at him in shock, unsure of how to approach him. Ash was the guy with the smiles, the one who made all the jokes. He could even make Ol' Barb, the lunch lady, laugh. He was the easygoing, laidback football player. He was not this guy.

His hair was a disaster, unkempt and unwashed. There were distinct dark bags under his eyes, eyes which had lost the luster they normally possessed. His clothes were rumpled and looked like they'd been worn for a couple days. I heard a soft click of nails on the wood floor and saw Bandit coming into the room. He rested his chin on Ash's knee. Ash raised his hand and patted his head absently.

"Ash, what are you doing here?" I asked hesitantly.

"I had nowhere else to go."

"What about…" I trailed off, "what about Heather?"

He didn't answer, and I felt my heart sink in my chest. I had a sudden feeling that Heather Carr was no longer a resident of this world. This still didn't explain why he was here.

"Ash?"

He looked up at me, and for a moment, I saw nine-year-old Ash, vulnerable, as the new student in a small private school. "My parents," he said, his voice hollow.

I stepped closer. "What about your parents?"

"They're gone." He sounded surprised, like he'd finally realized the truth of the statement. "They were sick, really bad. They kept begging me to take them to the hospital, but I couldn't…not after Madison."

I inhaled sharply, placing my fist against my trembling lips. I wouldn't cry. I couldn't cry.

"They came last night, the same people who came and took Maddie. I… He stopped and turned angry. "I hid. I hid in the closet and I just watched as they took them away. My parents. I just let these people take my parents."

I waited for tears to come, for him to yell or scream, to hit something, but nothing came. He just sat on the step, shaking like mad. I moved forward (to do what, I'm not sure) just as the doorbell rang.

Ash froze. "Don't answer it." He stood up, suddenly alert.

"Why not?" I asked confused.

"Shit keeps getting worse, Z. You can't trust anyone." He eyed the door cautiously.

"You worry too much, Ash," I said. "Neither one of us is sick. There is no reason for anyone to hurt us." I stepped toward the door as the bell rang again.

Ash grabbed my arm and pulled me back. "I'm serious.

Don't. At least, let me do it."

I rolled my eyes. I didn't know how to feel about this Ash, a determined, protective Ash, but he wasn't crying, and he wasn't thinking about his parents. There was nothing that could be done about them, not right now, not ever, most likely. "I don't need you to protect me."

I went to the closet and pulled out the case that was stuffed in the corner. I punched in the code; it was my parents' wedding anniversary, another sign that he'd never really moved on. I pulled out my dad's handgun, making sure there were bullets in it.

The person at the door had switched from ringing the bell to pounding on the door.

Ash raised his eyebrow at the sight of the gun but didn't say anything. I walked back to the door, the gun gripped tightly in my hand. I opened the door, slowly, peeking around the door to see who was standing there.

I gasped, terrified. I spun on my heel, slamming the door behind me. My fingers fumbled with the locks, my heart pounding in my chest. I'd imagined it; it couldn't be real. She couldn't be real. Lack of sleep was making me see things. Bandit started barking from where he was locked in the basement.

"What? Who is it?" Ash said, looking alarmed.

I looked at him, my chest heaving. I was going insane. "Madison."

His eyes widened, locking on mine. "Madison is dead," he replied, in a relatively calm voice.

"Zoey? Zoey, let me in."

We both froze as the voice drifted through the door. It was thicker, a bit raspier but there was no mistaking it—it was Madison's.

"Zoey, please. I'm so hungry."

"She's dead," I said, looking at Ash, whose face had gone pale white. "I'm hearing things."

"Then we're both hearing things," Ash whispered. He brushed past me to the window. His fingers shook as he slowly moved the curtain aside. He yelled, stepping back.

Madison's palms were pressed against the glass and she looked awful. Her beautiful straight black hair was in a tangled mess, and her eyes were wide, wet and crazed. The same outfit I had last seen her in hung loosely on her impossibly small frame. But the strangest thing...her skin was a pale but distinct shade of blue.

"Aren't you going to let me in, Zoey? I'm so hungry. Please. I'm starving," she said, sounding like she was in pain.

I was having a hard time keeping a grip on the gun in my sweaty hands. "You're dead. You died," I said, my voice shaking.

"Who told you that?" she asked, sounding more like herself. There was a distinct tone of surprise in her voice. "They lied."

"Madison, you were really sick," Ash said, slowly, looking like he was going to be sick at any moment.

"I'm fine. I'm perfect," she said, happily, a broad smile on her face. I shuddered at the sight of it. Each one of her tiny little teeth had been filed to a point, making her smile look scary as hell. She looked like a vampire, or a monster. I crept closer and noticed that her eyes were black: the pupil, the iris, and even the whites of her eyes were completely blacked. I bit on my wrist to keep from screaming.

I reached for my phone and remembered I had left it upstairs. I inched closer to Ash, hoping to take his phone out of his pocket.

Ash misunderstood. His arm came out and wrapped around my waist, pulling me tight against him. I was annoyed that he was constantly trying to protect me, but I couldn't deny the warmth I felt coursing through the side that was pressed to him. I did feel kind of protected.

Madison's creepy smile grew wider, and I had a sudden urge to bury my face in Ash's chest. He looked down at me, the same shock mirrored in his own expression.

"You guys are so cute together. I've been saying it for years," she said, clapping her hands together. They were covered in dry blood.

"You should go home, Madison," Ash said, loudly. "Everyone thinks you're dead. You should go see your parents."

Madison's face fell. "Don't you want to see me, Zoey? Ash? Didn't you miss me?"

"Maddie…" It was hard to recognize the person that was once my best friend, but there was still a part of her remaining, and it was tugging at my heart. I could never let Madison feel sad, and she was in obvious pain and sorrow, and I couldn't stand it any longer.

Tears were streaming down her face, dark against her translucent skin. "I'm so cold. I'm so hungry. Please let me in," she wailed, burying her hands in her hair. The sound made the hair on my arms stand on end. She looked pitiful, like a cowering animal, and I was terrified of her. I wrapped my arms tightly around Ash, reaching into his back pocket for his phone. I slipped it out easily and pulled away.

"What are you doing?" Ash hissed at me.

"Calling my dad," I said, trying to ignore the wails of Madison sending chills up my spine and the sounds of Bandit barking incessantly. I pressed the phone to my ear.

"Hello?"

"Dad, it's Zoey."

"Zoey! I've been calling you!"

I winced. "I'm sorry. I don't have my phone with me."

"Jesus, champ." His anger seeped in through the speaker. "It's not safe. You need to lock everything up, and shut off the lights. You need to hide."

"What are you talking about?" I asked, dread filling me.

"They're alive, Zoey, the corpses…all of the missing ones." His anger had evaporated quickly into fear.

"What are you talking about?" I repeated, more firmly, looking over at Madison, who was beating her fists against the glass.

"They're like zombies. Reanimated corpses. All the dead bodies have somehow awakened. Only they're nothing like we ever imagined. They're smart, fast…"

"Dad," I interrupted, surprised at the steadiness in my voice. "Dad, Madison is here except it's not really her."

"Don't let her in!" he shouted.

"I didn't!" I assured. I felt tears start to come. "What do

I do?"

"Lock the doors, close the windows, and shut off the lights. Get the gun. I'll be home as soon as I can." I heard him take a shaky breath. "I hate that you're alone."

I had started running around the apartment, locking windows and shutting off lights. "Ash is here, Dad. I'm not alone."

"Oh, thank god," he said. "Shit. Zoey. I have to go." There were sounds of crashing and gunfire in the background. "I love you."

"Dad? Dad!" I looked at the screen. Call ended. "Shit." I shoved it in my back pocket and flipped another switch off.

"Zoey!" Ash yelled. "Get over here."

I ran back to him. He had moved to the window and was staring out of it. "Where is Madison?"

"Out there," he pointed, sounding disgusted. "I think I'm going to be sick."

I glanced out the window and was nearly sick myself. Madison had someone pinned on the ground, and was bent over them. "Is she…is she…"

"I think so," Ash said, looking away.

I didn't hesitate. I yanked the door open and went bounding down the stairs, intent on stopping Madison at any cost. Her teeth, her newly sharpened teeth, were sunk deep into someone's neck, someone who was so covered in blood that I couldn't even tell who it was. I grabbed her arms and pulled hard, away from the body that now lay limp on the ground. I looked away but not before I saw chunk of flesh missing from the person's neck, and blood gathering in a puddle on the pavement. Madison struggled in my arms, her small hands reaching out for her prey.

"I'm hungry. I'm so hungry," she wailed. "Let me go."

"No, Madison," I said, struggling, as she pulled harder against my grip. "This isn't you." I had a brief thought of Madison's strict vegetarianism and how ironic it all seemed now.

"I just want to eat, please, oh god, I want to eat." Her limbs started flailing all over the place, making it more difficult for me to keep a grip on her.

The contents of my stomach turned and it was a miracle that I didn't puke right then and there. She was hungry, for human flesh, just like a zombie. My dad had said zombie over the phone but I couldn't believe it until now. She looked like Madison and sounded like Madison, but there were the eyes, the sharp teeth, the skin tone and the effort she was making to sink her teeth into someone's flesh.

Madison's teeth came sinking down on my hand, like little needles piercing my skin. I yelled out in pain, letting her go, but she stayed firmly attached to me, starting to rip into my flesh. My eyes went blind for a moment as the pain ripped through me. I did the only thing I could think of doing, and I fired the gun.

She stopped, shocked as the bullet went sinking into her stomach but she didn't pause. In fact, it seemed to make her angrier, and she moaned a little this time, sounding a little happier. I aimed again, and this time the bullet went straight through her head. She faltered and stared at me for a long moment before she keeled over.

"Oh god," I said, falling to my knees and cradling her in my arms. Dark red blood that was nearly black was gushing out of her wounds, and her eyes stared up at the sky, unseeing, as black as the deepest night, so unlike the beautiful eyes I had known before. "Maddie, I'm so sorry. I'm so sorry." Tears were gushing down my cheeks, and for a moment, the pain in my hand felt like nothing, nothing compared to the pain of losing Madison again. I had shot her in defense, but I had aimed to kill, and now she was dead.

"Z, you need to let her go," Ash said, suddenly at my side.

"No," I said, my grip on Madison tightening.

"You're bleeding; we need to get you inside and stop it."

"I don't care," I wailed. "I don't care. I killed her. I killed my best friend."

"Zoey, we need to go *now*."

I looked up at him and saw that he was staring over my shoulder. I turned and my heart started pounding harder in my chest. I picked up the gun that I had tossed aside. There were at least a dozen people heading right toward us. They were a far enough distance away, but I could still tell that their skin was blue, just like Maddie's, which meant bad news for us. I stood up, taking a step back. "Do you think…do you think they're slow? Like, in the movies?" I said, aiming the gun at them. I registered dimly that Ash had a fireplace poker in his hand and was holding it like a baseball bat.

At these words, the people started sprinting toward us.

The two of us turned on our heels, sprinted up the stairs, and slammed the doors behind us. My fingers fumbled at the locks, while Ash dropped the fireplace poker and started moving the armoire that stood just inside the entryway toward the door.

"Is it locked?" he yelled over the noise that was right outside our door. The sound of raspy breaths and hungry wails filled the air, and it was impossible to ignore.

"Yes," I said, taking a step back and helping him push the piece of furniture in front of the door. We both stepped backward, waiting, and a moment later, there was a slamming noise, like bodies hitting the front door. "Oh god, what do we do?"

"Shh, stay quiet," he whispered. "They can't get in. We need to fix your hand."

I remembered my injury, the small chunk of my flesh that Madison had managed to rip out before I shot her, and the pain came flooding back. I glanced down and saw blood dripping down my arm. "Damn, that hurts."

"Yeah, it got you good," Ash said, pulling me toward the kitchen, and running the water at the sink. The sound of water hitting the basin barely masked the sound of the people pounding at the door.

"It? That it is a person, Ash. She is a girl. She's Madison," I said firmly, wincing as the cool water flowed over my wound. Tears sprung up in the corners of my eyes, and I bit down on my lip hard.

"Was. And that wasn't Madison, Z. I don't know what it was, but it wasn't her. Madison wouldn't attack someone, and she sure wouldn't sink her teeth into you," he said, leaning over the sink and washing the blood away. I inhaled sharply. "Sorry."

"It's fine," I said, through clenched teeth.

"It's not too deep," Ash said, holding my hand closer to his face. "I mean, I'm not an expert, but it doesn't look like it needs stitches or anything. Do you have a first aid kit?"

"Under the sink," I said, tired. I walked over to the table, as Ash rummaged under the sink for the kit. I collapsed in a chair, my entire body shaking. He came over and sat in the chair next to me. Carefully, he wrapped my hand in gauze and taped it down.

"There," he said, before placing a soft kiss on the bandage.

I yanked my hand away from him. "Don't kiss me, Ash."

"Sorry," he said, but there was a tiny smile on his face. It was barely there, and after the probable deaths of his parents and the disaster that was taking place right outside my front door, I was surprised there was one at all. "Now what?"

I shook my head, pressing my lips together, scared to say a word. I knew the moment that I said anything, I would start crying, and I wouldn't stop. Ash stood up, gathered me in his arms and walked us down to the basement where he put me down on the couch. He grabbed a blanket from the armchair and placed it over me. He took a seat on the couch next to me and reached for the remote. The TV came to life, and he immediately switched it to a main channel.

The president was on the screen, speaking gravely.

"Turn it up!" I said, wrapping the blanket tighter around

me. Ash obliged, and the president's deep, reassuring voice came floating at me.

"…unsure of how these victims came to be roaming our neighborhoods, but we assure the American people that we are doing everything in our power to find out where they came from and how to handle them. We urge all of you to stay indoors and to stay vigilant, and await instructions…"

"Sounds like they have no idea what's going on either," Ash said, changing the channel. A scene of destruction filled the screen, and the caption on the bottom read, "Riot in Los Angeles." People were running in all directions, and you could just make out the distinct blue skin of the…zombies. A few of them were bent over bodies, and I knew exactly what they were doing.

Ash changed the channel again. This time we were looking at Chicago, and a scene so similar to the one we had just watched. Each time Ash changed the channel, we saw a different city under disarray: Los Angeles, Chicago, New York, Houston, Philadelphia, Phoenix, Dallas, Miami, Indianapolis, Boston, and so many more.

"Turn it off," I said, burying my head into the couch. "Just…turn it off."

Ash shut the TV off, and we were plunged into darkness, the silence enveloping us, the sound of sirens and screams closer than I wished. Brown eyes met blue eyes, and we stayed together, alone, waiting.

I curled up in the corner of the couch, staring at the blank TV until I fell asleep again.

CHAPTER
SEVEN

I WOKE UP A FEW hours later, disoriented in the dark room. A bit of light was peeking through the curtains, casting a ray of light across the coffee table and onto the couch. There was something solid and warm pressed against my back, and an arm was thrown casually against my waist. I could feel a slight warm breath on the back of my neck and for a second, I wanted to just lie there, safe and cocooned. The arm tightened around my waist, and I shifted a bit to look over my shoulder.

And immediately rolled off the couch. "God, Ash, what the hell?"

He rubbed his eyes, sleepily looking up at me. "What?" he said, stupidly.

"This is a cuddle-free zone," I said, grabbing the blanket from him and wrapping it around me tightly. "You may be in my house but stay away from me."

Ash yawned and sat up, stretching his arms out. "You were warm, and I was sleepy. I'm a cuddle bug, what can I say?"

I rolled my eyes. "Did you seriously just call yourself a cuddle bug?"

"You know it, babes," he laughed. I just shook my head, grateful for the fact that no matter what was happening, I could count on the infuriating nature of Ash Matthews. He glanced up the stairs. "Are they still out there?"

I followed his gaze, and I felt my fear, forgotten in the escape of sleep, come creeping back and seeping through my veins. "I don't know." Our eyes met, as my fingers clenched tightly around the blanket. "Should we…" I cleared my throat, "Should we go check?"

"Yeah, yeah, we probably should," Ash said, looking around, as if waiting for a better solution to burst out of the closet and shout, "I'm here!"

"We should go together," I suggested, "To be safe, I mean."

He looked relieved that I had been the one to suggest it. "Sure, yeah, if you think so."

I resisted the urge to roll my eyes again and tried hard not to throw something at him. I reached for the gun on the coffee table and tossed aside the blanket. "Let's go."

The two of us crept up the stairs, listening for any sounds that were coming up the stairs. We crossed the entryway, and I could feel my heartbeat vibrating through each step on the cold wooden floors.

Ash grabbed the fireplace poker off the ground and snuck up to the door, pressing his arm to the wood. He then lifted his eyes to the peephole and looked outside for a while.

"Well?" I whispered.

He stepped back, and sighed. "They're still out there. In the streets."

I moved across the entryway, my socks slipping on the floors, as I crept closer to the window. I peeked out the curtain, barely allowing a small space for me to look out.

There were at least a couple dozen…zombies out in the street. If it weren't for the distinct blue skin, it would be like any normal day. They were just milling around, not talking, just sitting on porch steps staring at street signs. They looked more like the zombies I had always pictured, from images I had seen in movies. "What are they doing? What are they waiting for?"

Ash came from behind me, looking out as well. "I don't know. But they're all…congregated together. Like, they're waiting for something."

The words had barely left his lips when there was a sudden movement. They all raised their heads in almost perfect unison and turned to face the east side of the street. Their eyes were wide as they watched something that neither Ash nor I could see. Frozen in place, captivated, they were insanely creepy to watch. I held my breath, waiting for something, any kind of movement.

Then I saw our neighbor Carl, an older man in his early sixties, walking down the street. He was a nice man, if not a little weird. He had kept to himself ever since his wife had died and tended to go on long fishing trips without telling anyone, so the postman and the dry cleaners would get angry and leave all his mail and clothes at our apartment. Now he was walking in front of my house, his dog Sandy on a leash in front of him.

"Carl," Ash said, sounding resigned.

"Is he insane?" I asked, incredulous. I reached for the doorknob, but Ash yanked me back.

"Don't be stupid, Z," he hissed. "You'll be torn apart..." His voice faded away as the zombies finally made their move. They moved almost as one as they came barreling toward Carl, at impossible speeds. They were so fast. Several of them dove onto the small dog, tearing it to pieces in a matter of seconds. The others went sprinting to Carl, who looked surprised. He attempted to fight them off for a moment until they overpowered him, and the sidewalk was covered in bits of flesh and dark, thick blood.

"I can't, I can't," I said, tearing my gaze away from the scene unfolding outside and the screams that were coming from Carl's torn face. I sunk to the floor, my back pressed against the wall and my hands covering my ears. "I can't do this. I can't handle this."

Ash bent down, his elbows on his knees. "Zoey, look at me."

I shook my head once, twice, three times, pressing my hands tighter against my head.

He reached down and took the gun from my hand and placed it carefully on the armoire blocking the door. His hands came up to mine, and he gently pried them off of my ears and forced my chin up so my eyes would meet his. "We're going to be okay. I don't know how, but we're going to be okay."

"I don't want to be okay. I want it to be the same, I want to go back," I said, rocking back and forth, my back slamming against the wall with each rock. "I don't feel safe."

He held my hands tightly in his. "I know, I know. But you are safe. You're with me, and I swear it to you, Zoey Valentine, I'm not going to let anything bad happen to you. I'm here, with you." His blue eyes were bright, and I could see the very beginning of tears in the corners.

I yanked my hands away from him. "I don't want to be here with you," I spat out viciously. "I'd rather be here with anyone else but you. Leave me alone." I sprang up, stomping up the stairs into my bedroom and slamming the door behind me.

If I had expected Ash to follow me upstairs, I was wrong. I paced back and forth in my room before reaching for my phone. There were a couple dozen missed text messages coupled with at least a dozen missed calls. I scrolled through my contacts searching for my dad, and pressed the call button when I found him. It beeped once long and loud, and "No Service" popped up. I typed out a quick text message, "Where are you?" and pressed send, but the same message came up again.

"Great," I muttered, tossing the phone back on the dresser, where it lay useless. I flopped onto my bed and tried to ignore the perpetual sinking feeling that was constant in my stomach. I tried to ignore the silence that was outside of my window. I expected screams, chaos, something, but it was eerily silent compared to earlier when they seemed to have descended upon the city.

I was stuck inside my house with no phone, and no one seemed to know what was going on. I was scared, terrified, and felt completely unprepared. I was stuck with the last person I ever wanted to be stuck with, but I couldn't get rid of him.

CHAPTER

EIGHT

IT HAD BEEN THREE DAYS since the zombies had appeared. We had no phone service, no internet, and I hadn't heard from my dad. The television didn't even work. Ash and I had scrounged up an old radio of my dad's and some batteries and tuned it to find a local radio station, but there was nothing there at all. We were living in complete silence and complete darkness. There was no power. We ate as much as we could from the freezer, old pints of ice cream, frozen vegetables over the stove, to keep it from going bad.

We didn't talk much. Ash showed signs of wanting to talk had no desire to rehash anything that had happened. Instead, we just tiptoed around each other, trying to read books and magazines by the light peeking in through the curtains or by the flashlights at night.

I spent a lot of time in the shower. It was the one place

in the house where Ash couldn't go. It was the only thing in the entire apartment that worked. I turned the knob, and water came out. I stood under the steaming hot water, trying so hard not to think about anything, except getting clean.

Every time we looked out the window, it looked like more and more zombies had shown up; more of them were wandering the streets. They were always covered in blood, and sometimes they even had limbs hanging from their mouths, like a snack they were saving for later. It was revolting, especially when a fight would break out over the smallest bit of flesh. They all had raspy breaths. It sounded exactly like every worse nightmare I'd ever had. Sometimes, in the middle of the night (or maybe the day, it was so hard to keep track), you could hear them as they made their way down the street.

The radio silence, the calm that seemed to have taken over the city, was unnerving. I was used to the sounds of the subway, cars honking at the kids playing soccer in the streets.

That's why, when the sound of gunfire reached my ear, I completely toppled out of my bed and landed on the hardwood floor with a crash. I lifted my head, and heard it again, the gunfire, and the sound of cars screeching by.

"Ash," I called loudly and uncertainly. "Ash!"

I heard a loud crash downstairs that reverberated through the house; I turned on my heel and raced downstairs.

"Zoey!"

"Dad!" I cried, flying into his arms. He was an absolute wreck; his shirt was torn, and his jeans were dirty and covered in blood. There was a hefty gash across his forehead, and a nasty bruise forming right on his jawline. He caught me up, just like when I was a little girl. "Dad, you're hurt."

"I'm fine," he said, hastily wiping at the gash on his forehead, smearing blood into his hair. "It's not bad. Where's Ash?"

"Here, I'm right here," Ash said, coming out of the kitchen still armed with the fireplace poker. "What's going on?"

I could hear sirens in the distance, mixed in with the occasional scream. The sounds of fallen footsteps as people ran past our brownstone reached my ears, and I could hear the rattling breaths of the zombies, just as Madison's had been. I wanted to cover my ears, to shut it all out. Instead, I grabbed the gun and retrieved the holster from the case that I had left open in the coat closet.

"They're all over the city," my dad explained, as he reloaded his own gun and slid it into its holster. He passed me a box of ammunition without meeting my eyes. I knew we were both thinking that this was never the purpose of my gun lessons. "We weren't sure what they were until people started reporting their dead family members alive, and that's when you told me about Madison." He took another gun out of the waistband of his jeans, loaded it and held it out to Ash.

Ash balked. "I don't…I don't know how to use one."

"Take it, kid," Dad said, his voice grave. "You just gotta aim."

He took it, staring at it for a moment before his grip

tightened on it. He took the holster my dad was holding and strapped it around his hips. "Well, I do play a lot of Call of Duty."

I threw him an exasperated look but turned back to Dad. "So what's going on? Why do you look so beat up?"

"They attacked the station. They've been attacking all of them, all the major cities: here, Los Angeles, Boston, Chicago…at least eight or nine cities." He reached into the closet, where the safe was and pulled out his extra gun case, the one I didn't even have access to. He yanked out three more guns and his rifle and packed them in his old gym bag. "We didn't know what to think. What do you think? But then they started attacking everyone, ripping them to shreds. They kept wailing on and on about being hungry."

"That's exactly what Madison was doing," I said, strapping my own holster around my hips.

"Where is she?" he asked, looking up from his task and meeting my eyes. I looked down, unable to answer. "Oh, okay, all right. Well, we need to get away. We need to go. The Awakened are everywhere."

"What? Awakened?"

Dad sighed. "That's what they're calling them, the… people. They're not zombies, and no one feels right calling them zombies. Someone on TV said Awakened, and that's what they are now. It doesn't matter right now. Let's go."

"Dad, they're everywhere," I said aghast. "We'll never get past them. They're fast…"

"I know they're fast, okay? And they're incredibly smart. This isn't like anything we ever expected. They're aware and able to communicate, and they look exactly like the people we know, except they're not. And they only seem to want one thing: us. So we need to go. Now."

I looked out the window and saw that there were even more zombies outside. There was a nondescript black SUV parked haphazardly on the sidewalk, and I immediately recognized it as a vehicle my dad sometimes used from the station. "There are just too many for the two of us, Dad."

"The three of us," he corrected.

I turned away from the window to look at him. "Excuse me?"

"The three of us: you, me and Ash," he said, grabbing a coat from the closet and shoving his arms in. "You've got five minutes to pack; we need to go."

"But Dad…" I protested, avoiding all eye contact with Ash, who was standing frozen in place.

He wheeled on me, anger and worry and panic on his face. "Seriously, Zoey Elizabeth? We need to go, and we need to go now. Ash is coming with us. We're not just going to leave him here."

I opened my mouth and closed it a few times.

Dad stopped what he was doing for a moment and ran his shaking hands through his hair, taking a deep breath and letting it out slowly. "They're bombing New York, and the surrounding areas."

It took a moment for this to sink in. "What do you mean?"

"Just go upstairs and pack, now," he said, firmly. "We don't have much time." He looked at Ash. "I'm sorry, but we don't have time for you to go home and grab stuff."

I raced back upstairs, yanking my duffel bag from underneath my bed and throwing it on top of the covers. It was my travel bag, the one I always used when I was forced out to Nebraska to visit my mom, every other Christmas and for half of Spring Break. It already had several pairs of socks and underwear tucked inside and toiletries like a toothbrush, deodorant and shampoo.

I took the gun holster off (why had I strapped it on over my pajamas?) and threw the pajamas I was wearing in my bag. I slipped on a pair of slim black jeans and a tight black shirt. I crawled into my closet briefly and yanked on my sturdy black boots. I caught my reflection in the mirror for a moment and noted how I looked like a heroine from a Resident Evil video game or something. I looked like I was trying way too hard, but what else did you wear when you were running away from zombies?

I yanked my hair back into its usual ponytail and strapped the holster back around my waist. I proceeded to grab as many clothes as I could find and shoved them in the bag. I looked around my room, wondering what I should grab. Eighteen years I had lived in this room, eighteen years of memories and accumulating a ton of stuff, and I had no idea what to bring with me.

I pulled a picture of my dad, Madison and I at the Mets game off my mirror. It seemed so small, like it was nothing compared to so many other things in this room. Should I grab the medals I got from playing soccer as a kid or the Honor Society certificates? Should I grab the diary I kept all through my preteen years, filled with a ton of hate words about Ash, and my middle school crush, and eventual boyfriend, Joel?

"Zoey! Let's go!"

I shook my head, dismissing memories and settled on the photo, my extremely worn and loved copy of Marion Zimmer Bradley's *The Mists of Avalon,* my Mets hat and, superficially, my iPod. I slung the bag over my shoulder and ran down the stairs. "Okay, let's go." I turned to Bandit. "Let's go, Bandit."

"Zoey, I don't think…" my dad said, looking stricken.

I looked back and forth between him and Ash, and I started to feel panicked. "No. No, you're not thinking. You can't be thinking…"

"It doesn't make sense to bring him," Dad said, softly. "I can't worry about Bandit. I need to worry about you, and Ash."

My fingers were lost in the shaggy fur of Bandit's head. "I can't…" my voice was caught on a sob. "I can't leave him, Dad. He won't understand. I can't just…"

Bandit could sense the tension in the room and barked softly, pacing in place. He was only six years old and still acted like an overgrown pup sometimes. I looked appealingly at Ash and Dad, but I knew it was a lost cause. My dad's face was full of defeat and sorrow, and Ash avoided my eyes completely.

I fell to my knees in front of Bandit and pulled him into my arms, burying my face into his warm, smelly fur. "I'm so sorry," I whispered to him. "I'm so sorry, Bandit. I love you so much."

I pulled back, leaving a damp spot on his fur. He was looking up at me, confused, and licked the tears from my face. I led him to the basement and shut the door. I couldn't bear to look at him as we abandoned him. I couldn't do it.

"Let's go," I said, sharply, refusing to look at either of them.

My dad was staring out the window. "There's a group of them about a block up. If we move swiftly and quietly, we can probably make it to the car before they notice."

"Brilliant," I said. I looked over at Ash, who was hoisting a backpack over his shoulder. He was pale, and he looked terrible. His hair was hanging in his face, and there was a slight tremble in the grip that he had on his own handgun. "Are we going?"

My dad looked around the brownstone, and I knew he was thinking similar things that I had been thinking upstairs. Like me, my dad had grown up in this house as a child, had lived in it his entire life. When my parents had gotten married so young and had no place to go, they moved into the basement and my grandparents had taken care of them. We had both taken our first steps here, had birthday parties and lived our lives here. I had my very first kiss on that porch step, had watched millions of Mets games and cooked too many dinners in that kitchen.

Bandit was whining behind the basement door; he always hated being locked up down there. My dad closed his eyes for a moment and then sighed. "Yeah. Let's go."

CHAPTER
NINE

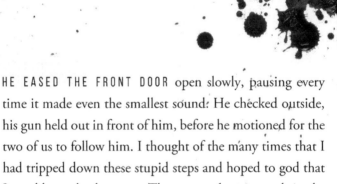

HE EASED THE FRONT DOOR open slowly, pausing every time it made even the smallest sound. He checked outside, his gun held out in front of him, before he motioned for the two of us to follow him. I thought of the many times that I had tripped down these stupid steps and hoped to god that I would not do that now. There was a heavy stench in the air, of blood and rotting flesh and death, and I tried so hard to keep myself from throwing up.

We had nearly made it to the car when there was a crack. My dad and I looked behind us where Ash's eyes and mouth were open wide, his foot on a stick that had cracked in half when he'd stepped on it. All three of us looked in the direction of the Awakened, whose scary black eyes were all focused on us.

"Shit," my dad hissed. "Get in the car. Get in the car

now!"

We dropped all pretenses of silence and sprinted to the car, flinging ourselves into the car. I had barely strapped myself in when my dad peeled out, taking out a few bodies that had thrown themselves in our path.

"They can't slow us down." Dad shouted at me as he sped down our street. "We only have two hours to be a safe distance away from the city."

"Safe from what?"

"They're nuking New York City and the surrounding areas. Brooklyn, Queens, Manhattan, all of it. They're doing it to all the major cities," he said, taking a swift left, throwing me into the window.

"What?" I shrieked and then clapped my hand over my mouth as the sound echoed through the car.

"They're just giving up? It's only been three days," Ash shouted from the backseat.

"They figured it would be better to just neutralize the problem off the bat," he explained, taking sharp turns and speeding to the exit out of the city. "They're nuking the other major cities too, the ones I was mentioning before, any area that has a huge population with the virus."

"Jesus," I said, paralyzing fear ripping through my body. They were going to blow up my city, the city I had grown up in my entire life. I looked behind me at Ash, who looked as shocked as me. "How do you know?"

He slammed on his brakes when we came up to several other vehicles before taking another right to go around them. "It was an accident." He didn't say more than that.

"How much time do we have?" I said. I felt the frozen pizza that Ash and I had cooked over the stove churn in my stomach, as we screeched through an alley, barely fitting.

"Two hours. Hopefully we can get as far away from the city as possible, and then we can regroup and find some supplies. I have some stuff, since we were supposed to leave anyway, but not everything. And Ash needs clothes." He glanced over at me as we went sailing out of the city. "And we need to stock up on ammunition, maybe grab a couple more guns."

"They're blowing up my city," I whimpered, turning around in my seat. "And we left Bandit." Tears filled up my eyes again, and my dad leaned over and squeezed my thigh briefly before returning to his tear down the highway.

There were cars everywhere, people everywhere, and there was a state of panic. The blue tone of the Awakened seemed to outnumber the regular, normal skin tones of people who weren't sick. I felt helpless strapped in this car as we barreled through. We were getting out, but none of these people knew. There was already so much chaos.

"Dad, why can't we tell anyone?" I said softly, pressing my hands over my eyes, shutting out the destruction, trying to ignore the raspy breaths and the screams. The air around me was filled with screams of pain and the screams of people calling out for help.

He shook his head, pained. "No, we can't do that."

"Dad!" I yelled. "What is wrong with you? All these people...they're going to die! We can't...we can't just let them die."

"Zoey…"

"No, don't. Just don't. We have to tell someone, anyone." I recognized dimly that I was having a breakdown, only my third of the week, in front of Ash. Again. One day, one day in this crazy messed up world, I would be composed and carefree and *awesome* in front of Ash Matthews.

He slammed on the breaks, causing me to fly forward. "I'm sorry, okay? I know, I know." His voice broke, and he looked over at me. I felt all of the fight go out of me. I had never seen my dad cry before. "I want to stop and save every single person back there, okay? I want to save all of the millions of people in Brooklyn and Manhattan and Queens, but I can't. And I just want to get you and Ash out of this city and to safety because that's the one thing I *can* do."

The car was quiet for a moment. Cars were honking at us, turmoil of the city was still all around us but the silence in the car was deafening.

"Some people will get out, okay?" He looked away and started driving again. "People are getting out already, trying to get away from…everything. But we can't save everyone."

We drove the rest of the way out of the city in silence. Staring out the window, I wondered how on earth we got to this point.

We had been on the road for about an hour when it happened. We weren't the only cars on the road, but no one had the same urgency that we did. They felt safe; they were outside of the city. But what was safety anymore? Was anyone actually safe anymore?

We were too far away to see anything, to hear anything,

but when the clock flashed over, we knew. We continued to drive in silence before my dad pulled off to the side of the road and held me. I kept waiting for the tears to fall, but they wouldn't. I just stared, stared at the woven patterns in the seat. I could see Ash through a crack in our entwined arms and saw his fist pressed firmly against his mouth, tears streaming down his face.

I don't know how much time passed while we all mourned the loss of our city before my dad pulled away and put the keys back in the ignition. "We need to get supplies," he said hoarsely, starting the car and driving again. It wasn't long before he turned off the main highway. He pulled a map out of the glove compartment. "I think we should stay off the main roads. It might take us a little longer, but I just think it's better."

I nodded, afraid that, if I said a word, I would burst into tears and never stop.

"There will be less people out on the back roads," Ash spoke up from the backseat. "Do we know how many zomb …Awakened are outside of the major cities?"

Dad shook his head. "They've only been awake for a few days. We have no idea how many there are or where they are. The major cities reported that they were in the street and attacking, like in Manhattan, but they could be anywhere. We just…we don't know." He pulled off the side of the road and drove through a thicket of trees. I glanced back at Ash as the car bumped over the uneven floor of forest, branches scratching at the side of the car.

"Dad, where are you going?"

"There's a town up ahead, only a few miles; I want to run in there and get supplies. But I don't want to put you in danger, and I don't want to risk our only mode of transportation." We were about a half-mile away from the road hidden enough that no one could see us. "You guys will stay here while I go ahead."

"Yeah, that's a terrible idea," I said immediately. "I'm going with you."

"Yeah, Mr. Valentine, I don't think…" Ash started.

"Frank," Dad interrupted. "Call me Frank. This is not the world to be bothering with misters."

"Frank, right," Ash said trying it out. "I just don't understand what the plan is."

He looked back and forth between us. "We're going to Nebraska. Last I talked to Jennifer, Zoey's mom, there was no virus there. Which hopefully means no Awakened either."

"Nebraska," I said, softly, feeling my shoulders sag. "With Mom, and Caspar."

"Casper? Like the friendly ghost?" Ash asked, his eyebrows furrowed. I picked up an empty water bottle from the console and tossed it at him.

"No. My stepfather," I answered, glancing at my dad, who usually developed a slight tick when Caspar's name was mentioned. Not that I could blame him. "So that's the plan?"

Dad unbuckled his seatbelt, and reached for the bag that he had stowed at my feet and pulled out two handguns. "Yeah, that's the plan." He met my eyes. "I'll be gone a couple hours, max. Stay down; stay low. Don't get out of the car for anything."

"Dad, I just…"

"No, Zoey," he said, firmly. "I'm going. We need to get to Nebraska. And don't think I'm happy about this, Zoey. I'm not excited for it either. But she's your mother, and we're going to be safe." He slammed the door behind him and started walking away, trudging through the forest.

"Yeah, we'll be safe. Just you, me, Mom, the man who ruined my family and the boy who spends most of his days making my life miserable. No problem," I muttered as he walked away.

"Z?"

I closed my eyes, briefly. It was the end of the world, or at least it felt like that, and yet I could still feel the pang of annoyance rip through me. There was something seriously wrong with me that I couldn't keep a hold of my perspective. "What, Ash?"

"You should get in the backseat with me."

I whirled around to face him. "You've got to be kidding me."

A small smirk appeared on his face. "That's not what I meant. But I'm interested in seeing where your mind was going with that." I stared at him for a moment not blinking, and he relented. "I just meant that it's probably much safer here in the backseat, where there are tinted windows, and you're not so obvious."

I squirmed, trying to work through this surprising logic. "Fine," I said, giving in. "But don't touch me." I climbed over the passenger seat, my gun firmly strapped around my waist, and flopped into the seat next to Ash.

There were at least fifteen minutes of silence before Ash spoke up. There was only so long he could stay still. I could already see his knees bouncing up and down, his fingers tapping on his legs. "So what's the deal with your mom?"

"What do you mean?" I said, looking out the window. I was amazed at the quiet of the forest. You could hear the cars driving by; a very faint sound in the distance but there was no other movement. No animal sounds, nothing. It was very weird.

"You have fought tooth and nail NOT to go to Nebraska, even though it is honestly the safest place for us to be, and I just want to know why." Ash shrugged, stretching his legs out in front of him and encroaching on what little space I had in front of me.

"Yeah, it's not really your business, is it?" I said, kicking his legs out of my way. They didn't budge an inch.

"Come on, Z. We're stuck in this car, okay? We can't go anywhere, and we can't talk to anyone but each other. I don't want to think about what just happened back home, and I know you don't want to think about your dad out there alone," Ash said. "I'm bored, and I'm going out of my mind. I need a distraction."

I blew out a raspberry, content in the sound that it made echoing in the car. "Agh, all right, fine." I turned to face him, flinging my outstretched legs over his lap. If he was going to take up this entire car, then so was I. "My parents separated when I was ten years old and were divorced by the time I was eleven."

"Yeah, I remember that," Ash said. "That's not new information."

"You asked me a question and I'm trying to answer it, okay? Can you maybe not interrupt me?" I said, throwing my hands up.

"Okay, okay, sorry," he said, calmly, smiling a little.

"As I was saying," I continued, giving him a pointed look. "My parents separated when I was ten. And I don't know, they sat me down like they had watched some parenting videos that taught them how to break the news to their kid. It was all staged, nothing like my parents at all. I had kind of known for a while that things weren't right. After my granddad died when I was about eight, my dad threw himself into work. He was gone all the time, and then my mom started being gone all the time."

"But I didn't notice. I was a kid so I just didn't even see it. I was so wrapped up in my stupid books that I couldn't look up for a moment to see that there was something wrong. So when they told me they had 'grown apart' and that they still 'loved me very much no matter what,' I just thought, I don't know, I thought it was my fault." I paused for a moment, swallowing hard.

"Zoey, it wasn't your fault," he said, scooting closer to me.

I glared at him and continued on. "Then my mom decides that she's going to move back to Nebraska, back to the house that she grew up in. Her parents had died in a car accident when I was about four, and the house just sat there while she was here in New York. And then began the battle of 'who gets Zoey.'"

I laughed, but there was no real humor in it. I wasn't sure when I would laugh again, for real. "And it was a battle, no lie. When they weren't fighting with me on the merits of Nebraska versus New York or the schools or the neighborhood, they would try to win my favor. My dad would take me to Mets games or take me to the Natural History Museum or buy me 'real New York pizza.'" I made air quotes sarcastically. "Did you know that's why I got Bandit? My mom thought New York was a terrible place for a dog, so she tried to convince me that a dog was worth moving to Nebraska. God, it was awful."

Ash's eyes met mine as he inched slowly over to me, like I wouldn't notice that I felt warmer the closer in proximity he came to me. He didn't say anything, kept silent. Ash had an interrupting problem, so this surprised me, but I went on.

"But the worst part is that it was both of them. No matter what happened later, it was both of them. They continued to do it for quite a few years after I decided to live in Manhattan. They played little games, and I was still young, and I didn't know who to please and who to listen to. They asked me to lie for each other, and it just got confusing. I felt like they were just constantly mad, mad at each other, mad at me."

I took a deep breath, and when it came out, it was shaky. Ash was right next to me, my shoulder pressing right into his arm.

"Then all the truth came out. My mom started seeing

this guy Caspar, Caspar with an 'A' which matched his super pretentious personality. This was before she left to Nebraska. She was renting some shabby thing in Brooklyn. And when I was there, he was just always there. When we went to the movies or the park or when she took me shopping, he was always there. She called him a friend, but I wasn't allowed to tell my dad about him. And I hated having to lie to my dad. I mean, okay, I lie to him about things all the time, like spending the night at Madison's house when I'm really going to midnight showings of *Rocky Horror Picture Show*, but this was just too much." My fists balled up as the memories came back to me. "My mom finally was making the move to Nebraska; she was leaving in a week, and she was still hoping to convince me to come."

"We were at a diner with my dad, and they were talking, but it was just, god, all kinds of awkward. My mom kept talking like my dad was just going to send me on the plane in a week, and I just…I don't know what happened." I broke off, and looked up at him. "I just got confused. It was so hard to keep everyone's stories separate, and the lies and the truth and the half-truths. I asked my mom whether Caspar was going with her to Nebraska."

"I knew immediately that I had something wrong, and not just because my mom had told me not to say anything. She looked horrified, angry, upset, and I had never seen her so red in my life. My dad…to this day, I still have never seen him as upset and angry as he was that day. What we've seen in the past few weeks, it's nothing. He started yelling, and she started yelling back. He was screaming 'how could you let him around our child?' and she was trying to calm him down. I didn't even really understand what was going on."

"Turns out, Caspar was my mom's boyfriend, and he had been my mom's boyfriend for quite a while. From what I gathered, Caspar had been around for about a year before my parents had officially announced their separation," I said, feeling the anger, the confusion, the frustration all piling back into my voice. "And I couldn't handle it. Before, I was angry at both of them, but suddenly I forgot about all the things I'd been mad about before."

I saw Ash's hand on his lap, inching closer to mine, and I found myself wanting to reach for it. I took a deep breath and clasped my hands together to keep myself from doing anything incredibly stupid. "And so I chose to live in New York, with my dad. She moved to Nebraska, and she married Caspar about six months later, where I was lovingly forced to be her maid of honor in a small casino chapel in Vegas, complete with a fat Elvis. I get to see the two of them twice a year, for either Christmas or Thanksgiving, and half of spring break."

I turned back to Ash and was surprised when his face was mere inches away from me, a hair's breadth away. His breath was hot on my cheek, and I felt my heart slamming in my chest at how close he was. There was a very serious expression on his face, not like any one that I had seen before, and I felt my breath catch in my throat as he moved closer.

Shit. Ash was going to kiss me.

CHAPTER
TEN

HE WAS SO CLOSE; I could see every single stupid, thick, black eyelash and every white vein spreading like lightning through his blue eyes. His lips came closer; they were so close. I wanted to pull him toward me and forget everything. I wanted to forget about my mom and Caspar and the fact that I had to be there out of all places in the world. I wanted to forget Madison and Bandit and my beautiful city. I wanted to lose myself in him, and feel anything besides fear or pain or heartbreak.

I couldn't believe how close he was and how I wanted to close the minuscule distance between us and feel something, anything but the pain of the past 72 hours. I wondered for a moment what Madison would have thought of this situation.

Just then, there was a loud snap, jerking the two of us

away from each other. I grabbed my gun, clutching it tight in my hand. I scanned the area around us, looking for any hint of blue.

"It was probably an animal or something," Ash said, pulling me closer to him.

The spell was broken though, as if the loud noise had pulled me out of a dream. I laughed shakily and pulled away from him, putting distance between us. I leaned against the window and faced him, my bent knees a barrier. "I hope so."

Ash stared at me for a moment but thankfully let it go. I was grateful for this. "I'm sorry."

I looked up at him surprised. My face immediately flushed. Sorry for what? For almost kissing me? "For what?" I asked.

"Your parents. It sounds rough," he said, leaning back and closing his eyes for a moment.

"Oh," I paused. "Thank you."

It stayed silent for a moment before he spoke again. "If it's any consolation, I think that you're lucky. Your dad is an amazing guy. And your mom, despite her faults, probably loves you just as much." He sighed. "The last few days that I saw my parents was the most time I had spent with them in years, and they were dying."

"What do you mean?" I asked. In the confusion and chaos of escaping the city, I had to admit that I had forgotten all about Ash's parents. There was no question about it now; they were dead, and I had not stopped at all to even give it a thought.

He smiled slightly, looking a little surprised at my

interest. "I love my parents. They're great, honestly. They give me anything and everything I could possibly want or need. But…" he sighed, almost angrily. "They're never around. They're so busy."

"Doing what?" I asked, thinking of Madison's parents and the society events they were always attending that kept them out often.

"My parents are…were lawyers," Ash explained. "And they were insanely dedicated to their job, and they were really good at it too. But it kept them out all the time, and when they were home, they were always on laptops, typing away into all hours of the night."

"I'm sorry," I said, meaning it. My dad was often out of the house, but when he was there, he was there 100%. We ate out, went to see movies and constantly went to the Natural History Museum. We had season tickets to the Mets. We saw and watched trashy cop shows (for my dad) and cheesy sci-fi movies (for me) all the time. I couldn't imagine being in the brownstone by myself all the time.

"It's fine. I just sometimes wish they would have made it to a football game, or watched me pitch." I opened my mouth to say something, but he immediately spoke. "Hey, you should sleep. I'll stay up and wait for your dad."

"Are you sure?" I asked. He nodded, not meeting my eyes. I turned away from him and curled up in a ball against the door. I didn't think I would be able to fall asleep, in a car, in the middle of a forest, with Awakened everywhere, capable of ripping me apart. But my eyes eventually got heavy as I slipped into a deep sleep, with my cheek pressed to the cold glass and my arms wrapped tightly around my knees.

It started off so normal. I was back in the quad at school, under the twinkling lights, in the same red dress I had worn only a few months before at the fall dance. Things were different though. It was colder, darker and the music was harsher than the kind of music that St. Joseph's Prep usually played. It was the kind of music that I would listen to on my stereo and dance around my room, feeling the aggressive beats move through my body.

I wandered under the vines that had been draped around, my fingers gliding over the thick branches and across the tough red skin of the apples that hung from them. It didn't make sense to me, and I vaguely had a memory of telling Madison that apples grew on trees and not vines.

I felt a sudden pang of hunger and wanted to rip all the apples off the vines and bite into their skin and rip them apart. I wanted to sink my teeth into them, and my hands grabbed at them, yanking them down, vines scattering around me, branches in my hair.

Everyone on the dance floor was standing still, facing partners, as if waiting for something. I made my way through the crowd, distracted for a moment at how graceful and silent my movements were. I stopped in the middle, spinning around, spinning and twirling, until I came to a halt and Ash was standing in front of me.

He looked beautiful, perfectly and achingly beautiful, and he was gaping at me, horrified. Despite his fear, he reached for my hands, pulled me closer and led me in a dance. It was formal, calculated, completely mismatching the violent music filling the air. His eyes never left mine, and I could almost see myself reflected in the empty pools of blue.

"You're beautiful," he said, his voice loud enough to hear over the music. "You're so terrifying but so beautiful." The world beautiful echoed off the walls, and went bouncing through the secluded area.

The unmoving people surrounding us started whispering "beautiful, beautiful, beautiful" over and over again, and I felt a shiver run up my spine.

"Terrifying?" I asked, confused. My voice sounded different, deeper. The rest of the dancers started moving, a slow waltz, slower than the two of us. They continued to repeat the word "beautiful" as if in a trance.

"Terrifying," Ash repeated, a distorted smile on his face. "And beautiful." He stopped for a moment and brought my hand to his face, pressing his full lips against a small blue hand.

I gasped, pulling backward, and stared, horrified, at the small blue hands that seemed to be attached to my own arms, blue, blue, blue. I wrapped my arms tight around my stomach, the sudden urge to vomit so strong, so immediate. I met Ash's smiling face and turned heel. I ran away, ran through the slow dancers, through the branches that I had left scattered on the floor, through the echoing hallways of the school and into the girls' restroom.

I stopped in front of the mirror and leaned over the sink, scared to look up. My heart was pounding in my chest, my ears, and my head, all the way down to my toes. I lifted my eyes and stared at the blue monster glaring at me in the mirror. Her hair was wild, covered in vines, her eyes were pure black, and there was no mistaking the blueness of her skin. I opened my mouth to scream and immediately saw the razor sharp teeth.

I woke up screaming.

A hand immediately went to my mouth, shutting off my screams. I went into a panic mode and clawed at the hand pressed against my mouth.

"Z, hey, it's me. It's okay," Ash said softly. "It's fine. It's okay. You had a nightmare but it's okay. I just didn't want you screaming. I'm going to lower my hand now, all right?"

I nodded, my heart pounding. He lowered his hand, and I let out a breath.

"Do you want to talk about it?" he asked, reaching to brush a loose strand of hair behind my ear. His face was only a few inches away from me, looking at me carefully. There was so much concern on that beautiful face, and I found myself straining toward it. I wanted to be held, rocked back to sleep when it would only be happy dreams. I may have left the nightmare of my dream, but the nightmare still existed in reality.

I shook my head, trying to reorient myself. I reached for Ash, to stop the spinning of the world around me, to stop the pounding in my head. I felt a slight relief that my hands were the normal olive tone that I was used to, and not blue. I had a sudden urge to look in the mirror to make sure that my eyes were still normal.

"Is she okay?"

I straightened up, finally noticing that my dad was sitting in the front seat. I met his eyes and I felt my heart squeeze again. What was wrong with me? I spent eighteen years keeping complete control of my emotions, and now I felt them threatening to pour over. "I'm fine, Dad. I'm glad you're back. Did you get…what you needed?"

He sighed, leaning his head back against the headrest. The keys sat in the ignition of the car, but he showed no signs of wanting to turn the car on. "I grabbed a few things that I hadn't been able to grab before. We have a lot of things in the back. I also got clothes for Ash." He nodded toward the trunk. "We have gas. I couldn't take chances that gas stations would remain open. There's food, but not a lot of it. There's plenty of weapons and ammunition back there."

He reached forward, turning the car on. The sound of the car starting in the middle of the darkened forest was loud, almost startling. "We should go."

"Wait," I said, clamoring over the seat to take my place in the passenger seat. "Dad, I need to know what's going on. Ah, no," I continued as he started to interrupt him. "It's unfair to me, to both of us, for you to hide it. I need to know."

Dad's hands gripped the steering wheel, his knuckles white. He looked back at Ash. "And you?"

I glanced back at Ash, who looked nervous. "I want to know. My parents were there, and they were sick. The same people who took Madison came and took them, and I don't know why, and I don't know what's going on."

Our eyes met, and I gave him a small smile, probably one of the first genuine smiles that I had ever given him. He answered with a smile of his own, and I realized again how ridiculously beautiful he was when he smiled. We both turned back to my dad.

He stayed quiet for a long moment, so long that I thought he was going to refuse, that he would put the car in "drive" and that would be it. Instead, he turned the car off. "What do you want to know?"

CHAPTER
ELEVEN

"EVERYTHING," I BLURTED OUT. "WHERE did they come from? What is going on? Where are we going? What are we going to do?"

"Yeah, everything," Ash echoed, scooting forward on the seat to get closer. His eyes were intent on both of us.

Dad ran a hand through his hair, and I noticed for the first time that there were streaks of gray there that hadn't been there before. My dad was not even forty, yet the world had given him gray hairs.

"They estimate about a third of the population has gotten the Z virus…"

"Wait, the Z virus?" I immediately interrupted. "What …the Z virus?"

A corner of his mouth turned up. "It's what they called the virus, or at least what they call it because they have all awakened as zombies…hence the "Z" part of the Z virus."

I really hoped that Ash would now stop calling me "Z."

"But they call them Awakened?" Ash said, voicing my own confusion before I had a chance to.

"It's confusing. I know. The virus is called the Z virus. The victims that are awake and walking around are called Awakened. I didn't make it up," he said roughly.

"I'm just saying, the name 'Z virus' isn't very original," I muttered. My dad shot me an impatient look, so I shut my mouth and motioned for him to continue.

"Like, I was saying, they're saying that it's affected about a third of the population, maybe more. It's mostly congregated in the areas with a bigger population, the cities they ultimately decided to eliminate. There's no way to tell how many of them have been awakened, but it seems to be about 90% of them. They have completely overrun the urban areas."

He sighed. "With about 100 million people out there with the ability to run faster than a normal human being and the desire to use their new razor sharp teeth to tear through human flesh, they obviously felt that it was a decision they had to make."

With the pain and shock of the recent demolition of the city I had grown up in, I didn't necessarily agree with that assessment. However, I kept my mouth shut so that he could continue.

"Everyone is insanely concerned about the fact they all seemed to awaken at the same time. Of course, that means when they got sick or when they died doesn't give us any clue to why or how this happened."

He sighed again, frustrated, and it sounded loud in the nearly silent car. "We were at the station, normal day. I was trying to keep up with the numbers, trying to see how badly this had affected our city when we started getting the phone calls. I immediately turned on the TV, and there was coverage everywhere, showing the Awakened. I was so... caught off guard. I've seen my fair share of shit here in New York but I've never seen this before and I couldn't think."

"Then you called me. I was so relieved. You told me about Madison, and I knew immediately what the media hadn't quite figured out yet. The Awakened were the virus victims, and they had somehow come alive again. I knew that we had to go; we had to go now, and that's when they hit the station."

"It was like it was planned. A group of them came in, quiet, nearly hidden. They were on us before we even knew they were there. They're so fast, sneaky, and they took down Briggs before we could even react. And we just started shooting, trying to take them out."

He stopped and looked at both of us, and his tone shifted. He slipped into a sterner voice, dropping the slower lilt of a storyteller. "This is important. If we had known, if we had figured it out sooner, we wouldn't have lost so many people at the station. Are you listening?"

We both nodded, looking like bobble heads. I felt a sudden urge to giggle at this and had to stamp it down.

"You need to be specific when you kill them. The head or the back of the neck. Every time," he explained.

"Okay, the head makes sense," I said quickly.

"But the back of the neck? How does that even make sense?" Ash chirped in.

"Yeah, I know," my dad said, shaking his head. "It was an accident. We just started shooting, and we were hitting their arms and their legs, their chests or their backs, and they just weren't going down unless we hit them in the head, directly in the head. We discovered the back of the neck on accident. Dolan was engaged in a kind of hand-to-hand scuffle with one of them, and he had another one creeping up behind him. I shot him, but I wasn't aiming well and hit him right in the back of the neck, and he went straight down."

"Are you sure though?" I asked. "That was one case. And does it have to be a gun?"

"I tried it a few more times on the way to the brownstone to get you and Ash. The head and the back of the neck. There's no other way, not that I know of. As far as whether it has to be a gun, I don't think so."

I started to feel panic. It was incredibly specific. We were running away from the central centers of outbreak, but I had no idea if we would run into any more Awakened while on the road. There was no telling if their population was decimated in the bombs. If I ended up in a scuffle with them, I had more of a chance at slowing them down but not stopping them from getting me. "Dad, my aim…it just isn't that great…" I said softly, my hand going to my holster reflexively.

"We're going to work on it," Dad said, sighing. "We'll

work on yours, and we'll have to teach Ash. And we're going to work on defensive fighting too."

"Well, at least I have practice in that," I said, under my breath. I knew I could hold my own against a human with average strength. I didn't know what the strength of an Awakened was, but I imagined it would probably be above human capabilities. It was my gun skills that were causing all the problems. "So…Nebraska?"

Dad nodded, turning the car on again. The familiar scent of gasoline and exhaust filled the air, and he started to back out of the woods, slowly, navigating around trees and roots and other obstacles in our path. "It's the safest place. There's been talk…of a place in Colorado, near Mesa Verde National Park, a sanctuary that has been built to be a safe zone."

"In three days, someone built a place to escape to?" I asked, skeptically. "It just…doesn't seem that likely."

"Rumor is that they built it years ago in event of any sort of catastrophe. Colorado is a rich, abundant area, but far enough from the coast, in case of, I don't know, tsunamis or some other natural disaster," he explained, finally making it to the edge of the road. It was pitch black, not a light in sight. We were far enough away from the local town to be blind to its light and there were no other cars on the highway. "It's a bunch of bullshit, people reaching out for something to have hope for in hopeless times. We're going to Nebraska."

He flipped his turn signal, most likely out of habit, and pulled back onto the winding road. I let us get a few miles, nearly to the town, when I asked one last question. "And... and the bombs?"

"After we had holed up in the station for three days, we were ordered to evacuate the stations, go home and lock ourselves in the house. That's the sort of order they've announced all over the country, to go home and lock yourself in. I was about to leave, but I wanted to grab a few things. I heard the commissioner, and I wondered why he hadn't left."

"I stopped, thinking maybe he needed help, but he was on the phone. I was surprised because the phones had gone out, or so I thought. I'm not sure who he was talking to, but I heard enough to figure out what was going on. They were giving up. They wanted to control the Awakened population as much as they could. Bombs were going to drop at nineteen hundred hours, which gave me a short window of time. So I crept away, grabbed the car that I had been stocking for our departure and came to get you."

"Now, go to sleep, both of you," he said. "I'm going to stop in a few hours, and we'll take turns keeping watch. I need sleep too."

"Okay," I whispered, resting my head on my hands against the door.

"Oh, and, Zoey?"

I looked up at him, waiting for a "good night" or an "I love you," maybe even an "I'm sorry." Instead he said in a very defeated voice, "Merry Christmas."

I felt my eyes fill, and I turned away from him, drifting back to sleep, hoping that it would be dreamless.

CHAPTER
TWELVE

A COUPLE HOURS LATER, I felt a hand shaking me awake. I jumped, startled, my hand immediately going to my gun.

"It's fine. It's just me," Dad said, soothingly. "I need some sleep. I haven't really slept in days. Do you mind taking watch?"

I nodded, rubbing the sleep from my eyes. I glanced at the backseat, where Ash was stretched out. His mouth was hanging wide open, and I wondered for a moment if he drooled. I smiled a little and adjusted my seat so that I was sitting upright. Dad lay back in his own seat and was passed out in seconds.

It was still dark outside, and we were in the middle of nowhere, no lights around to permeate the blackness that pressed against the windows. I pulled my phone out of my back pocket to check the time; it seemed to be the only purpose for keeping it now. The numbers blinked up 4:32 a.m. at me, and I was surprised at how long my dad had been driving and how close we were to morning.

I did the math in my head, trying to figure out where we could possibly be. There was still a thick forest around us, so we hadn't come near the flat plains of the middle states. We'd driven for about two hours before stopping for supplies, and my dad had driven for roughly eight to nine hours. I guessed we were somewhere in Ohio, maybe even Indiana. That left us with a lot of ground left to cover, at least 16 hours left in the car. We were all so exhausted, and I didn't know how fast we could make it there without making any stops.

I wondered for a moment whether my mom was even alive. I doubted that the Z virus had reached all the way to the tiny town of Constance, but how did I know? How did I know that Awakened hadn't escaped from the larger cities into the flatlands of the Midwest? Everything was so uncertain. The phones didn't work, and we had already tried the radio. Either we were too far from a signal, or they just didn't work at all. I didn't want to think about the fact that there was probably no one there to broadcast.

I looked back again and smiled slightly at Ash. His mouth was still hanging open, and drool was pooling down the side of his mouth and onto the thick, black upholstery. He looked so different in sleep, softer and more vulnerable.

I wasn't happy that he was along for the ride, that was my dad was now responsible for his safety too, not with the way he had treated me my entire life. But I was also happy that he was alive. He had been spared over millions of people in the city. He had no one left; his parents had been in the city when it had been bombed and torn to pieces. He hadn't even had time to accept it before being thrown in the back of an SUV and taken away from the life he had always known.

His eyelids fluttered a little and then flew open. He smiled when he saw me looking. I felt a small smile creep across my own face.

"Hey," he said softly. "What's going on? Why are you staring at me?"

"I wasn't staring at you," I whispered back. "I'm on watch. I was looking around."

His smile grew a little wider. "Okay, Z." He shifted upward, wincing a little. "Not the most comfortable bed. Is your dad asleep?"

I nodded. "Yeah, he drove for a while. He needs to sleep."

Ash looked around, his eyes scanning our surroundings. The darkness was beginning to fade and there was a distinct pale shade to the sky as the sun began to rise. "Where are we?"

"I *think* Ohio," I said softly. "But I'm not sure. We're far from New York."

He nodded, looking around some more. "You can go to sleep, if you're tired. I'll keep watch now." He pulled his gun out from underneath his seat and put it in his lap.

"I don't know if I can sleep," I admitted. I felt more exposed with the rising sun, light pouring into the car. I was afraid. I was afraid that every moment that I was asleep, I would be vulnerable.

"You don't have to sleep," Ash said, stretching out his legs across the seats. He was too tall to completely stretch out, so there was a slight bend to his knees. "We could talk."

"About what?" I scoffed. "You and I have nothing in common."

He looked nervous for a second, his knees bouncing again. I was starting to notice little tics about him. "We might have something in common. That we could maybe talk about."

"I don't really feel like talking, Ash," I said, quickly, turning back in the seat to face forward.

"Okay," he said, softly, his voice drifting up to me. "We can stay quiet."

"Okay," I said, closing my eyes and falling into silence.

"RAISE YOUR ARM, ZOEY. WE'VE been over this."

I sighed. My arms were heavy, but I raised them anyway. The bottle that my dad had set on the fence was several feet away. I had shot it at least five or six times already and hadn't come close. There were a couple bullets lodged into the wood fence. I shot again and just caught the tip, and it went toppling over.

After my dad had woken up, the sun had risen high enough that he could no longer ignore it. I had thought he would start the car up again and head out. After about twenty minutes of driving, however, he pulled into a field and had started impromptu gun lessons.

"Great. Good job, champ. We still gotta work on that aim, but it's getting better," my dad said, his hands on his lips, gun holstered around his waist and to his ankle. He looked just like a cop, even without the blue uniform. "Come on, Ash."

Ash stepped forward, looking nervous. He raised his arms, his eyes intent on the bottle, yards away. He shot and hit the fence underneath the bottle, wood splintering onto the ground. He shook his head, slightly.

"You're fine. Try it again."

Ash's eyes met mine, and I nodded quickly in reassurance. He took his stance again, breathed in and out and then fired another shot. This time he hit the bottle squarely, and it went flying.

"Fantastic," my dad said, a smile lighting up his face. He came over to stand next to Ash, clapping him on the shoulder. Ash allowed a small triumphant smile on his face as he looked up at him. They looked so much like father and son for a moment, their dark hair so similar, that I wanted to throw my gun at them.

I turned back to the fence, where one last bottle was standing. I aimed at it and raised my arm, just like I had been told a million times. A moment later, a tiny crack told me the bullet had made contact and the bottle landed a few feet away.

Dad and Ash looked up in surprise, from the fence to me. I walked past them, heading back to the car. "Yeah, I can hit the stupid bottle too," I muttered as I passed them.

"Oh, come on, Zoey, seriously?" Dad said, his tone full

of exasperation.

"I'm hungry," I said as I slipped my gun back in its holster and opened the back of the SUV. I dug through the bins that my dad had stored there until I found one stocked full of dry food. I grabbed a pack of jerky and climbed up onto the tailgate and tore into the package.

Dad and Ash had come up right behind me, following each of my movements with keen eyes.

"What?" I said, chewing on a particularly tough piece of jerky.

"Ash, can you go gather those bottles up? Put the ones that aren't too beat up back on the fence?" Dad asked. Ash nodded in response and walked away, his eyes lingering on mine for a moment. I looked away, staring at the gray sky in the distance. A storm was definitely coming.

Dad turned back to me. "What's going on, kiddo?"

I sighed. "The end of the world, Dad."

He gave me a look and hopped onto the truck bed with me. "Don't coddle me, Zoe," he said. "You've been in a mood all day."

"I have *not* been in a mood," I scoffed.

"You have been. You've been moping."

"Moping! Oh yes, moping!" I said, throwing my hands out and nearly losing my grip on the bag of jerky. "I mean, Dad, it's kind of the END OF THE WORLD. We have these Awakened everywhere, and they freakin' blew up New York. We're headed on this crazy cross-country road trip to Constance, to live with Mom and Caspar. So yeah, maybe I'm *moping* a little."

"Yeah, all that, I get that," he conceded. "But something more is going on here, and I think it has to do with that guy over there." He indicated in Ash's direction, who was busy lining the bottles back up.

"I have no idea what you're talking about," I said, shoving another piece of jerky in my mouth, in the hopes that my inability to talk around a hunk of meat would indicate the end of the conversation.

"It's not a competition," my dad said firmly. "It's about being able to defend yourselves. The Awakened are fast, and they can only be taken down in two ways. I want to make sure that, if we see any of them out here, that you guys will be able to take care of yourself."

"I know," I said, swallowing hard. "I know. I just…can you give me a little credit? I'm trying. I am. I know I'm not great at it, but I'm trying."

"I know you're trying," he said, defensively. "I give you credit. I think you're being dramatic, Zoey. You're making this a competition when it doesn't have to be."

"But it *is* a competition," I broke out. "It is! It always has been. I've been telling you nearly every day since Ash moved to New York that he teased me and made fun of me and played stupid pranks on me. I told you that I didn't like having him around. And you always just loved him. You're always talking about his stupid football or baseball accomplishments. You wanted him over for dinner. God, you wanted me to date him. You stuck me with him for hours a day for weeks while we waited to see what would happen with this stupid virus. So, yeah, maybe I'm just being a little dramatic because I'm so sick of all the Ash love."

I hopped off the tailgate and started walking away. I was nearly back to Ash when my dad caught up to me. I looked up at him, and he wrapped his arm around my shoulders, tight. He didn't say anything for a moment, but I knew. He was not an overly affectionate person, not one who was open with his words, but I knew. I nodded and stepped away from him.

"Let's work on some hand-to-hand stuff," my dad called out to us. "We won't always be able to use our guns."

Ash looked and nodded, sliding his gun into his holster. My dad had given us a variety of small knives, able to slip into a belt loop or into a belt. "I think I can handle that."

I laughed a little at that but walked over to the fence and hopped onto it, ready to watch my dad and Ash go through basic movements in fighting and self-defense. I didn't need him to tell me that I wasn't needed. I knew enough from all the classes he was constantly making me take. Every once in a while I spoke up to correct Ash's movements.

The day started to get a little warmer as the sun rose higher, and Ash peeled off his shirt and tossed it aside. I blushed a little at the sight of his nearly perfect body. It was unfair that he looked like this. People weren't supposed to actually look like this. Perfectly tan, hard muscles, strong arms. I waved a hand in front of my face, hoping that it was the heat of the sun and not the near naked boy in front of me that was causing my face to feel so flushed.

After about a half an hour of practicing, my dad clapped Ash on the shoulder again. "You're strong. It'll be to your advantage once your strategy gets better. We'll work more on it later. We have to get moving."

We piled back into the car. I leaned forward to fiddle with the radio again but there was nothing but static. People were taking the president's warning to heart and locking themselves down in the house. We drove in silence for hours, before my dad pulled off the road again, deep off the road.

Ash and I both looked surprised when Dad got out of the car.

"What are you doing?" I asked.

He poked his head back in. "We're going to camp outside. We're going to eat some food and be prepared the best that we can be. I'd rather be outside, ready to fight, than get ambushed in the car."

I exchanged looks with Ash as we climbed out of the car and followed him into a clearing. He was already scrounging around for wood and tossing it in the center. It wasn't long before he had a small fire going. It was freezing, and I pulled a blanket from the back of the car and wrapped it around myself.

After a small dinner of cold Spaghetti-os from a can, I curled up into a fetal position on the ground and drifted to sleep while staring at the fire, watching the flames flicker.

The dream started out the same. The situations were the same. I was at the dance; the lights and vines were stretched across the courtyard. I was in Ash's arms, dancing around, that uncontrollable hunger filling my entire body. Ash smiled down at me, his vacant, amazing smile and called me beautiful and terrifying.

It was darker somehow, the edges of the dream blurred into dark shadows. Every time I turned my head, I was met with a dark fog, suffocating me. I pulled away from Ash and ran away, struggling to find myself through the dark. I lost track of myself for a while, fighting my way to some light. I stumbled, fell to the ground, and all I could see were the ankles of the people passing me.

The hunger became too much to handle and my hands darted out quickly to grab the nearest leg to me. I dragged the person to the ground and sunk my teeth into the soft flesh of an arm. The person was screaming, pulling and tugging at me to get off but I was already latched on. I wasn't letting go. My teeth were tearing through skin and muscle and I was enjoying the sweet, coppery taste of blood. I caught my rippled reflection in a window and saw the blue skin and the black eyes, and the pieces of flesh hanging from my sharpened teeth.

I looked down at the person I had tackled and found Madison staring back at me, whimpering. "Don't kill me, Zoey. Please don't kill me. Please don't kill me again!"

"Madison!"

"Zoey, Zoey, shhhh."

My eyes flew open, and I woke up gasping. I looked around and saw both Ash and Dad bending over me. "I'm sorry," I whispered, squeezing my eyes shut.

"Another nightmare?" Ash asked, brushing my sweaty hair out of my face.

I nodded. "Yeah." I shifted uncomfortably and not just because I was lying on the hard ground. "Did I…did I scream?"

Ash nodded. "Yeah, you did."

I flushed. "Oh god, I'm sorry. I shouldn't scream. I'm so sorry."

"Hey, Z, it's okay. You're having bad dreams; it's natural to scream," he soothed.

"I have to agree with Zoey on this one," Dad said, sighing. "I'm sorry you're having nightmares, but your screams can attract people to us."

My face burned even hotter. "I know. I'm sorry," I repeated, embarrassed. Waking up in the middle of nowhere, screaming my lungs out in front of my dad and Ash and possibly within hearing distance of some Awakened was not something I had much pride in.

"It's fine. Let's just try and get some more rest before we head out again," he said, settling back down. "Then maybe we can…" He fell silent, suddenly alert. He raised himself to his knees, slowly and quietly, staring around us.

"Dad?" I asked, confused, my eyes darting around our surroundings. I was used to the well-lit city and couldn't quite adjust to the permeating darkness.

"Someone's coming," he said softly.

CHAPTER
THIRTEEN

"WHAT?" I WHISPERED, FEAR FILLING my body. I looked up at Ash, who looked equally as scared but determined. He stood up, his shoulders set.

Dad lifted a finger to his lips and slowly raised himself into a standing position, his gun aimed in front of him. I strained my ears, listening for whatever had stopped him, but I couldn't hear anything over the hammering of my heart. I reached for my gun, checking that it was fully loaded before clamoring out of the blanket that had tangled itself around my legs. Ash came to stand next to me, his own gun grasped in his hand. Together, the three of us stood, poised and ready.

Then I heard it, a sound so small there was no way I would have heard it if I had not been waiting for it. There was a shuffling of feet, more than one pair, coming our way.

They seemed to be moving at a decent pace, but there was no indication whether they were human or something more sinister. Every instinct in my body was telling me to run, to turn on my heel and go sprinting for the relatively safety of the car. I held my ground though, lifting my gun and aiming toward the darkness of the trees, where the footsteps seemed to be coming from.

After what felt like an eternity, people came out into the clearing, looking worse for the wear. They were carrying heavy backpacks on their backs and looked exhausted but alert. They stopped almost the moment that they saw us, hands out, and empty of weapons. While they held no weapons, I spotted a knife hilt protruding from a pocket and a rifle slung over a shoulder.

There were three of them, an older man and woman, and a younger man. The older man had to be in his late fifties, just a touch of gray touching his otherwise dark hair. He was bulky and wide but fit. He stood a couple feet in front of his companions, causing me to believe that he was in charge of the small group. The woman was around the same age as him. Though her hair was free of gray, her eyes showed wrinkles in the corners. The last man was not too much older than Ash and I, maybe in his early to mid-twenties. He looked very similar to the older man, despite his light hair, so perhaps he was his son. They didn't look dangerous, but looks could be deceiving.

"Evening," my dad said, his voice casual but his grip on the gun still tight and aimed at the newcomers. "What can we do for you folks?"

"We were passing through on a trail not too far from here when we heard someone screaming. We decided to check it out. We wanted to see if there was anyone out here who needed help."

My arms wavered a little, and I fought to keep them steady.

"That was my daughter," Dad explained. "We appreciate your concern, but she is okay. You folks can pass on now."

The three of them stood there, uneasy in the aim of three guns. The older man whispered something over his shoulder to the woman, presumably his wife, and she nodded. "Would you be so kind to share your fire tonight? We've been traveling a long way, and we have food we'd be more than willing to share."

Ash and I exchanged sideways glances before focusing on my dad. He studied them for a long moment. "I'm not sure that would be wise. I have two under my care; I'm sure you can understand my concern."

The man nodded. "I do. I have my own two to look after. The name's Garrity. Memphis Garrity. This here is my life, Julia, and our son, Liam."

He whispered over his shoulder again, while grabbing the shotgun that was strung across his back. I tensed, my grip tighter, my finger poised over the trigger. He smiled slightly and tossed the gun in front of him, so that it landed a few feet in front of us, much closer to us than them. It was followed by a couple of knives and a lone handgun.

"There. Now you're armed, and we're not," Memphis said, his voice calm. "We are travelers, just like you. We came from down South, in Atlanta."

"Did they bomb there too?" I asked, quietly.

Three pairs of eyes met mine in understanding and I felt a fresh wave of sorrow and regret and pain rush through me. This time it was the young man, Liam, who spoke up. "We were camping, ironically, when my fiancée called and told us about the Awakened. It was right before the phones went out. She told us to turn around and to not come back." His voice shook a little and I could see the red rims of his eyes, eyes that hadn't finished crying, not yet. "We've been headed away from there, ever since. We lost our car earlier."

I looked over at my dad again, who lowered his gun slightly. "Come share our fire. You'll understand if I keep your weapons."

"Of course," Memphis nodded. "We are very grateful."

Ash and I lowered our own weapons and walked back over to the fire, scooting over to make room for the three of them. My dad scooped up their weapons and stored them in the car, before locking it shut.

"That's a nice vehicle you got there," Memphis said, indicating toward the looming black SUV.

"I am...I was an officer for the NYPD," my dad explained, seeming more relaxed around the newcomers. He had a good read on people, and it seemed that, for the moment, he was choosing to trust them. However, he wasn't taking chances. He had Ash positioned next to Liam, who was much smaller than Ash, and he was next to Memphis. I was protected on either side.

"You're lucky then," Liam spoke up, his hands held out

toward the fire. Now that they were closer, I could see how cold they were. They were basking in the warmth of the fire, as it was the best thing they'd seen in days. "We had a few things with us, but you're probably way more equipped than we are."

"We've been making it," my dad, casually. "Have you seen any Awakened on your journey?"

They nodded. "We saw a small pack of them earlier today, when we lost our car. They're incredibly smart. I didn't expect for them to be working together, but they did, and they had a plan of attack. Luckily the three of us are hunters, and we took them down, but not before they had made quick work of our car." Memphis coughed slightly. "We've been walking all day."

"Have you seen any of them?" the woman, Julia, finally spoke up. Her voice was soft, in sharp contrast to her large figure. She was tall, definitely taller than me, maybe nearly as tall as my dad's six-foot stature, and had large hands that were clasped in front of her.

"Not since we left home," Ash said. "I didn't know they'd be out this far."

"We thought the bombs had taken care of them," Memphis admitted. "But then I realized that there must have been Awakened released in the smaller cities as well."

"Released?" I asked, confused.

He met my eyes, and there was something there in his eyes that made me feel comfortable. It felt good to see other people after two days on the road and days of near solitude back in New York. "Well, the way I figure it, the bodies of all these virus victims were stolen, right? And they all came back to life, as these Awakened, at the same time, right? Seems to make sense that it was done on purpose."

The three of us looked down taken aback at this statement but it actually sort of made sense to me. How likely was it that every single victim of the virus had magically awakened at the exact same moment, even though his or her times of death had been so drastically different?

"But why would someone want to do that?" I asked, thinking of the viciousness of the Awakened. They were an abomination, even worse than the zombies we had portrayed in books and movies for years. They were smart, and frightening. They worked together, and they were incredibly fast and strong. "Why would someone create something like that?"

"Think about it," Liam said, catching my gaze and staring at me intently. I felt my heart slam a couple times in my chest. He was good looking, even under all the dirt and grime. He had an all American look to him, blond hair and blue eyes, and was very tall and lanky. He seemed to take after his mother in that respect. He smiled at me, slightly, and I ducked my head. "What does one gain by releasing millions of incredibly fast, intelligent and strong beings into the world?"

Ash shrugged, but my father's lips grew thin, in a grim line.

"You're assuming that there is someone actually behind these Awakened," my dad said, sharply. "We don't know enough to assume that."

"But say they did. Say there is someone behind it," Liam insisted, passionately. "Why? What do they gain?"

"An army," I spoke up, softly. I shook my head. "None of this makes any sense."

"Well, whatever it is, we have to be sure to find someplace safe to be," Memphis said, digging through his pack. He pulled out a bag of trail mix and offered it to the group before chowing down.

"Where are you headed?" my dad asked carefully.

"Colorado," Memphis said, firmly. "To Sanctuary."

Ash and I exchanged bewildered looks, but my dad scoffed loudly.

"You're talking about the place near Mesa Verde. It's not real," my dad, a slight chuckle to his voice. "You won't find anything there. It doesn't exist."

"So says who?" Memphis asked, casually.

"So says me," my dad said, sounding irritated.

"Well you'll forgive me, sir, if I don't take that as solid truth," Memphis said, agreeably. "I think there's a place for us, a sanctuary in Colorado. There's been talk of it for years, and we're determined to find it."

My dad opened his mouth to say something again, and I knew it wasn't long before it turned into an argument. He was a practical, logical man, and he wouldn't believe in something based on rumors and heresy.

I started to interrupt, to intervene before it got further than it needed to, but Liam spoke first. "I'm parched. You folks wouldn't have any water to spare, would you?"

The two older men turned to look at him, almost

surprised that he was even still there. My dad's eyes met mine, and he said, "Will you get him some water?"

I nodded, standing up and brushing the dirt off my jeans. I knew it would only be another day until I would look as dirty and careworn as these three. I walked over to the car, reached into the back and pulled out a water bottle. I turned around, and bumped right into Liam. "Oh, sorry. I didn't see you there."

He smiled, a crooked grin that didn't quite seem to fit the rugged good looks of the rest of his face. It was endearing though, charming. "I just wanted to make sure you were safe."

A small smile twitched at the corner of my lips. "I can take care of myself."

"I don't doubt it."

I held the water bottle out to him. "Here you go."

He reached for it, his fingers brushing lightly against mine as he took it. "Thank you…?"

"Zoey," I supplied.

"Zoey," he repeated.

I paused, when I heard my dad's voice rise a bit, and I shook my head. I hoped they had moved on from the sanctuary talk, or it was going to be an extremely long night. "Yes."

"That's beautiful," he said, unscrewing the top of the bottle and taking a large swig. He offered the bottle out to me, and I shook my head. "So that's your daddy, I assume. Who is the other guy? Your boyfriend?"

"Oh, god no," I said quickly. "Ash is…well, was my

next door neighbor. He had nobody left, so he came along with us."

"Oh, I see," Liam said, his voice soft as he glanced over his shoulder at Ash, whose eyes were flipping back and forth between my dad and Memphis and myself and Liam. "Well, good."

I blushed and ducked my head, embarrassed at my obvious pleasure in his interest. I immediately changed the subject. "So are you guys really headed for Colorado?"

He nodded. "Yes, definitely. Sanctuary is there. I know it's there."

"But how can you be sure?" I asked. His confidence was unnerving, while at the same time it was addicting. He had a plan, a solid plan. It sounded insane, but he believed in it and his confidence in it was solid. "It's all just a rumor."

"Sometimes you have to have faith, you know?" he said, looking down at me. I leaned up against the car, and he leaned next to me, surveying the scene around us.

"I guess," I answered. "I'm not much one for faith."

He chuckled light. "So where are you headed, Miss Zoey?" I eyed him suspiciously for a moment, and he laughed again. "It's okay to tell me."

"Nebraska," I said, deliberately leaving out the specific town. "My mom lives there, on an inactive farm. It's a safe place, or so we hope."

"Sounds like you have to have a little faith in something too," he pointed out.

"You could be right," I admitted.

"Z?" Ash was suddenly in front of us, looking at Liam

with distaste on his face. "Come back to the fire. It's cold over here." He met my eyes, and I felt myself sucked into those baby blues. I found myself nodding.

"Okay," I agreed, looking up at Liam. "Are you coming?"

He smiled stretched across his face again, and he pushed himself off the car and started walking toward the fire. Ash grabbed my arm and pulled me to him. I collided with his chest from the harsh, quick movement and stepped backward.

"What?" I asked, looking back toward the fire, where the three strangers sat with my dad. He looked more relaxed, but he had shown no inclination to let go of his gun or to give them their weapons back.

"What were you guys talking about?" Ash asked, his voice casual.

I raised my eyebrow at him. "Nothing important," I answered, trying to walk past him. He stepped to the side, blocking me again.

"Zoey, just…just be careful, okay?" he said, under his breath. "You can't just trust anyone that walks into our camp just because they have a pretty face."

"You think Liam has a pretty face?" I asked innocently, my eyes wide.

"I'm serious," he said sternly. "Just be careful."

I pushed past him. "I never pegged you as the jealous type, Ash Matthews." I returned to the fire and sat down, exchanging a quick smile with Liam before turning my attention back to the conversation between my dad and Memphis.

It wasn't long before I was asleep again, sharing a blanket

with my dad and my gun tucked under my chest. Ash volunteered to take the first watch and set himself up against a tree. He still seemed very suspicious Liam and his family.

I had slept for a few hours before Ash woke me up, and we switched places. He smiled gratefully at me, and a rush of emotions went through me. It was getting harder and harder to ignore that I didn't hate Ash as much as I pretended I did. I watched him for a moment, as he settled under the blanket on the hard ground and fell asleep almost immediately.

Shaking my head, I sighed and refocused my attention of the area surrounding us. The sun was just beginning to peek through the crack in the trees. We had spent so many hours talking with Memphis, Julia and Liam that we had fallen asleep late. I knew that even though the sun would be shining on us in no time, they would stay asleep. Every face around me was the picture of exhaustion.

I felt my eyelids get heavy after an hour or so and contemplated waking my dad up to take over. I pushed through it though; he hadn't gotten nearly enough sleep, and I had to stay awake for at least a couple hours. It was only fair to the rest of them. I shifted, propping myself against a tree trunk and focused on the sounds of the forest. There was a light chirping from a group of birds, and the crackle of leaves being blown by the slight wind that had picked up through the night. Every once in awhile, there would be the sound of quick feet that would cause my heart to pound faster before a squirrel would dart out. I came to one conclusion: keeping watch, when you are really tired, is extremely boring.

I drifted off to sleep for a moment; that could have been a minute or maybe more because, next thing I knew, Liam had a concerned look on his face and was shaking me awake.

"Well, this is embarrassing," I said, rubbing my eyes, "falling asleep on the job."

"Shh," he said, quietly, his eyes darting around the trees. "They're out there."

"Who?" I whispered back, reaching for the gun in my lap and the knife tucked into my boot.

"Awakened."

I sat up straighter, my own eyes scanning the surroundings. I strained my ears listening for it and felt my heart jump into my throat when I heard it. It was low, barely audible, but I could hear the hoarse breaths coming from a distance away. "Oh god," I breathed.

"Zoey. Zoey, my family needs their weapons," Liam said urgently. I hesitated for a moment, casting a glance at my dad, asleep on the ground. "Please."

I handed him the keys to the car. "Get them quietly. You try to shoot me, I swear to god I will blow your brains out."

Despite the situation, Liam chuckled lightly. "Sounds about right. Wake everyone up."

I crept around the campsite, my ear cocked in the direction of the approaching Awakened. It sounded like they were moving slowly, which meant they were probably unaware that there were people in front of them. I woke my dad and Ash up first, whispering quickly. They woke immediately, grabbing their own weapons before waking Memphis and Julia. By this time, Liam had come back and was passing their weapons around."

The six of us stood poised, waiting in the silence for them to appear. My gun was clutched tight in my right hand and my knife in my left. I bounced from one foot to the other, anxious and ready.

CHAPTER
FOURTEEN

THEY CAME IN THROUGH THE trees, a pack of about a dozen. They stopped suddenly at the sight of us; I had been right when I had guessed about them not knowing we were there. Almost in unison, they crouched, prepared to fight.

"Leave us be," my dad called out to them, his gun raised. "Move on, and we won't hurt you."

A loud barking laugh came from a large man near the middle of the group. His teeth shone from between his pale blue lips, and I resisted the urge to throw up. I would never get over the sight of those animal-like teeth. "I don't think that would be in our best interest," he spoke, his voice filling the clearing. "We've traveled a long way, and we are so so very hungry."

The girl next to him whined loudly, like an animal poised and ready to attack. The hairs on my arms stood up at the sound.

"Easy, Cara," the man said. "We need to share amongst everyone in the group."

"I'm so hungry," she said, her voice like fingernails on a chalkboard. I glanced around me and saw that I wasn't the only one affected by her. Her black eyes stared unwavering at us, her tongue peeking out to lick her dry lips. "Let me go."

The man sighed as if bored. "If you must." He flipped his hand lazily, and as one, they came barreling at us.

I shot the first man that came toward me, missing his head, catching him in the shoulder blade. He went down, but was already struggling to stand up by the time I raced to him. I aimed a kick at his head, and sent spiraling back. I ducked in time to miss the arms of the girl who had whined earlier. I punched her in the face, aiming the gun straight at her head. She went down with a thump, blood pooling around her head.

I had no time to think of that though before turning back to my original opponent. He had recovered and tackled me to the ground, his strength unbelievable. I struggled for a moment, my gun slipping out of my hand and sliding across the ground. His mouth came closer to me, his breath hot and smelling vaguely icy on my face. With his teeth bared, he moaned with pleasure.

"I can smell your blood," he said, grazing his lips across my cheek. "It smells so good. Just one small bite, one teensy little bite. I promise I won't kill you. I'm just so hungry."

I leaned forward and head-butted him, sending him

howling back in pain. I took that opportunity to swing up at him with my fists, catching him in the jaw. His whines became more pronounced, and I reached up and around him, stabbing my knife deep into the back of his neck. I watched as his black eyes went wide. I raised my eye shaking fingers to his neck, but I didn't even know if they had a pulse. I pushed his body up as I dragged myself from underneath him.

"Zoey," Ash said, rushing over and offering me a hand up. I took it, and he hoisted me up. "Are you okay?"

I nodded. "Ash!" He spun around and immediately was caught, strong blue arms wrapped his chest pulling him away. I scrambled for my gun and aimed it at the Awakened. I hesitated; my arm was still shaky, and I didn't want to hit Ash. "Let him go!" I shouted.

My dad heard my shout and turned around, his eyes set on us. He started making his way over but was immediately stopped by a small Awakened woman. She had launched herself at him, and he was quickly distracted, fighting her off. I looked at our three temporary companions, but they were all busy taking down the rest of the group.

"Let him go," I repeated.

The man laughed. "Oh, sure, little girl. I'll let him go. After I enjoy a little snack." He proceeded to sink his teeth into Ash's shoulder. Ash cried out, his hands scrambling at the arms that held him tight. He started dragging him away, and I lost it.

I ran forward, jumping on the back of the Awakened, my gun pressed to his neck. The man dropped Ash, his arms coming up to claw at my grip, and Ash rolled out of the way. I fired and he went down. I fell onto the floor, the breath knocked out of me.

"Are you okay?" Ash asked, again, falling to his knees next to me.

"I'm fine," I said, sitting up and wincing. I looked around us and saw that the others had taken out the Awakened with ease. I watched as Memphis drove the butt of his gun at the head of the last one. I glanced around me, making sure there were none lurking in the shadows of the trees before turning back to Ash. "Let me see your shoulder."

Ash shook his head. "It's fine."

"It's not fine," I said firmly. "Come here."

He relented, failing to his knees next to me. I peeled back the torn fabric of his shirt, sticky with warm blood. I leaned forward and inspected the gash. "It's deep but you're not going to die. Unfortunately." I smiled up at him, and he smiled back looking surprised. "You probably need stitches though. I'm not sure, but I think so."

I pulled off the t-shirt I was wearing and pressed it against his shoulder. I was grateful that I was wearing layers and had thought to wear a tank top under the shirt I was wearing. Still the act of removing of an article of clothing in front of Ash made me feel incredibly self-conscious.

"Are you guys okay?" my dad said, crouching by us.

"He got bit," I said, looking up at him. "I'm fine. I think I may need to sew him up though." I lifted the shirt from Ash's shoulder and showed my dad the wound.

He nodded. "Yeah, it's deep. Let me grab the first aid."

He stood up and walked back over to the car, grabbing the first aid kit from underneath the passenger seat.

"Do you know how to stitch people up?" Ash asked warily, his face getting pale.

"Nope," I said, taking the first aid kit from my dad. "But no better time than the present to learn."

Ash winced but still had a smile on his face. "Well, if there's anyone I'd trust to sew me up, it would be you."

"Shut up, you," I said, pulling him toward me so that his shoulder was rested on my lap. I found a needle and threat in the pack, and poured some water across his wound, cleaning it the best I could. "This is going to hurt."

He took a deep breath, bracing himself as I sunk the needle into his skin. He squeezed his eyes shut, tense.

"I'm sorry," I apologized, feeling tears spring in the corners of my eyes. "I don't want it to hurt."

He laughed shakily. "It doesn't hurt in the slightest. Come on now." He winced again as I continued my precarious needlework. "Hey, Z?"

"Hmm?" I asked, concentrating on my work. The smell of smoke filled my nose, and I knew that the others were burning the bodies. I breathed out, doing everything I could to keep the Spaghetti-Os I'd eaten the night before in my stomach.

"Thank you," he said. I looked up from his shoulder, into his face, surprised. "For saving my life."

I was shocked. Ash had never said thank you, not sincerely, in the nine years I had known him. "Sure," I said, returning back to my work.

"You were like a warrior out there," Ash said, his head turned away from his shoulder. He was trying to remain steady, but I could read the pain in his eyes and in the furrowing of his brow. "I didn't know you could do that."

I shrugged. "Lots of years of karate and kickboxing and self-defense classes. I guess they finally came into use."

"Well, you were incredible," he said, inhaling sharply as I pulled the thread tight.

"She was beautiful."

We both looked up and saw Liam standing over us. My cheeks went red, and I bent over Ash's shoulder, finishing up the stitching and tying it off. I studied it for a moment. It was not a pretty job but it was adequate. He would definitely have a scar but at least he wouldn't bleed to death.

Ash frowned, sitting up slowly. He nodded gratefully at me. "She shouldn't have to fight like that," he shot at Liam, "beautiful or not."

"Thanks, Ash. Real smooth," I said, holding my hands covered in blood out in front of me and wrinkling my nose. I grabbed the water I'd used on his wounds and poured it over my hands.

"That's not what I meant, Z," he said, exasperated. "I'm just saying…"

I wiped my hands on my bloody, and now completely useless, shirt. "We're fighting for our lives and you still can't remember to call me by my actual name."

Ash started to retort but Liam cut in. "Sorry to interrupt, but I just came over to say goodbye."

"Say goodbye?" I echoed, confused.

He nodded. "We're headed up to Michigan to check on my dad's sister before making our way back down to Colorado, and your dad will be wanting to move on to Nebraska."

I nodded, surprised at my odd attachment to Liam and at my disappointment in his departure. "Well, I wish you guys luck." I held my hand out to him.

He ignored my hand, leaning forward to place a quick peck on my cheek, causing butterflies to rip through my stomach. Ash coughed loudly, but I ignored him. Liam pulled back, smiling that crooked smile. "You too, Zoey. I hope to see you at Sanctuary one day."

A corner of my mouth twitched up in a smile. "Maybe."

He walked away, heading toward his parents. They all exchanged words with my dad before shouldering their packs and heading back into the forest. I watched them with some trepidation. For a moment there, I had felt so alone. It had been nice to know we weren't the only three left fighting for survival.

"What a charmer," Ash scoffed as soon as they were gone. He leaned down to the ground, reaching for his gun. His face was pulled taught with pain, but he made no noise. I would have to remember to give him pain medicine later.

"You would know," I said drily. I glanced over my shoulder at the pile of charred bodies, just a pile of body parts and ash. I shuddered; it made me sick. These were humans, people who had lived lives before the virus, before they had died. I didn't know why they had awakened. I didn't know if there was a purpose to them. But that didn't matter. I felt a wave of remorse for them. They were beyond peace, beyond resting, and now were simply consumed by hunger and violence.

"Come on, Z, seriously? The guy is hitting on you in the middle of the zombie apocalypse! After his fiancée just died!" Ash said. "And he's such a Southern gentleman, kissing you on the cheek."

"Okay, one, it's not the apocalypse. Two, so what if he kissed me?" I said, starting toward the car. "And three, I'm pretty sure I detect a bit of jealousy back there."

Ash broke out in a grin, looking so much like his old self that I felt a pang go through me. "I don't like anyone looking at my girl that way. You know I'm the only one for you."

I rolled my eyes at him. "You're irritating," I said half-heartedly. "Let's get out of here."

After we had cleaned ourselves up and erased all signs that we had been there, we climbed back into the car and drove for a few hours. As the sun began to crawl higher, peeking through the heavy clouds, my dad pulled over and set up another practice. He set me up with bottles to work on my shooting while he sparred with Ash. He pointed out Ash's weaknesses, especially after the fight we had just encountered.

I focused on the bottles, occasionally shooting them off the fence but more often missing them. Every time I missed, I cursed loudly. I was so involved in what I was doing that I didn't hear my dad coming up to me until he was right next to me.

"You lack confidence," he said, his hands planted firmly on his hips. He looked exhausted, but still determined. Though he had washed most of the blood off from the fight, he was still dirty, and there was a definite scruff growing on his chin. I glanced at Ash and noticed the same thing, surprisingly. It made them both look older.

"I think it's more like a lack of aim," I grumbled, raising my gun and shooting again. It sailed too much to the left, and I resisted the urge to throw my gun and just roundhouse kick the bottle off the stupid fence. That was something I knew I could do.

"Look, Zoey, you're doing everything right, and yet you're still not hitting what you aim for," he pointed out. "You're not confident in what you're doing. You don't trust your own abilities."

"Right, okay," I said. "I don't trust myself." When he didn't move away, I spoke again, feeling exasperated. "Can you maybe not stand there and watch me? I can't concentrate."

He studied me for a moment before calling out to Ash. "Ash, why don't you work on your shooting for a sec? I want to have a word with Zoey."

Fantastic. I sighed, stepping out of the way.

Ash nodded, brushing against me as he took my place. A charge of electricity went zipping through me at the contact. Our eyes met for a second, and I temporarily lost my breath. He was worn, beaten from the past couple days on the road. His hair was a ruffled mess, there were dark purple bags under his blue eyes, and he had a shadow along his jawline, but he had never looked so tempting. I tore my gaze away from him and looked up to my dad.

"What? What is it?" I asked.

"Don't 'what' me with that attitude," he said. He led me away, enough from Ash that he could not eavesdrop. "I just wanted to talk to you. I wanted to see how you were doing."

"I'm fine," I said, automatically. "You don't have to worry about me, Dad."

He raised his eyebrow at me, looking so much like his old self that I nearly burst into tears. He was so young, only thirty-eight. He had only been twenty when I was born and the gray strands that were now in his hair worried me. "I always worry about you," he said. "I just want to make sure you're okay, as okay as anyone could possibly be. This isn't easy."

I shook my head. "I'm fine. I'll be fine."

"I know you're not thrilled with us heading to your mom's. And I know you're not thrilled with Ash coming along."

I nudged him in the shoulder. "She is my mom after all. It's just…that's rough too." I looked up at him. "I'd imagine it's worse for you."

He shrugged, but I could see the pain in his eyes. Despite them being separated and divorced for so long, I could see that my dad never really got over my mom. "It's for your survival, Zoey. We'll handle it as it comes."

"Exactly," I said. "We'll be fine."

"And Ash?" he asked, looking over my shoulder.

I looked back at Ash, who was standing legs shoulder

width apart, aiming for the bottles. My heart slammed in my chest, and I sighed. "It's not like I wanted him to die, Dad," I retorted. "It's just not easy to have your high school bully along with you, every moment of the day."

His mouth quirked up a bit, and I resisted the urge to smile as well. He knew me better than anyone. "I've been meaning to talk to you…"

"About what?" I asked, wiping my sweaty hands all over my jeans. I would have to change when I got back to the car. I felt disgusting and dirty. I ran a hand through my hair and winced at how greasy and stringy it had gotten over the past few days.

He took a deep breath and blew it out, looking embarrassed for a moment. "I wanted to apologize." I looked up from my thorough examination of my hair and narrowed my eyes at him. "You're right. I've always treated Ash better than I should have."

"Dad, it's not that important," I started to say, but he was already shaking his head.

"No, you were right. Ash was a bully, and I knew that he had sent you home crying, but I just liked the kid. I always thought he had a crush on you and couldn't quite figure out what to do about it. But that was no excuse. I should have been behind my daughter."

"It's okay," I said, secretly jumping for joy on the inside. Finally, after nine years, my dad was seeing. He was admitting. It shouldn't have been that important now, but it was. My dad's obvious affection for Ash despite his treatment of me had always bothered me.

"Thank you. It's not, but thank you. I should have never taken Ash's side when you guys were fighting. I should have taken you more seriously. I know you think I always wanted a boy, but really I just wanted you, Zoey. You're the best kid a parent could ask for."

"Aw, Dad," I said teasing him, trying to hide the emotions that were building up in the back of my throat. "Come on, there's no other person that I'd rather be with at the end of the world."

"Well, I'm going to take care of you," he promised, sliding his hands into his pockets. He nodded toward Ash. "I know he's been rough on you, but give him a chance. He's changed. The virus, the Awakened, it's changed him. And I've always thought he liked you."

I dropped my gaze to the ground. "Ash doesn't like me," I insisted, but I didn't feel so sure of that anymore. I sighed dramatically. "But I guess if we have to repopulate the earth together, there could be worse candidates."

He groaned, but there was laughter in it. I grinned. "Please, really? Don't talk about that kind of stuff with your old man. It's weird."

I laughed, and Ash glanced over at us, his eyebrows raised.

"Come on; let's get out of here," he said, grabbing my head with his arm in a headlock. "I love you, champ."

"I love you too, Dad."

CHAPTER
FIFTEEN

IT WAS A DIFFERENT DREAM this time. I was in the brownstone, trapped in my bedroom. Bandit was at the door whining, begging to be let out. I could hear the whispers of the Awakened in the streets. I was wrapped in the blankets on my bed, in the fetal position. Bandit's paws kept scratching at the door, and the whining grew loud and louder. I clapped my hands over my ears and whimpered. "No, Bandit. No."

He barked loudly, and I jumped at the sound. A moment later, there was a loud pounding on my bedroom door, shaking it in its frame. The doorknob rattled, but it was locked. I didn't remember locking it, and I remembered it was because my bedroom had never had a lock on the door. Bandit pranced nervously in place, barking at the door.

"Bandit," I whispered, fear shooting through my veins like ice. "Bandit, come here."

He ignored me, his ears perked up, alert and ready. He

crouched lower, his haunches up, as he growled at whatever was on the other side of the door. He was always the most protective dog. The door continued to rattle, and I knew it was only moments before it was ripped from its hinges.

It went flying, smacking into Bandit. He whimpered but held his ground. He went sprinting to the three Awakened that had burst in the room. The first one grabbed Bandit like he weighed nothing and tossed him across the room. My dog's body went slamming into the solid wall and fell to the floor with a thump. I screamed and screamed and screamed.

The three Awakened turned to me, and I realized with a jolt that they were the three I had killed in the woods. I scrambled backward, my back hitting my headboard with a smack. There was nowhere to go. There was one on each side of the bed, and the girl Cara at the foot.

"She smells so good," she said, her hoarse voice only a whisper, echoing through the room. "She's going to taste so good."

They came closer, pressing themselves against me, tearing away my clothes to sink into flesh. I screamed and screamed, but there was no one left. There was nobody left to hear my screams.

I woke with a start, sweat dripping down my brow. I realized that there were arms wrapped around me and recognized them as my dad's. I burrowed my face in his chest, inhaling his familiar scent. His arms tightened around me. I raised my head a little and saw Ash in the front seat. Our eyes met in the rearview mirror, and I nodded to the question in his eyes. I was fine. I would be fine. Eventually I would stop having nightmares like a five-year-old.

I sat up, rubbing my forehead, and yawned. I motioned

my dad to keep sleeping, and he slid back into sleep in seconds. I stretched, feeling cramps throughout my sore and tired body. I felt a pain in my abdominal area and frowned. It came again, worse than the last and I felt a swell of recognition rush through me. I paused, wondering if I could possibly be right, and started counting days. I frowned again. I just couldn't remember. Another wave of pain passed through me, and I nearly cried in frustration. This had to be the worst timing ever.

"Dad," I whispered, nudging him. He shifted a bit, but didn't wake. "Dad?"

He stirred and looked up at me, with sleep filled eyes. "What's wrong, champ?"

"Um," I started, looking up at the front seat of the car and hoping that Ash couldn't hear me. "You wouldn't happen to have any, um, female necessities with you? Like, you didn't grab any when preparing for this?"

He stared at me confused for a moment, and then it dawned on him. "Shit. No. I didn't think. I just didn't even think of it. You didn't grab anything before we left?"

I shook my head. "I wasn't exactly thinking of," I lowered my voice for a moment, "*tampons* when I was packing."

"Shit," he repeated. He sat, and peeked over the front seat. "Where are we, Ash?"

"Not too far from Iowa," he answered, quickly. "Maybe an hour or so."

Dad nodded. "All right. We need to make a pit stop."

Ash looked startled. "Why? Don't we have everything we need? We've only got about nine hours left."

169

We were getting so close. I couldn't wait nine hours though. I needed something. I wondered for an instant whether the Awakened could smell blood, like a shark or something, and had to bite down a frenzied laugh. "I can't wait. We need to stop."

Ash looked back at me confused before turning his attention back on the road. Thankfully he didn't ask. "There was a sign for a gas station about five miles back. It should be coming up soon. Will that work?"

I nodded. "Yeah. Yeah, that should work." My cheeks were flaming red. Who knew that such a trivial thing like a period would become such a hassle?

The gas station came up quickly, and Ash took the exit. It was lit up, and there were a few cars parked at the pumps pumping gas as if it were any normal day. I couldn't even remember what day of the week it was. Tuesday? I had lost track completely and my phone had died ages ago, taking my only source of calendar away from me.

I reached for the door handle as soon as we pulled in, but Dad grabbed my arm and pulled me back.

"Give me your guns, both of you," he said, holding his hands out for them. "Keep your knives, but hidden, tucked in your boots." We both handed over our guns. My dad dug into his pockets and pulled a rumpled twenty-dollar bill from his wallet. "Go on in, together. Act natural, get what you need, and get out."

"And you?" I asked, shoving the bill into the back pocket of my jeans.

"I'll be out here, keeping an eye out," he said. His eyes

were darting around the gas station, anxious. "It looks normal out there, but I don't know what's normal anymore."

I looked up at Ash, who was looking determined. "Let's do this." We both got out of the car and started walking to the mart. My eyes were darting around at the other people but I had to look casual. I couldn't believe that there was a gas station here, in the middle of nowhere, still operating. I had felt in the past few days that we were the only people left in the universe. It had felt like the world had gone silent.

Ash reached the door first and held it open for me. I walked in, glancing at the man behind the counter. He was reading a magazine and barely gave us a passing look as we walked in. "What are we here for?" Ash hissed at me as I walked through the aisles.

I burned with embarrassment. Having a period is a natural thing, I reminded myself, and it doesn't stop for anything, even when a third of the population is suddenly bloodthirsty. I didn't answer him and instead found a box of tampons on the bottom shelf, underneath the Nyquil and Tylenol. I grabbed it, and ignored the amused look on Ash's face. "Shut up." My fingers hovered over a box of Midol, and I reached for it. Ibuprofen was not going to be enough for this situation.

"Hey, I didn't say anything," he said, quiet laughter in his voice as we walked up the counter. I put both packages in front of the man, who rang them up, not bothering to say anything to the pair of us. I slid the dirty twenty across the slick surface of the counter and took back my change with shaking hands.

As soon as we walked around the mart, I stopped. Ash

noticed that I was no longer at his side and turned around to look at me questioningly.

"I have to use the restroom," I said, trying to put an easy smile on my face.

He nodded. "Okay, I'll wait for you."

I went around the side of the building and found the bathroom. It was dingy, dimly lit and extremely dirty. I made a face, wrinkling my nose before remembering that it was the first bathroom that I had seen in days. The novelty of "real" camping and peeing in the woods had lost its appeal almost instantaneously. I peeled my jeans off slowly, folded them and placed them on top of the paper towel dispenser. I removed my underwear, and tossed it in the trash; it was a completely useless pair now. I took care of business quickly and efficiently, as if it were any other day and any other normal period.

I sat down on the toilet after lowering the lid and cradled my head in my hands. I allowed myself to cry for about 30 seconds. They were quiet, desperate sobs. I couldn't distinguish whether they were real or if my hormones heightened my emotions. It felt stupid to be crying now, but I couldn't hold them back. I was struggling to hold it together, to keep myself together.

I had never even been camping. I had always lived a cozy, cushy life in my solo brownstone in New York City. Now I was dirty, disgusting, so hungry, tired and now I was on my period. I didn't know anyone else who would understand that this little extra bit was just the cherry on top of the worst sundae ever. My dad and Ash were tired, hungry and dirty like me, but they didn't have this. They wouldn't even have to think of something like, and for the moment, I sort of hated them for that.

I cleared my throat and calmed myself down. I used some scratchy toilet paper to wipe the tears from my cheeks. I took a couple deep breaths, washed my hands, ignoring my reflection in the foggy mirror, and left the restroom.

"Are you okay?" Ash asked, falling into step with me. "You were in there for a while."

"I'm fine," I said. "How do you know how long it takes?"

Ash grinned a little. "Don't tell me you're going to get all snippy at me now."

"Oh shut up," I said, feeling relaxed for a moment.

"I'm going to take that as a yes," Ash laughed. "Great. Now I don't have to just worry about an Awakened biting my head off."

I laughed, surprised at the sound. It had felt like years since I had laughed, genuinely. "Be careful, Ash. I might find you kind of tasty." I opened the passenger door of the car, noticing that my dad had moved back into the driver's seat.

He winked at me as I climbed into the backseat. "I always knew you wanted a taste of this."

My dad looked back and forth between us. "I really don't even want to know."

I buckled my seat belt and snuggled into my seat. "Let's go. We've only got eight hours until we reach Mom's house. We're almost there." I felt excited, for the first time, in such a long time, to see my mom and stay in a house with a bed and a shower.

CHAPTER

SIXTEEN

WE HAD ONLY BEEN DRIVING for a few hours when the rain
started. The sun had completely disappeared behind the
haze of dark gray clouds, and we went quickly from a light
rain to a heavy downpour. I had burst out laughing, filled
with joy at this small show of nature, this small example that
things weren't completely different. Ash and my dad were
staring at me for a long moment, watching as I rolled down
the window and stuck my hands out.

"What on earth are you doing?" Ash asked.

"I'm pretty sure that the rain is one of the most beautiful
things I've ever seen in my life," I said, as the rain washed
over my palms, washing away the dirt.

There was a chuckle from the backseat and I turned to
look at Ash. "What?" I asked. "Can't I enjoy a little rain?"

"I like that you're enjoying the rain," he admitted. "I

didn't think there would be anything left to enjoy anymore." He rolled down his own window, and a gust of wind came through, pelting Ash's face with rain. I giggled at the sight of his face dripping with rainwater. He grinned mischievously and leaned forward to shake his shaggy hair in my face.

"Hey now!" I yelled, throwing up my hands to block the spray of water. "I said I was enjoying the rain, not that I wanted it all over me."

Ash laughed and grabbed my wrists, pulling my arms and rubbing his wet head all over my face. He pulled back, his face only inches away from mine. "Is that better?"

I felt my breath catch in my throat, paralyzed by how close he was to me. Water was clinging to his thick, black eyelashes, and I was suddenly completely transfixed by his lips. His smile slipped, and his gaze held mine. My eyes met his, and I watched as they traced down my face to my lips. He bit his lip and looked nervous, his cool breath washing over my face. He was too close. His warmth was seeping through the contact and making my heart beat faster.

My dad coughed loudly and obviously. "Yeah, I'm still sitting here. Could you guys maybe think about doing that later?"

Ash blinked a couple times and pulled back, letting go of my wrists. I straightened up and cleared my throat, embarrassed. I chanced a look over at my dad and saw that he was barely concealing a grin. He saw me looking, and the almost-smile turned into a full-blown smirk.

"Don't you start," I said.

"I didn't say anything," he said innocently, abandoning all pretenses and turning to laugh at me.

"You're such a tease," I said. I glanced in the mirror and saw Ash staring at his hands, his brow furrowed. I looked back out the window and felt fear go shooting through me. "Oh my god, Dad!"

He looked away from me, back to the road. There were no less than two dozen Awakened standing in the middle of the road, as if waiting for us. My dad jerked the wheel, and the car lost control. It went barreling to the left, off the road and into a ditch. The car flipped once, twice before landing on its side. I heard screaming and it took me a second to realize that it was me; the screaming was coming from me.

My eyes flicked open, and I blinked a few times, wondering if I had passed out in the crash. I was disoriented and realized I was turned on my side, my shoulder pressed against the window that must have shattered on impact with the ground. The air bag had deployed, probably saving my life, and I pushed it out of my way as much as I could.

The car had come to a stop and was lying on its side. I looked up and over at my dad, who was talking quickly and quietly to Ash, who looked shaken but relatively unharmed. I looked down at my arms and saw cuts all over them, tiny pieces of glass embedded in my skin. It hurt, like needles in my skin.

Dad kicked the door open with his foot and began to climb out. His eyes met mine.

"Are you okay?" he asked quickly. I nodded, wincing as the pain shot through my forehead. I lifted my hand to my head and it came back warm and sticky. I whimpered. "I know it hurts, but we need to move. We have to move now."

I nodded again and reached overly slowly to unbuckle my seatbelt, while my dad struggled to lift himself out of the car. He leaned back over, extending his arm out to me. I grabbed it and let him pull me out. Ash was already out of the car, his gun pointed out in front of him. I reached for my own, and wiped the blood away from my eyes.

My heart sank. They were all around us. We were surrounded from all sides and outnumbered by about seven to one. We didn't have Liam, Memphis and Julia with us this time, and I knew that this was what my dad had been trying to prepare us for. I reached down to my foot, relieved to find my knife was still there. I slipped it out, clutching it in my hand tightly.

The three of us watched them for a moment, waiting for them to say something, for them to make a move, but they stayed still and silent. This scared me more somehow, and I felt my heart beat faster in my chest at the excruciating anticipation.

"Zoey," Ash whispered.

"Not now, Ash," I whispered back, making sure that my weight was balanced and that I had a firm grip on my weapons. I needed to be ready.

"Zoey, I need to tell you something," he insisted, his voice full of fear. I wanted to tell him to not be scared; I wanted someone to tell *me* not to be scared, but it was pointless. This was the perfect situation to be scared in.

I met his eyes for a moment. "Later, okay? You can tell

me later."

He looked like he wanted to protest, but instead, he nodded.

"Ash," Dad said softly, looking around at the Awakened surrounding us. They were so silent and so still. They looked dead, more so than they already were. I kept waiting as the seconds passed by. "Ash, whatever happens, you take care of Zoey. You protect her, no matter what."

I bit down on my lip hard, drawing the warm coppery taste of blood into my mouth. I refused to look at either of them, not even when Ash replied, "Yes, sir." I couldn't handle the waiting anymore, and I fired my gun at the closest Awakened near me. The bullet sailed straight into her forehead, my first perfect shot, and she crumpled to the ground. Everyone had watched in silence, but the moment her body hit the ground, chaos erupted.

No less than four or five Awakened ran straight at me. I ducked the arms of a small woman, sending my elbow into the chest of a man that came up from behind me. I kicked out, hitting him behind the knees and sending him to the ground. I used my knife to stab him in the chest, hoping it would keep him down for a moment. I whirled on the others, shooting one quickly in the head, just above the neck. It must have been good enough, because he fell, and immediately turned my attention to another. I dodged a kick, grabbing the leg and flipping the woman onto her stomach. I shot her in the head and felt an arm grab me from behind.

I was yanked backward, and I stumbled. They were

strong, stronger than their bodies suggested. They were light, much lighter than they had been before they had been Awakened, but they were strong and quick on their feet. The man who had a grip on my arm bit down on my skin, and I screamed. My hand scrambled for a grasp on the arm holding me in place, and I twisted, causing him to howl and pull back. I punched him in the stomach before taking a step back and quickly shooting him in the head.

The man I had stabbed had finally struggled to his feet and had a hold of me from behind. I struggled to throw him off, but he had a tight grip on me. His fingernails dragged across my exposed stomach, drawing blood in deep scratches. I tried to throw him over my shoulders, but he wouldn't budge. I continued to pull at his arms, and when he wasn't expecting it, I sent my elbow into his groin. He pulled back with a groan, and I spun around, kneeing him in the stomach. As he sunk to the ground, I pulled out my knife and stabbed him in the neck, blood gushing out and spraying all over my hands.

I was up to three kills, and I knew I had only made a tiny dent in the group that was attacking us. There was complete mayhem everywhere. Dad was standing up on the car, shooting as many Awakened that he could while Ash fought off a pair on his own. I didn't know what to do; I didn't know who to help. My world was spinning, and I couldn't stay balanced. I felt dizzy; maybe I was losing too much blood. I couldn't concentrate, and I knew I was vulnerable.

As if on cue, I was thrown backward, landing with a hard thump on the solid ground. I started to get up and found myself pinned to the ground. An Awakened held me down, his knees pressed into my thighs, and his arms holding my own down. I looked around in panic and saw my dad and Ash, lost in a crowd of fighting Awakened.

My captor grinned at me, sensing my predicament and enjoying the sight of me pinned to the ground. He reached for the knife in my hand, pressing his nails tight into my wrist until I was forced to let go. He picked it up, fingering the edge of it. He was young, maybe early 30s when he had died. There were traces of handsome features hidden underneath the chapped, blue skin.

"You know," he said, his raspy voice breathing onto my face, "my mom always told me not to play with my food, but you're just too pretty to eat so quickly." He pressed the tip of the knife to my neck, and a rush of fear, unadulterated, uncontrollable fear filled me. I started to call out for my dad, for Ash. He pressed the knife tighter against my throat, drawing a quick line across it. It was just a scratch, but I felt the sting of it, and I hissed in pain.

"Maybe if I make you less pretty, I won't feel so bad when I devour you," he said, studying my face curiously. He dragged the knife across the flesh of my bicep, cutting deep enough to send more blood running down my arm. Tears were rushing down my cheeks, and I heard a loud, desperate sob escape my lips.

He acted like he didn't notice, like he couldn't even see it. "When I was a man, I would have wanted you. I would be doing different things to you right now, and I could. I always took what I wanted. But I don't want you like that."

He sounded curious. "I don't have those kind of desires anymore. I just want to eat. I'm so hungry, and you're full of so much flesh."

I whimpered loudly as I tried to use my legs to push him off, but his knees pressed too tightly against my thighs, keeping me in place. The knife bit into the skin of my cheek, drawing blood there. I was becoming numb, and I could feel the sticky blood all over my body and wondered when I would die; when he would just kill me?

"I can't look at your pretty face," he said, his voice full of insincere sorrow. "How can I eat something that looks like you?" He started to slice the knife across my face, starting at my temple and dragging it deep across my forehead, over the tip of my eyebrow, across the bridge of my nose, down my cheek to the corner of my mouth.

I strained against him, trying to pull away from him. The pain ripped through me, worse than I could have ever imagined. Blood ran across my face, into my eyes and in my mouth. I couldn't see, and I couldn't breathe, and I couldn't stop screaming. The pain was never ending, and I wanted it to stop; I wanted to just die. I didn't want to feel anymore. He bared his sharp teeth, and they came down toward me, and I welcomed it, anything to stop the pain, to end it all.

I felt free for a moment, and I realized he was no longer pressed on me. Ash was yelling, stabbing the Awakened over and over again before pulling his gun out and shooting him in the face, sending a spray of blood across the dirt ground.

Ash sprinted over to me. "Oh god, Zoey, are you okay? Oh my god."

I was sobbing, sobbing so hard that I was having a hard time breathing. I couldn't see anything. The world was a haze, a haze of pain and blood. I didn't know which way was up or down. "No, no, no. Ash, it hurts. It hurts so much."

"I know, baby," he said, his voice breaking. Through the fog of my vision, I saw him pull his shirt off, and hand it over to me. "Keep that on your face, okay? We're almost safe. I'm going to keep you safe."

I pressed the white shirt, already covered in dirt and blood, tight against my face, covering my vision of Ash standing guard in front of me, shooting anyone who came near him. The white shirt soon became soaked with blood. I felt faint. I was losing too much blood, and I wanted to sleep. Sleep sounded so good; sleep sounded perfect.

A scream came from Ash's mouth, a sound of pain and torment that I had never heard from a person in my life, let alone from Ash.

"Ash? Ash!" I said, panicked, dropping the shirt.

He reached for me and picked me up, easily, scooping me up in his arms. "We have to go. We need to go now." He started to run, his breathing heavy as he carried me away.

"Ash, wait, where's my dad?"

He didn't answer, just continued to run.

"Ash!" I screamed. "Where is my dad?" I shifted in his arms, causing his balance to tip, and we both went spiraling to the ground. I lifted myself onto my arms, my stomach pressed to the hard ground and looked back over to the scene behind us.

My dad's body lay across the overturned car, and he was

limp as the remaining two Awakened bent over his body. Their teeth were buried deep into his flesh, pulling him apart. I was in shock. I couldn't react. It was like watching a movie. It didn't seem real because it couldn't be real. There was no way. I had just seen him fighting. Blood was dripping onto the dirt in front of me, gushing from my wound, and for a moment, the pain in my face was gone. I was paralyzed. I could do nothing but watch them tear apart the body that belonged to the most important person in my life.

"Zoey," Ash whispered, his wet, tear-stained lips near my ear, his body pressed on top of me. "We need to move. We need to go."

I didn't move. I didn't agree or disagree. I felt broken, fixed to the spot, incapable of movement, incapable of feeling anything. I watched, horrified, listening to the moans of pleasure coming from the Awakened. Their harsh, loud wails struck through me, and I pushed myself up and took the gun from Ash's hands before he could protest. I walked slowly toward them, limping with each step. They were so involved in their meal that they didn't notice me, not until I was right next to them.

Before they could say a word or make any sort of movement, I shot both of them, perfect shots in the middle of their foreheads. They fell to the ground dead, but the damage was done. My eyes landed on the wreck of blood and flesh that was once my dad and felt my knees grow weak. I had lost too much blood, and I slipped into darkness, collapsing to the ground. The last thing I remembered was the whisper of my name on Ash's lips.

CHAPTER
SEVENTEEN

I WOKE UP DISORIENTED WITH pain shooting through my forehead.

"Z, don't move," Ash said, his arms coming out to hold me down.

"Why?" I whimpered. "What's going on?"

"What do you remember?" he asked shakily. His eyes were red rimmed. He had been crying, and the tearstains on his cheeks were fresh.

I thought about it for a moment, but my head was pounding and thinking hurt; it hurt so badly. "There was a car crash. We fought Awakened," I said, slowly, trying to ignore the stabbing pain in my face. "My face...something happened to my face."

He nodded, his lips pressed tightly together. "I'm fixing it now, okay, baby. I'm taking care of it."

I finally noticed the needle and thread in his trembling hands, and I knew what he was doing. I felt the fear of further pain pass through me, but I tasted blood on my lips. "Ash. Ash, where is my dad?"

Pain flashed across Ash's handsome features, and he looked like he was going to cry again. "Zoey, he…he didn't …he couldn't…"

"What?" I asked, my voice coming out in a rush. "Where is he?"

"You don't remember?" he begged. I searched for the memory. Everything was hazy. All I could remember was fighting and the feeling of pain, pain that was still spreading through my body.

I searched through the memories of the fight and it hit me like a ton of bricks: my dad fighting over several Awakened as they tore into his skin. The memory of his limp body being torn to pieces burned in my mind, and I felt the loss wrench through me. My breathing came in short bursts, and the sky above me was spinning in endless circles. I wondered what a panic attack felt like.

"Where is he? Where's his body?" I managed to say, my voice barely more than a hoarse whisper.

"I pulled his body away," Ash answered. "I figured we could, I don't know, bury him or something. I don't know. Zoey, I'm sorry. I'm so sorry." Tears thickened his voice and he covered his eyes for a moment.

I shook my head, trying to forget, trying to wipe the memory from my mind. I tried to shift my vision to see him, to see his body, but pain ripped through my face as the cut pulled and tugged. "How bad am I?"

He breathed heavily, wiping the tears away from his eyes. "You're okay. You have cuts everywhere, but they're going to heal. They'll probably scar, but they're okay. But the cut on your face is bad. I need to sew it up."

"Can you…can you do that?" I asked, shivering. It was freezing, and I could feel a wetness seeping through my clothes.

"I don't know," he admitted. "But I'm going to try, okay? You're bleeding like crazy, and it needs to be sewn up."

I nodded once and squeezed my eyes shut. "Just do it. Please just do it and get it over with."

"Okay," he said, sounding uncertain. Then, he cleared his throat and said it again in a stronger voice. "Okay."

He poured some water on my face, careful not to get it in my eyes. That was the least of my problems. The water stung on my wound, and I could taste the blood and water pouring down my face. He hesitated for a moment before slowly starting to sew me up. Each prick of the needle was painful, and I could feel it slip through the tough bloody skin. I looked up at Ash and saw his unease. His hand slipped and the needle plunged into my eyebrow and I winced in pain.

"Ash," I whimpered.

He paused, the needle in his hands. "Does it hurt too much? God, Z, I'm sorry."

"Just please keep talking, okay? Tell me a story or something," I said. "Please."

"Okay," he said, going back to work on my cut. "Do you remember when we dissected that frog together in eighth grade?"

I squeezed my eyes shut, whether to block out the memory or the pain in my face I wasn't sure. "No," I lied.

"Well, I do. I remember thinking it was the most disgusting thing I had ever seen in my life, all those guts. I'm not going to lie; I nearly passed out, which would have been embarrassing. It would not be okay if I just passed out in class."

He paused for a moment reminiscing before continuing. The needle sunk into the fleshy skin of my cheek and I sucked in a breath, feeling the tugging of my skin. I focused on his blue eyes, falling into them. There was nothing else but his eyes and the rhythm of his voice. "But I remember looking at you, and you were so calm. You did everything so coolly and perfectly. It's like you knew. You took the scalpel from my hand and handed me the pencil. You told me you needed a new pair of gloves, which gave me an excuse to get away."

I remembered. I remembered being surprised at how awkward Ash had been with the dissection. His face had been so green, and I was scared that he was going to vomit all over the lab table. I had never seen that kind of vulnerability in Ash before, and definitely not at school where he was the badass on campus. It made me want to help him, to make him feel better.

"I don't know. It was just a great moment, you know? It was just one of those moments where I was reminded of how great a person you are. You could have let me throw up or pass out and be completely humiliated, but you didn't. It's something I'll always remember." He sat back, his hands covered in blood. "I think you're done."

I raised my hand to my face and felt the jagged stitches. Sitting up, I took in inventory of the rest of my body. There were cuts, some of them shallow and some of them deeper, all over my arms and on my legs showing through my ripped jeans. I lifted my shirt a little and saw four deep scratches in my stomach. They had been bleeding but not anymore. There was dry, crusty blood on my belly button.

Ash stood up and held out his hand to me, pulling me up. The world spun for a moment. I leaned over, breathing deeply to right myself. He reached for me, but I held out a hand to stop him. "I'm fine. Where is he?"

"I don't think you should…" Ash started to say, but it was too late. I spotted him, dragged off of the car and laying to the side of the wreckage, away from the other bodies. Ash had tossed a coat over him, hiding his face and torso.

I fell to my knees beside him, my hands reaching for the jacket.

"I don't think that's a good idea," Ash said, coming to kneel next to me. "You don't want to see him like that. You don't want your memory of him to be of this."

My hand stopped, my fingers falling on the soft fabric of the jacket. "I just…I can't believe that he could be gone." A sob was stuck in the back of my throat, and I felt the tears stinging the slash on my face. "I feel like if I see it, it makes it real."

"I know," he said, his voice soft. "But not like this. This…Zoey, it's not pretty. You don't want to see it." I looked up at him and saw that there were tears in his eyes. He had seen, and he could barely look at the covered body now. This was not his father, but he had cared for my dad.

"Okay," I said, nodding. "You're right." I stood up and stared down at the body that was once my father, the only good man I had ever really known and the only person I had always known I could count on. Now the only person I had left in the world, to keep me safe and get me to my mother's was Ash Matthews, and I hadn't quite figured out how I felt about that yet. "I want to bury the body. I want to bury my father."

Ash hesitated, looking around. There were bodies of Awakened all around us and they were starting to smell. "We need to do something about these bodies too. And I don't want to linger too long. But Zoey, we can't bury your father. The ground is frozen, we have nothing to dig with and I don't want to be here longer than we need to."

I looked back down at the body and back up at Ash. "You're right…"

"We could burn him?" Ash offered up tentatively, studying my face for my reaction.

I nodded, looking around me in a daze. "Yeah. Yeah, that's a good idea. Okay."

We made a pile of the bodies of the Awakened and set them ablaze first. I covered my face with my hand, trying hard to ignore the horrible stench from the bodies. I turned to my dad. Ash looked at me as if asking for permission, and

I nodded. I watched as my dad's body went up in flames, consumed by the fire.

"Do you want to say anything?" Ash whispered.

"I…I don't know what to say," I said, wrapping my arms tightly around myself. I was shivering like mad despite the incredible heat that was surrounding us. "I love you, Dad. You died protecting me, and I'll never…" I choked on the words. "I'll never forget that." I felt the tears again, and I held them back. I refused to let them fall. "Let's go. I just want to go." I turned away and walked back over to the mess that was the broken car.

We spent a good twenty minutes getting what we could out of the car. We grabbed packs and stuffed them with as many necessities as we could: clothes, water, the first aid kit, food and the map from the glove compartment. We started walking alongside the highway, walking for at least an hour before we stopped. I could still see the smoke in the distance, the lump in my throat growing larger and larger.

"What's the plan now?" Ash asked, after taking a gulp of water.

"We keep up with the plan that my dad had," I said, pouring some water onto the edge of my t-shirt and using it to wipe the remaining blood off my face. "We head to Nebraska."

He looked exhausted. "And how far away is that?"

I sighed. "We're probably about six hours of driving from Constance, which means, I don't know. Four or five days of walking?"

Ash's eyes grew wide. "Right. Okay. Five days."

My fingers were folded tightly into fists, the nails biting into the skin of my palms, and I could feel the stretching of the cuts on my legs. I was exhausted, so tired. Every inch of my body was in some kind of pain, and I was covered in dirty and blood. I needed to be clean again. I wanted to wash everything about this day off of me. And I was still on my stupid period.

"We have to do it, Ash," I said firmly, standing up and shouldering my pack again. "Now, let's go."

CHAPTER

EIGHTEEN

WE HAD BEEN TRAVELING FOR about six hours when we decided to stop. There was a thick forest, and we stumbled upon a small creek. It was frozen over in a thin sheet of ice that was easily broken through with the butt of my gun. It was too small to fully submerge ourselves in, but that would have been a bad idea anyway. It was freezing, and I had no desire to remove any clothing. The stream was adequate enough though, and I used some of the water to clean myself up, scrubbing as much of the crusty blood off my skin as possible. My teeth were chattering and the tips of my fingers were blue.

I was scared to build a fire, though we really needed one. We had already encountered a couple groups of Awakened while on the road, and I didn't want to call any more attention to ourselves than necessary. Lighting a fire would be risky. I bundled myself up tight in a coat and took the first watch.

We spent a couple hours in silence before I broke down and built a small fire. It was freezing, and I knew it would not be long before it started snowing in these parts. I pulled out my useless phone out of my pocket, where I had kept it out of habit. The screen was blank, dead, and I remembered when I could check the weather, the time, everything with the slight touch of the screen. Now, I didn't know if it would get hotter or colder, whether it was going to rain or snow. I didn't even know if we were going in the right direction.

I had been spoiled back home, and now, on the road, I was helpless. Now I felt completely responsible for the boy that I had a feeling I was falling for, the boy my dad had saved. I didn't know how to save Ash any more than I knew how to save myself. He was curled up on the ground, but awoke when I started the fire. He spotted it, eyes wide and grateful.

"Is that a good idea?" he whispered to me, reaching his hands out toward the fire. "We don't want any wandering Awakened to notice."

"At least we can fight them," I said back, wrapping my coat tighter around me. "I'd rather fight for my life than die of hypothermia."

He nodded. "Do you want to switch?"

I shook my head. "Go back to sleep. I'll wake you up when I'm tired. I could use some time to myself."

He nodded again, pulling the collar of his coat above

his ears and curled up closer to the fire. It wasn't long before his soft snores filled the air again. I sighed, settling up against a tree trunk, my gun in my hand.

I felt like laughing, and I didn't know why. Maybe it was the lack of sleep or the fact that I had so much grief and panic and fear piled up in me that I didn't know when it was going to burst out. I couldn't handle all these emotions piled up inside me, and for the moment, I pushed them down.

I felt stupid. I felt foolish. I read more than any person that I'd ever met. I worshipped strong female characters who knew how to fight, how to kill and save the day. I fell in love with the strong male leads. I escaped into these worlds, and I'd always wanted to live them. Worlds where things got worse before they got better but where the day was always saved—where the good guy always won.

The real world wasn't like that. I was more terrified than I had ever been in my entire life. I had a gun in my hand, but I didn't feel like a hero. I didn't feel like Arwen or Katniss or Hermione. I didn't feel brave, like a survivor. I felt like a little girl, who was scared and alone. The situation was hopeless. Unlike the books, I didn't think there was a way to beat the bad guys. I didn't even know who the bad guys were.

Where had the Awakened come from? Were the bodies stolen, or had they left on their own accord? Was Liam insane for thinking that someone had released them? Nothing made sense, and we knew so little. I had only one plan: to get us to Nebraska. I had nothing past that. I couldn't stop questioning absolutely everything. What if my mother wasn't even there? What if she and Caspar were dead?

I woke Ash up after a couple hours and slept next to the dwindling fire. I had trouble sleeping. I was exhausted, like there was nothing left in me to keep going, but the anxiety was keeping me awake. I shifted, tossing and turning on the rough ground.

Ash scooted closer to me, holding out his hand. I stared at it for a long pause, wondering what he was doing. He rolled his eyes, and ran his fingers through my hair. I closed my eyes, comforted by the feel of it. It felt like home. His hand reached for mine and I let him take it. I fell asleep, the heat of his palm against mine, feeling the gentle beat of his heart in the soft skin there, lulling me to sleep.

When I woke up, it was daylight and Ash was eating a small breakfast of jerky. He held the bag out for me, and I took it gratefully, running a hand through my damp hair. My stomach felt sorrowfully empty after the quick meal, but there was nothing else. What little food we had needed to last the entire journey to Constance. We didn't say anything to each other, besides to pass the water bottle back and forth. I was so tired. Each step felt like it could be the last, and I didn't think I could take another, until I did. I kept pushing myself. I refused to ask for a break, and we kept plodding along, keeping the highway alongside us.

We didn't see anybody else on the road; it was almost as if this major highway had been abandoned. I had driven this highway before, going back and forth between New

York and Constance. I knew that there were always cars on here, especially during the day. And there *were cars*, but they were abandoned, empty, stuck in a traffic jam that would never move.

It was a devastating example of what the world had become. I wanted to talk to Ash, to remind myself that I wasn't completely alone that I had someone with me, but it made me feel like we were the last two people on earth.

I felt like I was going to lose myself. I was already forgetting who I was.

Two days passed with no incident. We slept, watching watch over each other through the night, and walked as far as we could during the day. We didn't talk to each other at all, except to ask questions that required short yes or no answers.

It was the third day when we ran into the pack of Awakened.

We were stumbling along the woods looking for a clearing to set up camp for the night when we bumped into them. They moved so slightly, and they had been sleeping. I didn't even know they could sleep. Ash held his arm out to me, and I ran into him with a slight "oof" escaping my lips. He raised his index finger to his lips, his eyes wide. I counted the Awakened curled up together, using each other for warmth.

I wondered for a moment whether they needed it, if they even felt the elements. I shivered as we started backing up slowly. My eyes stayed on them the entire time, afraid they could hear me breathing, that they could hear my heart pounding like crazy in my head.

That was the perfect moment that my body decided to betray me. I tried to hold it back, but I couldn't help it. I sneezed. Loudly. Great, I was going to die because I sneezed. Ash reached out for me, and we both looked hurriedly over at the Awakened. They seemed to still be asleep, and I breathed a sigh of relief.

We turned around and started making our way in the opposite direction. I was afraid to breathe too loudly, afraid that the crinkle of the leaves under my boots would alert them to our presence. I could tell Ash felt the same because our pace was hurried but careful.

We had made it at least a mile away when Ash let out a breath and I paused, leaning against a tree, waiting for my heart to calm down. I was hot and sweaty, whether from the walk or the panic I was feeling I didn't know, and I peeled off my coat. I examined the cuts on my arm, relieved that they were beginning to heal. My nose wrinkled in disgust at the scars that seemed to be forming in their place. I was definitely going to look like a fighter from now on. My fingers ran along the jagged strings that ran through my face. I winced at how tender it still was.

"We should move on, Z," Ash said, taking a gulp from his bottle and holding it out to me. I shook my head and turned to walk away. I bumped into something, something solid and cold. I looked up and screamed.

The Awakened had caught up to us, silently. They had probably been following us ever since we had left them in the clearing, letting us get further and further away from the highway and deeper into the woods. Ash and I both grabbed for our guns in our holsters but there was no time. They looked starving, and they were on us in an instant.

"Run!" I screamed.

Ash didn't hesitate. We both turned and ran, sprinting through the woods, running for our lives.

CHAPTER
NINETEEN

I COULDN'T BREATHE. I FELT a stitch in my side as we went sprinting through the forest. Branches were scratching at my face and arms. There was the relieving sound of solid footsteps that told me that Ash was still running alongside me. In the not so far distance, I could also hear the light footsteps of the Awakened behind us. I jumped over a fallen log, a stray branch ripping into my jeans. I winced in pain but continued running. I would worry about it later. I wouldn't worry about it until I could stop.

Ash made a sharp right in front of me, and I followed him, each step sending another wave of pain through my legs. I needed to stop. I didn't know how much longer I could last. I listened to the voices behind us, wailing for us, begging for us to stop. I shuddered at the sound. I spotted a tree about twenty feet away, growing so closely to the others.

The branches of the trees overlapped and could potentially provide some cover.

"Ash!" I called, running to the tree and starting to find footholds to climb. He switched directions and came toward me, using his hands to lift me into the tree. I leaned down, extending my hand. He took it, and I pulled hard, helping him to reach the first branch. Together, we moved as quickly as we could, up higher in the tree, until the branches were so dense that we couldn't move any higher.

I pressed my body as close as I could to the trunk, breathing deeply and slowly, trying to calm my heart down, trying to make as little noise as possible. Ash was on the other side of me, his hands close to mine on the trunk. His eyes met mine and then looked down.

The Awakened had just caught up with us. They scattered in different directions, some of them heading further up the hill, and some of them heading east toward the river. A few of them stopped mere feet away from us. They started conversing between themselves but their voices were too low for either of us to hear. I couldn't believe their ability to communicate and work together. This was a large group, at least twenty. I knew it wouldn't be long before their heightened emotions got in the way and they started tearing themselves apart. I just hoped it would be long after they'd left us.

They stayed under the tree for a fair amount of time. It felt like hours, but I knew, logically, that it couldn't have been more than a half an hour, an hour at the most. I couldn't hear anything they were saying, just their distinctive hoarse and labored breathing. It filled me with terror, but I closed my eyes and focused on my heartbeat, the movement of my chest as it rose and fell with each breath. Finally, they took off, their quick steps soon fading into the distance.

We didn't drop right away. We waited, our muscles relaxing as the sounds faded and disappeared. After another half an hour, we descended, taking each step carefully. Ash jumped down first and held out his arms for me. I rolled my eyes at him and jumped down myself, landing awkwardly on my injured leg.

"Are you okay?" Ash said, grabbing my arm to hold me up.

"Yeah, I'm fine," I said, easing myself onto a log. "It's minor." I peeled the ripped fabric away from the gash and leaned forward to examine it. It wasn't that deep, but blood was getting everywhere. "Get the first aid kit."

Ash sat next to me, digging through his pack to pull out the first aid kit. He pulled out a bandage and the antibiotic ointment. He poured a little bit of water on it and used a cloth to wipe it clean. His hands were gentle as he spread the ointment over it, pausing when I winced. Once it was wrapped, I smiled slightly in thanks. "All better," he said.

"Thanks," I said, examining it a bit. It seemed these days that there would always be a spot on my body covered in crusty, bloody gauze. "When did you get so good at this?"

"I guess when you sew someone up, you just get good at the rest of it," he admitted. His eyes met mine, and I felt a flush go through me, at the ugly scar that was sure to be healing across my face. It was so tender, a constant reminder that it was there. Ash had done the best he could, considering.

I would always have a scar across my face, but it wasn't nearly as bad as it could have been. I ducked my head anyway. I had never been too overly concerned with my looks, but I had enough vanity and pride to be upset about it.

"Yeah," I laughed hollowly. "I guess you're right." I stood up and started shouldering my pack again.

"Zoey."

"We should get going," I said firmly, avoiding eye contact with him. "I know we aren't that far away from Constance."

"Zoey..."

"I also think we should get out of this stupid forest before it gets too dark. It'll be easier to see what's coming at us once we hit the flats."

"Zoey, come on."

"What?" I said, finally looking up at him.

"You still look beautiful," he said. "Whatever happens, you still look great."

"Oh. Okay." I knew this was the furthest from the truth. I was an absolute wreck. It had been days since we had been able to stop and bathe. My hair was greasy and stringy, pulled back into its usual ponytail. I was the dirtiest I had ever been, and I felt completely disgusting. Not to mention the fact that I had a huge gash across my face and several on my arms and legs. I was the furthest thing away from beautiful.

He stepped closer to me and I felt myself automatically step back, my spine hitting the solid roughness of a tree trunk. "I can tell you don't believe me."

"I believe you," I said quickly and softly as he stepped even closer. I felt warmth seep through me as he stepped even closer.

"I can show you, if you want me to," he said, his lips a brush of skin on my jawline.

I shivered. "I don't think that's necessary," I said, my voice shaking.

He chuckled lightly, his breath so light on my skin. He trailed light kisses right under my ear, down my neck, across my collarbone. I could hardly breathe. I felt my arms rise as if they had a mind of their own, and my hands latched onto his waist.

"Do you want me to stop?" he whispered, against my neck. He kissed it again, this time with more pressure, right on my pulse.

I felt another shiver go up my spine, and my fingers clenched tightly around him. He had asked me something, a question. I couldn't remember. I was in a fog being this close to him. He stepped even closer to me, his body aligned with mine.

His lips were dipping closer to my collarbone, and I felt the breath catch in my throat. He was so soft and warm, and close to me, and I still couldn't figure out why he was doing this.

"Do you want me to stop now?" his soft voice said again. "Do you feel beautiful?" His breath tickled across my check, where his lips were hovering right above my own. "Because you are so beautiful."

Beautiful and terrifying, I thought, just like my dream.

"Ash?" I said, my voice barely more than a whisper. My

heart was pounding so loudly. I had finally calmed it down from the chase, and now it was acting up again, but in a crazy, wonderful, stupid way.

"Yeah?"

"Stop. Please. Just stop, okay?" I squeezed my eyes shut, feeling tears spring at the corners of my eyes.

He pulled away, shock on his face. "Z…"

"Stop calling me Z," I snapped, pushing myself off the tree. I walked around him. "And don't touch me again."

He didn't say anything. Instead, he just followed me as I started to pick my way through the brush, wanting to head back toward the highway. The chase through the forest had thrown my direction off, and once I found the highway, I would be righted again. We had at least a day or two until we reached Constance, and I wanted to make it. I was determined to make it to my mom's house, alive, with Ash.

We were already in Nebraska. We were already so close.

"Zoey?" Ash asked, after a couple of hours walking.

"What?" I spat out. I caught the wounded look on his face before it disappeared and felt my annoyance disappear almost immediately. It wasn't his fault we were in this situation. It wasn't anyone's fault. It wasn't anyone's fault.

"Do you…do you think your mom will be there?"

It was the question I had been asking myself ever since we had left my dad behind in Iowa. We hadn't heard from her since we escaped Manhattan, and there was no way to get in touch with her. For all I knew, Constance was overrun by Awakened. For all I knew, they had already taken care of my mom and stepdad.

"I don't know," I admitted. "I don't know anything. All I know is that my dad wanted me to go to Constance, to my mom, and that's what I'm going to do."

I swallowed hard, holding back tears. "That's what he wanted. He wanted me safe. That's all he ever wanted, and I'm going to be safe, for him."

"I'll help you," Ash said, softly, "I promised." His eyes met mine. His face was a dirty mess. I could barely see his features through the dirt and grime but his eyes shone through, and I believed him. He had promised my dad just before he died. I knew that he intended to keep that promise.

"I know," I whispered. The trees were beginning to look sparse. I knew we were getting closer to the highway. I paused for a moment, orienting myself, and started to head west again. We were only walking for a few miles when we spotted a sign. I headed over to it, hurriedly. I traced the letters that read "Constance 100 miles." I nearly cried. "We're moving faster than I thought. We're so close."

Ash smiled, slightly. "You can tell. The forest has disappeared. It's so flat."

"Welcome to Nebraska," I said, drily.

"Z, a car is coming," Ash said, suddenly alert. He grabbed my hand and started pulling me toward the field, but it was too late. The headlights of the car hit us, lighting us up before we could make it far, and the car slowed.

"Hey! Hey! Hey, wait, stop!"

Ash continued to run, but I pulled back, turning around.

"What are you doing?" he asked, incredulously. "You're not seriously thinking of stopping."

"We haven't seen another human being in days. And he has a car, Ash," I pleaded. He held onto my arm firmly, and I couldn't pull myself away from him. I used my left arm to throw a punch at him, and he ducked, allowing me to yank my right arm free. I turned on my heel and started to walk toward the car. It was a truck, an older make definitely, and it was making a ton of noise. I looked around, nervously, expecting the Awakened to reappear. I walked cautiously up to the driver's side window as it rolled down.

An older man, probably in his sixties, was behind the wheel, looking down at me with concern. A woman around the same age was in the passenger seat, probably his wife.

"Honey, what are you doing out here?" she asked, a distinct Boston accent in her voice. I grabbed a hold of it, grateful to hear a voice that didn't sound raspy. Both of their eyes were normal, and they were dark skinned but not blue. I nearly cried with relief. She looked over my shoulder, presumably at Ash, if he hadn't run off without me. "Is it only the two of you out here?"

I nodded. "Just the two of us," I confirmed.

The man looked behind me and then his eyes met mine again. They found the scar on my face, tracing it from one corner to the other. I felt self-conscious and ducked my head. "Where are you headed?"

"Constance," I said. "Are you going that way?"

He nodded. "We're passing through, but I can give you a lift."

Ash had come up behind me. "I think we're okay. It's not far from here."

"It's 100 miles from here," I hissed back at him.

"It wouldn't be a problem at all," the man insisted.

Ash smiled at them, the wide charming smile that I was so accustomed to but hadn't seen in so long. I knew him well though, and I could see the strain in it. "Excuse us for a moment." He took my arm and led me a few feet away. "We don't even know them."

"Ash, I'm tired. No. I'm exhausted. We haven't had real food in days, and we're dirty and disgusting, and I'm covered in injuries. And we keep running into Awakened. I'm scared, and I just want to be safe. It's only an hour and a half drive. We only have to trust them for an hour and a half."

He hesitated. "I'm just…I don't know who we can trust, Z. I don't want us to make the wrong move."

"Look," I said slowly, "either we face down two regular humans, or we have to face another group of Awakened, that will try to kill us and eat us, or cut us to pieces. I'd rather take down those two. I'm tired of fighting."

He still looked unsure, but I knew my words had gotten through to him a little bit. "I'm tired too," he admitted.

"Well, then, let's do it. Please."

He was caving in. I opened my eyes wider, dipping my chin and biting my lip slightly. I hoped it helped that I already was really tired and dirty. "Okay. You win."

I grinned triumphantly and walked over to the car again. "We're going to take you up on your offer."

The man grinned, patting his hand on the truck, causing a loud sound to echo in the relative silence. "You can hop on in here with us."

Ash smiled, forced. "That's kind of you, sir. I think we will jump in the back of the truck, if that's okay."

"Are you sure?" he asked, his eyebrow raised. "It's mighty cold out here."

"We're sure," Ash insisted, pulling me toward the back of the truck. He let down the tailgate and helped me climb in before climbing in behind me. There were a few thick blankets in the back, smelling strongly of horse and manure but they were warm. I pulled one over me but couldn't stop the shivering that was coursing through my body.

"Come here," Ash said, holding his arms out to me. I hesitated for a moment before scooting closer to him, allowing him to wrap his arms around me, pulling the blanket over the both of us. The truck roared to life and bounced onto the road. Ash's arms tightened around me, and soon I fell asleep.

I fell straight into another nightmare. It was a variation of the first, the spooky slow motion night of the dance. I danced with Ash. I discovered I was blue. I ran through the slower dancers before crashing into the bathroom and finding the body on the floor. There was blood all over my hands and bits of flesh on my dress.

I had killed my father. The scene played over and over in my head, until I woke with a start, gasping for air.

"Another bad dream?" Ash whispered. I nodded, pressing my face into his chest. "I'm sorry. But I have some good news; I think we made it. I think we're in Constance."

I sat up, the blanket falling off my shoulders. We *were* in Constance, making our way down the small main street of the town. It was late, way past the prime hours of Constance, which meant that most of the stores were closed. There were no Awakened, which made me wonder if Constance really was safe. We passed the elementary school, and the truck came to a stop.

"Where am I taking you?" the man asked, leaning out the window to call to us.

"There are a few houses on the outskirts of town," I called back. "About a mile or two."

He continued driving, passing a few houses. I pointed out my mother's house as we came closer, my heart slamming harder and harder in my chest. It looked perfect, exactly the way it always looked. There were a couple lights on in the house, and my mom's jeep was parked in the long driveway. The man made the turn off and drove the bumpy road up to the house.

Ash hopped out of the back of the truck and held his hand out to me to help me jump down. There was wet, white crunchy show underneath my feet, and I shivered. He leaned through the window to thank the man, and after a few exchanged words, he pulled away, the truck groaning and coughing back down the road.

"Are you ready?" Ash asked, holding out his hand to me. "We made it."

"I'm terrified," I admitted to him, grabbing his hand and holding it like a lifeline. We walked up the frozen steps and crossed the porch to the front door. I raised my free hand, hesitating before knocking on the door, afraid of what I would find on the other side.

CHAPTER
TWENTY

MY MOTHER OPENED THE DOOR slowly, peeking out. Her eyes fell on Ash first and narrowed in suspicion. He stepped back, letting me step forward into the light. She threw the door open and stepped outside, a shiver going through her as the cold wind bit on her bare skin. She was wearing a long white sweater and jeans, with her long blonde hair pulled back into a ponytail. She looked tired but so young, so beautiful. It felt like it had been so long since I'd seen her.

"Zoey?"

"Hi, Mom," I said.

"Oh my god, Zoey," she said, grabbing my shoulders and pulling me into a hug. A flash of pain went through my face as it was pressed firmly against her chest. She pulled back and looked from me to Ash. "You made it. You were supposed to be here days ago. What happened? Where's

Frank?"

The words got caught in the back of my throat, and I shook my head, pressing my lips tight together.

"He…he didn't make it," Ash said, softly.

My mom's hand flew to her mouth, tears in her eyes, and I felt a surge of anger. She didn't get to feel that way. She wasn't allowed to be sad. "Oh my god," she repeated.

"Where's Caspar?" I said sharply, pushing past her to get into the house, immediately warmth seeping over me. I pulled my coat off, tossing it aside.

My mom and Ash followed me inside. Her eyes were still full of tears. "Caspar…he isn't here."

I faltered, turning back to look at her. "What do you mean, he isn't here?" I asked, looking around the entryway.

"He was…he was in Los Angeles when the Awakened hit the city. He was meeting with his publicist; he had just finished a book. He tried to get a flight out, but there were no flights leaving." She paused and took a deep breath. "I don't know if he got out when the bombs hit. The phones don't work."

I wanted to say something, anything. But I had nothing to say. What did you say about the man who you had held responsible for ruining your family? "Sorry," I managed to say.

"Who is this?" my mom said, looking over at Ash.

"This is Ash Matthews," I said. "He lives…lived next door."

"Ash Matthews," she repeated, looking up at him. He smiled at her, a hesitant, shy smile but containing all that

Matthews charm nonetheless. A small smile played on her own lips, and I resisted the urge to roll my eyes. "I remember you. You've grown up."

"Yes, ma'am" he answered, nodding his head.

She nodded and reached for the light switch. The lights came on and threw us all into clarity. She gasped as her eyes fell on my face. I turned away, a blush rushing through my cheeks.

"I'm tired," I said, avoiding her eyes. "I think I'll go upstairs and sleep."

"Zoey, what happened to your face?" she asked, horrified.

"Nothing," I said, heading for the stairs.

"We got attacked on the way here," Ash started to explain before I shot him a dark look. He was silenced immediately. He looked awkward for a moment, his hands sinking into the pockets of his jeans.

"Oh," my mom said, softly, sounding sad. "My poor baby. My poor little girl. You were so beautiful."

I felt something in me snap, and I spun around to face her, my face only inches away from hers. "Are you serious right now? That's what you have to say? Dad is dead, Mom. He is dead, and I had to burn his body on the side of the road by a cornfield that I'll never see again. I'll never remember where it was. And Caspar is probably dead too. People are dying. I just spent five days trying to get to you, starving and freezing and running from stupid Awakened, okay? And yeah, one of them cut my face. Whether I'm still beautiful or not isn't the thing to worry about right now. But I'm glad you have your priorities straight."

I flashed a look over at Ash and turned on my heel, stomping up the stairs, crossing the hallway to my room and slamming the door behind me. My shoulders shook, and I could feel the blood boiling under my skin. I clenched my fists tight before taking a deep breath and releasing them. I kicked off my boots and peeled all my clothes off, leaving only my tank top and underwear on. I climbed up into my bed and was about to turn off the light when Ash came in.

"Next time, it would probably be a good thing to knock, Ash," I said, dryly.

"Sorry," he said, not sounding very sorry. "Did I almost walk in on something exciting?"

"You wish," I said, pulling the covers up to my chin. "Did you need something?"

"Your mom sent me up here. She didn't look very happy."

"She tends to not look very happy when I'm around," I admitted. "What did you need?"

"I'm exhausted, and I just really want to sleep," he said, looking longingly toward the bed.

I shook my head. "No way. You're not sleeping in this bed. There's a guest bedroom down the hall."

He sighed. "I don't have to sleep in the bed. I can sleep on the floor. I just...I don't really want to be alone. Not yet."

I softened a little at the words. "No funny business?"

The corners of his lips twitched a bit. "No funny business," he promised.

I relented. "There's a trundle bed under this bed. You just slide it out. You can sleep there."

He smiled. "Thank you, Z."

"Zoey," I corrected sleepily, turning away as he slid the bed out from underneath mine. I heard him getting ready for bed, and the creak of the mattress as he lay down. I stayed awake, listening for the sound of his deep breathing and his soft snores before I fell into sleep myself.

When I woke in the morning, sunlight was streaming through the pale pink curtains that lined my large windows. I blinked several times, my eyes adjusting to the brightness. I rolled over, my hair tangled across my pillow, and looked down at the trundle bed. It was empty, blankets tossed to the side.

I climbed out of bed, my socks hitting the hardwood floors. I walked over to the dressers set right across from the bed and nearly cried with happiness at the sight of clothes in them. I wasn't completely positive that they would fit but they were my clothes and I wanted nothing more than to take off the dirty, bloody, torn clothing that I was wearing.

I grabbed a new outfit, a soft t-shirt and jeans, and a new pair of underwear and a perfect, clean bra. I held them close to me, smelling the lemon-scented detergent. I took them to the bathroom, and grabbed a towel from the cupboard. I stripped, tossing the dirty, offensive clothing in the trashcan. I would burn them later. I never wanted to see that clothing again.

The water was miraculously warm. It wasn't hot, like I would have hoped. Back home, I loved my showers hot and scalding, leaving my back bright red when I stepped out of the shower. But after washing in frozen cold streams, a lukewarm shower felt like heaven. I stayed under the water for what felt like hours, washing my hair, scrubbing it clean with coconut-scented shampoo. The bottom of the tub was a mix of blood and dirt, and I watched as it washed down the drain until the water at my feet was clear. I scrubbed and scrubbed until my skin felt raw.

I climbed out of the shower, wrapping the towel tight around me as I sifted through the drawers and cabinets in search of a comb. I found one quickly and went to work on the impossible tangles and knots that had worked their way into my hair over the past week. I winced as the comb tore out strands of my hair, falling in swirls toward the wet floor.

I found as many products underneath the sink as I could. I rubbed cocoa butter lotion all over my chapped skin, ignoring the puckered skin of my scars over my body. I brushed my teeth, feeling the glorious minty feeling in my mouth. I searched the drawers for make-up, powder, cover-up, something but there was nothing to be found. I sighed and put the clothes on, enjoying the softness of the clean fabric.

Voices reached my ears as I made my way downstairs and across the foyer to the kitchen. I paused when I heard the low rumble of Ash's voice and the clear mid-western accent of my mother's.

"She's been through a lot," Ash was saying. "I don't think reminding her of the cut on her face is going to be helpful for you. And I did the best I could to fix it. I'm not exactly a doctor."

"You did a fine job, Ash," my mom said, her voice soft.

I peeked around the corner, seeing the mug in front of her, clutched between her small hands. The smell of freshly brewed tea reached my nose. I inhaled, feeling a wave of nostalgia. No one drank as much tea as my mom did. "You've been protecting my daughter. You brought her home. I can ask for no more."

"I'm worried about her though," he admitted, his fingers tracing the grooves in the old wood table. "She hasn't cried. Since Frank, since New York…she hasn't cried. She's shed a few tears, but she hasn't cried."

"Shock?" my mom suggested, sighing. "Zoey has always been a tough one, refusing to back down. She's a fighter, always has been. She's never been an overly emotional or affectionate person. It got worse after her father and I got divorced."

I felt my face flush, and I knew I should move forward, but I was too fascinated by the conversation.

"But it's her dad. She needs to cry. She needs a good cry."

"Crying would be seen as a sign of weakness. And crying would mean accepting that he is gone, saying goodbye once and for all. I'm not sure she can handle that."

I couldn't take it anymore. I walked into the kitchen, making no indication that I had heard what they were talking about. "Good morning," I said.

"Afternoon," Ash corrected me, a lazy grin on his face. "You slept through the entire morning."

"I think I deserved it," I said, sliding into one of the rickety chairs next to him. "And the shower too."

"Did you leave any hot water for me?" he joked.

"It was admittedly kind of warm," I said. "But I wouldn't count on any of it for your shower."

He laughed, but I could see the worry in his eyes. He bit his lip, his eyes darting to my mom, but she didn't flinch. Whether or not she knew I had heard them didn't seem to bother her in the slightest.

"Are you hungry?" she asked, standing up and crossing to the stove. She lifted the teakettle and poured steaming hot water into a mug, dunking a tea bag into it. She placed in front of me. I wanted to pick up the cup and throw it, smash it on the wall, send the pieces flying across the floor but it smelled too good. It wasn't a cup of coffee-oh god, coffee-but it was the next best thing. "I could make you something."

"Yes, thank you," I said, stiffly.

She nodded, pulling her hair back into a messy ponytail before opening the refrigerator and rummaging through it. I leaned forward and was surprised to find that it was quite full.

"Where have you been getting the food?" I asked curiously, as she pulled out the makings for a sandwich.

"I was just telling Ash, things in Constance...they're quite different than what you've been experiencing. There were no bombs in Nebraska, not even in Omaha or Lincoln. People here...they just left. I don't know where, but they left. It's a ghost town, so the stores, everything, is just abandoned. So I went into town and stocked up."

"So...there are no Awakened here?" I asked confused,

as she slid a ham and cheese sandwich in front of me. I swallowed hard as I saw it was cut into four tiny triangles, the way I liked it when I was a kid.

She shook her head, taking her seat across from me again. "Nope. Well, at least none that have been spotted here. You guys say you were attacked by Awakened near the border, but none have made it to Constance. It's safe here. You're safe here."

"I'm grateful for you letting me stay, Ms. Flynn," Ash said. I flinched a little at the sound of his voice. It had felt like ages since I had heard his "charm" voice, the dip that he put into his voice that made it lower, sexier, and more apt to get people to fall madly in love with him.

My mom preened a little, and I felt a stab of jealously. Was I really getting jealous of my mom right now? My memory flashed to the feel of Ash's lips on my collarbone and I felt myself get hot. This was getting ridiculous. "Jennifer, please. And it's not a problem. I couldn't turn you out, not when you will be so safe here. And I could never do something like that to someone that Zoey cares about."

There was a long silence at the words. I turned away from them, a small smile creeping up on my lips. My eyes met Ash's, and he looked taken aback, and a little hurt at my reaction.

"Am I missing something?" my mom asked, looking confused. "Ash is your boyfriend, am I right?"

I coughed loudly, my face heating up. "Um, no. No, no, no. He's not my boyfriend. No way. Not in this world. No."

The corner of Ash's mouth turned upward a bit. "I'm not her boyfriend," he told my mom.

She looked back and forth between us. "Pity," she said, sighing, throwing me an exasperated look.

I rolled my eyes and stood up, already done with the conversation. "We need to get some things straight. We're safe…for now. But we spotted Awakened not even five hours away from here."

Ash and my mom exchanged looks but didn't say anything.

"I don't want to rain on your parade," I said, firmly. "I think we're safe here too. But I don't want to take that chance. We'll continue with practicing our shooting, Ash." I looked at my mom. "And you're going to learn."

She frowned. "I know how to shoot a gun, young lady."

I paused. "When was the last time you shot a gun?"

She paused to think about it. "Oh, well, probably back when your father and I were still together…"

"Exactly," I said, cutting her off before she could continue. "You're going to practice. We have an extra handgun that was…that was Dad's. You have to keep it on you at all times." I sighed, looking out the window at the flat lands that surrounded my mother's house. "You just never know what is going to happen."

I turned on my heel and walked away from them, back up the stairs to my room. I shut the door behind me, my eyes catching on the bookshelf that stood in the corner of the room. I rushed across the room toward it, my fingers tracing the spines. My heart was slamming in my chest, full of emotion, at the sight of my favorite titles. It seemed silly to miss books so much, but I had. There was nothing like curling up with a book, a blanket tucked around me, and falling into a world so different from my own.

Now I looked at the titles and wondered what could possibly make me feel better. So many of the titles on my shelves were fantasy and science fiction. I felt like I had fallen into my own sci-fi novel. I found it was not nearly as fun as it had been before. My hands fell on my worn copy of *Gone with the Wind*, given to me by my grandmother before she had died. Scarlett O'Hara had dealt with an impossible war and had overcome. I could too.

I pulled the book off the shelf and carried the tome over to my bed. I pulled the blanket up over my legs and settled the open book in my lap. I heard the sound of rain hitting the tin roof of the shed that was no more than a hundred yards away from the back porch. I tried remembering how long it had been since I had left New York and what today's date was. It was sometime after the New Year. It had to have been. It was winter, and I knew we would be spending a lot of time indoors. Together.

I yawned as I flipped through the title pages to the first chapter. I fell into the familiar words, the world of the South and Tara and the Civil war. It wasn't long before I had fallen asleep, my head resting against the hard wood of my headboard.

CHAPTER
TWENTY-ONE

I WAS WEARING A HOOP skirt in my dream, reminiscent of the beautiful dresses Vivian Leigh wore as Scarlett O'Hara in Gone with the Wind. *I was at St. Joseph's again, at the dance, but instead of apples hanging from the branches, there were peaches, and they dripped sweet nectar all over the floor. My satin slippers stuck to the floor as I made my way through the courtyard, lifting my overwhelming skirts. I could feel the pain of the tight corset around me and winced.*

"Miss Valentine, would you extend me the honor of being my partner for this dance?"

I turned, my skirt swishing around me, to find Ash standing in front of me, like always. He was dressed differently though, in the high waist trousers and coat of an old southern gentleman. He took my hands in his, led me out to the dance floor and pulled me into a proper waltz with a respectable distance between us, nothing like the dance we had shared at the Strictly Take-Out concert.

"Do you love me, Miss Valentine?" he asked, his voice echoing in the room. "Could you possibly love me?"

"Why are you calling me that?" I asked, my head tilted to the side in confusion. The classmates around me, dancing with us, started chanting my name, softly, as they danced in unison with us.

"I love you, Zoey Valentine," Ash said, ignoring my question and looking down at me with absolutely adoration. "There is no other girl in this world but you."

I frowned but let him lead me around the dance floor. I looked around me and noticed that the skin tones of my classmates were a distinct blue shade. I gasped, watching as they sunk their teeth into each other, devouring pieces of flesh before resuming their careful steps, as if there wasn't blood dripping down their chins, as if this was completely normal. I looked back up at Ash, who was grinning down at me, each one of his teeth filed into a perfect, gleaming point.

I pushed myself away from him, horrified. His quick hands came out to me, latching onto one of my arms, and he dragged me back to him. "Don't leave me, Miss Valentine," he begged, his voice a chilling echo.

"Leave me alone," I pleaded, trying to pull my arm free of his grip. "Please. Leave me alone."

"I can't," he said mournfully, his fingers tracing circles on my skin. He lowered his head to my wrist, sinking his sharp teeth into the skin there. Blood pooled around his mouth, and I screamed. A moan escaped his lips, a moan of pleasure, and I felt it up and down my spine. He captured my skin in his mouth again, tearing at the flesh there, and I woke up screaming.

"Shhh…shhhh. It's okay."

My eyes flew open, and I shrieked when I saw Ash's face so close to mine. I pushed him away, panicked, ready to fight him. He held my wrists and let me flail around, whispering softly to me. My heart rate slowed, and my surroundings came back to me. I was in my bed. I was at my mom's house. Ash was not an Awakened. It was fine. Tears streamed down my face, and I looked back up at Ash, ashamed.

"I'm sorry," I said, in between heavy breaths. "I'm sorry. Did I hit you?"

He smiled slightly. "You have a nice right hook. It's fine. Are you okay?"

I rubbed the sleepiness out of my eyes and peered up at him. "Yeah, I'm fine." I took a couple of deep breaths, trying to calm my racing heart. The room came more into focus, and there was a little bit of light from the moon streaming in through the blinds, casting Ash's face into view. It was full of concern as he waited patiently for me to calm down, his hands till grasping my wrists. I looked down at them. He followed my line of sight and dropped them. "I'm fine. I think I should just go back to bed."

"Zoey," he said, softly. I looked up at him. "I don't think you're okay. But that's not a bad thing. You don't have to be okay. No one would be."

I felt my lips tremble. I pressed them tight together, holding back the sobs that I had been holding in for days. I felt the tears well up in the corners of my eyes, dripping down my face, and I knew there was no force in the world to keep them held back any longer. I didn't want to keep them back. I was overwhelmed. I tried to be strong for so long, to take care of myself, to take care of Ash, to focus on our safety that I never gave myself a chance to mourn. I never mourned Bandit. I never mourned New York City. I never mourned Madison or the way my life was before. I never mourned my dad.

"It's okay to cry, Z; no one is going to judge you. I'm here."

I didn't know if it was his words whispered to me in the darkness or my dam finally collapsing, but the tears wouldn't stop. I covered my mouth, but the sobs came through loud and wild and full of pain.

"I killed Madison. I killed her, Ash. I killed my best friend." The words felt like they were being yanked out of me. "And my dad…and everyone. They're all gone. They're gone."

"I know, I know." His words were soft, gentle, understanding.

"Madison…Dad…Bandit…"

I cried until my eyes ran dry. It was an ugly cry. I knew my eyes were bloodshot, and my nose was red, and I knew I was covered in tears and snot. I was crying so hard I was choking on the sobs, finding it hard to breathe. I cried so hard that I didn't even realize that Ash had crawled into bed with me and had pulled me into his arms. I cried myself dry, until there was nothing left in me.

I stayed quiet for a few minutes, my forehead pressed to

his chest, breathing heavily before I said quietly, "I think you probably have to change your shirt now." I pulled back, placing my palm on his chest, and feeling the wetness of my tears and snot on it. I cringed. "I'm sorry. I cried all over you."

His arms were wrapped firmly around me, even as I pulled away. "It's fine. How do you feel now?"

I thought about it. "Better. Much better. Not good though."

"Good will come. Eventually," he said. "Don't rush for good. Just keep trying to get better. Just a little better each day."

A small smile crept up onto my face. "When did you get so smart?"

"I've always been like that," he said, laughter in his voice. "You've just never noticed before." His arms left my body, and I felt a rush of cold air around me. "Get some sleep." He started crawling over to his trundle bed.

I hesitated, and then said, "Ash?"

He looked back at me. "Yeah?"

"Can you…" I squirmed uncontrollably, hardly believing what I was about to ask him. "Can you stay here, with me?"

His eyebrow rose in confusion. "I'm not going anywhere." I didn't answer, just lifted the blanket and scooted over, not meeting his eyes. "Oh. Oh!"

The next few seconds were the like the longest seconds of my life. When I felt the bed sink down from his weight and the warmth of his body under the covers with me, I felt like letting out a sigh of relief. I didn't though of course; I just scooted over to lie down with my back to Ash. His hand crept across the blanket before meeting mine. I jerked back before letting his fingers intertwine with mine. The sound of deep breaths met my ears a moment later, and I fell asleep, my hand clutched in his.

THE NEXT TIME I WOKE, it was morning, and I felt warm. No, I felt hot, stifling. I noted that the blanket was not wrapped around me, but there was a solid presence against my back. I opened my eyes slowly and looked over my shoulder, finding Ash pressed tightly against me, his chest rising and falling with each deep breath. He didn't move, except to wrap his arm tighter around my waist. His hand was still intertwined with mine. I traced circles in his palm with the pad of my thumb. I was afraid to move or breathe. I didn't want to break the spell that was cast over the two of us that made it okay for us to sleep like that.

I wasn't sure how long I'd lain there before I heard a hitch in his breathing, and his grip loosened. I froze and then slowly looked over my shoulder again. Ash's eyes were open, drowsy with sleep. He yawned widely and then looked down at me, his hand rested gently on my hip. His eyes widened when he realized how close we were, and he pulled away.

"Shit. Sorry, Zoey," he said, pulling his hand away from my bare hip. Why the hell did I sleep in just a tank top and my undies? Why didn't I exercise more restraint when having St. Joseph's star quarterback in my bed? "I didn't mean to…"

"It's fine," I said, stiffly, pulling the blanket up over my legs. "Can you maybe just…get out of my bed? Please?"

He ran a hand through his messy hair, and I saw the slight shadow along his chin and jawline. I suddenly had the urge to run my hands across it, to feel the roughness of his skin. I leaned forward, our faces so close. He looked surprised, his sleepy eyes wide. My hand lifted to his face as if it had a mind of its own, and I found myself cupping his cheek in my palm. Ash was incredibly still, waiting to see what I would do.

My entire body was shaking, and I moved myself closer, pressing my lips tight against his before pulling back, shocked at my own movements. Ash watched me in shock, his breath coming out quickly before he darted forward and captured me back in a forceful kiss, his hand wrapped tightly around the back of my neck. I gasped and fell backward, my arms out in a shield. "No, don't…don't do that," I said, scrambling away from him.

Ash was still on the bed, his hair ruffled and his eyes wide from surprise, his lips red from the pressure. "Zoey…"

"No, just don't…" I said, grabbing shorts from the drawer and pulling them over my underwear. "Don't kiss me."

He sat back, rubbing his brow, looking perplexed. "Okay, I won't kiss you."

I was still trembling. "Good. Great." I spun on my heel and practically ran out of the room, doing the best I could to hide my flaming face as I went.

I spent the next few days avoiding both Ash and my mother in turn. When they entered a room I was already occupying, I found an excuse to leave it. I spent most of my time locked up in my room, reading. I knew I would eventually have to give in and focus on the survival of the three of us, but for now, I was ready to pout for hours alone in my bedroom.

On the fourth night that we were there, I woke again in the middle of the night in a cold shaking sweat, my sobs echoing in the silent room. I didn't say a word as Ash climbed into the bed next to me, pulling the covers over both of us. His arms wrapped tightly around me, his fingertips gently on my arms as he soothed me back to sleep. It became an unspoken agreement between the two of us. Most nights he skipped the trundle bed altogether and climbed under the covers, and the nightmares became few and far between.

We had been at the house in Constance for a couple weeks, and I was beginning to go mad. My mom's house was at least a mile or two outside the main center of town, and the only interactions I had were with Ash and my mom. Occasionally I kept company with my mom's old horse Kismet and my pony Pumpkin.

But the humans were the main source of the stir craziness.

My mom was acting as if the world was carrying on, as if the US government hadn't bombed several major cities into nonexistence, as if a third of the population wasn't transformed into something nearly unrecognizable. She spent most of her days cleaning the already immaculate house, taking care of the horses or reading.

She also made everything difficult when it came to survival. She held my dad's old gun as if it had offended her. Any attempts to teach her any sort of combat, even the most basic of self-defense, was contested until it was pointless to continue.

Ash wasn't much help with this. In the relative safety that Constance and my mother's house provided, he had gained an inflated sense of security. At night, he was sweet, though he never said a word as he climbed into bed to comfort me. During the day, he had returned to his normal self. His confidence was back, possibly borne of the consistent showers that had not been available to him. He joked often with my mom while they cleaned together, and he returned to teasing me.

I felt trapped and alone in my own house.

I opened the fridge door in search of something to drink. I had spent the morning running around the property, determined that I would not become lazy and complacent in the safety of the house. I sighed in exasperation when I spotted something in the vegetable crisper that definitely didn't belong there.

"Mom, seriously?" I yanked the gun out from the drawer and held it out to her. She was sitting at the dining room table, a romance novel open in front of her as she sipped her tea. She made a face and took it. "How on earth did that end up in the vegetable drawer? Honestly?"

She shrugged, seeming unconcerned. "I went into the fridge to get some milk for my tea and must have left it in there by accident."

"You need to keep it with you at all times, Mother," I said, slowly, trying as hard as I could to keep a fair level of patience in my voice. "That's what the holster is for."

Her eyes flashed up at me, her tone was firm. "It's excessive, Zoey. It's unnecessary. We are safe. I can defend myself if need be, but there is no need for me to carry the gun with me at all times."

I opened my mouth to protest but shook my head. "Just keep it with you." I slid it across the table to her, where it bumped lightly with her cup of tea, some of it splashing onto the table. I felt a pair of eyes on me and looked up to the doorway. Ash stood there, watching our exchange. My eyes went to his waist, and I was relieved to see his gun was holstered there. Despite everything else, at least he had managed to do that.

"I'm going upstairs," I said to no one in particular, stomping past Ash and making my way upstairs and into my bedroom. I closed the door quietly behind me. I crossed over to the bedside table and opened the tiny drawer that was there. I kept pictures in there of Bandit, Madison and my dad, pictures to tide me over when I spent random holidays with my mom and Caspar.

I climbed up onto my bed, folding my legs underneath me. I held the pictures in my lap and flipped through them slowly. Bandit and I when we first brought him home from the shelter. The red bow around his neck was larger than his head was as a small puppy. There was a picture of Madison and I at Coney Island, the pink stickiness of cotton candy on both of our cheeks. The picture had been taken just as Madison had burst out laughing, her small mouth open wide. There were several pictures of my dad and myself: at Katz Deli, at more than one Mets game, at my junior high school graduation, the two of us at Christmas.

I felt the tears prick at the corner of my eyes, but they didn't fall. I was beginning to think that I was all dried up, incapable of crying anymore. I felt the emptiness deep in my heart, in my stomach, my whole body, but I couldn't find it in myself to cry anymore.

I jumped when the door burst open. I was poised to yell at Ash for not knocking for the millionth time when I looked up and saw my mom. She closed the door behind her, crossed the room and took a seat at the chair set up in front of the small desk she had added in my room a couple years ago. She had a serious look on her face, and I wondered for a moment if I was going to be scolded for nagging. I set the pictures aside, laying them gently on the table beside the bed.

"We need to talk," she said.

Yeah, I was definitely in trouble.

"About what?" I asked, avoiding eye contact with her, my fingers tracing the raised scar on my hand where Madison had bit me.

"About the fact that you act like every minute spent here is the worst, as if you're in some sort of prison."

I looked over my pillow, my headboard, out the window,

anywhere but her eyes. "I have no idea what you're talking about," I answered, my voice full of impatience. "I am grateful to have made it to Constance. I'm grateful that I'm relatively safe."

She sighed, running her hands through her blonde hair, so unlike my own dark hair. Sometimes it amazed me how little I looked like my own mother. "I don't disagree with you, Zoey. I believe you are happy that you are safe. I don't think you're happy that you're safe here with me. Or Ash for that matter."

I squirmed uncomfortably. "I brought Ash with me, all the way from New York. I kept him safe, and he kept me safe. You will never understand what we went through to get here."

"I know I won't, but…"

"Was there a purpose to you being here in my room?" I interrupted.

She drew herself up straight, all pretenses gone. "Zoey Elizabeth, I am so tired of this. I am so tired of your shit. I've been putting up with this nonstop attitude of yours for years now, and I'm so tired of it. I am your mother, whether you like it or not. I've apologized a million times, done a million things to get you to forgive me. You refuse to forgive me. And now, in the situation we are in, you can't find it in yourself to forgive me now? Your dad is gone, and Caspar is probably gone too. We are all each other has left."

She took a deep breath and continued. "Now can we do this, please? I will work harder to learn to defend myself, if that's what you want. But only if you promise to try and give me a chance. Because I can't be the only one who is trying. It's not fair. Ash is changing, and I'm trying to change. It's your turn."

"You didn't even know Ash," I muttered, but I knew she was right. They both obviously were trying. They were still infuriating but they were trying. My mom gave me a look and I sighed, feeling frustrated. "It's just not that easy. I'm asking you to defend yourself, to do something you should be doing anyway. You're asking me to forgive you, like you forgot to pack my lunch for school or lied to me about Santa Claus. It's not that easy. It's not that simple."

"I'm not saying anything about easy. I'm talking about necessary. This is not the time for us to be like this. It's not the time for both of us to basically tiptoe around each other. What if I die? What if I die, what if you die, and this is how it is between us?"

I inhaled sharply, turning to glare at her. "Don't say that. Don't even say that."

Her face softened at my words. "I still think we're safe, but you're right. We should do better to protect ourselves. I should take you more seriously." She stood up and came to sit next to me on the bed, brushing a strand of hair out of my face. "I promise to try harder if you promise to try as well."

A rush of sadness and affection burst through me at her touch. I wanted to lean into her, smell her scent (vanilla, always vanilla), and feel that safety that I had felt when I was a kid when she used to sooth away all the bad dreams. I was still wary, oh so wary, but she had a point. We couldn't go on like this anymore, not with the world like it is. I knew, at the very least, my dad would want me to try. He sent me here for a reason, and it was to be with people who loved me.

"I can try," I said finally.

Her face burst into a smile, and I had to hide one of my own. I don't think she had ever expected me to agree. "Okay then."

I nodded. "Okay."

PART 2

CHAPTER
TWENTY-TWO

AS MUCH AS I WISHED for things to magically be fixed as soon as we'd had that talk, it wasn't that easy. You couldn't just make six years of pent up anger, upset feelings and resentment go away overnight.

But things did get better.

We fell into a routine. We woke up in the morning, ate breakfast, and then spent most of the morning and early afternoon working on shooting and self-defense combat. We would break for lunch. After lunch, we'd work on plans, plans what we would do if Constance didn't work out. We stocked up things in the barn, ready to grab at a moment's notice if needed.

We also released the horses. We couldn't afford to feed them, and we felt better knowing that they would have a chance on their own. If Awakened hit the farm...well, let's just say they wouldn't be on my list of things to protect.

After we worked on that, we would drift apart. We each made our own dinner whenever we felt hungry and disappeared to different parts of the house. I often took a plate up to my room, eating with a book in hand. Ash took to joining me in the room and perusing the books on my shelves.

"I can't believe you've read all of these," Ash said one evening, running his fingertips along the spines. "Some of these are thicker than my arm."

I shrugged, my eyes darting quickly over the words on the page.

"I think you especially like this one," he said, tugging at one of them and opening it in his lap. "It's falling apart."

I looked up from my book and smiled slightly at the huge tome in his lap. It really was falling apart. What was left of the cover was ripped off the back and the pages were brown and soft from so many readings. The cover had lost its bright color. It was beautiful. "It's my favorite."

"*Mists of Avalon,*" he read aloud. "What's it about?"

I folded the page down of the book I was reading and set it aside. I brought my knees up to my chest, my chin resting on them. "It's all about those King Arthur legends but told from a different point of view. It's strong on the female characters, which is what I like. A lot of the female characters of the original stories are so…one-dimensional, so lacking. This story changes that. Besides, I just love the Arthurian legends anyway."

He raised his eyebrow at me. "Interesting. I don't know

how you read so much."

I thought about it for a moment. "There's just something about reading a book that makes life so much better. No matter how bad the world is, you can always escape into a *different* world. It's a beautiful feeling."

Ash looked at me, nodding as he slid the book back onto the shelf and continued looking. "Ah, yes. *Goosebumps,* some good ol' R.L. Stine. This is much more like it."

I laughed and turned back to my book.

We had been in Constance for months. The days passed by and it started to seem surreal that the Awakened had even happened. Everything felt so...normal. Sure, we were practicing our gun skills every day, and Ash was getting better at trying to take me down. But it felt normal.

The weather was beginning to turn; the sun was out longer, the cold seeming to fade. Winter was finally breaking, and the beginnings of spring were finally beginning to show. I felt more confident in our abilities to survive in Constance, away from any Awakened, during mild temperatures of summer instead of the biting cold of winter.

We were spending an afternoon taking the winter things down from the house, opening the windows and doors to let some spring air in. I was taking the big blankets from all over the house, folding them and piling them up to be put in the barn.

I was eating lunch with Ash when my mother came in, a bandana tied around her long blonde hair.

"Can you run to the barn and grab the bins in there?" she asked. "All the blankets should fit in those. We're going to have to start planning for summer." Her hand was held to her forehead while she stopped to think. She began muttering other suggestions to herself and I resisted the urge to laugh.

"Yeah, sure," I said, taking my dishes to the sink. Ash started to stand up, but I waved him aside. My hand went automatically to the gun, hanging in the holster at my hip, and I felt a sense of relief and comfort at having it there. I ran my hands under the cold faucet real quick and then headed outside toward the barn.

I immediately halted mid-step when I heard it: the loud breathing, raspy, rough and absolutely terrifying. My hand flew to my gun, but I hesitated, unsure if I was really seeing what was in front of me.

It was an Awakened, on its own. He was probably mid-forties, maybe early fifties, dressed in a tattered business suit, not unlike the men I was used to seeing all the time back home. He was staring at me blankly, and I felt frozen in his stare, unsure if he was going to say something, or whether he was even aware of me standing in front of him.

I shook my head, pulling myself out of the hesitation, and yanked my gun out of my holster and shot him. The first shot hit him in the shoulder and dark blood came pouring out of the wound.

He looked down at it unfazed and back up at me, his eyes making contact with me. "That hurt, you know," he said, his voice causing me to shiver with disgust. I aimed again and this time I was much closer, the bullet sailing straight through his cheek. Before he could react, I'd shot one last time, and he went crashing to the ground. I lowered my arm, shaking, and crossed over to the body. I pulled out the knife that I tried to keep with me at all times and stabbed him in the face. Blood spurted up at me, covering my hands. I looked down at the body, feeling like I was about to lose my breakfast.

"Zoey?"

I looked up and back at the house. Both Ash and my mother were standing there, looking horrified.

"Is that…" my mom asked, lowering her hand from where it was covering her mouth.

"Yes," I answered, looking over my shoulder at the body on the ground. I was shaking uncontrollably, and my eyes met Ash's for a moment in solidarity. "I need to get rid of the body."

"I'll get it," my mom said, though she looked absolutely sick at the idea.

"It's fine," I said, sliding my gun back in the holster. My shaking fingers caused me to miss a few times, and I almost threw it on the ground in frustration.

"Zoey." I looked up at her, and saw that she had calmed herself and now looked determined. "I'll clean up the body. Go inside. Clean yourself up."

I climbed up the steps of the porch and made my way to the front door. I found my way blocked by Ash. "Move," I said, sharply.

"I was coming outside to help you," he said, "with the bins, I mean. I can't believe there's an Awakened here."

"Was here," I said, a flash of anger bursting through my

veins. He had seen the Awakened, had seen me hesitate, and he hadn't even moved. He hadn't even thought to help me. The rational part of my brain was telling me that I was overreacting, that I wasn't thinking logically. "Move," I repeated. When he stayed there, in front of me, I pushed past him and made my way into the house and into the kitchen, ready to get the hot and sticky blood off my hands.

I leaned against the kitchen counter, letting the water run, focusing on the sound of the water hitting the stainless steel sink, anything to get my mind off the Awakened that I just killed in the front yard. I could hear my mother moving around in the shed outside, trying to find some way to dispose of it. I couldn't think about it. Every time I fired a gun, every time I hit something, I couldn't think about it. I was killing people, humans that had lives and families, until they got the stupid virus and had become these hungry, blue, terrifying monsters.

"Are you okay, Z?" Ash had followed behind me, and I felt my teeth start to grind.

"I'm fine, Ash," I said tersely. "No thanks to you."

He walked next to me and shut off the water. "Hey, I knew you had it. You're like a little spitfire with that gun of yours."

I shot him a scathing look over my shoulder, ignoring the heat I felt where our shoulders touched. He stepped even closer, the distance between us so small that I could feel the heat radiating off of him. I remembered the moment, at the side of the road, when he'd pressed himself on top of me, keeping me quiet while an Awakened ripped shreds out of my dad's body before I woke up out of my stupor and shot him. My memory switched again, to when we were in the woods and the feeling of his lips on my neck and collarbone before he'd pulled away, or I had pushed him away. I felt a wave of hot lava sweep through me and felt ashamed.

"You know, shooting one of the Awakened? That was awesome. Like, freakin' badass, Z. Every time you shoot one or take one down, it's just the sexiest thing I've ever seen."

"Yeah, thanks," I said, avoiding looking at him in the eye or getting closer than necessary to him. Sharing a bed with him at night was rough enough as it was, even if I could admit to myself that I liked it. But now, when the nightmares seemed far away, in the light of day, I wanted him away from me.

Ash didn't seem to feel the same. He stepped in front of me, forcing me to step away from him, my back crashing into the counter. "What are you doing?"

"I don't know," he said, curiously. "Something I've wanted to do for weeks. Something I keep hoping you'll let me do." His hands came up to my waist, pulling me flush against him and I gasped quietly at the quick movement, my palms flat against his hard chest. "I feel like you want to, but I don't know. I can't seem to get a read on it."

I didn't answer and taking this as permission, he brought his mouth on mine. His tongue made a smooth movement of my bottom lip before sliding between them.

I wanted to push him away. I wanted to hate him, but it was the last thing I felt. It was *never* what I had ever felt about Ash Matthews. My hand reached up and grabbed a handful of his shirt, pulling him closer to me. I poured everything I had been feeling in the past few months into the kiss: the fear, the grief, the panic. I felt his hands move from my waist to grip my thighs as he lifted me onto the counter.

My fingers slipped into his belt loop. I pulled him closer to me, kissing him faster and more desperate than I had ever kissed anyone. I could feel him, every bit of him against me as we kissed. I wanted him more than anything; I couldn't get enough of him. My hands fumbled at the hem of his shirt, and I started to tug it over his head before pulling him back to me. My hands were flat against his warm chest, and I wanted to rip my own shirt off. I wanted us to be bare, skin-to-skin.

Ash's lips were on my jaw, my neck, dipping down to my collarbone and into the neckline of my shirt. I gasped as his hands lifted the shirt over my head, in one swift movement. He tossed it aside, before his fingers found their way up my waist, grazing my stomach, causing goose bumps to ripple across my body. His hands dipped underneath the fabric of my bra and cupped my breast; he pressed his lips tight against me again. I moaned, the sound loud in the echoing kitchen. My legs were wrapped around his waist, and he was moving against me, sending waves of pleasure through my body.

"Ash," I panted, surprised at how desperate sounding his name was on my lips.

"Jesus, Zoey," he breathed, his forehead pressed firmly against mine. "You are so goddamn beautiful." I flushed at his words and kissed him harder.

His hands were at the button of my jeans, unsnapping them with ease. His fingers were sliding below the waistband on my pants to brush them lightly against them. A brand new feeling was shooting through my body. I heard myself moan again, my hands gripping his arms tightly, my knuckles white. His lips were back on mine, his tongue sweeping against my own, and I felt incredible; everything felt so incredible.

His hands came up to my breasts again, and I knew in a moment that my bra would be off, that more of my clothes would end up on the floor, and I registered vaguely that my mom was right outside. She could walk in any moment. I dismissed it as another wave crashed through me. My fingers fumbled, shaking, at the button to his jeans, pulling the zipper down. We were grabbing and pulling at each other, as if we could pull each other closer than we already were. Every move was desperate and hurried. I wanted to fall into him.

Who had I been kidding for so long? Why had I been denying it for so long? I was in love with Ash Matthews. I had been since his stupid bowl haircut and impossibly blue eyes had walked into my life in the third grade.

I gasped, pulling back, grabbing the gun from where I had set it on the counter and pressing it lightly against his stomach. "Don't touch me again, Ash, or I swear I'll shoot you," I said, trying to ignore the heavy breathing we were both experiencing, and the fact that we were both slowly losing our clothes.

To my surprise, Ash laughed, as if having a barrel pressed to his hard stomach was something he experienced every day. His stupid sexy naked stomach. How had I let myself get so far in? "You seemed to be enjoying it, the way I see it. It's the end of the world, Z. You'll ask for it again."

I pressed the gun harder against him. "No, I won't."

He pulled away, creating a bit more distance between us, one of his hands pressed against my bareback. His other hand dipped lower again, right between my legs, right at the spot that had caused me to shudder with pleasure before. How was it possible that I wanted him to stop and continue at the same time? "Why do you keep denying this?" he whispered, his lips against my ear.

"Denying what?" I cried, pulling away from him and tugging his fingers away from me. I suddenly felt embarrassed, sitting on the counter, my face red, my breathing heavy, with my legs wrapped tightly around his waist. My pants were unbuttoned, my shirt laying forgotten on the ground and the straps of my bra were falling down my shoulders. But I didn't feel like some kind of sex goddess anymore, just a girl that had gotten carried away in the moment. "Denying that you're driving me insane, that you've been driving me insane and teasing me since the third grade?"

"Those were only ever jokes, Z. I was kidding with you," he said, sounding confused. He still had a firm grip on me, and I knew it wouldn't be long before my mom walked in on us in this precarious situation.

"It's *never* not felt that way," I said firmly. "You've made my life at school miserable since you made fun of me your first day at St. Joseph's. You've made me cry with your all your teasing. How can I sit here and just let this happen and just forget all of that? We can't tear each other's clothes off without any regard to the past. Or at least, I can't do that."

"I made you cry?" he asked.

I sighed. "Yeah, you made me cry. Not recently but yeah. Several times. You hurt my feelings. You made me feel so low."

He paused for a long moment. "I never meant it that way, ever. I panicked that first day. I was the new kid, and I wanted to fit in and make friends. I knew immediately that I had been stupid to you, and I wanted to fix it, but I was nine! I didn't know how to fix it, come on."

"I don't think being mean was the way to go about it," I said, my voice loud. "Pelting me with water balloons while I walked Bandit or filling my locker with glitter or stealing my clothes so I'd have to wear my PE clothes all day? You thought that would make up for it? Not exactly the right way to apologize, Ash."

"I was an idiot, Zoey! I *am* an idiot. I liked you!" he said, sounding frustrated, his fingers flexing tightly around my waist. "I liked you, and I'd messed up, and I didn't know how to fix it. I kept thinking, if I could make you laugh, you'd see that. I didn't know how else to show you. I have never liked anyone that much, so much that it never goes away."

"Wait, what?" I said, shaking my head, hardly daring to believe the words that were coming out of his mouth. "Did you just say…"

"I…like you, Z," he said softly, his blue eyes meeting mine. "I have ever since my first day at St. Joseph's. I remember you in your little plaid uniform dress, and your hair was so long. I swear it was past your butt. You had this huge book in your hands, so big that I thought you might tip over from the weight. But I cared too much about fitting in, and I chose that over helping you that day in the cafeteria. And I guess I never grew up and learned how to tell you. I just made a big joke out of it all because I couldn't handle how much I liked you, and how much I still like you."

I paused, a flurry of emotions rushing through me. I felt happy but wary, excited but anxious. "I don't know what to think," I admitted after a long pause.

"I know. I can understand that," he said, his hands moving from my waist to my back.

I covered my face with my hands. "I seriously, I don't …I don't know how to handle this. I mean, you like me? That doesn't just erase all those things you did to me. I don't know what to say. I don't know what you want from me."

He laughed, one quick laugh, full of nerves. This surprised me; I had never experienced that coming from Ash before, not when it came to me. He gently pried the gun out of my hands and put it on the counter next to me. "Can you please just kiss me again?" he said, his voice low and full of desire. "I can't stand being this close to you, and not kiss you."

I bit my lip, thinking about it for a moment. I lowered

my hands and raised my eyes to his and nodded. He broke out into a smile, and his hands came up to cup my face as he lowered his head toward mine. His eyes flicked upward and suddenly got very wide. "Zoey." His hands dropped.

I pulled back, alarmed at the terror that suddenly filled his voice. I stared at him, trying to meet his eyes, but he was focused on something behind me. I turned to look over my shoulder and felt a chill of terror seep through my body.

A group of Awakened was sprinting straight toward our house; at least they were a good distance away. And my mom was outside, oblivious. I stared at her and noticed that, yet again, no matter how many times I told her, she was without a weapon.

"Shit!" I said.

I hopped off the counter and grabbed my gun. We both went sprinting outside, right toward her. She was at least a hundred yards away, right by the barn, a black bag next to her.

"Mom! Mom!" I screamed at her, running faster than I had ever run before.

She looked at both of us in shock, taking in our disheveled appearance. I remembered for a moment that we were both shirtless, our pants unbuttoned, caught unawares by a pack of Awakened. And they were running straight at us.

"What are you two doing?" she asked, her voice loud and yelling at us. They were right behind her. I needed to make it there before them. I needed to get there.

"Mom, behind you!"

She turned around, as if in slow motion, just as they came up to her. I reached her and shot the closest one to her but not before they had latched their hands tight on her shoulder, their teeth on her neck. The bullet went sailing past the Awakened that grabber her and straight into the one just a beat behind her.

"Shit," I said, darting forward to kick the woman attached to my mom's neck. She fell to the ground but was up on her haunches in a beat. This time, I aimed the gun for her head and shot, and her body crumpled to the ground. I turned just as Ash shot the man who had attached himself to my mom's leg.

She was whimpering, fighting with another Awakened at her head. She wasn't strong; she hadn't trained; she was a freakin' preschool teacher. I yanked the man off of her, sending my elbow into his throat before shooting him. I stood, my eyes darting in all directions as the Awakened surrounded us. I looked behind me as Ash kept guard on the other side. My mom was on the ground between us, blood gushing from her neck and leg. She was whimpering in pain, and I wanted her to get up, but she wasn't going to.

"How many on your side?" Ash hissed out the side of his mouth.

I scanned the Awakened around me. They had slowed down and were just standing there, staring. I waited for them to say something, to do something, but they just waited. "Seven," I said back.

"There's five on this side," he said.

"Of course, why would it be even?" I grumbled.

"Give us the blonde," one of them spoke, his guttural voice sending shivers up my spine, so different from the ones Ash was creating earlier. "Give us the blonde, and we'll let you and your friend there go free."

"Do you think we're stupid?" Ash growled at him. "We're not giving you anyone."

"Let us all go," I said, trying to keep the tremor from my voice. "I'll let you all walk away, scot-free. But if you make a move, if you try to take either one of them, I will take you down."

They stayed silent for a moment before bursting into laughter. I had never heard them laugh before, and I decided right there and then that I never wanted to hear them laugh ever again. There couldn't be a worse sound in the world than that one. I felt chills go up and down my spine, and it wasn't because of the breeze on my bare skin.

"Suit yourself," he said, shrugging.

They came at us all at once, and it was in that immediate moment that I knew that we were overwhelmed, completely outnumbered. This was when I knew I was going to die. After so many months of fighting and surviving, this is where it was going to end: in the middle of nowhere.

I immediately went to duck around the first man sprinting toward me, but I was a beat too late, and he went careening into my stomach. I fell to the ground, slamming my head against the rough dirt. For a moment, all I could see was the glaring sun in my eyes. It was blocked quickly by a looming shadow, and I quickly rolled over, just missing the man's grabbing hands. I pushed myself up off the ground, feeling bits of dirt sticking to my sweaty palms. He was coming back for more, a grin on his face, blood staining his teeth. I shot him quickly, a perfect shot to the head.

I didn't stop to marvel at my success. I immediately dove onto the back of another Awakened, taking them down as quickly as I could.

"Zoey, Zoey, Zoey."

I turned at the whimpering sound of my name and saw my mom propped up against the door of the barn. She was covered in blood, and I couldn't even begin to tell where it was coming from.

She was going to be okay. She was going to be fine. I repeated it in my head like a mantra. She was going to be okay.

"Get in the barn, Mom. Get in there and lock the door," I said firmly, turning away from her.

I caught Ash at the corner of my eye, taking two Awakened down so quickly that I wanted to stop and clap or throw my arms around him and kiss him. I shook my head and started shooting at the remaining Awakened that were coming toward me. One by one, they went down, and all I could see in front of my face was red. I was on fire; I wasn't even a person anymore. I was a weapon, and I wanted to kill. I wanted to kill these stupid Awakened that had taken away my city, my father and attacked my mother.

I was still shooting an Awakened on the ground when I felt a strong hand on my arm. I turned, quickly, ready to fight.

"They're dead, Zoey" Ash said, his hand gripping my

arm tightly. "You got them. You can stop shooting. They're gone. You can stop."

My arm fell to my side, and my gun dropped to the ground. He grabbed me tightly, pulling me close to him, and I felt his heart beat on my cheek. For a moment, I felt safe.

"It's okay. It's okay," he said. "Let's go find your mother."

I pulled back, remembering. "Mom." I spun on my heel and saw the barn door standing slightly open with just enough room for a person to squeeze their way in. Blood was pooled at the entrance and streaked across the hay that was spread inside. I followed it quickly, my eyes darting all about. I spotted her, lying against a bale of hay, her eyes closed, her breathing heavy. "Oh, no. Mom." I ran the last few steps to her, and fell to my knees next to her.

She was completely torn up. There was blood everywhere, and I couldn't even see where it began or where it ended. I shifted her a bit, and she groaned. I pulled my hands back, afraid to touch her. I didn't want to hurt her any more than I already had. "Ash, we need to take her into the house."

"Yeah, you're right. I can get her." He leaned over and took her into his arms gently, like she was a doll. A whimper escaped her lips, and I saw a flash of pain cross Ash's face. We made our way out of the barn and across the lawn to the house. On the way, I gathered up the gun I had dropped, ignoring the bodies strewn all over the ground.

"Put her in the downstairs bathroom," I said, as we went into the house. He nodded, pushing the door open with his foot and walking in. he bent down, slowly, laying her as carefully as he could into the bathtub.

I pushed past him, grabbing the removable showerhead from its hook and turning the water on, waiting until it got a little warm. I started to wash her down, my hands shaking as the blood ran on the sides of the tub, toward the drain. There was so much of it. There were gashes and bites everywhere, consistently gushing blood. "She's covered, Ash," I trembled. "I…I don't know where to start."

"Zoey…" My mom's voice was weak, her eyes still closed.

"Don't," I interrupted her. "Don't talk. Save your strength." I looked over my shoulder at Ash. "Get me towels, a bunch of them." He was staring at me. "Now, Ash!"

He shook himself out of his daze and turned on his heel. I could hear the hard falls of his step as he ran upstairs to the linen closet, the familiar creak of the doors, and he was back in a moment. He dropped them next to me, and I started pressing them over the wounds. There were just so many, and the towels were crimson before long.

"Zoey, please."

I could feel tears in the corners of my eyes, and a large lump was in my throat, threatening my ability to breathe. "You're going to be okay, Mom. You're going to be okay. I'm going to fix it, okay?"

Her eyes fluttered open and met mine. Her eyes were red and, for a moment, I wondered if any other color existed. All I could see was red, the deep red of her blood that was now covering the bathroom. "I love you, Zoey."

I shook my head. "No. No, you are not talking like that. I refuse to let you talk like that." I ran the stream of water over her body, and the water started running pink, and I felt a brief sense of relief. The bleeding had slowed, and I cleaned the wounds as best as I could, feeling helpless. I could fight. I could pack a punch, and I had a stupid blue belt in taekwondo, but I couldn't fix this. I didn't know how to fix this. She just wouldn't stop bleeding. She needed a hospital, but I don't think those existed anymore.

"I love you," she repeated, her eyes falling closed again. I held my breath for a moment, my hands frozen, until I saw the subtle rise and fall of her chest. She was alive, for now. I stood up and walked out of the bathroom. Ash followed me, looking at me in concern.

"I don't know what to do," I admitted.

"I don't think she's going to be okay, Z," Ash said, softly.

I nodded. She wasn't going to be okay. I wanted her to be okay, but I had learned in the past few months that wanting something meant nothing; even need was a silly thing to contemplate. The only thing that worked was what you got. "We should get rid of the bodies."

"The bodies?" he asked.

I nodded toward the front door. "The bodies of the Awakened. There are quite a bit out there, and we should get rid of them."

"Burn them? Bury them?" he asked. He looked disheveled, defeated and torn. There was blood and dirt streaked across his entire body, his jeans slung low on his hips, and I had never seen him look more beautiful in all the years I had known him. I wanted to run to him, to pull him to me and never let him go, but I couldn't move. I couldn't even feel.

I sighed, wiping a hand across my forehead. I was covered in blood, and I was sure I had just gotten blood all over my face now too. "We should bury them."

He nodded, disappearing into the kitchen for a moment and reappearing with both of our shirts. It was hard to believe that less than an hour ago, Ash and I had been tearing each other's clothes off on my mother's kitchen counter.

I took my shirt back, pulling it over my head. I was shivering like crazy, but I didn't think it was because I was cold. "There are shovels in the barn. Let's go."

CHAPTER
TWENTY-THREE

SHE DIED TWO DAYS LATER. I changed the bandages. I washed her. I gave her antibiotics that I found in the medicine cabinet in the upstairs bathroom. I took care of her the best that I could to the best of my limited knowledge. I wrapped her in a ton of gauze and prayed and prayed and prayed, but she died.

My mother was dead.

I could barely look at the body that was lying in front of me. We had moved her upstairs, to her bedroom. She had been in and out of consciousness, mumbling nonsense or calling out for Caspar. She wasn't herself anymore. She was sick. Her skin had burned hot with fever. She died in her sleep, free of the pain that had ben plaguing her for days.

Ash and I were both orphans now.

"Zoey…"

I shook my head, refusing to look at him. It couldn't be happening. Not another person. Not now. Not ever. I felt the emotions boiling up in my stomach, up my throat, threatening to burst out. It was taking everything I had not to lose it. I had to keep myself sane; I had to keep myself calm. I had to survive, and I couldn't lose my grip.

"Zoey?"

Ash was standing behind me, looking down at my mother's body with a deep sadness on his face. "Are you okay?" he asked, reaching for me.

I ducked out of the way, heading downstairs and into the kitchen. "We need to go. This area isn't safe anymore. We need to pack up and head out of here, make a plan," I said.

"Zoey, no. There's time for that. We're safe for now. We need to bury your mom."

I swallowed hard. "No, I just…I want to leave. We need to go."

He crossed the room, coming to stand in front of me. I took a step back, overwhelmed by the heat radiating off of him. I kept shivering. "We are safe. I promise. You need to mourn your mom, Z. You need to give her what we couldn't give your dad."

"I don't want to bury my mom," I said through clenched teeth, my fingers lost in my hair. The bubbles were bursting in my throat, and I was about to spill over. "I don't want to mourn her. I don't want to care anymore. I just want to die."

Ash's face paled for a moment, but he didn't react to

me. "No," he said, firmly. "You aren't going to die. I'm not going to let you die. Your parents would want you to live. They would want you to keep fighting. You've been so brave and so strong, and you have to keep fighting. It's what they would want."

"They would want to be here with me, Ash. They would want to be alive," I said, my voice raising.

"Of course they would!" he said, his voice remaining calm. I wanted to tear at him. I wanted to break the smooth look on his face. How could he feel that way? How could he not be bursting and ripping apart at the seams? "But they can't. They can't be here, Zoey, and I'm here. And we are going to do this, okay?"

"I don't want to!" I screamed, reaching for the nearest thing to me. My hands found the salt and pepper shakers on the table. I threw them at the wall, sending salt and pepper scattering across the tile floor. I started grabbing things off the shelves and counters and throwing them, tossing them to the ground, feeling a sort of relief when they hit the ground or the wall. "I don't want to. I'm tired, and I don't care anymore. I don't want to do it anymore. Don't make me!"

Ash had backed up, out of the zone of fire, but he made no move to stop me. His eyes were wide as he watched me throw the coffee pot across the room, landing with a tinkling crash against the door.

I looked around me at the disaster I had created and felt the breaths coming in and out quickly. I searched for something else to throw, but what else was there? I sunk to the floor, bits of glass and other things biting through the worn fabric of my jeans. I cradled my head in my hands and rocked back and forth.

Rough but gentle hands reached for me, pulling me up. I didn't hesitate, my arms going around his neck. He pulled me tighter against him, his arm wrapped tightly around my waist. "I know, baby. I know." His words were watery, and I swallowed my tears back down again. A dry sob escaped my throat as I pressed my face into his neck. "Shhh, I know."

"I don't want to do it anymore. I can't…I can't do it anymore. Everyone is gone, and I can't do this anymore. Ash, I just don't think I can do this anymore." I felt the last bit of energy drip out of me, and I knew that, if he hadn't been holding me up, I would have fallen down.

"You can," he said, pressing me tighter to him. "I know you can."

"I'm just so tired. I'm so tired, Ash," I said, my arm losing their grip around his neck. My eyes were beginning to close. I was exhausted, worn out. "I can't hold on anymore." I didn't know if I meant I couldn't hold on to myself anymore or if I couldn't hold onto him. Maybe both.

"It's okay; I got you," he said. I vaguely registered him scooping me up in his arms before I lost all consciousness.

I blinked once, twice, three times before opening my eyes fully. Sunlight was streaming through the thin white curtains that bordered the window by my bed. I was confused for a moment, the sunlight hitting my cheeks and warming them. I sat up slowly, hearing deep breaths and peered over the edge of my bed. Ash was curled on the trundle bed, asleep, his hair falling over his eyes. Flashes of memory hit me: Ash catching me as I fell, carrying me up the stairs to the bed and nightmares. More nightmares than I could possibly remember. I shuddered, rubbing my arms.

Ash shifted. His eyes opened, and they met mine. He smiled slightly and sat up. "You're awake."

"How long was I out?" my voice was rough from disuse.

"A couple days," he said, yawning, running a hand through his hair. He was in desperate need of a haircut, but I kind of liked his hair like this. It made him look rough, like a fighter.

"A couple days!" I sat up straighter, flinging the covers off of me. "Where is…where is…" I couldn't bring myself to say the words. My mother? The body? Neither felt right.

"I buried her, in the backyard, near the garden," he said, his eyes meeting mine for a moment. "I hope that's okay. I just thought she…she would like it there."

I nodded. I felt the sensation, the urge to cry, but I had no tears left. I was out. "She would. She loved that garden."

"Are you still intent on leaving?" he asked, getting out of his own blankets and standing up.

I thought about it for a moment. I thought of surviving her on the farm, with my mom's body in the backyard. We could do it. We had the garden, the barn. We had access to food. But the Awakened had caught up to us here, and I didn't know if we were safe anymore. "Yes. Yes, I think that's a good idea."

"Okay," he said firmly. "We'll go." I felt relief go through me and wondered how this had happened. How did I end up with the boy I had loved for most of my life?

His eyes met mine and I felt a wave of love pass through me. I didn't know if he felt the same way or if it was just a passing attraction because I was the last girl available on earth. But I loved him. I wanted him safe.

He said softly, "Z, I'll get our things ready to go." He paused. "You should say goodbye to your mom." He smiled again and headed out of the room.

I glanced out the window, seeing the fresh mound of dirt that was just outside the garden, and swallowed hard. As if they had a mind of their own, my feet started moving, out of the room, down the stairs. I paused at the kitchen, noticing that the mess I had made was gone. I felt another wave of affection for Ash and continued out into the garden.

Her grave was simple, no marker, and perhaps, as time went on, something would grow on top of it, but it was something. It was much more than I had been able to give my father. Ash had done the best he could for her. I sunk to my knees, feeling the soft, cool dirt through my jeans.

I had a chance here, a chance I hadn't had before. I had a chance to really say good-bye to one parent where I had not had the chance before. But what could I say? What could I say to a mother that I spent so much of my life resenting and was only beginning to know?

"I'm sorry," I whispered to the dirt in front of me. "I'm sorry that we didn't have more time. I'm sorry that I could not protect you. I wanted so badly to protect you. We were just beginning to know each other again and...and..." I swallowed hard and took a deep breath. "I love you, Mom.

I love you so much. Say hi to Dad for me, okay? Tell him he owes me some pizza."

I wasn't sure how long I stayed there. It could have been five minutes, or it could have been five hours. I just sat there, staring at the grave in front of me, wondering how it was possible that I was now an orphan.

Ash came out, dressed in a dark blue hoodie and jeans with a pair of Caspar's boots laced tight on his feet. He had a backpack hoisted on one shoulder and his gun strapped to his waist. He was carrying a second backpack in his hands. "I have your stuff. I was sure you would want to change though."

"Yeah," I said, looking down at my sweatpants. I didn't remember putting these on. I raised my eyebrow at Ash. "Did you change me?"

Ash raised his own eyebrows in response as we made our way back to the house. "I have no idea what you're talking about."

I shook my head, a small smile at the corner of my lips. We made our way back into my room. I started pulling clothes out of the drawers, reaching for the hem of my shirt. "Turn around," I told him.

"It's nothing I haven't seen before," he said, a small smirk on his face.

It felt wrong to smile, so incredibly wrong, but sometimes I couldn't help but smile around him. He made me smile. "Turn around, Ash," I repeated.

I reached for the hem of my shirt and tossed it across the room. I pulled a white t-shirt out of the pile and wrinkled my nose. It would be dirty in a day. I settled on an olive green shirt instead and yanked it over my head. I grabbed a sturdy pair of dark jeans and slipped them on. I looked around for my boots and found them under the bed. My hair was a tangled mess and I dragged a hairbrush through it before pulling it into my standard ponytail. I looked at myself in the mirror and felt like Katniss for a moment.

Ash came over to sit on the bed, setting my backpack aside. "Where do you want to go?"

I bit my lip, hesitating before turning around to face him. "I was thinking…I was thinking Sanctuary."

He looked at me for a moment before a smile spread across his lips. "You're joking, right?" I didn't answer. "Z, we don't even know if that's real."

I sighed, sitting on the bed next to him. "I know. God, I know. But how can so many believe in this if it didn't have even an ounce of truth to it?"

"Z," he said, sounding a little frustrated. "Tons of people think Area 51 is real, right?"

"We don't know that it *isn't* real," I said weakly.

He sighed, his arm coming out to snag me around the waist. I squeaked but didn't protest. "I just…I don't know about this. We're going off what we heard from Memphis, Julia and Liam." He said Liam like it left a bad taste in his mouth.

"You just don't like Liam," I said, looking up at him.

He avoided my eye contact. "I don't like anyone who flirts with a girl just days after his fiancé died from a nuclear bomb. And who thinks that this magical place exists."

"I'm not saying a magical place exists, Ash," I said, impatient. I brought my knees up to my chest. "But what if a bunch of people are there? What if people went to Colorado to find this place and stayed? What if there's... something safe out there? It may not be Sanctuary, but it's something."

He looked down at me, his blue eyes bright, and ran a hand over my head, his fingers brushing the strands of my ponytail. "You really want to go?" he asked.

I nodded. "I just think...where else do we have to go? What else can we possibly lose? We should try."

"Okay."

"Okay?" I asked.

He smiled, his lips pressing against my forehead. I felt a shock go through me, and I bit my lip. I was having a hard time adjusting to this new Ash. "Yeah, okay. We'll go."

I nodded, leaning into him.

We stayed like this, comfortable in our close proximity for a few moments longer before we both sat up and made our way downstairs. I glanced out the window and thought of something. "Hey, Ash?"

"Yeah?" he said, peeking out of the kitchen.

"We should take the jeep," I said. Why hadn't I thought of it before? I walked into the kitchen with him, grabbing the keys off the hook where they had hung for months. I rifled through the junk drawers, looking for the maps my mom kept in there. I found one and took it to the dining room table, unfolding it, tracing the route from Constance to Mesa Verde. "It would take us about 12, maybe 13 hours. Walking…it would take a week, probably more."

"The jeep," he repeated. "God, why didn't I think of it?"

I shrugged. "I didn't either until I saw it outside. But it makes sense, and it's definitely safer."

"You're so smart," he said, giving me a squeeze around my waist. "And we can take more things in the jeep. Just in case."

We spent the next twenty minutes packing things in the back of the jeep, clothes, blankets, flashlights, all sorts of things and as much of the nonperishable food as we could find in the house. I placed the map on the front seat and turned back to the house. I spent so little time here in my life. I had kicked and screamed every time I was forced to come out here, and it wasn't home like the brownstone was, but it was the place that I was able to say goodbye to, and I would.

"Are you ready?" Ash asked, coming to stand next to me.

"Yeah," I whispered. "Let's hit the road."

CHAPTER
TWENTY-FOUR

THE CAR WOULDN'T START.

I guess I shouldn't have been surprised. It had been sitting on the driveway, idle and unused for months. My forehead was resting against the steering wheel and I wondered if my brilliant idea hadn't turned into the biggest disappointment.

Ash was sitting in the passenger seat next to me, not saying a word and I was happy for that. I might have bitten his head off. I grumbled under my breath. The gas tank was, miraculously, full, and we could easily make it most of the way to Colorado. We could always walk the rest of the way, if it was absolutely necessary.

That is, if the car wanted to start.

"Try it again," Ash said finally. "You never know."

"Yeah, right, you never know," I said bitterly. I slid the

key back in the ignition throwing a prayer up. "Come on, baby; I believe in you. You'll take us to Colorado." I turned the key, and it made the same familiar whining noise. "This is absolutely ridiculous."

Ash sighed, leaning over to reach for the keys.

"It's not going to turn on," I said firmly, sitting back in the driver's seat. We hadn't even left, and we were already hitting roadblocks. What did this say about this crazy trek we were making to Colorado?

He ignored me, reaching across me to turn the key. The engine sputtered a bit, whined and then roared to life. He grinned triumphantly, turning to look up at me. I was torn between smacking him in the head and making out with him. I smiled grudgingly at him, and pushed him back into his own seat.

"Let's just get out of here, okay?" I said, putting it in gear and starting to back out of the long driveway. When we reached the road, I turned and looked one last time at the house, saying a silent goodbye to my mother before driving away.

The first five hours of the drive went by quickly in a comfortable silence. Ash fiddled with the radio every half an hour or so, trying to catch a signal of something. It had been so long since we had contact with anyone besides each other and my mother that I think we were desperate to know that there were others out there.

The roads were empty of people, but like the roads we had seen back in Nebraska, there were empty cars everywhere, abandoned. Every time we passed one, I turned away, afraid to look at it.

The first time we passed a real city, we slammed on the breaks and looked down at the ruins that were left. There was nothing, just…nothing. I stared at it for a long time before forcing myself to turn away and drive.

We stopped later that night, pulling over and taking the time to get some sleep. Ash reached for my hand before falling asleep, and I let him, feeling comforted by his soft, warm palm against mine.

My dreams were restless, not quite nightmares but enough to make me toss and turn in the hard driver's seat. I woke up more than once, distracted by the bright moonlight streaming through the large windows. I sighed, looking over at Ash, who looked so peaceful in sleep. He shifted a bit; his hand tightened around mine, and I felt for a moment like he was squeezing my heart. When we got to Sanctuary, we would figure it out. I would tell him how I felt, and we would figure it out.

Sanctuary, the possibility of it being real seemed so far-fetched, like the stories I was told as a kid of Santa Claus and the Easter Bunny. Could a place of safety, of utopia even exist? What would we do if there wasn't anything there? I had a vision in my head, of the two of us in animal pelts living off the land like Adam and Eve or something. I bit back a laugh at the image. There had to be something there. There just had to be.

I sat in comfortable silence, keeping a watch outside while Ash slept silently beside me. He slept so quietly that I felt the need to check on him constantly, to make sure that he was still breathing. We were both orphans now, and he was all I had left in the world. Even if he didn't feel the same way (and my heart clenched painfully at the thought), I needed him. I could not survive if I lost him as well.

He woke up about an hour later, rubbing the sleep from his eyes. "Have you been up for long?"

I nodded. "I couldn't sleep." He frowned at me, but I shook my head. "It's okay. There's only about seven hours left until Mesa Verde, and I can drive that straight."

"No way, Z," he said. "It's my turn to drive. You're not driving the whole leg. You need to rest." I opened my mouth to protest, but he reached over and grabbed the keys from the ignition before I could stop him. "We're not going anywhere until you switch places with me."

"Okay, okay," I said, rolling my eyes. "I'm not going to fight you that much. If you want to drive, you can drive."

He smiled widely at me, the first real smile I had seen from him in days, and I found myself smiling back. He got out of the car and walked over to the driver's side as I climbed over to the passenger seat. I buckled myself in and grabbed the map from where it had fallen on the floor.

We drove for another hour before we spoke again. Ash yawned, rubbing his eyes and looked over at me. "What's your favorite color?"

I looked at him, surprised. "Excuse me?"

"What's your favorite color?" he repeated, yawning even bigger than the last time.

"Are you really asking my favorite color right now?" I asked, kicking off my boots and propping my legs up on the dashboard.

"Yes," he answered. He noticed my silence and looked over at me. "I'm tired, and I don't want to fall asleep. And I realized that there is just so much I don't know about you, Zoey Valentine. I want to know more."

I paused for a long moment before I nodded. "Okay. Why not? My favorite color is orange." He smiled widely, and I couldn't help it; I had to smile back.

We played for about an hour before I fell asleep, right in the middle of a story about Ash's most embarrassing moment. My sleep was restless, so I woke easily when I heard the sound of Ash's hurried voice. "Zoey. Zoey, wake up!"

I came to with a start, looking around. "What? What is it?"

"There's a car," he said in a hushed voice, his hands tight on the steering wheel. He was driving faster than he had been earlier, his eyes constantly darting to the mirrors.

I felt a drop in my stomach as I turned around slowly to look out the back window of the car. There, in the just near distance, I could see the pinpricks of headlights heading in the same direction as we were. "How long have they been back there?"

"About twenty minutes," Ash answered, his voice shaking. "I thought maybe it was just someone on the road, like us. Like that couple that gave us a ride to Constance. So I started taking random roads, random turns, and they've remained behind us the entire time."

"Maybe...maybe they're just curious about another person on the road. I mean, we've been driving for hours and haven't seen anyone…" I said, my voice shaking as I watched the pinpricks grow a little larger as the vehicle grew closer.

"Yeah, maybe," Ash said softly, his eyes flashing back and forth between the road in front of him and the rearview mirror.

They were just far enough away. "Turn off your lights, and make the first turn you can," I instructed him.

He hesitated and then turned off the headlights, throwing us into near darkness. I was never more grateful that the jeep was black; I remember my mom wanting a yellow one. He eased the jeep off the road and began driving in the opposite direction of the highway. He drove slowly, painfully so, but I concentrated on the car that was approaching us, closer and closer. I hoped it would pass us, keep driving. It had to.

"Stop," I said, putting my hand out. He crawled to a stop, and cut the engine. We both shifted in our seats, peering over them to look behind us. The car was crawling on the highway, moving painfully slow. They slowed, impossibly, near to a crawl, as they passed near the spot where we had driven off and continued on. I breathed a sigh of relief, but it was premature.

"Zoey," Ash said, his voice sounding strangled. I looked at the car, and saw it was backing up, making its way off the road toward us.

"Oh god," I said, terrified. "Oh, god. What do we do?"

He turned back in his seat, his fingers fumbling with the key at the ignition. The engine popped to life and he quickly threw it in gear and took off.

"What are you doing?" I asked as he sped away.

"I don't know, Zoey; I have no idea, But I don't like that this car is showing way too much interest in us, and we need to go. Now." His hands were tight on the wheel, and I could feel the jeep protesting as the speed increased.

"How on earth are we going to lose them, Ash?" I asked, watching as the car behind us sped up, matching our speed and closing the distance between us. "We're the only cars out here. It's not like we can get lost with all the cars out here."

"I don't know, Zoey!" he shouted. "But they're obviously following us, and I don't like it, okay?"

"Okay, okay," I said, breathing heavily. The car was gaining us, getting closer and closer, and it was close enough that I could see that it was a large SUV, black or maybe dark blue, with heavily tinted windows. It looked like a car that my dad would have driven. This made me nervous. This was not a typical car; most people did not drive cars like this. "Ash, they're right behind us."

He didn't answer; just pushed his foot harder on the gas, but the jeep only increased speed by a couple miles per hour. It was old, outdated and had been pushed farther in the last few hours than it had in the past few months. We both gasped as the car pulled next to us. "Shit," Ash said under his breath.

The window of the SUV rolled down, and a man peeked his head out, motioning for us to roll our own window down. He was older, maybe in his late forties or early fifties, judging by the small amount of gray dotting his hair and beard. He was yelling at us, but I couldn't hear him over the sound of both engines as they sped along. He was dressed nicely, I could see the beginnings of a tie at the base of his throat, and I felt uneasy, uncomfortable. I hadn't seen anyone dressed so nice, so impeccably since we had left New York. This wasn't right.

The car moved closer and closer to us before bumping into us. The jeep shook, but Ash's hands were still gripping tightly on the wheel, and he managed to keep us aligned. "Did they just hit us, or was that an earthquake that shook the car?" he asked, a shaky laugh in his breath.

"No, no, they hit us," I said, my hands gripping the dashboard tightly. I felt like I was going to be sick. We only had to drive half a day. Half a day to reach Colorado, and we would have been able to find a place of safety. And yet, here we were. A shock ran through my body as the SUV made contact with the Jeep again, this time much harder than before. "Oh my god."

"What do you want me to do, Z?" Ash asked, through clenched teeth. His eyes were intent on the rugged terrain in front of us as the Jeep bounced over rocks and grass. I didn't know where we were heading, whether we would end up in a town or at a cliff. I could see hills in the distance, and I didn't know what was over there. The SUV hit us again, shaking the entire car.

"Stop," I said, the word bursting out of me. "Just stop the car, okay?"

He looked over at me incredulously but slowed down,

bringing the jeep to a stop. We were both breathing heavily, and our eyes met as the SUV came to a stop about one hundred yards in front of us. A couple doors opened, and two men descended from the car and started coming over toward us. "Should we get out?"

The question was answered for me. They stopped in front of our car, stopping in the light of the headlights. The sun was coming up, a soft haze to the right of us. One of the men, the one who had been waving to us before, motioned for us to get out of the car.

"I'm getting out of the car," Ash said, not taking his eyes off those watching us. "Don't get out. I'm going to come around the other side to get you."

"Ash, you don't…you don't have to do that," I protested softly, meeting his eyes.

"Stay in the car, Z, okay?" he asked again, and I nodded, watching as he opened the door slowly and got out of the car. He walked across the front of the jeep and came to my side. I held my breath as he did so, watching the eyes of the men in front of us, as they too watched him. He came up to my door and opened it. "Ready?" he asked.

"Yeah," I said. "Yeah, I'm ready." I unbuckled the seat belt and lowered myself out of the car. Ash shut the door behind me and laced his fingers through mine. We walked slowly toward the men, though Ash made sure he was a few steps ahead of me, shielding me from the strange men in front of us.

"Hello there!" The older man, the one who had been in the passenger side window, was the one who called out to us. He waved his hand in greeting.

I looked up at Ash, and we both looked back at the man, not saying anything.

"The name's Rich," he said, putting his hand down. "Don't be frightened. I'm here to help you. I'm from the government. We've been looking for you."

"Looking for us?" I managed to squeak out. "Why would you be looking for us?"

"Well, because you're survivors!" He took a step closer to us, holding his hands out. "We've been looking for survivors all over the place. There aren't many of you left, and we want to be able to take care of you."

I thought about this for a long moment. He was dressed perfectly, in a suit, and I could see the gun strapped to his waist, just underneath his jacket. "You're from the government?" I asked, my voice shaking.

"Yes, of course. The government has managed to put together a small force to find the survivors, bring them together and keep them safe so we can start over."

"Where?" Ash cut in. "Where are you bringing them?"

"There's a place in southwest Colorado that everyone is heading to, and it's a safe place," he explained.

Ash and I exchanged looks, and I knew we were both thinking the same thing: Sanctuary. Could it possibly be real? Could they have found us before we found them?"

"How far away is it?" I asked, feeling a sense of relief.

"We're not too far out of Deer Trail, so maybe six or seven hours. You two should grab your stuff, and we can take you there. What are your names?" he asked.

I hesitated. "Zoey. This is Ash."

"Zoey and Ash," he said, a smile on his face. "It's great to meet you. I'm glad you two are safe. Grab your stuff, and we can head out." He started walking backward to the car, and I felt a sense of unease return. This was too easy. He expected us to come with him, readily, no questions asked. And it still didn't explain why they felt the need to ram their car into ours.

"Well, we do have our car," I said, trying to sound breezy and free of panic. "We could follow you down there." He met my eyes, frowning, and I continued. "We have a lot packed in the car, things maybe you could use at this...at this place, and I would hate for a working vehicle to go to waste."

The frown remained on his features. "I don't know if that would be wise, Miss..."

"It's just Zoey," Ash said, tugging my arm to pull me closer to him. "And I don't understand. What's the harm in us driving our own car?"

"There's no harm...Ash, was it?" Rich said with a small smile on his face. I shivered. The smile was wide, charming, but it didn't match the darkness in his eyes. "I just think it would be safer for you to travel in our vehicle. Don't you think I'm right, Crosby?"

Rich's counterpart, a large, muscled man who looked massively bored, grunted in response. He sighed, looking around.

"Well, perhaps we might just continue on our own," Ash said, pleasantly. I could see the strain in his eyes, the tightness of his mouth. "We appreciate your help, but we've been surviving well so far, and I'd feel better if it were just the two of us." I nodded in agreement.

Rich sighed, looking disappointed. "I thought you were going to make this easy, kids. I so hoped you would make this easy."

"Make what easy?" I asked, suddenly terrified. Both Rich and Crosby reached for something in their pockets, and I reached for my gun before remembering. They were in the car. *They were in the car.*

They didn't pull out weapons. Instead, they both reached for...a needle? It was a syringe of some sort, and I remembered the men coming to get Madison after the concert that night. I stepped closer to Ash and his arms went around me.

"We could do this the easy way or the hard way," Rich said, holding up the syringe. He sighed again. "God, I hate sounding like a cliché."

"Can we just do this already? I'm bored," Crosby said, tearing open the package and looking at the needle carefully.

Rich waved his hand lazily, and Crosby came toward us, right to Ash. Of course he would. Ash was tall, over six feet, and muscular from playing baseball and football, and he was looming over me protectively. Of course he would be seen as the threat.

Crosby reached for Ash, and I went ducking under his arm, and right to Rich. Rich looked surprised as I threw a punch straight at his nose, and he went down to the ground. He cried out in pain, his hands coming up to cover his face.

I turned around and saw Ash taking Crosby down. "Ash, Ash, let's…"

He looked up from Crosby's body, and his eyes grew wide. "Zoey!"

An arm wrapped tightly around me, yanking me backward into something solid. I felt the slight pinprick of the needle against the skin of my neck, and I froze. Ash had frozen too, his hand still in a tight fist above Crosby's stirring head.

"I wouldn't do that if I were you," Rich said, his voice a breath on my ear.

"What is that?" Ash asked. "What's in the needle?"

"It'll just knock her out, but I don't want to have to do that. I'd rather have you awake when we get to Sekhmet."

"Sec-met?" Ash sounded it out, the word unfamiliar on his lips. It felt…familiar to me, like I had heard it before but couldn't quite place where. "What's that?"

"It's where we are taking you, young Ash," Rich explained. "It's a place…it's a place of dreams." He pulled me closer up against him, and I flinched. "Would you like to dream, Zoey?"

"Leave her alone!" Ash dropped his grip on Crosby. He stepped over Crosby's body and came running at the two of us, and the last thing I remembered was the needle piercing my skin, and then the darkness hit quicker than I could have ever anticipated.

TWENTY-FIVE

I WAS AWAKE, BUT I couldn't open my eyes. Sounds surrounded me. I heard whispers of unfamiliar voices and the squeaks of shoes against slick floors. My eyelids felt heavy when I tried to open them. There was a bad taste in my mouth, and I licked my lips, which felt dry. I tried to lift my hands thinking that maybe I could peel my eyelids open, but they wouldn't move. They were held down by something.

"I think she's waking up," a hushed voice said with a slight accent. It was familiar, like I had heard it on the radio or over the intercom at school. It was not someone I knew. But it enticed me to try and wake up.

My eyelids opened, and for a moment, all I saw was white. The lights were burning bright, making me feel fuzzy and disoriented. I blinked a few times and then looked around at what was around me.

It looked like a doctor's office but not quite like any doctor's office that I had ever been in before. The counters were a spotless white, and I was strapped to a chair, like the one I sat in when I went to the dentist. There were computers, machines set up all over the place. There were a handful of people in the room sitting at the computers; one of them was in front of a large touchscreen looking at a very complicated chart. An IV was attached to my hand, and there was a consistent beep ringing through the hush of the room, sounding very much like a heart monitor. Were they monitoring my heart?

The strangest part of the room though was on the ceiling, right above my head. It was an incredibly large lion's head attached to the body of a female, with the letters SF boldly intertwined around her body. I looked around and noticed it on the computers, the machines. It was everywhere, like a symbol, like a mascot.

I didn't know where I was, except that I felt like I was in a weird sci-fi movie or an alien was about to burst from my chest or something. What I did know was that I was exhausted. Even if I hadn't been strapped down, I didn't know that I could move my arms or legs. They felt heavy, like they weren't even a part of my body. I felt dead. Was I dead?

"You're not dead, Miss Valentine."

I jumped. Had I actually asked that question out loud? I turned toward the voice and was met with a face, a face that was blurry in my memory, but I knew that I had seen it before.

It was a woman, probably in her late fifties to early sixties. Her skin was dark, the color of melted chocolate on a hot summer day, and her hair was deep black, impossibly black, except for the streaks of silver that weaved through it. She was tall, taller than most women that I had met in my life, but it also could be the way she carried herself, poised, ready, standing with her feet together, examining me carefully.

"How do you know my name?" I asked, my voice rough. My tongue felt like sandpaper, and I was having a hard time getting the words from my brain to my lips.

"It is amazing how easily you can find a person just by taking one simple fingerprint," she answered, stepping closer to me. One of the other people in the room, a young man, came up to her and whispered in her ear. She nodded, and he immediately turned and walked away.

My fingerprint. Searching for the memory in my brain was like fighting my way through an impenetrable fog. And then I remembered. I had been fingerprinted when I was about thirteen years old, as a precaution. Of course. Everything my dad had done in my life had been a precaution of some sort. "Where am I?" I managed to ask.

"You are at Sekhmet Facilities, Miss Valentine, in the medical rooms," she answered. She had an accent, British with a touch of something else, something unfamiliar to me.

There was that word again: Sekhmet. "What is... Sekhmet? Sekhmet Facilities?" Each word came out carefully. I wondered if this was what it was like to learn to speak. I was unsure of each word that came from my mouth.

"Sekhmet Facilities is my research institute. We do

quite a variety of things here," she explained. "Do you know who I am? Well, no, of course not. You probably don't." She laughed, and it sounded beautiful, full of chimes and bells. I had never felt so charmed by a laugh before. "My name is Doctor Cylon. Razi Cylon."

I squinted at her for a moment, and it dawned on me where I had seen her before: a news conference on my television so many months before. "You're from the CDC. I remember you on the news."

She hesitated, biting her full bottom lip. "Well," she said, carefully, "it is true that I was once affiliated with the CDC, but my primary focus is Sekhmet and the objectives of the company as a whole."

She was speaking, but her words made no sense. She raised a hand to my face, her nails a bright crimson red, to brush back a strand of my hair and tuck it behind my ear. I recoiled from her touch. Her hands were cold, unnaturally cold, and the mere touch of her skin on mine had sent shivers up my spine.

"I don't…I don't understand."

Dr. Cylon motioned for someone, and they immediately brought a chair and placed it next to mine. She lowered herself into it gracefully. "Have you ever heard the story of the goddess Sekhmet, Miss Valentine?"

I shook my head slowly. "I don't think so."

"I am not surprised. I know that they tend to focus on the Greek mythologies in most American schools. The goddess Sekhmet is an Egyptian goddess, protector and warrior for the pharaohs. She was also a goddess of healing, very powerful. In fact, her name is derived, often times, as meaning 'one with power.' She was fierce, often depicted as a lioness. She's a good likeness for the cause, wouldn't you say?"

I was even more confused than I had been before her explanation, though it did explain the weird half-cat/half-woman that was all over the room. "I don't understand," I repeated. "What cause?"

She stood up abruptly. "I'll show you." She leaned over me and pressed her fingertips to the cool strips of metal that were encasing my wrists. She paused before unlocking them. "I must warn you, Miss Valentine, that if you try anything, there are several people in this room alone that would be on you in an instant. I would not bother to try."

I nodded quickly. I hadn't even thought of fighting. Was there a reason to fight? I couldn't even think straight. There was a pounding in my head, and I still felt like I was stuffed with cotton. And I was thirsty, incredibly thirsty. I was unstrapped in an instant, and I sat up, rubbing my fingers over the sore spots of my wrists. I had no idea where I was. I had no idea what Sekhmet Facilities were or what their cause was. I had no idea...

"Ash!" I blurted out abruptly. "Where's Ash?"

"Your companion is perfectly safe. He is in another wing of the facility," Dr. Cylon answered vaguely, leading me through the room and out the door. We walked down a long, blinding white hallway, and I shivered. It was freezing. I realized that I was no longer wearing my own clothes. I was instead in an outfit not too different from those that nurses wore in hospitals, in plain shades of gray and brown. I had a bulky gray tunic that fit snug across my chest, and baggy brown pants. They were thin but comfortable, and yet I still felt slightly like a prison inmate.

"I want to see him," I demanded, though my voice sounded weak even to my own ears.

"All in good time, Miss Valentine."

I pressed my palms tight against my eyes. "Stop calling me that. My name is Zoey."

"If that's what you prefer," Dr. Cylon said agreeably. We had reached a door, at the end of the hallway. She pressed her fingertip to the pad, and it blinked green. She reached for the doorknob and ushered me inside.

Just inside the door was a pair of Awakened.

I rushed backward and my back smacked into the door. My hand reached for the handle, and I turned, but it wouldn't budge. It was locked, and I had no way of getting out. I reached for my gun, but of course, I didn't have it. It was probably still in the Jeep, lost in the middle of Colorado.

"Relax; they cannot harm you," Dr. Cylon said, standing very close to them. She pointed to the ground, and I noticed what I had missed before. The two Awakened were chained, their ankles attached to a chain that was hooked to the ground. They had no more than a foot or two of room to move.

"Why...why are they here?" I asked, shaking. I didn't move from the door. The two Awakened were staring at me intently, salivating over the sight of me. I waited for them to say something, anything, but they didn't. All I could hear was the harshness of their breathing.

"You wanted to see the cause, did you not?" the doctor asked, one perfect eyebrow raised in confusion.

"I…well, yes, but…" I sputtered. I turned away from the Awakened and met her eyes. They were a deep, dark brown, nearly black, and framed by the thickest eyelashes I had ever seen.

She gestured toward the Awakened. "This is the cause. This is *my* cause."

CHAPTER
TWENTY-SIX

I BLINKED A FEW TIMES at her, looking between her and the docile Awakened. I kept waiting for them to speak or attack. They were so calm; I had never seen them so calm. "I don't know what you mean. The Awakened are your cause."

An amused smile crossed her lips. "Ah, yes, the Awakened. That is what the civilians have taken to calling my creations. I admit it is better than calling them by their proper name: SK-521. Much more of a mouthful, I suppose."

"Your creations?" I asked horrified. "You created them?"

"Well, of course I did," she said, looking over at the creatures adoringly. "They have been a central part of the plan, of my cause."

"They've killed so many people," I said, my voice shaking, thinking of the Awakened that had torn both of my parents to pieces. "They've torn the world apart."

"Don't give them more credit than they deserve, Zoey," she said, her voice suddenly harsh. "They are my creation. They are acting on my will. I am the one with the power and the control." She pulled something out of her pocket, a small tablet. Using her finger, she navigated through a series of menus before selecting a single button.

It was like a trigger. The two Awakened chained to the floor were suddenly loud, demanding, and struggling against their bonds. They reached for us, their voices a high-pitched wail in the echoing room.

"I just want to eat! Please, please let me eat. Her flesh smells so good. Please, oh god, please, just one bite!" The closest one to me, a male, was reaching, stretching with all his might toward me, his black eyes focused on me. I bit my hand hard, struggling to keep the bile from rising in my throat.

Dr. Cylon watched them for a moment before pressing on her tablet again, and they once again became subdued. I looked over at her in shock, and she smiled, quite triumphant.

"I control them all. Would you like to see?" she asked. Without waiting for an answer, she brought up a screen on the tablet, one that looked like a rough map, with blinking numbers across it. "There are groups all over the country, and I control them. I can make them hungry or docile. I can make them attack. Most of the ones out in the open are free. The ones I've kept to myself in here...well, let's just say it's a bit distracting to have them wailing about all the time."

I stared at the screen for a moment. The numbers were

so many; they overlapped each other. The country was far more overrun with Awakened than I could have possibly imagined. I wondered if any of them had managed to die in the nuclear blasts. "But how do you control them?"

"It is simple," she said, walking away from me and up to the Awakened. I gasped at her close proximity to them, but they just stood there, silent and calm, not noticing her. She turned the male around, showing me the back of his neck. With her finger, she pressed on the base of his neck, and a piece of flesh popped out.

I was going to throw up. There was nothing left in my stomach, but I knew I was going to throw up. This was sickening. Between the tiny bit of flesh was a piece of metal, gold and shining. It looked exactly like...

"A computer chip," Dr. Cylon said, finishing my thought. "It is in the back of the neck of every SK-521 out there. It is what awakened them, and it is what gives me the control that I have. They each have their own individual signal, and those individuals have their groups as well. I can control their every action...or simply those of the group they belong to."

"But...but why?" I demanded, my hands rolled up into tiny fists. I wanted to shake her, punch her and throw her against the wall. Why on earth would she ever create something like this? I watched her place the cube of flesh back in its place, right at the base of the neck. No wonder that was a prime spot to aim for when trying to take one down.

She placed the tablet back in her pocket. "Come," she

said. "I will show you."

We left the room, and I heard the click of the lock behind us. I was on autopilot. My feet were doing the work for me, making sure that I walked alongside her as she took us down a different hallway, which led to an elevator. This time, she typed in a code, and the doors immediately opened. She stepped inside, using her hand on my arm to guide me inside with her. The elevator glided smoothly upward and immediately opened at a new floor.

I gasped.

She nodded, looking proud. "These are our research labs. They are quite impressive." We went through a series of doors and walked alongside a hallway until we reached one last door. She typed a few numbers into the keypad and pressed her thumb to another pad, and the door slid open.

We were inside an office, not unlike any other office you would see. There was a large desk, on top of which sat a sleek, high-tech computer. The walls were covered in frames, most of them degrees of some sort. I saw Harvard, Oxford and a few others that I couldn't make out. There were bookshelves along the walls filled to the brim with books, scores and scores of books. The back wall was completely glass and looked out on a huge room. I peeked out, and saw dozens of people, all in white lab coats. Some were on computers; some were working with what looked like chemicals. I even saw a group, bent over an Awakened with a scalpel, cutting into its blue flesh.

"This is where everything started, Miss Valentine," Dr. Cylon explained, her voice barely more than a whisper. Her eyes were intent on the scene below her, watching it with a mix of adoration and pride, like she was watching her child learn to walk for the first time. "This is where Sekhmet was born. This is where the Z virus was created, and the victims were…awakened, as you would say."

I shook my head, trying to clear my thoughts, to get a sense on the situation that was in front of me. This was too much. "You created the virus as well?"

"That was the beginning of everything. That was the plan from the beginning," she said. She ran a hand through her hair and gestured for me to sit down in one of chairs in front of the desk.

There was a loud thump as I sunk into the chair. I felt like I was going to pass out and immediately ducked, putting my head between my legs.

"Are you not feeling quite well? Do you require anything?" Her accent made everything she said sound so incredibly charming, but her words were toxic and hard to process.

I shook my head and sat up. "But why? Why would you create the virus? Why would you awaken the victims? It's sick! People are dying!"

"As they should," she said softly, but fiercely. Her eyes fell on the lone picture frame on her desk, and her expression softened for a moment. She flipped it around, and I saw the face of a young man, handsome, looking much like the woman sitting across from me. "This is my son. His name was David."

I swallowed hard. "Was?"

"He died." Her words were hard, blunt. "Four years ago, when he was eighteen years old."

"I'm sorry," I blurted out without thinking.

She nodded, a hard sadness in her eyes. "Ever since he died, I've been on this cause, working my way up the ranks at the CDC, creating this facility, doing what I can to change this world."

She took a deep breath. "David was a beautiful person, the most beautiful person I have ever met in my life, and I do not say this only as his mother. He was intelligent and kind and so incredibly selfless. He could have done so much."

"I worked hard, going to school, doing everything I could to give him the best life I was capable of. His father wasn't around. But we did the best we could, the two of us." Dr. Cylon sighed, remembering. "When he was fourteen years old, he came to me and told me that he was gay, that he had known for a while that he was gay and could not keep it a secret from me any longer."

I was mesmerized, addicted to the story. I had no idea what it had to do with the Awakened or the existence of this facility, but I had a feeling I was going to find out.

"I was shocked, but I think deep down I had always known this about him. We had come from a traditional family, but I loved my son, more than life itself. I loved him no matter who he chose to love."

Her hands reached for the portrait again, and she picked it up, looking down at the face of her son adoringly. "The world, it would seem, did not feel the same. He always had a hard time being accepted, but he took it with so much strength. He held his head up high. When he left for university, I had no doubt in my mind that he would succeed."

"It was two weeks before his winter holidays that I got the phone call. He had not shown up for finals, none of them. I hadn't heard from him in a few days, but he was an avid student, and I assumed he was too busy studying. It was no matter of concern; I would see him in a few days."

"What happened?" I whispered.

"He was killed, murdered by two of his fellow students," Dr. Cylon said, her voice returning to its harsh nature. "They followed him one night as he left the library late at night. They invited him out for drinks, but they had no intention of friendship. They beat him until he stopped breathing."

I gasped. "That's horrible."

"Yes. It tore me apart. David was the beginning and the end of everything that mattered to me. His death nearly killed me." She took a deep breath and straightened herself up. "But it gave me a mission, Zoey."

I felt my heart sink.

"The world is wrong. The world is broken. When we came to this earth, whatever way you believe, we were a clean slate. But over the thousands of years that we've been here, we have dirtied that slate. We've become an embarrassment, an abomination of the species. We are weak. We need to start over."

"I created the virus. It was so easy to do," she said, a

note of pride in her voice. My sympathy over the loss of her son was dissipating quickly. "It was created to target the immune system. Those with the strongest immune systems would survive. I wanted the strongest of us all to survive. We released it in the water supply. So simple."

"I don't see the point," I admitted, my voice low. "Why kill off those with weak immune systems?"

"I wanted the strongest of us to live. I wanted to rebuild the world, to start fresh, but I still needed people. So I worked out a way to have the strongest of us all survive," she explained, looking at me as if I were simple. "Free of disease, free of alcoholism and affinity to drugs, free of the darkness that creeps up and makes us so evil."

"So you created the virus," I said, feeling anger rising in my throat, "to rid the Earth of the so-called weak ones. But the Awakened? What was the point of those?"

"That, I must admit, was a stroke of genius, on my part." She smiled widely at me. I stared at her, my face hard, refusing to show her any form of emotion. I was angry, furious and terrified at the woman standing in front of me. "We stole the bodies, because we wanted to study them to see the effects of the virus, but we didn't need so many. We had been working on these chips for so long, and it suddenly clicked together. It took a while, but we managed to use the chips to reverse the effects of death. We had our own built-in army."

She stood up and walked back to the window overlooking the labs. Her hands were folded behind her back as she surveyed the scene below. "Of course, they turned out a little differently than we had expected. The unfortunate look of them, well, they ended up looking quite scary. I'm not quite sure what caused the blue tint to their skin pigment, but frankly, it wasn't that important." She shrugged her shoulders elegantly.

I stood up as well, my fists clenched. I could be across the desk and have her down on the ground in less than two seconds. I wanted to. "You're not making any sense, Dr. Cylon…"

"Razi," she cut in. She smiled over her shoulder endearingly, as if smiling at her daughter. I felt the fire of anger in my stomach and had to resist the urge to punch her.

"Razi, fine," I said, dismissively. "Fine, you had an army at your disposal. But why release them? Releasing them caused even more people to die, especially after they dropped bombs on the major cities. I thought you wanted to rebuild the world with the survivors."

"Oh, I did. I do." She turned away from the window and came over to me, her dark eyes meeting mine. "But I wanted the strong, the strongest of the survivors. I wanted those who could survive no matter the conditions. Those who would survive the outbreak of the SK-521s, sorry, the Awakened, would be the strongest. The bombs were unfortunate but that was outside my control." She sighed, a sorrowful look on her face. I had never seen such a forced expression.

"I want to create a utopia with the smartest, strongest people that are left in the world. The people who want to live are the ones that I need to create it. I've created a virus, awakened millions of dead people and perfected an army. Sekhmet, the warrior goddess of the Egyptian pharaohs, would be so proud. I am fighting for the world. I am healing it."

She looked at me appraisingly. "You are one of those, Zoey, one of the survivors. I am so proud of you. I am so excited that you are here to become part of this new world."

I swallowed hard. I wanted nothing to do with this new world that she had planned. She was playing God, taking nature into her own hands and I wanted no part in it.

"What do you think?" Razi asked, spreading her arms wide, as if to show off the encompassing nature of her facility. "Are you ready to join my utopia?"

"I want to see Ash," I said immediately. "Now."

She sighed, looking at me with disappointment. She was quiet for a long time, and I was sure she was going to refuse me. "I see," she finally spoke. "Very well. I will take you to him."

We left her office behind and continued through a winding maze of hallways, elevators and even a few flights of stairs. We kept going lower and lower, the air around us becoming thicker and colder. I could see white puffs of breath escaping my lips, and I wrapped my arms tight around me as I followed her.

"Where is he? Ash? Where did you put him?" I asked, looking at the doors we were passing. They were strong, steel, with a small window at the top. They looked like prison doors and I knew, deep in my gut, that Ash was behind one of these doors.

I was right. She stopped in front of one of them and pressed her thumb to the pad. The door sprung open, and she stepped aside, letting me walk in.

Ash was on a chair, not unlike the one that I had just been occupying earlier. His own room was so different though, so dark in contrast to my lighter room, and there was no one in here, just the steady beep of his heart on the monitor. He was completely out, but looked unhurt.

I spun around, facing Razi. "Why is he here? Why isn't he upstairs, with me?"

"He's sick," she said simply. I looked at her, horrified. "Nothing serious. We think bronchitis, perhaps strep throat. He was trying to hide it from you, but we noticed it right away. He will heal but…" She sighed again, looking disappointed. "He is not strong, not like you. He really serves me no purpose."

"He serves *me* purpose," I protested. "He's important to me."

"That is human weakness, emotions," she said, sharply, pushing me out of the way, to stand next to Ash. "To be part of this new world, you need to find a new mate, a strong one. Holding on to those who would only make you weak is a false move, Zoey."

Razi leaned over Ash, running her long fingers over his forehead, smoothing out the wrinkles of stress. "I'm not cruel though, of course! I will allow you to say goodbye."

This was all happening too fast. It seemed like it had only been hours (though I had no idea how long I had been under) that Ash and I had been on the road, heading to what we thought was Sanctuary, and now we were captured, kidnapped by this crazy doctor playing God who I was pretty sure was going to kill the boy I loved. I was not ready to say goodbye. I was not ready to join this ridiculous utopia that she thought she was creating. She was crazy, and all these people that she had upstairs working for her, they were crazy as well. They had been killing innocent people on a false cause, and they weren't stopping anytime soon.

She woke Ash up gently, coaxing him awake. His eyes flew open and darted around wildly, taking in his surroundings. His lip curled at the sight of Razi; this was definitely not the first time that he had seen her, and his previous experience had not been good, judging by the disgusted look on his face. His eyes wandered and fell on mine, and I felt a sense of relief as I crossed the room toward him.

"Zoey," he breathed. "You're all right."

I nodded. "Of course. Are you okay?"

He coughed loudly. "Of course I am. Never been better." He tossed a glare at Razi who didn't flinch as she watched us. "What are you doing here?"

"I'm…I'm…" I started to say. I could feel tears building up, and the words got caught in my throat. How could I tell him that we were trapped, stuck with the people who were responsible for the deaths of everyone we loved and cared about?

"She's come down here to say goodbye to you," Razi cut in, pressing a few buttons on the machine. There were so many wires connected to it, and I was sure that at least one was connected to Ash in some way. I watched her apprehensively, afraid that there was one button, a simple button, that could just end his life right then and there.

Ash turned to glare at her, and I stepped back. "Should I be grateful to you, Doctor Cylon, that you brought her down here to say goodbye? Did you tell why I am forced to say goodbye to her? Did you tell that I didn't fit into your ridiculous idea of a perfect world?"

I gaped at him. "You know?"

"Of course," Ash spat out, though his venom was aimed at Razi, not me. "She told me that you were the only one that they wanted. You were strong, and I was weak, and I would only hold you back." He met the doctor's eyes squarely. "They're going to kill me."

"No!" I shouted, looking over at Razi, who was still regarding me calmly. "No, you can't do that. This is ridiculous."

"I am building a perfect world, and I cannot afford you to be emotionally weak. He is sick; his immune system is not as strong as yours. He would be a waste to keep around," Razi explained, no remorse in her voice.

"You're sick," Ash yelled at her, struggling against his bonds. "You're a sick woman, and you're acting like you're God, like it's a game, but you're taking away innocent lives. Who gave you this power? Who decided that you could do this?"

Razi didn't answer. She blinked her large dark eyes at us and used her hands to wipe off imaginary lint off the perfect creases of her blazer. She was too far gone to be reasoned with. She'd been planning this for the past four years, and there was no stopping her from her objective now.

"You should just kill me too," I said angrily. I saw Ash shake his head out of the corner of my eye, but I refused to look at him. "I want nothing to do with this new world you think you're creating."

"That is not going to happen. Say your goodbyes," she said, firmly. "I'm tired of this. I have better things to waste my time on."

Ash shifted, turning his head toward mine, a smirk on his face. "Can I get one last goodbye kiss, Zoey?"

All the words that I wanted to say, the "I love you" that I needed to say, were stuck. I couldn't get them out. Now was the time. It didn't matter if he didn't feel the same; I needed to say it now. I leaned forward and pressed my lips tightly to his, feeling the sparks dart through me. I went to pull away, but the look in his eye stopped me. "Now," he whispered.

It took me a moment before I realized what he said. I nodded slightly, watching Razi out of the corner of my eye, just a short length of space away from me. She was completely unprepared.

"Now!" he urged, and I moved. I whipped around, catching Razi around the waist, spinning her to face me. I caught a quick look at the surprise in her eyes before kneeing her in the gut and sending an elbow to her throat and then her head. She collapsed quickly, slumping to the ground.

"God, I always forget how fast you are," Ash said, staring at her body on the ground. "Get me out of here, will you?"

I raced back to his side, yanking the needle out of his hand and the wires pasted to his chest. I fumbled at the metal cuffs around his wrist unable to find a clasp. I thought of Razi's fingers, gentle on the cuffs that had released me earlier. "Hold on."

I went back to her body and lifted her up, buckling a bit under her weight. I lifted her hand and pressed her fingertips to one of the cuffs. It sprang open at the touch. "Perfect." I reached over, pressing her fingertips to the other cuff, and Ash sat up, pushing her off his lap and back onto the ground. She flopped back, smacking her head on one of the machines that surrounded the chair. I had hit her hard.

"Let's get out of here," he said, grabbing my hand and heading for the door. He looked left, and right, both leading into long hallways. "So, uh, any idea on how to get out of this place?"

"No idea," I answered, promptly. "Come on, let's go. We'll figure it out."

"Make it up as we go along," Ash said as we went left and headed quickly up the hallway. "That's always my favorite kind of plan."

"Shut up," I said mildly as we came up to another fork. I immediately turned right and was relieved when I saw the door to the stairs. We had to make our way upstairs. We could only find a way outside the facility if we made our way upstairs. We moved quickly up the stairs, careful to keep our steps as quiet as possible.

We finally reached a door that led to an actual floor. I peeked through the window and saw no one around, so I pushed the door open slowly. I motioned for Ash to follow me and we crept through the empty hallways, peeking in doors. There were a lot of empty rooms just like the one I had found myself waking up in, but none of them led to an exit. None of them even had windows.

"We have to find a way out of here," I said as we continued hopelessly down the hallway. Ash squeezed my hand in response, and I immediately felt calm. It felt silly that a simple hand squeeze could make me feel better, but there it was. The warmth of his palm was the perfect comfort.

"There they are!"

We whirled around and saw several people at the end of the hallway, pointing at us. I looked up at Ash. "Run!"

We took off, running as fast as we could, skirting around a corner into another endless hallway. There were no other sounds except the falls of our footsteps and the heavy breathing as we sped through the hallways. I could hear them behind us, and I flashed back to us running through the woods, away from the Awakened.

We hadn't made it more than a few feet before I went flying into a wall, landing with a smack. I fell to the floor and rolled onto my side. I saw a pair of heels clicking down the hallway toward us and felt a sense of dread.

"Did you honestly think that you would be able to get away?" Razi's voice sounded annoyed but also a bit amused. "Someone pick her up."

I was yanked to my feet, my arms held by two overgrown goons. I glared at both of them and saw Ash held up in between another two goons, both of whom seemed to be even larger than the ones holding me. Where did they get guys like this? Was there some sort of "evil company lackey" school that these guys went to? Was there a Craigslist ad that read, "Need ginormous men to work for evil genius"?

Ash coughed loudly, and I met his eyes, wincing at the blood dripping from his nose.

"You were foolish, both of you," Razi said, looking back and forth between us. "Trying to escape from Sekhmet was bold, almost worth admiration but very idiotic. I'm only trying to help you."

I met her eyes and noticed the bruises that were already forming on her face. Rich stood just behind her, and I had to suppress the smirk that was threatening to burst out onto my face at the bandage that was across his nose. I did that, and I was damn proud of it.

"We don't want your help," I said, firmly.

She pressed her fingertips to her temple as if I was giving her a headache. Good. I wanted to give her a headache, and stomachache, and all sorts of things that were massively unpleasant. "Don't make me regret choosing you, Zoey, to be part of this new world. You are one of the strongest I've seen. You're a survivor. You just proved that again, by attempting to escape. Let me help you," she pleaded.

"No. Definitely not," I answered again.

"Very well." Razi shrugged and motioned to her minions.

"Dr. Cylon, should we stick to the original plan for the boy?" Rich said, coming up to stand next to her.

She eyed Ash carefully and my heart slammed in my chest, beating a rhythm against my ribcage. "No, no, I don't think so." Her eyes met mine and a smile crept across her face. "I think for now, I'd prefer to keep Mr. Matthews around. He might work as great…motivation for Ms. Valentine."

The sinking feeling in my stomach multiplied as I realized what she meant. Ash and I looked at each other. They would not kill him, not yet, and now it was up to me. My compliance would be the only thing keeping him alive. The men holding him nodded in understanding and started pulling him away.

"No," I said, struggling against the large hands holding on to me. "No, please, don't take him, please. I'll do whatever you want, just please don't hurt him."

"It is far too late for that, Zoey," Razi said, her voice clipped and brisk. "But I love your attitude change."

I watched helplessly as they dragged Ash down the hallway. He struggled, trying as hard as he could to break free of their grip. They pulled him to the elevator. His hands gripped the doors as they began to close. I strained against my own hold, but it was useless. I wasn't moving. "Ash!"

"Zoey! Zoey!" Ash's voice echoed through the hallway, and I was desperate. I was dreading the doors closing, that watching him being dragged away would be the last time I saw him, that it would be the last memory I ever had of him.

"Ash!" I looked at Razi, fury blazing on my features. "Stop them!" I screamed.

Ash's fingers were slipping as the doors for the elevator began to close. "Zoey! Zoey, I…"

The doors of the elevator slammed shut, and then there was silence.

TWENTY-SEVEN

I AWOKE ONCE MORE IN the same room that I had been before, but this time I woke to an eerie silence. The machines were still there making soft noises, but there was a distinct lack of people. The lights were dimmed. I moved to sit up and noticed something else; I was not strapped down as I was before. I blinked in surprise at my hands and pushed myself off the chair.

The floor was cold under the soft fabric of my socks as I moved quietly toward the door. I reached for the handle, but it failed to turn under my palm. I was locked in. I should have known better. I sighed. Leaning against the door, I took a look around my surroundings.

The room was fairly large, much larger than it had seemed before, with several people inside of it. The chair sat in the middle of it, surrounded by several clean, smooth, empty counters. There was a sink in one corner, and a shower in the other, with no curtain or door for privacy. Most of the machines that had been beeping earlier were gone, but there were still a few, including the large touch-screen.

I crossed the room toward it, pressing my fingers to it. The screen came immediately to life, sending brightness into the room. There was only one option to press, the epitaph of the lioness woman, so I selected it gently. A request for a password immediately popped up, and I sighed in disappointment.

A smell reached my nose, and I squinted around the room. There was a tray I hadn't noticed before, just beside the chair. It looked like what you got when ordering room service at a hotel. I moved over to it, my stomach rumbling. I couldn't even remember the last time I had eaten. I lifted the cover and was surprised to find a full meal there; a lightly seasoned chicken breast, a pile of peas and chopped carrots, and a mound of mashed potatoes covered in a dark gravy. My stomach rumbled again. When was the last time I had eaten a full meal like this?

I reached for the fork that lay on the tray beside it and was halfway to scooping up the mashed potatoes when I paused. This food had come from somewhere within this facility, and I trusted no one in here. It could have been poisoned or filled with a serum that made me grow an extra arm or something. My eyes darted around the room, and I finally noticed it, the small black globe on the ceiling in the corner of the room, the camera. I looked at the food again longingly and forced myself to put the fork down. I could not give in so easily.

A few hours later, it was proving to be more difficult than I thought.

There was nothing to do, nothing but count the ceiling tiles or trace patterns in the speckled tile on the floor. I walked back and forth; I sang songs; I did everything I could without going crazy. I had no concept of time. I had no way of knowing how much time had actually passed. No one came to my room. There wasn't a peep except for the now familiar hum of the machines housed with me. I worried about Ash, and I avoided the tray of food, pretending like it was not even there.

Thinking of Ash occupied the majority of my time.

I felt positive that he was alive, but in what condition, I didn't know. After seeing him, it had become more apparent of how ill he had been. It wasn't serious, but it was enough to worry me, and I had no doubt in my mind that they weren't feeding him antibiotics and chicken soup. But Razi did seem intent on keeping him alive, to use him as a tool to get me to obey her wishes.

But what were her wishes? What on earth did she want from me? I was a survivor, representing the sort of ideal that she was looking for, but there had to be more of us out there, more than just a dirty, disgusting, confused eighteen-year-old girl. What could I possibly provide for them? I was no stronger than the goons she had sent after me, and no smarter than the team of scientists and doctors she obviously had.

I couldn't take it any longer. My hunger was gnawing at me from the inside. I had experienced a lack of food in the past six months but not like this. I went with very little, but never had I gone with none at all. I grabbed the plate off the tray, knocking the fork to the floor with an astonishingly loud clatter. The food was cold, but tasted like heaven. I ignored the fork that lay on the ground beside me and dug into the food, tearing off strips of cold chicken with my fingers and stuffing it in my mouth.

When I had nearly licked the plate completely clean, I set it on the floor, feeling a pain in my stomach. I knew it was in part because I had eaten entirely way too much way too fast, but I also knew a part of it was guilt. I had not even lasted a few hours. Who knew what was in that food?

I drifted in and out of dreamless sleep, not bothering to stand up and return to the chair. The ground was cold, hard and uncomfortable beneath me, but I barely registered this through my exhaustion. I kept imagining the sound of footsteps just outside the door, but when I crept over, there was nothing, and I started to wonder if I was going insane from being alone.

Time passed. I didn't know how long. It could have been hours or days. The only sign of life besides me was the delivery of food. I never saw it appear. I would fall asleep, my head rested against the tile in the shower, or lying across the smooth counter top, and when I would wake, a new tray would be there, ready with a new meal for me.

I gave up on the idea of avoiding food. I was hungry, and the taste of real food, the first real food I'd had in so long, was too much. My body was growing used to it and would growl audibly each time a new meal was delivered. I would consume it fast, stuffing the food in my mouth before I could really think about what I was doing. After the deed was done, I would be filled with an overwhelming wave of guilt and would retreat back to my corner, my knees curled up to my chest.

A week must have passed, maybe longer, when someone finally came into my room. I was dozing only half conscious when the lights in my room came on fully and I jerked up, startled. The door opened slowly. A week ago, I would have run for it, pushed whoever was there out of the way and ran for my life. Now, I could only look at them, my eyes glazed. There was no energy. I was only a listless bag of bones.

There were two men, young men, probably mid to late twenties. They were both dressed in similar outfits to mine, nurses' scrubs, but theirs were pure white, and had the Sekhmet goddess stitched on the front pocket. One went immediately to the large screen, typing quickly and navigating so quickly I could hardly keep up. The other came toward me, and lifted me to my feet. I didn't fight him; I just leaned uselessly on him. My eyes met his for a moment, and I noticed that he was fairly good looking. I wanted to speak, find some sort of sympathy in his kind, brown eyes. Maybe he wanted to be here just as little as I did.

He stuck me hard, with a needle, right above my hip, and I immediately lost any sort of sympathy for him. I glared at him, but he ignored me. A strange sensation was filling my body, and I started to lose feeling in my legs. I slipped, heading toward the ground.

He caught me before I could fall and swung me up into his arms. "Damn it. I didn't really want to have to carry her all the way there," he said, his voice full of disgust.

His companion laughed. "You shouldn't have stuck her with that so early then. Besides, you're the one that volunteered to come and get her. Hoping she'll be your match, Tommy?"

Tommy looked down at me, his eyes thoughtful. "Well, she sure is pretty enough. Except for her messed up face." He laughed, tracing a finger lightly over the curve of my scar. I reached up to smack him, but my arm wouldn't move. It lay curled against my chest, useless.

The other guy, who still remained nameless to me, continued to work on the touch screen for a few more moments before we departed the room. Tommy held me in his arms as we traveled down the hallways to the elevators. I watched the numbers as we moved upward. We had been on the second floor. I stored that away for later, thought I didn't know what good it would do me. We traveled only a few floors, the doors opening up at the 5th floor.

They took me through another series of long hallways before coming to a pair of double doors. The other guy (I had taken to calling him that, like it was his name or something) pulled a keycard from a key ring on his waist and ran it through a scanner. The door automatically opened, and we went into a very large room.

The room was massive. It alternately looked like a

doctor's office and a gym. There was medical equipment everywhere, but there was also a treadmill, a stationary bike and a lap pool. There was a small group of people that looked like nurses or doctors, wearing the same uniform that Tommy and his companion wore. In the middle of them, looking quite pleased, was Dr. Razi Cylon.

Tommy carried me across the room, depositing me on the hard, paper covered medical bed. There was a tingling in my fingers and toes as whatever Tommy had injected me with started to wear off.

Razi leaned over me, examining me from head to toe with her careful eyes. "Did you inject her already?"

"Yes, ma'am," Tommy said. "I was going to wait but given her tendency to fight, I thought it best to do it when she was cooperative."

Razi nodded. "That's perfectly adequate, Mr. Riviera. You are dismissed." Tommy and his companion nodded and exited the room. "How are you feeling?"

I opened my mouth to speak and nothing came out. It was too dry, my lips nearly welded together from the lack of use. I felt like the Tin Man from the Wizard of Oz.

Razi waved to someone, and they brought over a bottle of water. She unscrewed the cap and handed it to me.

I grabbed it and gulped down the entire thing, the plastic crinkling to nearly nothing under my palm. I wiped the corners of my mouth with the back of my hand, letting the bottle fall to the ground. "You're strangely nice for a kidnapper," I croaked finally.

She sighed, her shoulders rising up and down delicately.

"I am not a kidnapper. Soon you will understand that I am only trying to help."

"You locked me in a room for days," I remarked, running a hand through my disgusting hair. I hadn't bothered to use the shower in the room, afraid that they would be able to see me through the camera. "I don't see how that's trying to help."

"I was…" she paused, mulling over the words, "preoccupied and could not come to you sooner. That won't happen again. You are very important to me and to everyone here at Sekhmet."

I looked around and saw that she was not lying. There was a group of five adults in the room with us, the nurses or doctors I had noticed before, and they each had their own expression of eagerness on their faces. I shook my head. "Why? Surely you have managed to track down other survivors."

Razi laughed, and the other doctors were a beat behind her. "Well, of course we have. But you are special to us." I opened my mouth, but she cut me off. "You will find out in due course, I promise you this." She stood up, offering me a hand.

I stared at her hand with disgust and kept my hands folded in my lap, clenched tightly together. I would not punch her again, not now, not when the game was so obviously in her favor.

She raised an eyebrow at me. "It would do you quite well to cooperate." She held out her hand once more, and this time I took it, allowing her to lead me across the room.

The doctors tittered around me, helping me to lift off

my scrubs and replacing them with a hospital gown. I felt a dark flush go through me, at these strangers seeing me in my underwear, especially my dirty underwear, but it didn't seem to register on their faces. I might as well have been a golden retriever in a vet's office.

They took my weight and measured my height. I gaped at the numbers at the scale; I had lost a considerable amount of weight since leaving New York. I ran my hands over my body, feeling more bones than I ever had before. My hands cupped my breasts and I sighed. Even now they remained a ridiculously large size.

They poked and prodded me, taking my temperature and my blood pressure. They looked in my ears, up my nose, down my mouth and made me take a vision test. One doctor took blood, missing the vein in my arm several times before finally securing the needle. Another doctor conducted a full reproductive exam, including setting up my feet in stirrups. I ignored the flames that were licking at my cheeks, and stared at the ceiling, hoping that it would all be over soon.

They even made me pee in a cup—right in front of them.

After they examined me to their satisfaction, they helped me back into the clothes I was wearing before and took me over to the gym equipment. I was told to lift weights, touch my toes, and bend in all sorts of ways while they wrote on their clipboards. I was in another place, going through the motions as they guided me through. I didn't feel present; I didn't feel real.

"Get on the treadmill," one of the doctors said, pressing

a few buttons on the console. I hesitated, and he glared at me, casting a glance over at Razi, who was sitting in a chair, watching with careful eyes.

I climbed up on the treadmill, my hands sliding over the smooth rails. My legs were like jelly, and I didn't know how they expected me to run.

He started me off at a slow speed, more of a crawl, and I took careful steps forward as the conveyor belt moved, my hands locked on the handrails. He watched as I did so, making little notes on his clipboard. I wanted to grab it and crack it over his head, but I continued walking. Every few minutes or so, he would increase the speed until I finally was at a steady run.

My heart was pounding in my chest, and I could feel a stitch in my side, but the sight of all these quiet, watchful adults terrified me, and I kept the pace, focused on the bright red numbers on the console in front of me. A mile passed, then two and then three, and I wondered when he would make me stop. I was tired, oh so tired, and I didn't want to do it anymore.

Miraculously, right before I hit the four-mile mark, he decreased the speed tremendously, and I spent the remainder of it walking slowly on my wobbly legs. The conveyor belt came to a rest, and I nearly collapsed.

"That is enough," Razi spoke, her loud voice carrying across the large room. "Bring her back over to me."

The doctor grabbed my arm roughly and pulled me across the room to Razi, depositing me in a chair in front of her. I collapsed in it gratefully. I watched as she flipped her way through the clipboards they had handed her, nodding and shaking her head at whatever she read there.

Finally, she looked at me, an encouraging smile on her face. "I have a very important question for you, Zoey, and I need you to answer as honestly as you possibly can. It is vital."

I didn't answer, and she took that as acquiesce.

"Zoey, when was your last menstrual cycle?"

I opened my mouth to reply and then immediately shut it. I hadn't thought about that in so long, months. It wasn't the first thing on my mind. Surviving, having enough to eat, training to be able to fight the Awakened were all things that had been more important to me. How had I not noticed? "Um, December? I think December?"

"Right around the first attacks?" she supplied and I nodded, wrinkling my brow, confused. I was steady, on a perfect 28-day cycle ever since I was fourteen years old.

Razi noticed my confused look as she made notes on the clipboard in front of her. "It's not surprising given the circumstances. I would imagine that you have not eaten well in the past months, and I have no doubt that you've been under high levels of stress."

"You could say that," I muttered under my breath, rolling my eyes.

She ignored me. "Often times, a women will stop ovulating and skip periods because of changes in the body. An abrupt change in diet, an emotional upheaval, massive amounts of stress are all examples of what would cause your period to stop." She paused, her pen poised on the paper.

"There is no chance of you being pregnant, is there? I will not be getting that surprise when your test results come back?"

I couldn't help it. I laughed. "Definitely not."

She nodded, satisfied. "You're healthy, incredibly so, given the circumstances. So many of the survivors we've managed to track down aren't nearly as healthy and vital as you. You have a strong body. You will do well for us."

I smirked. I couldn't help it. I was scared, tired, hungry again and still thirsty. Sarcasm was my last refuge. "What am I going to be doing? Manual labor? Literally building the utopia?"

Razi smiled, oblivious to my sarcasm and attitude. "You are going to be much more important to us than that, Miss Valentine. You are very precious to us." He turned to her lackeys. "Let's get her started on an exercise program. I want vitamins added to her diet and a healthy amount of liquids. I want her to be ready and fertile, soon."

I shot up in my seat, looking at her with surprise. "Excuse me? Fertile?"

Her smile grew even wider. "We've managed to bring in so many women to Sekhmet, but so many of them have been older, no use to use where we really need it. Finding you, Zoey, so young and healthy and full of vitality, was a godsend."

It dawned on me suddenly, why I was so important above the rest. I was young, untouched and unblemished by the effects of aging. Sure, I had scars but those weren't genetic. I was fairly healthy and was just stock full of exactly what they needed to build a new race. I could give them new lives, new people to breed to their ideals. I felt sick to my stomach.

"You're going to use me to build your perfect race," I spat out, repulsed at the thought of someone touching me. My thoughts flashed to Ash, and I felt a pang go through my chest.

"We hope to find more young girls like yourself soon," she said, shrugging her shoulders. "I would not want the burden to fall too heavily on your shoulders. But, yes, we want you pregnant and soon."

"You're disgusting. You're horrible, vile, wretched, and I hate you!" I spat out at her, standing up. Hands immediately grabbed at me, but Razi looked bored.

"Take her back to her room," she said, dismissing me, "her new room."

They dragged me, kicking and screaming, back to the second floor. They didn't take me back to my first room; instead they took me to a new one. I was practically thrown in the room. I tripped, crashing to me knees on the ground. I turned to run back at them, but they slammed the door in my face. I was alone again.

CHAPTER
TWENTY-EIGHT

MY NEW ROOM HAD A CLOCK.

It wasn't the only thing in the room, but it was the thing in the room that I hated the most. It hung high above the door. I immediately went to grab a chair, to tear it down from the wall so I wouldn't have to agonize over time passing but it was a no go. The chair, along with the rest of the furniture, was bolted to the ground.

My new room felt like a hotel room, much more comfortable than the room I had before. This one had a bed, at least a full size, with a thick gray comforter and two comfortable pillows. There was a separate bathroom, equipped with a sink, toilet and shower. There was a desk, though I wasn't sure what I would need it for. There was also a dresser, full of clothes identical to the ones I was already wearing, including clean underwear. I lifted them out, feeling the soft fabric under my fingers. They weren't anything that you would find on a rack at Victoria's Secret or anything, but it was definitely better than the ones I was currently wearing.

Directly across from the bed was the entrance to the bathroom, complete with a sink, toilet and shower. I ran a hand through my greasy, tangled hair and reached for the knob. I was shocked when a blast of hot water came bursting out of the showerhead. I peeled my clothes off leaving them in a pile on the floor and stepped into the shower, pulling the door closed behind me.

After I showered, I went back into the room with a towel wrapped tightly around me. I stared at the clothing in the drawers, wishing that I had anything else to put on except those. I stared at them for a long time before caving in and slipping into a brand new pair of underwear, clean pair of socks, a bra and a dark green scrub like shirt and baggy brown pants. I felt like a tree.

I climbed into the bed, not bothering to pull the covers down. I lay on my back, staring up at the ceiling. I noticed a small black globe above me and swallowed hard. I didn't even want to know what that camera was for. I drifted to sleep, my eyes glued to the camera that was sure to have someone monitoring me.

I woke up the next morning (or at least, I thought it was morning) when I heard a loud pounding on the door to my room. I sat up quickly, my hand immediately going to my hair. It was still damp and stuck up in random places, and I yawned. The loud knocking sounded through the room again, and I felt a wave of irritation roll through me. Was the knocking really necessary at this point?

"What?" I grumbled.

The door swung open, and the nurse from the day before, Tommy, came in, this time without his companion. He wheeled a tray in front of him. I looked at it and saw the familiar silver gleam of the dome that covered a meal. He rolled it over to the bed and lifted the cover without any flourish. Underneath was a simple breakfast of oatmeal, eggs, orange juice and toast. I looked up at him, raising my eyebrows.

"You're not leaving the room until you eat, so I would suggest you eat," he answered, sitting in the chair in front of the desk.

"I'm not exactly inclined to leave the room, so that's kind of an empty threat," I said, folding my arms across my chest, refusing to acknowledge the loud grumbling that was coming from my stomach.

Tommy smirked. "You're a feisty one, aren't you? You're lucky you're young and at a great breeding age, or Dr. Cylon wouldn't put up with this."

"Ah, yes," I said, ignoring the way my heart beat frantically in my chest. I was not a cow. I was not a pig. I was a person, and I wasn't going to be sent in for breeding. "My whole purpose for being here. I'm still not going to eat."

"You will if you want your little friend to stay alive," he said. His voice was casual, like he was merely commenting on the weather and not the life of an actual human being.

He had given me some information though: Ash was alive.

Or they could be totally pretending he was alive in order to get me to do what they wanted. I had to believe he was alive. I had to do whatever I could to keep him alive.

I lifted the fork and dug into the eggs. They were sunny side up, and I grimaced. Not my favorite but my stomach gurgled happily. Tommy relaxed, and we remained in silence as I finished up most of the breakfast. I gulped down the orange juice and set the cup down on the tray. Everything was plastic, I noted. I sighed. They weren't stupid enough to stick a real knife in my hand, or a glass that I could break and use as…well, some sort of a weapon.

"Happy?" I asked.

"Let's go," he said, standing up and reaching for me. I leaned backward, away from his touch, and he glared at me. "It really would make your life so much easier if you didn't fight me on this."

"Where are we going?" I said, continuing to lean away from him.

He smiled, and a flash of perfect, white teeth blinded me. He was incredibly handsome, so much that he would have stopped me in my tracks had I seen him walking down the streets. Despite this though, I felt no attraction at all. I didn't feel revulsion or hatred toward him either. I felt nothing. Absolutely nothing.

Before I could even think to stop him, a pair of silver, gleaming cuffs were wrapped tightly around my wrists, bind them together. I looked up at him, feeling a flutter in the pit of my stomach. They felt heavy against the pale, thinness of my wrists, and I swallowed hard. "Really? Handcuffs?" I asked, trying to keep the anxiety from rising in my voice. "There's a compliment in there somewhere."

Tommy grabbed me roughly, pulling me through the door. He guided me down a short hallway which came to an end at a crossroads. He took the left hallway, and we made our way into an elevator. It was quiet, barely making a sound as we moved up a few floors. I made a mental note that I was on the seventh floor.

The elevator was small; only a couple more people would have been able to fit inside with the two of us. It was mirrored, and I caught myself staring at my reflection. It had felt like ages since I had looked at myself in the mirror. I was smaller, thinner. My cheekbones stood out in my pale skin, something I was not used to. I had always had a dark olive tone, courtesy of my dad's Italian background, but it was all but a memory. The scar across my face was pink and raised, so obviously marring the beauty that I once believed I had.

The shirt I was wearing billowed around me, tight across the chest, as usual, but much roomier everywhere else. I pressed a palm to my ribcage and winced at the hard bones I felt there. I felt so tired, and I looked it too.

The elevator doors slid open almost silently, and Tommy directed me down another few hallways before sliding a thin black card, credit card sized, through a slot, taking us into a small room. It was simply furnished; there was a wooden table in the middle, with sturdy chairs placed around it. A bookshelf was in the corner, stocked full of books, though I could not see the titles from where I stood. There was also a flat screen TV. I stared at it for a moment wondering what would happen if I turned it on. Surely, there were no television stations left to broadcast anything.

Tommy forced me into a chair, and I started to glare up at him when he leaned over and removed the handcuffs from my wrists. I rubbed them, feeling the absence, and sat back in the chair. I watched as he went over to a panel on the wall, something I had missed before, and pressed a few selections on the screen before turning and walking out of the room. He spared not a single glance back at me.

I sighed, pressing my palms tight against my eyes. I wanted to lie across the smooth cold surface of the table, fall asleep and possibly never wake up. The books that were sitting neatly on the shelves seemed to be calling my name, but I couldn't muster up the energy to get up and look. I scanned the ceiling for the familiar black globe that told me they were watching and wasn't shocked. I had no doubt that there was someone watching my every move. I leaned back in my chair, feeling like I was being put through some sort of test.

I was just about to give up and either grab a book or turn on the television when the door swung open and Tommy returned. I opened my mouth to say something but felt the words catch in my throat as someone came into the room behind him.

He didn't look much different than the last time I had seen him, except that he had the same tired look that I did, the look of defeat, the look of constant survival. His sandy blond hair had grown a bit and was just touching the collar of his shirt. He had thinned out a bit as well, and I could see that the pants he wore were slung low on his hips, barely held up. Green eyes met brown, and the corner of his mouth twitched, just slightly.

"Zoey," he said simply. His southern accent was still there, thick, drawling and almost comforting.

"Liam," I answered in shock. There was a part of me that was compelled to get up, run to him and throw my arms around him but it was as if my body had a mind of its own, and I stayed glued to the hardwood chair.

Tommy glanced between us, his eyebrow raised. "You two already know each other?"

Liam looked back at him, a barely concealed look of contempt on his face. "You could say that."

Tommy didn't show any sign of noticing Liam's negativity. "Well, this might make your job a whole lot easier." He stared at me for a beat, studying me; I felt a blush creep onto my face and looked away. "Okay, um, enjoy yourself." He left the room.

Liam and I studied each other for a long moment before he crossed the small room and sat in the chair across from. "Zoey," he repeated.

"Liam." I couldn't believe that he was sitting in front of me. Of all the people in the world, he was the last person I expected to be sitting in a seat across from me. I remembered the way he had made me feel all those months ago and knew it had been nothing, absolutely nothing, when compared to the overwhelming way I felt for Ash. My heart clenched at the thought of him, and my hands circled in tight fists, my fingernails biting in the soft flesh of my palms.

"I can't believe you're here," he said, leaning back in his chair and staring at me.

"I can't believe *you're* here," I said, shaking my head. "You're literally the last person I ever expected to see here…or anywhere really. I thought you were on your way to Sanctuary."

"I thought you didn't believe in that," Liam said, his mouth curling up in a smile. It was not as strong as it once was, but it still made me feel like smiling myself.

I traced the patterns of wood on the table with my fingertip. "I don't know what I believe anymore."

Liam stayed quiet for a long while before speaking again. "We were making our way out to Sanctuary, camping out before we made the last trek out to Mesa Verde when we were ambushed by Awakened. A group of men came out of nowhere and helped us take them down. My dad thought they were from Sanctuary and was ready to trust them, but…but I knew something was wrong."

"Are Memphis and Julia here too?"

He shook his head. "I told them to go, run. They weren't happy about it, but once the men started pulling syringes out of their pockets, I made them. The men didn't seem so keen on catching up with Mom and Dad. Makes sense now though."

"What do you mean?" I asked.

"Haven't they told you why they were so excited to find you? This whole place was buzzing when you came in,"

Liam said, the sarcasm spilling from his voice.

I felt a flush fill my cheeks again at the though. Everyone in this place knew about me when I was brought in, and they knew exactly why. "Right. I guess Memphis and Julia aren't exactly at the child-bearing age." I stopped. "Wait, why did the put us together? Why…"

"Think about it, Zoey," Liam said, his arms folded tight across his chest. His arms were so much thinner than the last time I saw them, and I felt an uncomfortable twitch in my stomach at the sight of the translucent tone of his skin.

It took me a moment to process what he was saying. Everything was moving so slowly. Then it sunk in, and I felt the flush on my face deepen, threatening to set my face on fire. "They want you…and I…they want us to…" I couldn't even get the words out. "Oh god."

"At twenty-four years old, I'm a perfect age to become a father, at my peak," Liam said. "Their words, not mine. All they needed was someone for me to 'mate' with." His words were dripping with disgust. I wrapped my arms tightly around myself. "There are plenty of women here around my age, but they aren't qualified to be mothers, I guess. They have their own jobs in this crazy place."

"I'm guessing Razi filled you in about her crazy idea," I said, feeling like I was about to lose my breakfast at any moment.

"Of course," he said, his accent even more prominent than before. "They were all so excited when I was brought in, though not nearly as excited as when you were found."

"So we're the Sekhemet Adam and Eve," I said, trying

to keep my voice light. My hands were shaking in my lap. My eyes met his and he nodded. "Oh god."

"Not exactly the response that I was hoping for," Liam said, lightly.

I winced. Liam was attractive, more than attractive. He was exactly the kind of boy that Madison and I would have drooled over and teased each other about at late night sleepovers. He was beautiful, and at least I knew him. But he wasn't... "Do you actually want to be part of this plan?"

"God, of course not, Zoey," Liam answered angrily. His hands hit the table with a loud smack, and I jumped. The sound echoed through the cold, empty room, lingering. "Do you think I wanted to be locked in some room all day, experimented on and prepped to repopulate the world that Razi destroyed? I don't want to be forced to do things like this. I don't want you to be forced to do something like this, but I don't see that we have much of a choice. And at least I would take care of you. At least I care about you. You could have gotten off much worse. We both could have."

I flinched at the harsh sound of his voice. It was so different, a stark contrast to the light tones that I had been used to for months while living with Ash and my mother. "That's not what I meant."

Silence filled the room for a long moment, and my eyes fell to my clenched hands in my lap. They seemed to be the one thing that hadn't changed since the Awakened had changed everything in my life. They were rough, calloused, scarred, but they had been like that ever since I had learned to fight. Nothing about them seemed girly or feminine, but they were familiar, and right now, they were shaking like crazy.

"I know that's not what you meant," Liam finally spoke, his voice light and low, "but you can't imagine the relief I felt when I realized it was you. Everything about this sucks, and there's nothing I can do to change it, but if I have to do this, if I have to go through with this, at least it's with you. You're beautiful, Zoey, and you made such an impression on me, in such a short amount of time."

My fingers twisted the hem of my shirt into knots. I felt a sort of comfort at the sound of his words, and my hand went consciously to the raised scar across my face. It was hard for me to remember that I had once felt beautiful, that I had been so sure of myself. The wound across my face had taken all of that away. "Liam, it's just that..."

"How did you get here, Zoey?" Liam interrupted. "What happened to your dad? And...the other guy that was with you? Are they here?"

A lump formed in my throat, and I choked on the words. "My dad...he...he's not..." I took a deep breath. "He's dead. He died about six months ago."

"Six months ago?" Liam spoke softly. "I'm so sorry, Zoey."

I shook my head. "Thank you."

"Where have you been this entire time?" Liam asked. He hesitated for a moment and then stood up, moving around the table to sit in the chair that was closer to me. "Did you make it to your mother's?"

I nodded. "It didn't work out there. We left, and we were going to find Sanctuary. I still don't know if it exists, but I had to believe in something. I had to go somewhere. That's when we were taken."

Liam scooted closer to me, and my body relaxed at the warmth that was emitting from him. His arm came around my shoulders, and I let him pull me closer. I needed the comfort; I craved it. "Who? Who was taken?"

"Me," I said, my head leaning against his chest. "Me and Ash." Ash. I felt tears well up in my eyes, but I refused to let them fall, not now, not with them watching on the cameras.

His arm tightened around me. "Ah," he said, his voice full of understanding. "Ash. Are you and he…"

My head bobbed around in a sort of nod and shaking my head gesture. I shrugged. "I don't know. I think so. I know I…" The words refused to leave my lips. "I know how I feel, and I think I know how he feels."

Liam pulled away, catching my gaze in his. "I don't understand. Where is he? Did he die too?"

I hiccupped. "No. No, he's…he's okay. He has to be okay. He's sick, so he's not good enough for me." Liam's eyes grew wide and I shook my head again. "No, not like that. He has a cough or something, but apparently that's all it takes to be completely wrong for Razi's world. I don't know where he is. They say he's alive, but I don't know."

"Zoey…" Liam started to say but I cut him off.

"What of the outside world?" I asked. "I've seen nobody, heard nothing. I felt like we were the only ones left for so long."

Liam looked pained for a moment. "We, my parents

and I, encountered a lot on our journey over here. We went north and tried to find some family, but they were gone, whether they were scared away by the bombs or the virus, we didn't know. So we kept traveling."

He continued to speak, but his words came out harsher, louder, full of desperate anger. "The world is fucked up, Zoey. There's nothing left. They bombed the major cities and then continued to bomb. There's nuclear waste everywhere; the country is barely livable anymore. The army took over and just kept killing. Awakened or human, they weren't taking any chances. There's not much left out there. No one really knows who is in charge, and it's just a disaster. People have gone underground."

I swallowed hard. "And the rest of the world?"

"No one knows," he admitted. "Or if they know, they aren't telling. She probably knows." He tossed a scathing look at the camera fixed above our head, and I knew who the "she" was. It was not hard to guess. "We've been on our own."

"Perfect," I said, slumping back in my chair. "We're stuck."

"Zoey, come here," Liam said, leaning toward me. My mouth fell open in shock, as his hand wrapped around my neck. I was frozen solid. His lips fell on my ear, and his other hand reached for my hair. "Don't move."

"What are you doing?" I asked, trying to pull away.

"Shh," he said, softly, holding me in place. "They're not going to let us out of the room unless we give them what they want." He paused. "Everything is going to be okay. I promise." I didn't answer, though I felt weirdly reassured by his words. "Okay?"

I nodded, feeling the coolness of his breath on my cheek. "Okay," I said back.

He pulled back, just a few inches, biting his lip. His eyes raised to the camera that was just above us. "Forgive me for this." He pressed his lips tightly on mine, and I resisted the urge to push him away. His lips were soft against mine, and I felt myself responding for a moment before pulling away.

"Stop," I said, harshly. "No." I held my hands out in front of him. "Don't. Don't do that again."

He had a look of sadness on his face. "If you want to survive, Zoey, it has to happen again."

At the sound of his words, the door opened, and a nurse that wasn't Tommy stepped into the room. He came straight for me, placed the handcuffs back on my wrists and escorted me out of the room. I struggled to look behind me.

The nurse laughed at me, the sound vibrating through my body. "Don't worry. You'll see your boyfriend soon enough."

I felt the anger boil up inside me, too hot and too wild to even think about controlling. The handcuffs may have hindered my arms, but I wasn't helpless because of them. My left foot came out in a harsh kick against his leg. He cried out as he stumbled into the wall. He turned to me, arms out, and I aimed another kick at him.

He ducked, and my kick went flying past him. I growled in frustration, hating that my hands were bound, hating that this threw off my entire balance. I put my arms out and pushed him as he came closer to me, ready to kick him once more. I was stopped before I could make contact. A large hand landed on my arm just above my elbow, and I was yanked backward.

"Has no one learned anything about this girl yet?" a clipped voice said. I raised my eyes and met the dark, cold and calculating eyes of Dr. Cylon. "Her feet should be bound as well."

The nurse looked appropriately chastened, rubbing the spot on his leg where I had made contact. "Yes, ma'am," he finally said, after a few moments of uncomfortable silence.

She nodded. Dr. Cylon looked irritated, but she was doing a fantastic job at keeping it from seeping into her voice. "You're dismissed." He dipped his head and turned on his heel, making his way quickly down the hallway.

My arm throbbed under the strong grip of the hand that held me in place. I glared up at the man, one of the goons that I had met the night they had taken Ash, but he stared off into space, looking bored. He pulled on my arm and started to drag me down the hallway.

Dr. Cylon followed us, her heels clicking on the cool tile floor as we hurried away. "Do not make this harder on yourself, Zoey. You'll do better to accept your role here at Sekhmet."

I didn't answer her. I kept my eyes drawn to the speckled pattern on the floor, refusing to look up at her, refusing to acknowledge her at all.

"Very well," she answered, sounding disappointed. "Take her back to her room."

CHAPTER

TWENTY-NINE

MY TIME AT SEKHMET WAS growing longer and longer, as days turned into weeks.

It was the same schedule every day. I woke up to a loud pounding on the door, which was usually Tommy coming to bring my breakfast. After breakfast, I was taken back to the room where I had been examined before. I would run on the treadmill, be put through several other exercises and examined some more. It was almost a shorter version of what they had originally done. I went through it as if on autopilot, ignoring the hush of voices that were all around me as I ran or lifted weights or stood on the scale.

I was gaining weight, getting stronger. Even though I took every opportunity to be as unwilling and uncooperative as possible, they took care of me, making me believe that I really was as important to them as they had made it out to be. I was fed well, three meals a day. If I had a particularly good day, though I wasn't sure what I did to make it so, I was rewarded with dessert, usually something simple like chocolate pudding or fat red strawberries. I hate eating the food, hate taking anything from them, but hunger won out, and I consumed everything they brought me.

After lunchtime, I would be brought back to the small room, where Liam would meet me. I didn't know what they hoped to accomplish from that. Perhaps it was some sort of sick version of dating, where we were forced to spend time together, in order to make it easier when we...when we...did what we were there for. Most of the time, we just talked, talked about our lives before the virus and the Awakened. We talked about Ash and Liam's fiancée, Cathy. Often times, I would fall asleep in my chair, and Liam let me, choosing to the read books that lay on the shelf in the corner of the room.

Some days, I let Liam kiss me. Those days were the ones where I tended to get a smile from Dr. Cylon, who often accompanied me on my walks from my room to other parts of the compound. Other days, flashes of Ash's face made me sick to my stomach, and I couldn't even stand the sight of Liam in front of me, especially when he looked hurt. It wasn't his fault that we were in this situation, but I couldn't make myself care for him that way. I couldn't make myself give it up to him.

After my "dates" with Liam, they would take me back to my room, where dinner would be waiting for me. I usually took that time to take a shower and then stare at the ceiling, my eyes glued to the camera that was mounted there. All the thoughts and worries and anxieties that I hid during the day usually came pouring out at this moment, and I usually blinked back tears while trying to remain as stoic and hard for the cameras as possible.

It was the same thing every single day. Every day. They became a blur of monotony and boredom, and I lost track of how many days had passed. I kept thinking of Ash, somewhere else in this compound, or so I hoped. I hoped with everything that was left in me that he was still alive.

One of the Sekhmet doctors pried my legs apart, and I sighed, focusing on the goddess on the ceiling, refusing to be a part of this experience at all. Every day, every single stupid day, I was forced through this stupid exam. I didn't know what they expected to find. I was watched all the time, every moment of every day, and they would know immediately if something had happened between Liam and me.

Maybe it was better if Ash wasn't alive.

I shook my head and went through the motions of the exam, relieved when it was over and I was escorted back to my room.

Lunch sat on a tray on the desk when I was let back into my room.

"You have one hour," Tommy warned, using a small key to unlock the handcuffs that were around my wrists and ankles. They seemed so unnecessary now. There wasn't much fight left in me anymore.

I nodded, sliding into the desk chair and lifting the cover off the tray. I hesitated, as Tommy started to make my way out of the room. "Tommy?"

He spun around, his eyes focusing on me sharply. I didn't blame him. I never addressed him directly, and I had certainly never called him by his name. "What?" he said. His voice was softer than I had expected, with no hint of anger. He sounded more…wary than anything else.

"How long…" my voice cracked from its lack of use. "How long have I been here?"

He stared at me for a long moment, determining the weight of my question and wondering if he should answer me. He bit his lip and then nodded to himself. "A month," he said finally.

I nodded, turning back to the desk. A turkey sandwich, complete with lettuce, tomato, onions, avocado and Swiss cheese sat on the plate, with a small side of fruit and potato salad. My stomach rumbled at the sight of it. "I'm nineteen," I said, softly. "I turned nineteen. I missed my birthday." It seemed silly to be thinking of a thing like birthdays right now, but it was true. Sometime in the past month, in my time here at Sekhmet, I had turned a year older.

There was a sharp intake of breath behind me, but by the time I turned around, he was gone, the door slamming shut behind him. I heard the lock turn and then the soft sound of footsteps as he left.

True to his word, he was back an hour later. He looked different, his posture was lazier than before and his eyes refused to meet mine.

I was sitting on the bed staring at my hands when he'd

returned. I stood up and held my hands out to him, ready for the heavy manacles to go around my wrist. When the familiar cool metal didn't come, I looked up at him, confused.

"You're staying in your room today," he explained quickly. He still refused to meet my eyes and I frowned. He stepped aside as the door opened once more.

I felt a large pit in my stomach as Liam came through the door, with the other nurse, Patrick. Patrick unlocked Liam's handcuffs and smirked at the two of us. "You two have fun now," he said, amusement coloring his voice. He grabbed Tommy's arm. "Come on, let's go."

"Yeah. Right," Tommy said, his voice low. He looked up, and our eyes met for the first time. I leaned back, away from him. There was something there that hadn't been before. Before, there had been nothing in Tommy's eyes. This was his job. Now there was emotion there, and I couldn't even place a name to it. I turned away, not wanting to see this, and didn't look up until the door had slammed shut behind them.

"Zoey."

I looked at Liam, my heart pounding in my chest, aware of the silence in the room, aware of he large bed that stood just feet away from the two of us. My eyes flew up to the camera up above us and I flinched, almost imperceptibly. "I suppose it's time then," I said, surprised at the way my voice stayed even and strong.

He came over to me and took me in his arms, hugging me tightly. "Zoey, I'm sorry. I am so sorry."

I felt the tears streaming down my cheeks, seeping into the soft fabric of Liam's shirt as I pressed my face into his chest. My arms raised and wrapped around his waist, pulling him closer to me. "I don't want to…I don't…" I choked out the words.

His body stiffened up, and I knew that I had hurt his feelings again. This caused another fresh wave of tears to well up and spill out over my cheeks. "Oh, Liam, I'm sorry…"

Liam pulled back and raised my chin so that I was looking at him. He looked fierce and firm. "No, you have nothing to be sorry for. You never have to apologize to me."

I pulled away from him and perched on the bed, cradling my head in my hands. "I'm a virgin, Liam," I said bluntly.

The bed dipped as he sat down next to me. "I had a feeling." I looked up at him quickly, and there was a faint hint of a smile on his features. "It's not an insult, Zoey, calm down. But you really seemed against this, more so than I would expect for someone who wants to survive so badly."

I blushed and turned away from him. He reached out for me again, pulling me into his lap, and I sighed, leaning my head against his chest. I felt so tired, and the warmth of him against me felt so good and so comfortable. I felt my eyes flutter, my eyelashes scratching against the cotton of his shirt. "Thank you."

Liam nodded and pulled me in tighter. We stayed like that for a while, so long that I lost track of time and fell asleep.

I dreamt for the first time in ages. There was something about this place that kept me from entering the world of dreams. There was a part of me that had been relieved, knowing that I could lay my head down on my pillow and not enter into scary worlds. There was no one here to hold me and rock me to sleep after I woke up screaming, so I was grateful for the absence of nightmares.

But I missed real dreams, dreams of worlds outside this compound. I missed dreaming about happier times. The dream that I had while wrapped in the arms of Liam was a good dream. It was almost like it was on fast-forward, and I wanted to reach out and grab it, stop it before it could leave me.

Madison and I were on the subway, on the way to Coney Island, which was a tradition of ours. She was addicted to cotton candy and liked to eat as much as she could before running to the roller coaster and riding as many times as she could. She always made me sick just thinking about it, but it was something she just loved to do. We were squished together at the end of the car, bent over something that I couldn't see. I was smirking while Madison laughed out loud, her hand covering her open mouth. She looked beautiful, her skin a creamy white, her dark almond shaped eyes wide.

The image shifted, and I was at the baseball park, four rows behind the Mets' dugout. I had a hot dog in one hand and a soda in the other, and I was cheering loudly as a homerun went sailing out of the park. Soda sloshed down my arm as I jumped up and down, and I heard the familiar boom of laughter next to me. I turned and saw my dad, a Mets cap on his head. He high fived me and whistled loudly as the stadium exploded in cheers.

In a moment, I was on the back of my pony, Pumpkin. I must have been about six or seven, and I was absolutely terrified of him. He was gentle and calm, but that didn't stop me from having a near panic attack every time my mother tried to bring me near him. I could feel the power of his body beneath me when I sat on him, even at that age. I knew this was not something to mess with. I felt a strong hand at my back and looked down at my mother. She was smiling at me, speaking words of encouragement, and I felt a sense of relief that she was there.

My mother morphed into Ash, and I wondered if it was possible for your heart to stop beating while you were dreaming. He was smiling down at me, strong and beautiful. He looked like that Ash I had known from months before, free of the scars and the heartbreak. He leaned down toward me, his lips on mine, his hands at the hem of my shirt, pulling it over my head. He pressed me up against the wall, trailing soft kisses along my collarbone, leaving me breathless.

I woke up with a start, aching, my fingers folded in a fist, clutching Liam's shirt tightly. We were lying on the bed together, facing each other. There was a respectful amount of distance between the two of us, and I felt a gush of affection toward the boy that lay across from me. His eyes fluttered open, and I smiled at him. He smiled back and pried my fingers off his shirt.

"Are you okay?" he asked. I nodded and looked over his head to the clock that ticked incessantly above the door. I frowned. "What is it?"

"It's way past dinner time." I sat up and looked over at the desk, which was empty of its usual food tray. "Have they not come by with dinner?"

Liam shook his head slowly, his brow furrowed. "Maybe they were waiting…"

"Right," I said, interrupting him before he could continue. "Well, it's not happening tonight." My voice was firm, and Liam raised his eyebrows at me. "Come here, and give me a kiss. That'll have to be enough for them tonight."

He laughed, a real laugh, and I felt myself smile back at him. "Okay," he agreed, sitting up, his hair sticking up on one side. I leaned closer, using my fingers to flatten it down. He froze and looked down at me, and I swallowed hard.

"I'm going to have to give in soon, aren't I?" I whispered to him. "If I want to survive. If I want Ash to survive."

He didn't answer, but he didn't have to. I sighed shakily and stood on my tiptoes for a kiss. Our lips met, and I waited for him to pull away. He always seemed to know how much time was necessary for each kiss, what would keep them happy. He hadn't pulled away and I found myself responding to him, more so than I had before.

Liam's arms came up and wrapped around my waist, pulling me against him. His lips pressed harder to me, and I gasped. He pulled back and stared at me for a long moment, his eyes wide. The look in his eyes was pleading, and I found myself falling into it. My hand reached up to his chest. I felt the contours of his body as my hand traveled up his chest, across his collarbone, and came to rest at the back of his neck, where the end of his hair curled. I ran my fingers through it, and he closed his eyes, sighing.

"You're not helping, Zoey," he admitted.

I didn't answer, lifting my other hand to his arm, feeling the muscles underneath my fingertips. I traced the veins, raising the light blond hairs, and smiled slightly at the goose bumps that formed there.

"Zoey…" he warned.

I had no idea what I was doing, except that the dream was so fresh in my mind and his body was pressed right against mine, and I was responding to it. I wanted to touch him. I kissed him nearly every day, and he always kissed me softly, affectionately. He never forced me further. He saw me as a person, as Zoey the girl. Not as Zoey the Eve of Sekhmet, the girl being forced to restart the human race. I was lonely, and my entire body ached for this, ached for love and affection. My hand left his arm and came to the hem of his shirt. My fingers traveled under the hem, against the warm, hard skin of his back.

"Shit," he said, and his mouth came back down on me again. I gasped and threw myself into the kiss, my hands pressed tight against his back and neck. He kissed me long and hard, pressing his tongue against my lips until my mouth opened and our tongues battled together. I whimpered, and a growl ripped through his body. He lifted me and placed me on the bed. I looked up at him, breathing heavily. "Zoey…"

"Come here," I said, raising my arms to him. "It's okay."

His eyes closed for a moment, and then he came over to

me, his body covering mine. I arched toward him, loving the feeling of his hard body against mine. His lips found mine again and we kissed again, over and over again, our soft sighs and moans the only sound in the world.

Liam's hand came up to my shirt, tugging on the hem and I reached for his hands. He looked up at me, frozen, and I shook my head, pulling the shirt over my head myself. Our faces were both flushed, and my legs went around his waist before I could think about what I was doing.

"Oh, Zoey," he breathed, his lips grazing the soft skin of my stomach. His lips left a hot searing trail of kisses from my stomach up to my neck and back onto my lips. He moved against me and I felt the pleasure crash through me.

"Liam," I whispered, my hands reaching for his pants. His hands met mine and together, we pulled his pants off, revealing a plain pair of boxer briefs, tented up. He reached for my own pants, and they joined his on the floor. He came back on top of me, moving himself against me. We were both panting, and I yanked his face back to mine, my kisses desperate and hurried.

His fingers were at the clasp of my bra, and he easily twisted it off. It fell slightly, revealing the top moons of my breasts. He lowered his lips to them, leaving hot kisses on the skin. I felt a moan escape my lips, and my hands went to his hair, my fingers weaved in the strands, as I pulled his head tighter against me.

"Oh, Liam," I breathed, arching myself closer to him. My eyes fluttered open and closed and fell on the black globe that was affixed to the ceiling above us. My eyes widened. It was like a bucket of cold water had been dumped on me. Liam's lips were still on me, trailing down my stomach, lower and lower, toward my underwear. I felt a wave of panic shoot through me.

"Stop," I said, pulling my fingers away from his hair and pushing his shoulders. "Stop."

Liam looked surprised, and he stumbled back a bit. His face was flushed, his lips full from kissing. I looked down and saw that he was still definitely aroused. "What's wrong?" he asked, his hand against my bare hip.

I felt tears threatening to spill again, and I hated that I was in this situation, that I was practically naked and that they could see this, all of this. I hated that I was feeling this way, and with the wrong boy. "Just, stop. I don't want to do this," I said, my voice coming out breathless and rushed.

He pulled back, his face clouded. He crawled off of me, reaching for his discarded pants, and pulled them up over his hips. I could see that he was still hard and there was a part of me that was turned on by it and wanted to pull him back on the bed with me. He turned away from me, his eyes on everything else in the room, everything but me.

I reached for the blanket, pulling it over me, embarrassed at how little I wore. Without the pressure of his body against mine, the coolness of the room was more apparent and goose bumps rippled across my skin. I shivered. "Liam, I'm sorry. I'm so sorry," I said softly, my voice thick with tears.

He sighed, and I realized how exasperated and hurt he really was. "Zoey," his voice coming out like a bark, a warning.

"You're great, Liam, and I like you…I like you a lot," I said, feeling like it was not coming out right. It was coming out all wrong. "But, you're not… you're not him." My body was still tingling but it wasn't the same. What I had felt with Liam was the flame of a candle, warm and comforting. When I had kissed Ash on my kitchen counter, it had been a forest fire, threatening to burn down everything in its wake.

Liam's eyes met mine and my bottom lip trembled. He sighed again, but it wasn't angry anymore. It was more resigned. The door opened and Patrick reappeared, looking both amused and frustrated. I wondered who was behind the cameras and how much anyone had seen of what had just taken place between Liam and I. "Let's go," he snapped at Liam.

I pulled the covers up higher, trying to cover everything. "Liam…"

He was halfway out the door but he stopped and looked over at me. My words failed, getting stuck in my throat. I wasn't even sure what to say to him anymore. How many times could one person apologize?

Instead he spoke up. "It's going to be okay, Zoey. I promise." The door shut heavily behind him, and I was left alone once more.

CHAPTER
THIRTY

AS SOON AS THEY HAD left, I crawled out of my bed, refusing to look toward the ceiling. I took a long cold shower, shivering under the biting water, washing away the feel of his lips on my body. I stayed in there for at least an hour before climbing out and wrapping myself in a towel.

I lay on the floor, wrapped in my towel. I wasn't sure how long I stayed there but long enough that my hair was starting to dry, the ends curling. I picked myself off the floor and slid into some clean clothes. I spared the camera one last loathing look before crawling into bed and falling asleep.

I woke with a start in the morning, with a hand pressed tightly against my mouth. My eyes flew open in panic, and I reached for the hand, trying to pry it off. My legs kicked, and I heard a low "oof" as I made contact. The hand on my mouth loosened, and I opened my mouth to scream.

"Jesus, Zoey, shut up for a second." The voice was low, rough and full of pain. I was satisfied to know I had caused actual pain. "I'm trying to help you, okay?"

My body grew still, and I blinked in the relative darkness. I could just barely make out the features of the person perched on the bed, and for a moment, I couldn't believe my eyes. "Tommy?" I whispered.

"Yeah," he answered. His hand was pressed tightly against his stomach. "Did you have to kick so hard?"

"What the hell are you doing?" I answered, ignoring his question. I sat up, running a hand through my hair. I looked up at the camera and back down at him.

He shook his head. "It's not on. None of them are. They malfunction sometimes; it's normal, so no one will suspect I did it on purpose. It'll give us at least fifteen minutes of privacy."

Things were not making sense to me. "Why do you need…" I started, as a horrible thought occurred to me. "Oh god, please don't touch me."

He threw me a scathing look, and for some reason, I was comforted by it. It was a look I had grown used to with Tommy, and it was familiar. "Jesus, Zoey," he repeated. "I'm not going to touch you. I'm here to help you."

I stared at him warily. "Help me? Help me how?"

Tommy glanced upward at the camera and then at his watch. He sighed. "Your boy came to me, okay? He asked me to help you get out, and so that's what I'm going to do."

"You're…you're going to help me get out?" I stuttered. "But why?"

He seemed to think about it for a moment, taking time to ponder his answer. "Well, I guess…I guess because I like you."

I leaned away from him, my wariness of him growing even more. "Oh," was all I said.

I could barely see him roll his eyes in the darkness. I had just noticed that the light was on the bathroom, lending us enough light to see each other but not to cause any alarm to anyone who might pass through. "Not like that, Zoey. Not everyone is groveling at your feet."

"Shut up," was all I answered. I sat up straighter. "You're going to help me. You're going to help me get out of Sekhmet. How the hell are you going to do that?" my voice grew louder with each question, and I saw him flinch.

"Keep your voice down," he hissed at me, his arms coming out to grab my wrists. "Do you want the whole compound to hear you?"

"Sorry," I said, looking down at my wrists. His hands were huge, and wrapped around both wrists with no trouble. It was weird how I was noticing things about him now, in the darkness, that I had never known in the light, when he had escorted me everywhere, for days.

"Did anyone ever tell you that you're ridiculously loud?" he asked. He didn't make it sound like a compliment.

"You were saying about getting me out of here?" I reminded him.

His eyes flicked down to the watch at his wrist again. "Right. We're going to get you out of here. It's not going to be easy. They're watching you like crazy. I can assist, get you a keycard, that sort of thing, but a lot of it is going to be on you."

I nodded, immediately caught up in this. I hadn't even heard the plan but the direction he was going in made it sound dangerous and impossible. Dangerous and impossible sounded so much better than staying here and waiting for them to force me to have children. "Tommy, I'm ready to do anything. I don't want to be here."

He nodded again, looking nervously at his watch. "We'll talk about it when I come later to escort you to see Liam. There are cameras, but they don't pick up sound. I'll stand at the door, where the cameras won't catch me, so they won't be able to see me talking to you. We'll figure it out, okay?" He stood up, smoothing out the invisible wrinkles of his pants. "I have to go."

"Okay," I said, pulling my legs up and resting my chin on his knees. "Wait, Tommy?" He paused, looking back at me. "Liam asked you to do this?"

He nodded and, saying nothing more, left the room.

I went through the motions on autopilot, my mind stuck on the possibility of finding a way out of here. Hopefully we could figure out a way to get a keycard into my hand, and then I could be free, free to make my way to Sanctuary or anywhere that wasn't here.

A face came flashing into my brain and I stumbled, tripping on the conveyor belt of the treadmill. I fell and immediately felt it scrape my knee. The doctor surveying me immediately pressed the stop button on the treadmill, watching me carefully as I lifted myself up, shaking.

Ash. Ash was still here. I had to believe that he was still here and that this plan included him as well.

As soon as Tommy escorted me to the small room after lunch, I turned to Liam. He had beaten me to the room and I wondered if that had been done on purpose, in order to prevent Patrick from staying in the room as well. "Ash," I said firmly. "Is Ash going to get out too?"

I saw Liam and Tommy exchange knowing looks, and I felt my heart sink. "No," I said. "I won't leave without him."

Liam stood up, coming over to comfort me. I pushed his arms away, glaring up at him. "Zoey, we don't even know if he's alive."

I looked at Tommy, who looked tired. There were bags under his eyes and I wondered if he had gotten any sleep the night before. "I don't know, to be honest," he admitted. "They say he is. Dr. Cylon says he is and that we're to mention him any time you don't feel like cooperating. But no one has actually seen him in weeks, Zoey."

My head began to shake back and forth, repeatedly. "He's here. I know he is. If you're getting me out, you're getting him out too."

Leaning up against the door just out of sight of the camera, Tommy sighed, exasperated. "We're risking so much just to get you out of here. We can't risk it anymore to rescue someone we don't even know is here."

"What about Liam?" I shot back.

They exchanged another look, and Liam spoke up. "This plan is for you, Zoey. That's it."

They were both looking at me, with firm looks on their faces. I saw the pity in their eyes, and I turned away, unable to look at them. They were asking me to leave the one person that I had left in the world, who would probably be killed if I left. I suddenly felt unsure in the idea of escaping.

"Zoey," Liam warned. I looked up at him shocked; surprised that with so little time spent together, he had already begun to recognize my facial expressions. "Don't even think about it. We're getting you out of here. Maybe, if we find out more information, we can get Ash out too. But for now, we're focusing on you."

I swallowed hard, pushing down the tears that were threatening to crawl up and take over. "Fine," I agreed. I crossed the room and sat in the chair across from Liam. "What are we going to do?"

MY BREAKFAST CAME ON THE same tray that it normally did in the morning. Tommy walked into the room, setting it down on the desk. His moves were jerky and unsure, and I wanted to throw something at him. Everything about what he was doing just screamed that something was wrong. His eyes met mine, and I tried to tell him to calm down, in one look. His head dipped slightly, in a barely perspective nod.

I waited until he left the room before lifting myself off the bed and crossing to the desk. I slid into the chair and ate my breakfast slowly. Each bite felt like cardboard in my mouth, but I forced myself through it, trying to ignore the bubbling of anxiety in my stomach. I ran my fingers along the edge of the silver tray and stopped when I felt something sharp poke the tip of my finger. Just a tiny bit of hard, black plastic was poking out, and I knew immediately that the first part of the plan had been successful.

I sat in my chair, my heart beating faster in my chest, feeling the sting of the camera on my back. Before I could really think about what I was doing. I flung the tray across the room. The remaining food went flying, scattered across the perfect gray carpet. I pressed my hand to my mouth, hoping that it looked like I was crying. My other hand flew to the stomach, and I pretended to retch. I reached absently for the tray and flew to the bathroom, trying to look like I was about to be sick.

The door shut behind me, and I winced at the sound. I had no idea if anyone actually bought my performance, but there was too little time to be bothered by it. My fingernails slid along the groove of the tray and I pried it apart. Sitting there, in the middle of the broken tray, was a thin, black keycard. My fingers reached for it, trembling, knowing that if I were caught with this, it would not be good. I slipped it into my bra, hoping that it would not show through the fabric. I took a deep breath before exiting the bathroom.

Tommy had returned, and I glared at him, the tray clutched tightly to my chest. "Are you ready to go?" he asked. He had finally schooled his features into a look of indifference and was holding out the handcuffs toward me.

I threw the tray at him, and he ducked at the right moment. "No!" He looked up at me, and I nearly laughed at the expression on his face. He had been expecting the tantrum, but he clearly thought I was going a little over the top.

"Zoey, calm down," he said, his arms held out to me. "We're going to see Liam now. You're not doing your evaluations today. Don't you want to see Liam?" His voice was soft, like he was talking to a small child or even an animal. It would be the way they expected him to talk to me.

I reached for the food that had scattered on my bed and flung it at him. The food went flying past him, out the open door. My eyes stayed glued on it, and for a moment, the two of us were frozen. He shifted a bit to block the door, and I mouthed "I'm sorry" before running at him.

My fist met his gut before he could even react, and I felt only slightly bad at the power that I had put behind it. He doubled over, wheezing in pain, and I kicked out, sending him flying to the ground. I kicked once more before leaping over him and running out of the room.

The past few days, Tommy had given us the best details he could on the best escape route out of the compound. He couldn't provide us with maps, so we repeated the route over and over, until I could say it without even thinking. As soon as I ran out of the room, my mind went blank, full of anxiety and the fear of being out of the room without an escort. I blinked once, twice and then shook myself awake. I ran down the hallway and made a left. I heard footsteps and stopped, pressing myself to the wall. I dared a peek around the corner and saw no less than five or six security guards peeking into my room. Dr. Cylon was just a beat behind them, looking calm.

I heard her gasp as she entered the room, and Tommy's frantic voice carried down the hallway. "She attacked me before I could get the cuffs on her, Doctor, and she ran out in the hallway. She's heading toward the fifth floor, where the boy is."

I froze, playing over the words in my mind. Tommy had planned to make an excuse, a fake plan on where I was heading in order to give me a better head start. This was not in the plan, to mention Ash and I wondered for a moment if that was really where he was. I glanced down the hallway, where the empty stairwell waited for me. Liam and Tommy's warnings about rescuing Ash were screaming in my head, but I ignored them. I had to try. I had to, didn't I?

A shot rang out, vibrating in my ears, cutting off Tommy's explanation, and I flinched. The world was spinning, and my hands clutched the wall for support. I listened hard, waiting for Tommy's voice, but it never came.

Instead Razi spoke up, her voice echoing from my room to where I stood in the hallway. "Thank you, Mr. Riviera. That will be all," she said, and I felt the food I had just consumed rise in my throat. "Find her."

I shook my head and started running toward the stairwell, hearing the heavy footsteps behind me. I pulled out the card tucked into my bra and slid it through the pad at the door. It blinked green, and I yanked it open. I glanced around, looking for some indication of what floor I was on and saw a large number seven printed on the wall. I knew we were underground and I had to go up a couple flights to level five. My legs burned as I ran up the stairs.

I came to a halt at level five and hesitated. I knew I should keep going, stick to the plan, but every rational part of me was shutting down in favor of searching for Ash. Would it really be worth leaving the compound if I left Ash behind?

The answer came to me clearly. No, it wouldn't be worth it. I opened the door to level five and slipped into the quiet, dark hallway. I crept along the hallway, hating the slow pace I had to set. I ducked, doing my best to stay out of line of the cameras that lined the hallway.

Footsteps sounded from the hallway directly in front of me, and I froze. There was the familiar sound of harsh voices, and I looked around frantically. There was a door across the hallway from me. I crossed it, slid the card in the slot and closed the door quietly behind me.

I was in a room that looked like a storage closet, only slightly larger. There were several boxes of medical supplies and a whole wall of canned food. A small window was cut in the door to the room, and I peeked out carefully.

There were three men standing just outside the door, holding guns and looking around. They were opening the doors of the other rooms in the hallway. My heart was slamming hard in my chest, echoing in my ears. I was surprised they couldn't hear it. They were creeping closer and closer to the door that I was hiding behind, and I knew it would only be a moment before they discovered my hiding place. I looked around desperately for a way out.

A small vent was hidden in the corner room, nearly

concealed by the cans of food that were stacked to the ceiling. I spotted a step stool and carried it over to the vent. When I reached the third step, I looked at the shelves in front of me. They were sturdy, made of a strong aluminum, maybe even steel. I wasn't sure if they could take my weight but there was no time like the present to find out.

I glanced over my shoulder. The men still hadn't come to this door. I couldn't see them, which bought me a little time, but they were coming closer. I started moving cans aside, clearing space on the shelves for me to climb. When I had just enough room. I placed my hands firmly on the shelf directly in front of me and pulled myself up, climbing up the distorted ladder. I reached the top and lifted myself up to perch on the top shelf. There wasn't a ton of room between the shelf and the ceiling and I found myself crouched over.

I pushed up at the vent, relieved when it lifted easily. The open space left was just big enough for me to fit through, and I boosted myself up, crawling into the small space before slowly lowering the vent back into place, and not a moment too soon.

The men came in the door slowly, their guns raised as they surveyed the room. One reached for the switch by the wall and flipped it up; light filled the room. I flinched away from it and scooted as quietly as I could away from the slits in the vent. They moved throughout the room, peering under the shelves. I watched as one backed up into the stepstool, sending it crashing to the ground. I covered my mouth to keep myself from gasping out loud. I had completely forgotten about that.

"What was that?" one of them said, his voice coming out gruff. He sounded bored.

"Someone left out a stepstool," was the answer. He came right into my line of sight, and he looked up, and I froze. "Stupid kids. Let's go; this room is clear."

They lingered a little, thoroughly checking the room, before leaving and locking the door behind them. I let out a sigh of relief and surveyed my surroundings.

I was obviously in a ventilation system, probably the air conditioner because I was immediately cold. The hairs on my arms stood up, and I rubbed them. It was a fairly decent size system; I had just enough room to crouch down. I started to crawl away from the direction that the men had headed in, hoping to find myself in a different area.

My hands and knees started aching almost immediately as I crawled through the small, suffocating space. There were bends and turns, and I kept going, turning left or right as I saw fit. I had no idea where I was heading. I only stopped to look down through the vents that I passed on my way. I felt like a spy, someone out of an action movie and I had to bite my lip to keep myself from laughing.

I had no idea how long I'd been crawling through the ventilation system when it started to slope down. I tried going down slowly, putting pressure on my palms to keep myself from slipping down the slick metal. When it finally leveled out again, I realized that I had come to a dead end with one large vent, large enough for me to fit through. I peeked out and saw metal steps. I must have ended up in the stairwell. Again. I hesitated for a moment and then reached for the vent, pushing it out.

It landed with a loud clatter on the metal floor beneath me and I paused, my heart doing a series of flips in my chest as I waited to see if anyone had heard it. When a few uneventful moments passed, I crawled out and fitted the screen back on the vent. I walked over to the number and saw six. I had gone down one floor. I immediately started running up the stairs.

I reached level five again and found myself in a different part of the compound. This must have been a different stairwell, because I recognized nothing around me. I crept through the hallways, listening for the sound of footsteps, but this wing felt relatively abandoned. There was also a distinct lack of cameras, which both relieved me and made me feel nervous. I glanced around, wondering if there were smaller, less detectable cameras in this particular hallway.

I continued on, pausing at each door and peeking inside to look for Ash. I was so tired, and I had no idea how large this compound was, or even how large each level was. It could take me ages to track down Ash if I had to stop and peek inside each and every door.

Just as I was thinking this, I reached a fork at the end of the hallway. A sign was there, pointing in each direction. Miraculously, perfectly, unbelievably, the arrow pointing to the left had small block letters printed above it reading: Detention.

My heart burst open, and I sprinted down the hallway, not bothering to mask the hard sounds my feet made as they hit the linoleum floor. There were doors in this hallway, the same as before, but the windows had small bars across them, and each one had a small door in the center of it, about the size of a dog door. I started peeking in the windows. Empty. Empty. Empty. Empty.

Wait.

I halted and returned to the door I just passed and felt my heart leap up into my throat. There was someone in this room, the first person that I had seen, and I knew almost immediately that it was Ash. I examined the lock on the door and was relieved to find that all it required as a key card. I hadn't thought for a moment if I would have needed a fingerprint or password to get anywhere in the building. I'd had a direct route out of here planned by Liam and Tommy, and none of it included anything more than the keycard that was tucked into my bra. I yanked it out, sliding it through and watched as the light blinked from red to green. I reached for the door handle and pulled the door open.

CHAPTER
THIRTY-ONE

AS SOON AS I OPENED the door, Ash looked up and froze, his eyes wide. I wanted to rush at him, but he looked absolutely shocked to see me in front of him.

"Um, hi," I said stupidly.

He blinked a few times and stood up. He was dressed in the same clothes I had last seen him in, complete with small bloodstains on them. My fists clenched in fury. His hair was a tangled mess, and there was a dark shadow along his face. I had never seen him with facial hair before. I noticed that it made him look older, much older. There were deep purple bags beneath his eyes, and his blue eyes had lost a little of the luster that I was so used to seeing.

But he was Ash. He was alive. He was standing in front of me, alive, and I had never seen anything so perfect and incredible in my life. He was *alive*.

"Zoey?" he asked, sounding unsure of himself. I was so relieved to hear him sound so normal. There was no hint of a cough anymore.

I nodded, suddenly feeling nervous. "Yeah. Yeah, it's me."

He shook his head. "I don't understand," he said, his voice low. "Why?"

I shifted back and forth, glancing at the open door. There was a camera inside his room, which was no larger than a closet, and I knew it wouldn't be long until someone found us in here. "Well, I'm breaking out. And I came to get you. We should probably leave though. Now."

To my surprise, he looked angry. "Are you crazy?" he said, his voice rising slightly. "Zoey Valentine, what the hell were you thinking?" He stepped closer to me, his fists clenched at his side.

I flinched, backing up. "Wait…what…"

"Zoey, you had a way to get out of here, and you came here to get me? Why would you do that?"

"I…I…" I faltered, speechless in my shock. His eyes were trained on mine, and he was angry. "Ash, I…"

He cut me off, pulling me to him and crushing me in his arms. My arms came up automatically to wrap around him, and we stood like that for a moment, just holding each other. I felt myself relax for the first time in weeks, feeling safe in his arms. He pulled back and pressed his lips tightly to mine. "You're so stupid," he whispered to me.

"Thanks," I said, laughing slightly under my breath.

"You're alive, Zoey," was his reply. "You're alive."

"Yeah, I am," I said, pulling back. "But I won't be much longer if we don't go. Now."

"Right," he said, and he was back to business. I grabbed his hand and started pulling him out the door and into the hallway. "Do you have a plan to get out of here?"

I glanced over my shoulder at him as we made our way back to the stairwell. "Mostly."

"Mostly," he scoffed, but he continued to follow me. I pushed the door open to the stairs and was immediately met with a gun in my face. The three men that had chased me to this level were standing in front of me.

"Run!" I screamed, and we both turned around and went tearing through the hallways. I followed Ash as he weaved his way, turning left then right and then left again. We had no destination, and I could hear the hard fall of boots against the floor just right behind us. I felt a pain in my side, and I remembered that I hadn't really eaten today, and I was feeling it.

"Come on, Zoey, come on, baby," he yelled back to me as we sprinted down a long corridor.

"Wait," I said, looking around me. I recognized the hallways that I had come in earlier and knew there was another stairwell just around the corner. I ran past Ash and found it. I reached for the handle, praying that there would be no one behind it.

The stairwell was open, but it wouldn't be for long. "Come on," I said to Ash, and we started running up the stairs. I could see the strain in Ash's face, and I felt it in my own body. Even all the running I had done on the treadmill the past few weeks hadn't prepared me for this. There was a difference between running on a treadmill, not going anywhere, and running up the stairs, your heart pounding in fear as you ran for your life.

"Here," I told him, as we reached a door that read the letters "AG."

"What does that mean?" Ash panted, indicating the AG.

"Tommy said it was the above ground level, the only one that's above ground. It houses all the vehicles that Sekhmet keeps," I explained, my voice lowered. I raised myself on the tips of my toes to peek out the window and saw the level looked abandoned. Tommy had explained that most vehicles were used at night, where they had the cover of darkness as an advantage. The vehicles sat unused during the day, perfect for stealing a car, not so perfect for getting away. "Okay, let's go."

"Tommy?" Ash asked, his eyebrows rose as we made our way down a long hallway that led to a door.

"It's a long story," I said. I reached up to brush a loose lock of hair out of his face, and he reached up to grab my hand. He pressed his lips against the soft skin of my palm, and I felt a shiver go through me, and I turned away to swipe the keycard at the door.

It opened up into a large room, like an airplane hangar, and it was no wonder. There were lots of cars in there tucked to the side, more cars than I could begin to count. There were at least three helicopters and two small planes, one of them a large 747. I stopped underneath, wishing that I could fly. That would be a perfect getaway. I shook my head and turned away.

"There they are!" Voices rang out across the vast room, echoing off the walls.

"Oh my god," I said, immediately running toward one of the vehicles. "Let's go."

Shots rang out behind us, and I kept running, running faster than I ever had before. These were not Awakened. Awakened had to catch up to me in order to hurt me. These guys could hurt me from much further away.

Ash stumbled, rolling into a somersault and landing hard on his stomach. I skidded to a stop and reached for him, helping him to his feet. He gasped, his eyes squeezed shut in pain before he continued to run beside me. We ducked in between planes and helicopters, making our way over to the cars that lined the furthest wall.

Ash was right at my heels, and I could tell he was limping from his fall. We reached the cars, and I started counting, one, two, three, four. There was a small SUV there, the exact one that I was supposed to be looking for. I yanked the door open and threw myself into the driver's seat. He fumbled, surprised, and moved to the passenger door and lifted himself into the seat.

"Why the hell are these open?" Ash said, gasping, immediately pushing the lock button on the door.

"Please save all questions for the end of the tour," I said, reaching for the keys Tommy said would be tucked into the visor. Sure enough, there was a slick silver key, and I stuck it in the ignition and turned; the engine flared to life. I glanced over at Ash and saw that his eyes were wide.

"What the fuck?" he said. His words were coming out in gasps, and his hand was clutched tightly over his stomach. I felt my stomach drop, wondering if he had somehow hurt himself when he had fallen.

"They're very trusting at Sekhmet, apparently," I said, wryly. "Too trusting. It works for us though. Get the guns."

He raised an eyebrow. "Excuse me?"

"Under the seat," I said, reaching down to put the car in gear. I watched as Ash fumbled under the seat and pulled out two handguns. He handed one to me and jumped as he looked out the windshield.

The men had caught up with us, and there were at least six or seven more of them than there had been before. They were coming at us slowly, their guns raised, each step solid and sure as they approached the car.

"What are you waiting for?" Ash asked, the gun clenched tightly in his hand, his eyes trained on the men in front of us.

I tucked my own gun next to me, hoping that I wouldn't have to use it. I had killed plenty of Awakened, but I had no desire to kill these men, even they had no qualms shooting at me. Tommy had assured me that the vehicles were bullet proof, but the delicate clear glass in front of me made me nervous.

"Zoey, go," Ash urged, his fingers tapping nervously on his knees. His voice still sounded strained, and I shook my head. Just a few more steps, just a few more...

I slammed my foot on the gas, and we went spiraling out of the spot, heading toward the men. They shouted in surprise and went diving out of the way. The tires squealed as I gripped the steering wheel and tried to gain control of the car. I weaved in between planes and other vehicles that lined the hangar. I was so glad that Mom had taught me to drive. There was no reason to drive back in New York, but Mom had insisted, and I had never felt so grateful for it.

"Over there," Ash wheezed, pointing toward the exit that I had seen just a beat after he'd pointed it out. I headed in that direction. I glanced at him and gasped.

"Oh, Ash, what happened?" The car wavered, as I looked him closer. There was blood covering his hand and I looked down at his stomach. There was a large, dark red stain spread there. "Ash!"

"Watch out!" he yelled, and I looked up, just in time to jerk the wheel, to avoid crashing into a helicopter. I felt the tears spring up in my eyes, wondering how on earth I had missed that Ash had been shot. "Just go. Just go."

"Ash, Ash, Ash," I whimpered, pressing my foot harder against the gas pedal. We were nearly at the exit, just nearly to the sunlight. It was streaming in through, and I ached for it, eager to feel the warmth on my skin. I heard Ash groan, and I felt myself slow down. Where were we going to go? Where was I going to take him?"

"No," he said, interrupting my thoughts, as if he could hear what I was thinking. "Don't you stop, Zoey, don't you do it. Keep going." He coughed, pressing his hand tighter against him. "Drive, baby."

I nodded, not trusting myself to speak. Tears were streaming down my face, and I focused on the rumbling of the engine beneath me, the pressure of the pedal under my foot as we closed the distance between the exit and us.

There was a line of guards at the exit, their guns raised. As we grew closer, they started firing, the bullets hitting the window. Tommy hadn't lied; the cars were definitely bullet proof, though there were small cracks were they had landed. I flinched as they rained down at us and kept going at them, full speed.

I could feel every muscle in my body tense up. I was going to hit them. They weren't going to move, and I was going to hit them. There was no time to stop. Stopping would be the worst thing for us to do; I had to keep going. I felt my eyes shut, and a scream ripped through my throat as I barreled through them. I felt warmth on my skin, and my eyes flew open. We were out.

The exit opened right out onto a dirt road. I followed it, glancing backward every so often, my foot still planted firmly on the pedal. There was no one behind us, and this did not bode well. They wouldn't let us go. Maybe Ash, they saw no purpose in him, and maybe they knew that he was hurt. But would they let me go?

I kept driving, easing up on the speed, taking inventory of the car and my surroundings. The car was full of gas, and I knew there would be minimal supplies in the back, provided by Tommy. I felt his loss again, like a punch to the gut and hoped we would make it out to justify his life. We were in the middle of nowhere, surrounded by trees everywhere. I glanced behind me and saw that there was still no one behind me.

Ash groaned again, low, as if he didn't want me to hear him.

"Ash?" I asked, my voice wavering as I looked over at him. My knuckles were white as I gripped the steering wheel. "Baby, are you okay?"

"Just. Drive," he said. His eyes were squeezed shut, and his forehead was pressed to the glass. The car was full of the slow, ragged breaths coming from his mouth.

I took one last look behind me, just to make sure there was no one there, and looked back over to Ash. "I'm sorry." His eyes flew open and met mine. He opened his mouth to speak, but I kept talking. "This is going to hurt." I jerked the wheel to the left and we went spiraling into the forest, hitting the ground beneath our wheels rough and hard. Ash winced, but I kept going. I had to keep going.

I navigated through the forest, around trees, not caring if they were scratching up the paint. I hit one tree hard, and the side mirror cracked and hung against the side of the car, useless.

The forest wasn't very thick, probably because there was a road right on the other side but that's what I was hoping for. They would expect me to take their dirt road to the actual road but they would never expect me to make the rough trek through the forest. We bounced around, no matter how gentle I tried to be, and I felt Ash's gasps all the way down my spine. I had to get him somewhere. Sanctuary, we would find Sanctuary and they would fix him.

"Zoey."

We hadn't spoken for a while, letting the minutes tick

by in silence as we listened, listened for the sound of someone following us. I jumped at the sound of Ash's voice and looked over at him. "Yeah?"

He raised a shaking hand and pointed. "The road," he coughed. A dribble of dark red blood sputtered out of his mouth, and I immediately looked away, my stomach clenching. My eyesight followed his finger, and sure enough, there was the road. I felt myself relax against the seat, relieved to see it.

There was a slight incline as we reached the road, and I had to press hard on the gas to get us up and over and onto the smooth pavement of the road. I immediately turned left, away from the compound. We drove for a few minutes in relative silence, watching the empty road before us. Then I saw something in the distance.

I squinted and slammed on the brakes, as two cars, two black SUVs approached us, at top speed. I started to turn around but there was no time. One slammed right into us. I let go of the steering wheel. Screams filled the air as we spun in circles. My hand reached out and I grabbed Ash's in mine, hoping we would come to a stop soon.

We came to a halt, but I didn't move. My body was pressed against the sticky leather and everything in front of me was still spinning. I closed my eyes, pressing my lips together. I felt the bile rise up in my throat and the scent of blood was everywhere. "Ash?" I whispered, squeezing the hand that was still clutched in mine.

"Yeah," he whispered back. His face was pale, and the dark circles under his eyes stood out even more. "I'm here."

The doors were wrenched open, and a hand reached out and grabbed me, pulling me out of the car. My hand was yanked out of Ash's grip as I was dragged out of the car. The hand belonged to one of the goons I had seen before. He had a tight grip on me, his hand burning into my arm, and he practically threw me in front of the one person that I most definitely did not want to see.

"I have to admit," Dr. Cylon said, her arms folded tightly across her chest, "I'm actually impressed that you managed to make it this far. Of course, you had help, but that was already taken care of."

I looked up at her towering over me and glared at her. She had killed Tommy. That was how she had "taken care of it." One person stood up to her and her crazy idea, and that was how he was rewarded. I felt a rush of pain again at the thought.

One of the other goons came and deposited Ash at my feet. He wavered for a moment, struggling to stay up, before collapsing in a heap. I dropped to my knees, reaching for him. His breathing was hard and labored, and there was blood everywhere. "Hang in, Ash," I said, leaning over him. "Please hang in."

"We could help him, you know," Razi said, looking down at Ash. She was giving him the barest of glances, as if he was no more significant than the small spider that was crawling against the hot pavement by my knee. "If you return, willingly, I can help him."

Ash coughed hard, and blood dribbled down his chin. His eyes were closed, and if it weren't for the subtle rise and fall of his chest, I would have thought he was dead. My eyes met Razi's, and I hesitated.

"You are not a fool, Zoey. You know that you tried your best, but you are outnumbered. There is no one else that can put your friend back together. Come back to Sekhmet. Fulfill your destiny, and we will take care of him. You have my promise on that." Her hands were folded in front of her, and her face was steady and calm.

Everything seemed to be spinning around me, and all I saw was a blur. I was going to be sick, I wanted to be sick, to empty myself of every bad feeling I had felt in the past few months. There was nowhere to run, no place to go, and Ash was dying. Would it be so wrong to go back to Sekhmet and have Liam's children, if it kept both of us safe and alive?

Ash's hand was clutched tightly in mine, and I felt his fingers squeeze around mine.

"No," he said. I looked down at him in surprise. "I know what you're thinking." I opened my mouth, but he shook his head, a slight smile on his face. "I always know what you're thinking. Don't do it. It's not worth it. They won't fix me. You know they won't, Zoey. And you'll be stuck forever."

The realization went rushing, ice cold, through my veins. I could never, for one moment, believe anything that she had promised me. She had locked me up, kept me from the one person I had left, killed people, all for her insane vision.

"He underestimates how much you mean to our vision, Zoey," Razi said, stepping closer. For the first time, I felt a flash of doubt in her features. For the first time, I really realized how much I meant to her. "I will fix him. I promise."

I opened my mouth to answer, but a loud crack sounded before the words left my mouth. The man holding my arm fell in a heap next to me, a clean bullet hole in the center of his forehead. I gasped, falling backward on the heels of my palms. Another shot rang out and hit the man on the other side of me, the one who had grabbed Ash. He hit the ground a moment later.

Ash's eyes flew open. "What is going on? Zoey?"

One by one, the men around us went crashing to the ground, perfect shots in their forehead. Dr. Cylon was looking around frantically, watching as they fell around her. She looked panicked, scared. She started running back to one of the SUVs when it went flying to the side. A beat up pickup truck had come peeling out of nowhere, slamming into the SUV. Dr. Cylon stepped back, her eyes wide. She moved toward another SUV, but a deep voice rang out.

"Stop." That was it, one word. But it rang out strong, as if the person behind expected nothing less than completely obedience.

Razi froze in her steps. She looked so different than I had seen her in the last few weeks. She had lost the perfect, calm composure that I had come to expect from her. She was breathing hard, looking around, as if looking for an escape.

A man stepped out of the truck. He was tall and strong, though he looked like he was in his sixties, his dark skin wrinkled. A rifle was clutched in his hands, and he aimed it at Dr. Cylon. His eyes locked on mine, and I felt a rush of reassurance at the sight of him. "Get him in the truck."

I didn't hesitate. I couldn't explain it, but there was something about this man that made me want to trust him immediately. He had obviously come to our rescue and at the moment, I didn't know why, but I couldn't afford to question it. I reached for Ash, wrapping my arm around him and lugging him to his feet. He buckled, and I nearly dropped him. "Come on, Ash," I whispered desperately. He was a foot taller than me and at least fifty pounds heavier than me.

I felt him nod against me, his hand pressed tight to his ribcage, and we started moving slowly toward the truck.

"They aren't going anywhere," Razi's voice rang out. She was trying hard to insert authority into her voice, but it came out shaky. "They belong to me."

The man stared at Dr. Cylon, calm, so different from the sort of calm that I was used to with Dr. Cylon. It was reassuring, a calm that exuded confidence and intelligence. "I'm afraid that they don't, Doctor. It's in your best interest to let them come with me."

She blinked once, twice, three times, looking at him as if she couldn't quite believe he was real. "You're from…"

He nodded. "Of course I am. We've been keeping our eye on you, but you still managed to make all this happen. Now let me have the children."

"I can't," she burst out. "I need them. I need *her.*"

He shook his head, staying silent. Ash and I made slow

progress around them, working our way to the truck. We took it one step at a time, each one sending a jolt of pain through Ash's body, judging by the look on his face.

"I need *her,*" Razi repeated, her eyes meeting mine. There was a desperate hunger on her face, and I shivered, thinking of the doctors poking and prodding me, the cameras following my every move and the feel of Liam's hands on me. She fell to her knees, her eyes taking in the bodies all around her. There was a stark look of defeat on her face. "There are more men, back at my compound. They will come looking for me. You are outnumbered."

The man raised the gun. "I don't think so."

Razi reached a shaking hand out, and her fingers closed over the handle of a gun, left behind by one of her dead bodyguards. I froze, watching it all in slow motion. Ash went crashing to the ground, and I reached for him. Razi raised the gun, a manic look in her eyes as she turned the gun toward the two of us. I flung myself over Ash, burying my head in his chest, as one last shot resonated out. I waited for the pain, but it didn't come.

I dared to lift my head and saw Razi's body lying on the ground, the gun still clutched tightly in her palm. Blood was gushing out of the wound in her neck. The man stared at her for a moment, before coming toward us. "Get up."

I scrambled to my feet, reaching for Ash. The man pushed me aside, lifting Ash with ease, and carrying him to the passenger door of the car. I walked quickly, next to them, reaching for the handle. I got inside with no hesitation and reached for him. The inside of the truck was huge, large enough for at least three people to sit comfortably. The two of us pulled Ash into the car, getting him as comfortable as possible, his head resting in my lap. The man walked to the other side of the truck and climbed back in, turning the ignition on and speeding off.

"Take his shirt off," he said in a low, deep voice. I looked at him, surprised. "You need to put pressure on that wound."

I nodded, slowly peeling the shirt off of him, careful not to jostle him too much. The wound was near his ribs, and it made me sick to look at it, but I focused on pressing the fabric against it. He was still conscious but barely, his breathing coming out shallow. "Who are you?"

He didn't answer for a moment, just continued to press his foot hard against the gas, speeding down the highway, away from the mess we had left behind. "Bert," he finally said. "Bert Washington."

"Zoey Valentine," I said, running my fingers through Ash's hair. He was so pale, so quiet. "This is Ash."

"He your boyfriend?" came the gruff reply.

I paused, and there was a rough chuckle. I looked down at Ash, startled to find him smiling.

"I want to be her boyfriend, but she's been holding out on me," he joked.

I laughed, nervously. "Shut up, you." I leaned forward, placing a rough kiss on his lips. "Just don't die, okay? Please don't die," I whispered.

We drove on for about twenty minutes before Bert took a turn and drove down a bumpy road that led to a small house. It was small, only one story, the blue paint chipped and faded. He pulled up to the front and threw the car in park. "Let's get him inside."

At these words, Ash began to cough uncontrollably, and blood splattered down his front and all over my arms. "Ash?" I said, my voice rising. "Ash!"

"Get him in the house," Bert said again more firmly. Ash began to shake violently in my arms and I pulled back, afraid to touch him. "He's going into shock; we need to hurry." He got out of the car and came to the passenger side, scooping Ash into his arms as if he weighed nothing more than a rag doll. He hurried in the house.

I took a couple deep breaths, feeling the heat of blood on my fingertips. Then I let myself out of the truck, slamming the door behind me, and followed them into the house.

Bert had him set up in a bedroom. There was a ridiculous amount of medical supplies there, way more than seemed necessary for a normal, everyday house. "My wife, she was a doctor," he said, bent over Ash. There was foam at the corner on his mouth and his eyes had rolled back, showing only the whites. I wrapped my arms tightly around myself, holding myself together, trying to stop the shaking that I seemed to have no control ever.

"Is he going to be okay?" I whispered.

He glanced over his shoulder at me, as if realizing I was still there. "You need to leave the room."

I lurched forward, reaching for Ash. "No...no, I can't leave him."

"Miss Zoey," he said, "he will not get any better if I can't concentrate on him, completely. I can't do that if you are still in the room."

"But...I just..." I looked over his shoulder at Ash.

"Please."

Ash's chest was bare and blood was pooled, sticky and dark, all over his chest. I could tell he was still breathing but for how much longer?

"Zoey."

I nodded absently, backing out of the room, my eyes on Ash until the door was shut in my face. I pressed my palms against the wood of the door, still wishing I could be in there. I turned away from the door, ready to explore my new surroundings, if only to get my mind off of what was going on inside that room.

There were three more bedrooms, all of them on the small side, except the master bedroom, which was slightly bigger. They all seemed to be unoccupied by anyone. They lacked any personal touches, no photographs, no posters on the wall, nothing. The rooms almost looked like hotel rooms. One bedroom had a bookshelf but even the comfort of books felt far away from me.

I made my way through the hallway, back toward the front of the house, running my hand along the cool surface of the wall. There was a small sitting room, complete with an outdated TV and a computer that looked like it might take the entire electrical capacity of the house to turn on. I went to the kitchen, simply furnished with a refrigerator, a small table with four chairs, and a couple other appliances.

I crossed the tile floor and opened the door. There were several jugs in there: water, milk, something that looked like it might be apple juice and orange juice. I reached for the water jug and searched the cabinets for a glass, pouring the water to the very top. I took a shaky sip and sat down at the table, ready to wait.

The only light coming into the small kitchen was the dim glow of the moon. There was a switch to the overhead light, but I couldn't bring myself to stand up to turn I ton. I drank my water slowly, ignoring the grumbling of my stomach as I waited. I stared at the tile on the floor, trying to make pictures out of the random gray swirls.

My mind drifted as I thought about Ash, and all the times that I had spent with him in the past nine months or so: dancing with him at the concert, ordering Chinese food in and watching Buffy, trekking through the woods, kissing him on my mother's kitchen counter.

I jumped at the sudden sound of soft footsteps. I looked up just in time to see Bert enter the room. He flipped the switch, throwing the both of us into brightness. I flinched, lifting my hand to block the light. I stood up. "Is he okay? Is he…"

He sighed, crossing the kitchen and pouring himself a glass of water. "He's going to be okay."

I felt the surge of relief flow through me like an electrical current. I was paralyzed by it, unable to think of anything else. He was okay. Ash was okay. I needed to see him. I put one foot in front of the other, like learning to walk for the first time.

"He needs rest," came Bert's deep, resonating voice. I had never met anyone with a voice like that, so deep that it almost didn't seem real. "Let him be."

"I want to see him," I said firmly, stopped in my tracks.

"He needs rest," he repeated. "He's asleep, and he needs to be alone. Give him that. Please, I ask only this of you."

I turned around, away from the hallway, to face him. "I have no idea who are you or where you came from. You're asking me only this, but why would I believe you? You just saved us, but why?"

He sighed again, sliding into a chair. He looked tired, worn out. The wrinkles that I had noticed earlier stood out even more, and he winced, stretching out his left leg gingerly. "Sit down."

I wavered, and then sat down in the seat across from him. "So?"

"Has anyone ever told you that you have an attitude?" he asked me. He spoke slowly, choosing every word with care.

"This wouldn't be the first time," I admitted. "But I've been yanked all around this country, told a million different things, shot a gun way more than I have ever wanted to, just escaped from a high security compound and watched the boy I love get shot in the ribs so yeah…a bit of attitude is kind of necessary at this point."

Bert studied me for a moment, his eyes fixated on me. "I think that your friend…"

"Ash," I interrupted.

"Ash, then," he said, smoothly. "I think Ash would like

to hear this too."

I opened my mouth and then closed it. "You're probably right about that. But I can't just stay here, not knowing anything about you. I'm kind of rattled already."

"I do not deny that," he said. "It's not often that someone tries to break out of Sekhmet. Most go willingly."

"You know of Sekhmet. How is that possible?" I asked, my hands folded on the table in front of me.

"That is a story for later. What you need to know is this: I worked for a place, a safe house, for many years. Some people have heard it called Sanctuary. We have been aware of Sekhmet for years." He paused and took a deep breath, looking a little overwhelmed by the words. "I've been going out on drives often, even since the Awakened struck and they released the bombs, looking for those are searching for Sanctuary. What I ran into today…I hadn't expected. But I was prepared."

Words failed me. It was the barest of explanations, but I knew that this was the most I was going to get out of him until Ash was well enough to hear the story as well. I was left with a thousand more questions than I'd had five minutes ago. My head was going to explode at any moment, and I felt a slight throb right above my right eye.

"It's late. You need rest too." He stood up, taking his glass and my glass and carrying them to the sink. He rinsed them, placing them in the drying rack and started heading down the hallway. I stood up, assuming that he wanted me to follow him and found myself in one of the small rooms. There was a twin bed and a chest of drawers. "There are clothes in the dresser that should be fairly close to your size."

He stepped aside, letting me pass into the room. I slid a drawer open and found a few worn pairs of sweatpants. I lifted one and felt the soft fabric under my fingertips. I couldn't wait to get out of this scratch khaki pants and this stupid tunic. "Thank you," I said simply.

Bert nodded. "There is a bathroom down the hall, if you'd like to shower. And my room is just across from it. If you need anything…"

"I will come and find you. Got it." I nodded. After the day I'd had, I was ready for a shower, to crawl into bed and just be alone with myself for a little bit. I waited for a few moments, as he hovered in the doorway and then made his exit. I sighed and braced myself against the dresser. Less than twenty-four hours had passed since I had left Sekhmet, left Liam behind, heard Tommy get shot and watched as Ash had bled all over me. I looked down and saw the blood all over my shirt and grimaced.

The bathroom was small but efficient. I turned the knob on the shower and was pleasantly surprised when the water was fairly warm. I stripped off the dirty clothes and shoved them into the tiny trashcan that was behind the toilet. I let the warm water run all over me, letting it wash away all the blood that had covered my body. I nearly cried when I spotted shampoo and body wash. There was even a razor sitting on the side of the tub. There was a soft layer of hair on my legs. I reached for the razor, ready to have some sort of semblance of normalcy back in my life.

I made my way back to the room, feeling refreshed and

clean. I paused at the door to the room where Ash was. My hand reached for the doorknob, and it turned with ease under my palm.

"Not yet, Miss Zoey."

I jumped, startled at the voice in the darkness of the hallway. "Jesus, Bert, creep much?"

"I know you want to see him," he said, standing in the doorway of his room. "But not yet, I will let you know."

I swallowed hard, nodding and turning away from the door. I flipped the light switch in my new room and crawled into bed, pulling the blanket up and over my head. I felt all that happened in the last few hours, and the tears came flowing down my cheeks and soaking the pillow beneath me. I cried until I couldn't cry anymore and fell into a restless sleep.

CHAPTER

THIRTY-TWO

THREE DAYS PASSED BEFORE BERT let me see Ash.

I spent those days in relative quiet. Bert was a man of very few words, and most attempts at real conversations ended up in silence. He sat on the couch often, reading books or solving a crossword puzzle.

I tried many times to sneak over to Ash's room. He was in a room connected to the second bathroom, so there was literally no reason for him to come out. Bert went in, disappeared in there for hours. He went in with food and came out with empty trays. Every time I tried to sneak in, Bert appeared out of nowhere, reminding me that he wasn't ready, that seeing me would overexcite him.

I spent most of my time outside. Bert informed me that we were in Colorado on the outskirts of Mesa Verde, and it was beautiful. There was forest everywhere. Everything was so green. Bert had said it was due to the recent rains that I had missed during my time underground. There were a few books in the house, and I lost myself in a beat up copy of *The Sound and the Fury*, sitting in the bed of Bert's truck.

I kept thinking of everything that had happened since I had left New York. It felt like that life was a dream. I barely remembered wearing my St. Joseph's uniform, or even my cheerleading uniform. My memories of planning school dances, going on walks with Bandit, eating hot dogs with my dad at baseball games and hanging out with Madison were all a blur. It felt like a lifetime ago, and I was afraid of losing them.

I missed them all. I missed them so much; it physically hurt. My dreams weren't nightmares anymore, but they still left me sad and breathless. While I was busy worrying about Ash in the next room, I kept forgetting that there were people that weren't here anymore. I kept thinking of all the people we had lost and how I had almost lost him too. I couldn't take it anymore. I couldn't take any more loss than I already had. I had lost my parents, my best friend, my dog. Everything and everyone I knew was gone. All that was left was Sekhmet and the Awakened.

The memory of Razi Cylon filled my every thought. She was gone, shot in the throat, left to die on the warm concrete of the Colorado highway. But every memory of that place was embedded in my mind, in my very soul. She had taken every bit of self-respect I'd had and thrown it away. I'd been poked and prodded and inspected like a sample under a microscope. I was watched constantly, and I often woke up breathless, afraid that she was still here, waiting for me.

Bert was quiet and patient. I would hear him walk by the door of my room during the night and pause by my door. I wasn't sure what he was listening for, but it felt good to know that he was there and that I wasn't alone.

On the third day at Bert's house, I woke up later than normal, the sun streaming through the blinds and casting shadows over the bed. I yawned, and dragged myself out of bed, wondering if I could just stay in this house forever. In the shower, I spent way too much time washing my hair and making sure my legs were silky smooth again.

Bert was already sitting at the kitchen table with a jug of orange juice and a couple empty glasses. "Stove," he said, as I came in. I rolled my eyes and walked over, pleased to see that there was a pan of eggs and another pan of potatoes sitting there. My stomach gurgled happily, and I piled some on a plate. I slid into a seat across from him and poured myself a glass. I had barely lifted my fork to my mouth when he spoke.

"He's doing well. He's weak, but he's doing well. He's very strong," Bert said, not looking up from his book. "But you can see him."

"What?" I said, disbelieving. "I can see him?" He nodded, and I started to stand up.

"After breakfast, Zoey," he sighed, and I sat back down.

I scarfed down my breakfast, shoving the food in my mouth and practically choking on the orange juice as I gulped it down. I took my plate, fork and glass to the sink and rinsed them quickly before turning back to him. I smiled wide. "Can I see him now?"

"Yes. You can see him now."

My smile grew wider, more genuine, and I practically sprinted down the hallway to his room. I paused right before the door. I took two deep breaths and reached for the doorknob.

I opened the door slowly, the doorknob squeaking as I turned it. I peeked around the door and found Ash sitting up in bed, a book in his lap. He was wearing a clean white t-shirt and a pair of jeans, his bare feet out in front of him. His hair was damp. I could see the bandage through his shirt, and I felt a wave of sorrow sweep through me. I backed up, going to close the door, when it screeched loudly. I winced at the sound.

Ash's eyes lifted and met mine, and a wide smile spread across his face. It was so different though; there was shyness to it that hadn't been there before. "Hey," he said, softly, closing the book and putting it to the side.

"Hi," I whispered back. "I just wanted to check to see if you were okay. I'll let you rest."

He shook his head. "No, come in, please. It's only been Bert in here for days, and the guy isn't much for company."

I thought of the many silent hours spent in Bert's company and laughed. I pushed the door the rest of the way open and closed it quietly behind me. I dragged the desk chair across the floor and sat in it, next to Ash. He looked mildly disappointed but kept his comments to himself.

"Are you okay?" I asked, reaching for him but then pulling my hand back. I folded my hands together and held them in my lap.

"I'm fine," he assured me, "fit as a fiddle, whatever that means."

"I've been…" I swallowed hard, overwhelmed by the sudden emotions that were flooding in. "I've been so worried about you."

He reached for my hand and pulled it close to him, placing it on his chest. "Zoey Valentine, worrying about me? The world must be coming to an end."

"Don't joke," I said, my voice dipping in a barely held back sob. "I thought you were going to die. You were shot, and there was so much blood, and I thought you were going to die."

"Hey, hey, hey," he said, his voice gentle. His grip on my hand tightened, and I looked up into his pale blue eyes, full of something I was almost afraid to identify. "I'm okay. I'm going to be okay. Look at me, Z."

I looked up at him, trying as hard as I could to control the tears that had been threatening to spill for days. My lip quivered as I attempted a smile.

"I was scared for *you*," he said, slowly. "I promised your dad, and I promised your mom that I would protect you. When I was shot, the only thing running through my mind was that you would be alone and there would be no one left to protect you. I didn't care about me."

I ran the back of my hand across my eyes, taking my tears with me. "You shouldn't…you should never think that way. You are important. You matter to me."

He took a deep breath and let it out slowly, my hand

rising against his chest. "Can you please come here? You're so far away."

The bed was fairly large, with enough room for the two of us to lie together, if we didn't mind being close. I wanted to be close to him, to touch him and make sure that he was real. Not being able to see him the last few days was torture. I hesitated, and then climbed up into bed with him. The roughness of his jeans grazed my bare legs and I was grateful for my brief moment of vanity in the shower.

We stayed quiet for a moment, and I stared at the ceiling, ready to count the squares, if that's what it came down to. There was a heat spreading through me, and we were still a few inches apart. Ash sighed and then, in one quick movement, pulled me toward him, his arms wrapped tightly around my waist.

I squeaked at the sudden closeness, my cheek pressed against his chest. "I don't want to hurt you. You're still healing."

He chuckled a little, and the sound vibrated through his chest and my face. "You can't hurt me. The only way you can hurt me is if you leave me alone with Bert again for three more days."

I laughed. "Come on. Bert isn't that bad."

He squeezed his arms tighter around me, and I found myself wrapping an arm around his waist, ready for snuggling. "No, no, he's not. He took us in. He saved your life."

"And yours," I pointed out, my fingertips pressed lightly to the bandage on his ribs.

He shrugged. "You were more important. And you saved my life. You saved me from Razi and her psycho doctor clones. You were fearless. You could've left without me, but you didn't."

"I wouldn't ever leave you behind," I said sharply. "Don't even say that."

He pulled back a little, his eyes finding mine. My eyes took in his gaze, hungrily. I would never get tired of looking at him. If it was he and I together, for the rest of our lives, against the world, I would be okay. I would be more than okay. "Well, we're together, and that's all that matters."

I hesitated, wondering if it was the right moment to tell Ash about Sanctuary. I decided it could wait. He felt safe right now, and I didn't want to ruin it for him, not yet. I didn't want to tell him that we would have to make yet another journey. "Yeah, Ash, that's all that matters."

He raised a bandaged hand to my face, and lifted my chin so that our faces were even closer than before. "Are you okay, though, Z? I mean, sorry, Zoey."

I felt a shock rip through me at his correction and a blush rushed through my face. "It's okay, Ash. You can call me Z," I said, softly, staring at a point above his head, afraid to look him in the eyes. "I kind of like it."

His hand shot out, wrapping around the back of my neck and dragging me toward him. "I have a confession to make too."

"Oh, yeah?" I squeaked, my gaze on his lips. I missed kissing him. Had it been that long since I kissed him? I wanted to kiss him again. "What's that?"

He sighed, his eyes raised to the ceiling. He looked back down at me, a sheepish look on his face. "My real name is not Ash. My name is actually Ashley. My mom had a slight obsession with *Gone with the Wind* and named me after some buffoon named Ashley. I got teased a lot about it at my old school and begged her to let me shorten it to Ash when I moved to New York and started at St. Joseph's."

My lips twitched a bit as I took in this piece of information. Ash stared down at me expectantly, and I couldn't hold it back any longer. I burst out laughing, giggles ripping through my body. I hadn't laughed like this in ages, and I couldn't stop. Tears had sprung in the corner of my eyes, and for the first time in so long, it wasn't because I was sad.

"Oh, go on and make fun of me," Ash said, his eyebrows narrowed at me. He had a grin on his face though, and I launched into another set of uncontrollable giggles.

"Sorry, Ashley," I burst out. "I'll try not to make fun of you."

"Come here, you," he said, launching himself at me. I squealed and pulled back, flopping backward on the bed. I moved to roll away, but he grabbed a hold of me, his large hands holding my arms down, his body half pressed against me.

The giggles faded from me as I stared up at him. My breath got caught somewhere in the back of my throat as a wave of desire swept through me, pinning me to the bed, underneath the heat of his body. He was studying my face, looking for permission, and I gave it with a small nod. His hand came up to cup my cheek, and he pressed his lips against mine.

I'd like to say that I was cool and calm and demure when he kissed me, but that was not the case. I clung at him, desperately. I had been so worried about him, and I poured all the love I had for him into the kiss. His tongue probed at my lips, and I opened myself up to him. I grabbed at him, pulling him closer to me, and I heard him gasp. I pulled myself away, my mouth a round O of surprise. "Ash, I'm sorry."

He smiled but there was pain in it. "It's okay. Just...be careful of my ribs."

I nodded, one swift up and down movement. I pressed my palm against his chest, feeling his heart beat against the soft flesh of my hand. "I'm so sorry. I can be gentle with you."

Ash bent lower over me, his hands lingering as he traced the curves of my body with his fingertips. "I don't want you to be gentle with me," he admitted, his voice low.

A shiver ran through me, and I arched my back, pressing myself closer to him, as I pulled him back to me for a kiss. He moaned, a deep sound in the back of his throat, as I bit the soft skin of his lower lip. My hands were tracing the fine contours of his chest and stomach and tugging at the hem of his shirt. He pulled back for a moment, allowing me to lift his shirt over his head and toss it to the floor.

"Zoey," he said, his voice soft. My name sounded like music when he said it, like hitting just the right notes on a piano. He unbuttoned my blouse, his fingertips grazing the skin underneath. His lips were at my throat, biting softly at the skin there, causing goose bumps to ripple across my arms. I shrugged out of the shirt and pulled him down on top of me, amazed at how our bodies fit together. My feet just reached the tops of his, as our legs tangled around each other. Ash was moving against me, his breathing hard and labored.

Ash sat up, and I felt a breeze of cold air rush across my skin at the absence of his warm skin against mine. He tugged me up, into his lap. His hands were lost in my hair as he leaned down to kiss me again, his tongue sweeping over my jawline, over my lips before plunging between them. I was drowning in his kiss and the way he made me feel. I rolled my hips against him, and I felt him gasp. His palms were pressed hard against my back, making quick work of the hooks of my bra.

I inhaled sharply, as my bra straps fell down my shoulders and revealed my breasts. I yanked myself back, suddenly self-conscious. I was aware of the nakedness, the bit of me that I had never shown anyone. And now it was marred, scarred and cut from the Awakened I had battled. I felt the raised skin of the scar on my face and an embarrassed flush filled my face. I started to pull back, but Ash's arm shot out, wrapping around my waist, and holding me close to him, my bare skin pressed against his.

"No," he whispered softly, his lips at my forehead, my temple, and the soft skin below my ear. "Don't cover yourself up. You're beautiful, Zoey, every single bit of you." His soft lips traced the sensitive skin of my scar. "You're a fighter, and it's the sexiest and most beautiful thing I've ever seen. Don't ever cover yourself up. Don't ever be ashamed."

I swelled and bloomed under his words, and a small smile crept onto my face. I was bursting to tell him how I felt, but the terror was too much to handle. I brought my lips back to his, hoping he would understand.

He pushed me back onto the bed, tossing the bra to the side. "You just lie there and look beautiful, baby. Let me show you how beautiful you are."

A bigger smile grew across my face. "I think you showed me back in the woods."

"Not like this," he said, his voice low and full of desire. I felt it from my spine down to the tips of my toes. His lips traced a wet, searing trail down my neck to my collarbone, between my breasts. One of his hands cupped my breast, his thumb tracing light circles on the smooth skin. His mouth came down on the other breast, his tongue a soft sweep on my nipple. I gasped, surprised at the immediate pleasure that sped through me. I whimpered as his warm tongue traced the circle again.

"Ash," I breathed in, my teeth biting down hard on my lip. I was in a haze, wondering how it was possible to feel this way. My hands were lost in the softness of his long hair, and I could feel the roughness of the stubble on his chin against my bare skin.

"Hmm?" he said, switching his mouth to the other breast. I sighed, my head thrown back against the pillow. "Do you want me to stop?"

"Oh, god, no," I said, my breaths coming out fast and hard. My hands were at the buttons of his jeans and they unbuttoned easily. I found myself pushing them down. Ash's hands reached out to grab mine and stopped them from undressing him.

"No, you first," he insisted. His eyes met mine, and they were so full of desire and want and need, and I wanted to stay like this forever, in this bed. His hands were tugging my shorts off, and his hands were on me, soft against the skin there. My fingernails dug deep into his arms, my gasps coming out quicker. I started shaking, knowing what was coming next. I was both excited and terrified.

Ash must have sensed some of my unease because he pulled back. His blue eyes were now full of concern, as he leaned over me. "Are you okay, Zoey? Do you want to stop?" he asked, his own breathing labored. He was so sexy and so incredibly beautiful, and in this crappy world, he was the one bright light left. "We can stop if you need to. But we should do it now because I honestly don't know how much longer I can let this go…"

My fingers traced circles on his arms, and I thought for a moment, looking up at him. "I'm scared…and nervous. I'm not experienced. I've never…I'm not…I haven't…" I took a deep breath, trying to compose myself. "I've never done this before."

Ash smiled at me, an achingly perfect smile that made me melt into a puddle right then and there on the bed. "It's okay, Z. We can do this together."

"But you and Heather…" I protested.

He looked uncomfortable for a moment. "Zoey, I'm not going to pretend that I haven't done something that I have. I wouldn't do that to you. But I can tell you this: whatever I had with Heather pales in comparison with the way I feel right now."

My skin was still tingling from his touch. "How do you feel now?"

"I want you," he said immediately. "Every bit of you. No one else matters. No one else has ever mattered but you."

"I'm scared," I repeated, my voice barely above a whisper.

His hands were lingering on my hips, his eyes intent on mine. He looked nervous. "I've been trying to tell you for weeks and weeks, but it never felt right. It never felt like the right moment and I wanted it to be the right moment for you, for both of us." He took a deep breath, shaky and unsure. "I love you, Zoey."

I had known for so long, or at least I had suspected, hoped, ever since we had fought the Awakened that had killed my dad. But I had never believed it. Not after he had sewed me back together and told me I was beautiful. Not when he had climbed into my bed and soothed me to sleep after the nightmares. Not even when he had lifted me onto that kitchen counter and kissed me with incredible passion. No, I hadn't believed it. Not until now, when he said the words out loud.

"Zoey?" He sounded scared. No. He sounded more than scared. He sounded absolutely terrified. He had just bared himself to me, and I was having a hard time getting the words out in my surprise at his words.

"Ash," I said, my voice soft, pulling him down for another desperate, searing kiss. His mouth explored mine tentatively as my tongue traced the curve of his bottom lip. I pulled away, my lips still grazing his. "I love you too. God, I love you so much."

He came crashing down on me, his movements fast and full of need. His lips were on mine, pulling me into a never-ending kiss, as he yanked on the waistband of my panties, sliding them down my legs. I kicked them off, sending them flying in an unknown direction. We were both frantically pulling at his pants, and his boxers, until we were both naked, pressed against each other. I wrapped my hand around him, and a shudder ran through him, a low growl escaping his lips. I smiled, pleased that I could make him feel that way.

"Are you ready?" he asked, his voice just above a whisper.

I nodded, and he was careful, sliding in slowly. I winced, tears filling my eyes. He took it slow and before I knew it, pleasure was spreading through me, causing me to pant. I met his eyes, and I knew he was feeling the same.

"You're so incredible," he said, the words coming out in quick breaths. "You're so beautiful, Zoey."

No, I thought, you're the beautiful one. My fingernails dug into the firm skin of his back as a new feeling swept through me, causing me to arch my back and cry out, my face pressed into his neck. He was a beat behind me, a low moan in the back of his throat. He collapsed against me, and my arms went around him, automatically, tracing the scar that had risen on his shoulder.

"Can I say it again?" he asked, his voice vibrating against my skin.

"Say what, baby?" I asked, out of breath, my eyes closing.

He laughed lightly. "I have to admit, I like when you call me baby." A lazy smile grew across my face. "I'm just going to say it again. I love you, Zoey."

I felt my heart skip a beat at the words. They would never get old, never. "I love you too. I always have, since we were kids."

He sighed. "Me too." Before I could say anything, he had fallen asleep. I grabbed the blanket and pulled it over both of us. For this one moment at least, we were together, and we were safe. We had each other.

THIRTY-THREE

WE WOKE HOURS LATER. I jolted awake, hot and sweaty. Ash was still asleep on top of me, his breathing heavy. My hands were lost in his dark hair, and I felt a rush of affection go through me. He shifted and raised his sleepy eyes to mine. A lazy grin stretched across his face.

"Good morning, baby, or afternoon, I suppose," he said, softly, raising himself up on his elbows. He winced, and his fingers went to his bandage.

"Are you okay?" I asked, reaching for him. He nodded, his fingers moving from his bandage to my thigh, up to my hip, across my stomach, between my breasts to cup my chin. He leaned down and my lips met his eagerly. We spent the next few moments lost in each other.

I pulled away, reluctantly. "As much as I want to keep doing this, I think it probably would be a good idea to get out of bed."

He sighed, but there was still a smile on his face. "You're right. And a shower sounds amazing right now."

"Is that okay?" I asked, as he lifted himself off of me. Cold air rushed across my body, causing goose bumps to ripple across my skin. I grabbed the blanket and pulled it across me again. "With your injury, I mean?"

"Should be," he said. He pulled on a pair of jeans, not bothering with underwear, and leaving the zipper down. I felt my breath quicken at the sight of him. His hair was messy, tangled from my fingers, and his skin was pale, but his chest and abs and hipbones were slim and fit. I bit my lip, wanting pull him back into bed.

He noticed me looking and winked at me. "It's very hard to leave you like this, all naked, wrapped in that blanket. It's kind of irresistible, actually." He sighed again. "But you could always join me in the shower."

I blushed. "I don't think that would be wise, not in Bert's house."

"Later?" he asked, bending over me to kiss me again.

"Later," I agreed, eagerly. He grinned and walked over to the door, turning the knob. I hesitated and then spoke up. "Ash?"

He looked back at me. "Yeah?"

I looked down at the bedspread, tracing the patterns with my finger. "You should make it quick. We need to talk to Bert."

He frowned. "Why? What's wrong?"

"He said...he said Sanctuary is real," I blurted out. "It's

real and he knows where it is. He…used to work there."

Ash's hand was still on the doorknob, but he made no move to open it. Instead he stared at me. "It's actually real…" he said softly. His eyes met mine, and I saw that they were full of barely disguised hope.

I nodded. "We need to find out more information, and…we need to ask him if he can take us there."

"You don't think we can stay here?" he asked, his brow furrowed in confusion.

I shook my head. "We can't. I can't…we need to talk to Bert. He'll explain everything."

"I don't want a shower anymore," Ash said firmly, grabbing his shirt from the floor and pulling it on. "Let's go talk to him now." He turned around and sped out of the room.

I sighed and got out of bed, locating my various articles of clothing strewn about the room, putting them on. I stumbled on something and saw a book laying on the ground, the one that Ash had been reading when I had come into the room. I lifted it up and felt the corners of my mouth turn up, almost involuntarily. In my hand was the most familiar book to me, one that I had read so many times it nearly fit in my hands perfectly. *The Mists of Avalon.* I knew it wasn't my copy, but it felt just like my own. Someone in this house loved this book as much as I did. I closed it, and pressed it to my chest, overwhelmed with emotions for a moment. I placed the book back on the bed and followed Ash out of the room.

They were both in the kitchen. Bert was sitting at the

worn table, a beat up book of crossword puzzles in his hands. Ash was standing in front of him, his arms tight across his chest.

"What's going on?" I asked, as I entered, running a hand through my tangled hair. I slid into a chair across from Bert and looked back and forth between them.

"He didn't want to say anything until you got here," Ash said, his voice terse. There was the sound of pencil against paper as Bert continued working on a crossword puzzle. "Never mind that he told you about Sanctuary before I knew anything about it."

"Ash," I warned.

"Well, come on, Bert, you going to finally fill us in? Maybe tell us how you were randomly there to save our lives? How do we know you're not working for Sekhmet?"

"Ash," I said, louder. He turned to me, his eyes meeting mine, and I silently pleaded with him to stop. His face softened, and a small smile hinted at the corners of his lips. I felt a rush of affection pummel through me. "Sit down, okay?"

He glared at Bert, who was still steadfastly ignoring Ash, and slid into the chair next to me. His hand reached for mine, and my fingers slid between his.

The puzzle book was finally put down, and Bert raised his head to look at the both of us. "I wish I could keep you both here but I can't. I have to take you to Sanctuary. It's my job."

"Your job?" I said, worry in my voice. "I thought you said you *used* to work for Sanctuary?"

"I did." Bert's deep voice filled the echoing kitchen, each word slow and careful. "I was part of security at Sanctuary for most of my life, until my wife died. She was a doctor at Sanctuary. We dedicated our lives to the place, a place where we could go should the worst happen."

He sighed, looking out the window. Ash's hand tightened around me, and I scooted my chair closer to him. "When my wife died, I couldn't be there anymore. It hurt too much to be there. So I left. But you can't just leave Sanctuary. So, yes, Miss Zoey, I do not work there anymore but my life is dedicated to it. I can never truly leave it. And I must take you there."

"But what is Sanctuary?" I asked, biting my lip nervously. "I don't understand."

"During the 1950s, when the idea of nuclear war started to become a real fear, there was a group of people that realized that bomb shelters were not going to save us. We needed a place, a place where we could seek refuge. Back then, it was nuclear war, but as time passed, we knew that it was more than that: natural disaster, civil war, economic breakdown."

"Zombies?" I asked.

A small smile crept onto Bert's lips, and I was surprised at it. "No, no, that was the sort of thing we never would have thought. But despite having never been prepared for that, Sanctuary is still perfect for it. It was created to be a perfect refuge. It's built into the cliffs of Mesa Verde National Park, and it was created with every need in mind. There are doctors and scientists and teachers and everything else needed for a new society to grow. A good size population can live and survive in this underground fortress for years, waiting for the world outside to be ready to start over again."

"I met my wife when she was a student at Columbia University, in the '70s. She was studying to become a doctor, and I was working the late night shift on security duty on campus. She always called for an escort, and I volunteered more than once to escort her to her car. Prudence was a beautiful lady, incredibly beautiful, and even smarter than she was beautiful."

"One night, it was pouring rain, and when I came to meet her, to walk her home, I was drenched to the bone. I had forgotten my damn umbrella. When I left Pru at her doorstep, she hesitated. I had never seen her do that before. She always charged forward. She was a force of nature. But that one time, she hesitated. She handed over her umbrella to me and told me to meet her for coffee the next day. 'To return my umbrella' she said. We met for coffee in the morning and continued to do so for two months. It was easy. It was magic. We had been together ever since."

I was afraid to speak, afraid to break the story that Bert was telling us. I curled my hand tighter in Ash's grip, hoping he would get it and that he would know how much I loved him.

"We were married a few weeks after her graduation, just a small thing down at the county offices. She was offered a job, in an ER wing at Robert Wood Johnson in New Brunswick. New Jersey. Things were working out quite nicely."

"And Sanctuary?" Ash interrupted, his tone harsh.

"Ash, shut up," I said. He looked at me in surprise, and I raised my eyebrow at him. "Let him continue, okay?"

Ash grumbled under his breath but remained silent.

"Pru and I lived in New Jersey for…about five years when a man came to visit her at the hospital. He said he was part of a secret project, one that would change the world. He was looking for the best and the brightest."

"Now, we both thought it was a bunch of smoke and mirrors, wishful thinking, until they convinced us to come and visit Sanctuary. By that time, it had been up and functioning for nearly thirty years. It wasn't perfect, but it was on its way. They had everything and they needed to bring people in: doctors, teachers, architects, scientists, everyone that would be necessary to build Sanctuary."

He looked up at us. "What people fail to understand about Sanctuary is that it is already there. It has always been there, functioning like it's supposed to for years. People live there. Children are born there. It's been there, waiting and watching for the moment that it would be needed."

"That's so…unsettling," I admitted. "That this group of people have been there, all along, without us knowing, kind of makes me feel weird, like I was being spied on."

"I'm sure you wouldn't like to hear about Area 51 then?" Bert asked, a low chuckle in his voice. I wasn't sure if he was kidding or not, and I wasn't sure I wanted to know the answer. "Once Pru and I had seen what Sanctuary was and what it could accomplish, we were both in. I had fought in Vietnam before I became a security guard, so they welcomed a soldier. Even soldiers were needed in the future."

"Pru worked herself to death in Sanctuary, and I do not say this lightly. She worked harder than anyone I've ever known, and she gave her life to make that place what it is. Sanctuary is not perfect. It never will be, but it's as close as we're going to get to it. It's the only place left that we have. Whatever is going on outside of this house, in this country, in the world, they know. They have everything, and they know everything. Sanctuary was created for just this kind of world."

I opened my mouth and then closed it again.

Ash finally spoke up. "Is it safe? I just want Zoey to be safe."

"And Ash," I said quickly, looking at him anxiously. He nodded in reassurance and turned back to Bert.

"It is the safest place in the world to be," Bert said, his hands folded on the table in front of him. "You do not have to go. We do not force anyone to go, but...it is probably in your best interest to go. It will keep you safe from Sekhmet."

"How do you know about Sekhmet?" I asked, feeling my heart pounding in my chest at the mere mention of Razi's corporation. I closed my eyes, seeing red behind my eyelids. We had left her dead body at the side of the road, but just the memory of her would haunt me for as long as I lived.

Bert sighed, leaning back in his chair. "Sekhmet has been around for quite a while, longer than anyone really knew. Being a part of Sanctuary meant that you were privileged to information that most people are not. The higher-ups in Sanctuary knew that this organization existed. We knew where they were located. They didn't seem to be a threat so they were ignored. We had no idea what they were up to and frankly, most people didn't care." He ran a hand across his face. He suddenly looked incredibly tired. He was only in his 60s, maybe his 70s, but at that moment, he looked much older. "I am not there to know. I don't even know who is left there, but I can imagine the regret that some may feel."

"But it's done, right? It's gone. With Razi dead…" I said, my voice soft. Images flashed across my vision: being strapped to a medical chair, Liam's soft hands on my face, running with Ash through dark hallways, and I felt a shudder run through me.

"That, I cannot say," Bert said, his left shoulder lifting slightly in a shrug. "Dr. Cylon was just one woman, and she had worked for long enough to get quite a system under her belt. They will be weak without her. What happens after this is hard to say."

I stood up. "I just…I need a moment." I turned on my heel and walked out of the kitchen. I pushed my way out of the swinging screen door and took off down the porch and across the lawn. I stopped right in front of Bert's truck. I wanted to kick it, but I was afraid a well-placed kick would rip off the fender, so I resisted. I lifted myself into the back and plopped down. The sun was streaming down on me, and I leaned backward, soaking up as much vitamin D as I could.

I was worried. Everything seemed to be coming to an end, a conclusion. We found what we were looking for. Sanctuary was real, and it was a place where we could be together and be safe. I was tired of watching people die, and I was tired of being hungry and running for my life. I was ready to stop.

But Sekhmet had left me wary of trusting anyone in the world besides Ash. Razi Cylon was evil. She had wanted to better the world but had gone about it the wrong way. She forced me into her world, examined me, pushed me and used me. She kept Ash hungry and cold, and she had treated Liam like a toy.

My heart squeezed painfully at the thought of Liam. I had no idea where he was now or if he was even alive, but I had to hope. I would always hope that he would be okay and that he would make it to Sanctuary.

"Hey there, beautiful."

I sat up and looked down at Ash. He had his hands buried deep in the pockets of his jeans, and I could see a small sliver of skin peeking out between the white hem of his shirt and pants. "Hey," I answered.

He grabbed the edge of the truck and hauled himself into the back with me. His face contorted as he did so, his hands going to the bandage underneath his shirt. The truck bed creaked as he made his way over to me and sat next to me. I slid closer to him, his arm falling across my shoulders. It felt so weird from him to be close to me as he was nuzzling my neck, yet it felt like it was supposed to be like this all along. "Are you okay?"

I shrugged. "I don't know," I admitted. There was a bit of movement out of the corner of my eye, and I jerked. A butterfly flew across my face, passing over the truck, and continuing on its way. I sat back, trying to calm my heart. "Well, maybe, I'm not okay." I looked up. His eyes met mine, unwavering, so trusting. "But I will be."

"Yeah, yeah, I think you will be," he said, his other arm coming up to wrap around me, pulling me tighter to him.

"What do we do now?" I asked him. "Sanctuary?"

He paused for a moment, the gentle rise and fall of his chest soothing to me. I pressed my cheek against him, more than willing to just fall asleep there. "It's what we came to Colorado for," he finally said.

"What do you think we should do?" I pressed him, feeling anxious.

"Zoey," he said. I pulled back and shifted myself so I could look at him. "I trust you. You've gotten us so far already, farther than anyone else could have. I think we should go to Sanctuary, but the decision is ultimately up to you. I'll follow you wherever."

My lips came down on his, hard and fast, and he responded eagerly. After a few moments, I pulled away, my breathing heavy. "I think we should go too," I whispered. My hands were wrapped tightly around his neck, and I was breathing everything that was him, everything that made him Ash. "I just want you to be safe."

He smiled, and I felt the pull of his lips against mine as he did so. "Okay, we'll go," he whispered back. "We'll be safe."

I barely let him finish when I pulled him back to me. I had waited way too long for this, and now that I knew, now that I would never question it again, I didn't want to ever have to waste a moment with him. I could feel a laugh in the back of his throat as he responded, but I didn't pause, not even for a moment. I climbed in his lap and swept my tongue along his jawline, causing him to shudder underneath me. His hands were at the hem of my shirt, his fingers spread against my bare back.

"I love you," I said, hurriedly, pulling at his shirt.

"I love *you*," he said, pulling me closer to him. I felt him harden underneath me and a wave of pleasure swept through me. My fingers fumbled at the button of his jeans, and he laughed. "Um, Zoey?"

"What?" I said, as my lips found their way down his neck.

"Ah, uh," he groaned, his eyes closed. A small smile escaped my lips, and I rolled my hips into him. He let out a low growl and grabbed my arms. "Zoey," he pleaded.

"Ash," I teased him, running my hands through his hair. He needed a haircut, but I liked the longish look on him. He reminded me of some of the emo boys I had been obsessed with my freshman year of high school, and it only turned me on more.

"Zoey," he said, his voice low against my cheek. "As much as I would love to continue this, maybe we shouldn't do this in the truck bed, in Bert's truck bed within easy viewing of his front window."

I pulled back, my face flushing. "Right. You're right. That was dumb."

His arm reached out, catching me around the waist. That wide smile was across his face, cocky and charming, and I found myself leaning toward it. "Never dumb," he said, shaking his head. "Let's go continue this inside, okay?"

I nodded, eagerly. "Okay."

We stood up, walking carefully across the truck bed. Ash jumped down and reached up for me. I stuck my tongue out at him but let him help me down. His hand immediately reached for mine, and we crossed the lawn together and went back in the house.

Bert still sat at the table in the kitchen, looking as if nothing had passed in the last hour. The puzzle book was already in his hand again, and his pencil was poised above the open page, a crease of concentration on his forehead. He glanced up as we came inside and said nothing.

"We'll go," Ash spoke up for the both of us.

He dipped his head, his eyes returning down to his book. "We'll leave in the morning."

Ash nodded in response and pulled me down the hallway, back to the room that we had been in before. He shut the door and turned the lock, and I felt a nervous giggle escape my lips. He raised his eyebrow as he spun around and pressed me up against the locked door. His hands came down below my butt, and he lifted me. My legs automatically wrapped around him, my hands gripping his arms tightly. "Something funny?"

I shook my head, feeling my heart beat rapidly in my

chest, threatening to burst out of my ribs.

"Good," he said, in a low voice. His lips came down on mine, and I found myself eagerly kissing him back, low whimpers escaping my lips in between kisses. My shirt was off and tossed to the ground before I could even protest. Goose bumps rippled across my skin as the soft cotton of his shirt rubbed up against me. He was still hard from before, and he was moving against me, causing me to pant in between kisses.

"Let's go to the bed," I suggested under my breath. He grinned and carried me over to the bed. I fell back on the bed, with his body lying next to me. I brought his face back to mine and rolled on top of him, catching him by surprise. His hands came up to my hips and thrust himself upward into me. I gasped in surprise, and a chuckle went through his body. "Something funny?" I parroted his words back to him.

He sat up, propping himself on the pillows, pulling me along with him so that I was straddling his lap. "Never," he whispered.

I smiled down at him before covering his mouth with mine.

I WOKE WITH A START the next morning with only one word on my lips. "Sanctuary." I looked over and was unsurprised to find Ash lying awake next to me. He looked over at me and gave me a nervous smile. His hand reached for mine, and I immediately grabbed it.

"You ready to do this?" he asked, his voice full of sleep. He cleared his throat, sitting up. I watched as the blanket fell to his hips, revealing his naked chest, and I felt a deep ache at the sight of him. I placed a palm over his warm chest, right above his heart, and smiled.

"You know, you have got to stop ogling me like this," he yawned. "I'm starting to think you love me only for my body."

I shrugged. "Well, at least the truth is out now."

He laughed. "Are you ready to do this?" he asked again.

I nodded, feeling the anticipation build in my stomach. "Yeah, let's do this."

We moved slowly, despite our confident words. I took my time in the shower, reveling in the water that came out of the spout. It wasn't hot, not like that showers had been back at Sekhmet, but it was warm enough. I felt more comfortable in this shower though. I didn't have the overwhelming feeling that someone was watching every single move I made. I stayed in the shower, longer than was necessary, wincing at the wrinkles that sprouted across my fingers and toes from being under the water too long. I dried myself off and slipped on a nondescript black shirt and a pair of jeans. I had never asked Bert where he had gotten clothes that had fit the two of us so well, and I wasn't sure I wanted to hear the answer.

When I returned back to the bedroom, Ash was sitting on the bed, fully dressed, his hands clasped tightly together in his lap. He was staring at them, his brow furrowed, lost in thought. I paused in the doorway to study him. I leaned against the doorway, and the floor creaked underneath my feet. His eyes shot up to meet mine, and the left corner of his mouth tilted up for a minute. He stayed sitting for a long moment before standing up and walking toward me.

"Let's go," he said, taking my hand and pulling me out the door.

THIRTY-FOUR

THE DRIVE TO SANCTUARY WAS short, maybe only an hour, maybe two. I kept my hand clutched in Zoey's the entire way there. I was trying hard to keep up a strong appearance for her, but I was terrified. Her face remained calm, her eyes staring out the window at the blur of trees and empty homes. I watched her, unable to tear my eyes away. I had been in love with her for as long as I could remember, and all I wanted to do was protect her and keep her safe from all the bad things in the world. I had to remind myself how incredibly strong she was, how capable she was.

She shifted in her seat, and I felt myself fill with warmth as she turned those wide brown eyes at me. They were beautiful, dark, nearly the color of milk chocolate, framed by the thickest black eyelashes I'd ever seen. Sometimes I just wanted to lean into her, just to feel those eyelashes against my skin as she kissed me. She was beautiful, and I wondered if she even knew how beautiful she was.

I couldn't help it as a smile spread across my face. She beamed back up at me and squeezed my hand tightly. My mind flashed to the night before, the way our limbs had tangled together, the way her face had looked when I made her feel good. I leaned over and pressed my lips tight against her forehead.

We had been driving straight on a lonely highway for ages before Bert finally pulled off and took a series of turns. He led us up a long, windy road where we passed a sign that read "Mesa Verde National Park." There was a ranger station at the entrance, but it remained empty, and there was something almost haunted about the sight of it. My eyes were glued to it until it passed out of sight. I shifted back in my seat, feeling the warm leather of the seat sticking to the fabric of my jeans.

I didn't know how long it took us to drive up the cliffs, but eventually Bert pulled to a stop. There was nothing around us but trees and the hard red and white rock of the cliffs, and I looked up at Bert, curiously. "This is the best way to get to the entrance." He took out a piece of paper that showed a roughly drawn map scrawled in red pen. He handed it over to me, and I studied it. Zoey leaned over, pressing her cheek against my arm as her eyes roved over the paper.

"It should be simple enough," Bert said, his fingers tapping the worn brown steering wheel. He looked at the two of us. "Should only take you a couple hours, at the very most. It's not very hard to find, but this is the most direct route."

I nodded, slipping the map into my pocket and grabbing the pack I had brought from Bert's house. It had a few articles of clothing in there, some snacks and water bottles, and the book I had found amongst the shelves at Bert's house. As soon as I'd seen the familiar title, *The Mists of Avalon,* I knew I had to grab it. It wasn't her copy, but the book was important enough to Zoey to bring it across the country with her, and I wanted to have one for her, always. Zoey slid across the seat and pushed the creaking passenger door open. She hopped down and turned back to me. I slung the pack across my shoulders and climbed out after her.

Zoey turned back to the truck, her eyes bright and wide. "Thank you, Bert, for everything." I could hear the emotion in her voice and knew how hard it was for her to show it. "Take care of yourself, okay?"

Bert smiled at her, a full smile, and I was taken aback. I hadn't seen a smile like that from him the entire time we had been at his house, and believe me, I had tried hard to get one. He was quiet, stoic, kept to himself and definitely not quick to smile. I saw the way he looked at Zoey and knew that there was a part of him that had quickly come to care for her. "You take care of yourself, Miss Zoey," he spoke. He looked at me. "Take care of each other." He turned the key in the ignition, and the truck fired back to life. With one last glance at us, he turned the truck away and began the slow, winding drive back down the cliffs.

We trucked through the forest for what felt like an eternity, the sun beating down on us. Zoey stayed quiet the entire time, never complaining, even as she drained the water bottle I handed to her. Every step was like a burning flame in my ribs, but I pushed forward. Bert's map was a drawing of landmarks; turn left at a boulder in the rough shape of a bear, things like that. We were looking for a gap in the cliffs, something most people wouldn't notice but would be marked by a single symbol.

Zoey halted when we reached the ruins, built right into the side of the cliff. They were old but incredible, and the two of us paused for a moment to take them in, to wonder about the people who had once lived here. I was mesmerized at the sheer size of the dwellings, cut out of the cliffs, high above the forest floor. We stared at them for a long time before Zoey tugged on my arm, a strange look on her face.

"I think I found it," she said, her voice low.

She led me closer. Hidden just beyond some of the dwellings was a crack in the cliff just large enough for a person of decent size to squeeze there. I had to wonder if people actually used this entrance all the time. There was no way. There had to be an official entrance. For now, though, it seemed that this would be the way we go. Right above the entrance, two large circles were carved, intertwining, almost like a Venn diagram.

"I'll go first," I heard myself saying. I took the pack off my shoulder and handed it back to her. She had her arms folded tightly across her chest as she watched me. My body was pressed tight against the stone as I turned sideways and pushed my way through. I was grateful, for the first time, for all the weight I had lost in the past months. I blinked a few times, trying to adjust myself to the darkness that was on the other side. I didn't hear anything, but this had to be the right way. No more than a hundred yards away was a light.

"Well, I think I just lost about twenty pounds squeezing through there." I heard a light laugh coming from the other side. "But it's safe."

Zoey came squeezing after me, a look of panic on her face as she took in the darkness around us. She steeled herself, her hand reaching for mine. I thought for a moment that she might falter, but instead, she pushed her shoulders back and started walking toward the light.

When we reached it, we realized it was just the first in a series of overhead lights, lighting the way down a tunnel. We continued to follow them, like a trail of lit up crumbs, leading back home from the witch's house. Soon, the dark crumbly cliff walls disappeared, and we found ourselves in a hallway, not unlike the one at Sekhmet. I felt my heart slam into my chest as I began to spot the cameras dotting the hallway, every few yards or so.

"I'm scared," Zoey said, her voice so soft that I was unsure if I had even heard her correctly. I wanted to pull her toward me, wrap her in my arms and never let her go. I knew what it meant for her to admit that.

There was a loud bang, and the sound of a door opening. It echoed down the hallway toward us, over-whelmingly. We both stepped closer to each other, stopping in our tracks, afraid to move.

It had been no longer than a minute or two when I heard it: footsteps, light and unhurried, heading down the hallway toward us. I took a step forward, subtly placing myself between Zoey and whoever was coming toward us. She didn't notice. Her eyes were focused on the space in front of us, waiting to see who would appear.

Eventually someone came within our eyesight, and we both looked at each other quickly before turning our eyes back to the figure. It was a woman, I noticed as she came closer. She was small, almost as small as Zoey, dressed impeccably in a blazer and skirt, reminding me of the women I sometimes saw on political shows. She had dark black hair streaked with gray, and I placed her around my parents' age, forties, maybe fifties. She had a pleasant look on her face, not quite a smile but still welcoming. She stopped about six feet in front of us.

"Hello," she said, her voice strong and deep in the cavernous hallway.

I went to speak, but the words were stuck, and I was grateful when Zoey spoke. "Hello," she said. I felt her nervousness in the shaking of her palm against mine, but her voice was clear and steady. "I'm Zoey, and this is Ash."

The woman smiled wide and swept her arms out in greeting. "Zoey. Ash. Welcome to Sanctuary."

EPILOGUE

SHE HAD WATCHED THEM FROM the moment they had left the old man's house. Bert Washington, she didn't know him well; in fact, she barely recognized him from the files she had managed to glean from Sanctuary years before. He had aged quite a bit since then, more than she would have expected. They felt safe and hadn't noticed that she had been following them for miles, staying far enough away that they wouldn't notice her car in the distance.

The car hit a rough patch on the windy road as it went over a rock. She winced as the jolt sent a wave of pain through her body. Her driver looked over at her, concern on his face, but he knew better than to say anything to her. She was the leader. She was strong.

She had let them escape, and now they were soon to be in the safety of Sanctuary.

"Did you want me to continue following them, ma'am?" the driver spoke, his voice full of unwavering devotion. He would do anything for her, anything she asked of him.

"No." She watched as the two climbed down a steep hill, just visible from the window of her car. She was obsessed with them, and she wanted them, needed them. She would get them.

She turned away from the window, her eyes shining with purpose. "No, I think not. We can leave."

The driver looked taken aback and began to sputter his next words. "But ma'am...don't you...don't you want to bring them in?"

A smile spread across the face of Razi Cylon, her first smile in days. She glanced back one more time as the two teenagers made their way toward Sanctuary. "No," she answered. "I don't need to bring them in. They will return to me, all on their own." She sighed, pressing her fingertips lightly to the bandage that was wrapped around her throat. "Let's go."

ACKNOWLEDGEMENTS

Back when being an author was just a crazy dream of mine, I said…one day when I finally got to do this, I wouldn't make them the longest acknowledgments ever. I obviously broke that promise.

First, I have to give a major shout out to my family. My mom, for giving me my insane love of reading and writing. My dad, for…well, everything, including, but not limited to: buying me food, fixing my car, helping me pick out my prom dress and picking me up at Six Flags when I was sick even though you told me not to go because, duh, I was sick. Love you! My siblings, Robby, Jess, Dink, Joey and Stevey…you guys are insane but I wouldn't trade you for anything else. You guys would be my Awakened fighting team. My dog Scout because she always seems to know when I need her.

To my best friend Allison Lane, who is not a book nerd but always reads my books and thinks it's badass that I can write. That's true friendship. Thanks for always loving me and being there and for having an alcoholic beverage of some sort ready for me, always. And random pictures of Robert Downey Jr…

To the girls that literally make every single day amazing:

Sylvia Torres, Alexandra Campos and Cassandra Gomez. We are the fearsome foursome, and I would not be able to get through each day without the three of you. Thanks for the adventures, the shoulders to cry on, the millions of laughs, the craziness, always the FOOD, the everything. You guys are my parabatai, my wifey and my little sister. In that order. Those golden chairs are waiting for you always. #NoEasyDays

Thank you Kim G Designs to for designing an AWESOME cover and to Nadege Richards for the equally awesome interior of the novel as well. Casey Ann Books…thanks for that trailer! You guys make my book look infinitely cooler than it actually is.

HUGE thanks to Gina Elliott and Logan Gulley for editing this thing. Seriously. It's a wonder that I know how to spell. Or grammar. Can I grammar? I don't think so…

To every amazing person in the LADA: you rock. Jonathan Lesso, thank you for so many years of love and support. Isabel Naquin, thank you for being one of my biggest fans right from the beginning.

Thank you a million times to the beta readers: Alexandra Campos, Ashley Smith, Jackie Connet, Jackie Zwirn, Krystal Maestas, Lindsey Berg, Marlee McMahan and Taylor Helm. Thank you for loving The Awakened when it was just a first draft and helping me make it what it is now!

A major, huge shout out to the band, Set It Off. When I first started writing this book, I was feeling major down in the dumps. I couldn't get the words on paper and I felt like

I just wasn't on the right path in my life for me. I went to go see one of my favorite bands, Story of the Year, when I discovered Set It Off, who opened for them. There were two songs that just STUCK to me: "Nightmare," which eventually became the unofficial theme song for this novel, and "Dreamcatcher." Cody, the lead singer, kept talking about living your dreams, and working hard, and not listening to what everyone says about going down the "right" path and not listening to your own dreams...and it just really resonated with me. Their album, *Cinematics*, stayed on repeat in the entirety of this novel. This novel would NOT exist without them.

To all the bloggers and readers and fangirls and boys that I've met through all these years of blogging and reading: you guys are rock stars. Thanks for always reading and believing. You're such a huge part of this. Thanks for fangirling with me, and just being my friend, whether you're someone I see all the time, or whether you're someone I've never met before. My book friends are the best! This book is yours too!

Courtney Saldana and Allison Tran: for being the BEST librarians in the entire world, for always giving me a chance as a blogger, and for never ever giving up on me. Lita Weissman at Barnes and Noble...you are the best ever, and don't ever stop being the awesome, passionate, fantastic person that you are!

All the authors that I've had the pleasure and HONOR of becoming friends with over the past three and a half years...there's just so many: Jessica Brody, Leigh Bardugo,

Andrew Smith, Aaron Hartzler, Tonya Kuper, Morgan Matson, Cassandra Clare, Robin Benway, Valerie Tejeda, Catherine Linka, Lauren Miller, Michelle Levy, Cinda Williams Chima, Cora Carmack, Gretchen McNeil, Josephine Angelini, Marie Lu, Carrie Arcos, James Dashner, Tammara Webber…I literally could go on for ages. Thank you for being my friend, for always encouraging me, telling me to NEVER give up, and for giving the best advice.

Thank you to baseball and books and cupcakes and Asian food for keeping me sane. Writing is hard!

To all the aspiring writers out there: DON'T. GIVE. UP. Don't do it. Ever. It may seem easy to, or it may seem like it's never going to happen, but it is. Don't ever give up. Write, write, write. Never stop.

A HUGE, GINORMOUS, MASSIVE thank you to Benjamin Alderson, aka BenjaminOfTomes, aka the founder and brains of OfTomes Publishing. Thank you so much for loving this book and for giving it the chance that I've always thought it deserved. Thank you for making this real!

Lastly, thank you to YOU, the reader, the person holding this book, in whatever format you chose…you are the literal best. Even if only one person (besides my dad) buys this book, you're making my dream come true. Hugs and kisses!

ABOUT SARA

Sara Elizabeth Santana is a young adult and new adult fiction writer. She has worked as a smoothie artist, Disneyland cast member, restaurant supervisor, nanny, photographer, pizza delivery driver and barista but writing is what she loves most. She runs her own nerd girl/book review blog, What A Nerd Girl Says. She lives in Southern California with her dad, five siblings and two dogs. Her debut novel is The Awakened. Visit her at sesantanawrites.com for more!

13897742R00260

Printed in Great Britain
by Amazon.co.uk, Ltd.,
Marston Gate.